An excerpt from *Breaking the Rancher's Rules* by Cat Schield

"It might not seem like it, but I'm not usually in need of rescuing."

"Maybe if you can go a day without risking life and limb, I might believe that."

Giselle placed her palm against his cheek and turned his face until his gaze met hers. "I could do that, but I'm starting to think being saved by you is the best part of my day."

She rose up on tiptoe and brushed her lips against his cheek. The fleeting touch sent Lyle's heartbeat into overdrive. As if by mutual agreement, the angle of their heads changed. Lips followed, a tentative brush and retreat that confused Lyle.

She'd started this, so why was she hesitating? From her flirty profile pictures, he expected boldness. She appeared to be a woman who knew what she wanted and went after it. Why was she toying with him? Or was this a clever ploy to make him think the kiss was his idea?

An excerpt from *The Trouble with an Heir* by Stacey Kennedy

"You're a Winters, and I'm working for the Del Rio family. I am loyal to them."

The side of his mouth curved. "You're pulling out the feud card even when you're not part of either family?"

"Yes, because I'm working for the Del Rio family," Jessica countered. "Whether you like it or not, there is a feud between your families, and I am firmly on their side."

Marcus paused, his eyes searching hers, then suddenly he took a step closer. "I bet I could bring you over to the dark side."

Her core heated and she felt the warmth creep along her cheeks. She should step away, but she figured this was some power play he was trying to win.

Holding her ground, she took the final step between them, their bodies nearly touching, the energy sizzling in the small space that separated them.

CAT SCHIELD

&

USA TODAY BESTSELLING AUTHOR
STACEY KENNEDY

BREAKING THE RANCHER'S RULES

&

THE TROUBLE WITH AN HEIR

Special thanks and acknowledgment are given to Cat Schield and Stacey Kennedy for their contributions to the Texas Cattleman's Club: Diamonds & Dating Apps miniseries.

Recycling programs for this product may not exist in your area.

ISBN-13: 978-1-335-45781-3

Breaking the Rancher's Rules & The Trouble with an Heir

Copyright © 2023 by Harlequin Enterprises ULC

Breaking the Rancher's Rules
Copyright © 2023 by Harlequin Enterprises ULC

The Trouble with an Heir
Copyright © 2023 by Harlequin Enterprises ULC

Scriptures taken from the Holy Bible, New International Version®, NIV®. Copyright © 1973, 1978, 1984, 2011 by Biblica, Inc.™ Used by permission of Zondervan. All rights reserved worldwide. www.zondervan.com The "NIV" and "New International Version" are trademarks registered in the United States Patent and Trademark Office by Biblica, Inc.™

For questions and comments about the quality of this book, please contact us at CustomerService@Harlequin.com.

Harlequin Enterprises ULC
22 Adelaide St. West, 41st Floor
Toronto, Ontario M5H 4E3, Canada
www.Harlequin.com

Printed in U.S.A.

CONTENTS

Cat Schield is an award-winning author of contemporary romances for Harlequin Desire. She likes her heroines spunky and her heroes swoonworthy. While her jet-setting characters live all over the globe, Cat makes her home in Minnesota with her daughter, two opinionated Burmese cats and a goofy Doberman. When she's not writing or walking dogs, she's searching for the perfect cocktail or traveling to visit friends and family. Contact her at www.catschield.com.

Books by Cat Schield

Harlequin Desire

Sweet Tea and Scandal

Upstairs Downstairs Baby
Substitute Seduction
Revenge with Benefits
Seductive Secrets
Seduction, Southern Style
The Trouble with Love and Hate

Texas Cattleman's Club

How to Catch a Bad Boy
On Opposite Sides
Breaking the Rancher's Rules

Visit the Author Profile page
at Harlequin.com for more titles.

You can also find Cat Schield on Facebook, along with other Harlequin Desire authors, at Facebook.com/HarlequinDesireAuthors!

Dear Reader,

Being part of any Texas Cattleman's Club series is always a joy for me. I hope you all enjoy reading the stories as much as we love to write them. *Breaking the Rancher's Rules* is my eighth book. While every series has been so fun, I love this particular story for the hopefulness of my heroine and the sunshine she brings to my grumpy hero.

Embracing optimism isn't always the easiest thing to do in the wake of the difficult last few years we've gone through. That's why I gravitate toward romances. What can be more uplifting than to go on a journey with two individuals whose hearts are healed by love? In the real world, we might not always get our happily-ever-after, but we can be swept up in great stories and find inspiration watching someone struggle and win.

I hope you enjoy Giselle and Lyle's story and that their romance makes you smile.

Happy reading,

Cat Schield

BREAKING THE RANCHER'S RULES

Cat Schield

For Charles Griemsman and Stacy Boyd.
Thank you.

One

"Don't get mad…"

Weary resignation flooded Lyle Drummond at his younger sister's words. Whatever she'd done had to be something god-awful if she'd tracked him down at six thirty in the morning.

Lyle finished applying wound balm to a cut on his favorite gelding's hock before he straightened. "What have you done now?"

He'd been unprepared at twenty-two, when their mother had died in a tragic car accident, leaving him in charge of thirteen-year-old Jessica. Until that moment, she'd been his pesky sibling, someone he could ignore or indulge depending on his mood.

"You know k!smet, that new app that went viral last month after what happened at ByteCon?"

Lyle frowned at her. What was his sister playing at? She knew that he knew. Lyle's best friend, Trey Winters, had financially backed the app that had been the brainchild of Misha Law. With rumors swirling about Misha's company going public, she'd presented the app's newest function at the technology convention, being held for the first time in Royal.

Everything had been going smoothly until the "Surprise me!" feature had matched Maggie Del Rio and Jericho Winters. Since the Del Rio and Winters families had been engaged in a decades-long quarrel, the pairing had sent shock waves through the convention, the town of Royal and both families.

After ByteCon, Trey had suspected something was wrong with the app since it matched his brother with a Del Rio. He'd stormed over to Misha's company to demand answers. As they worked together to solve the issues with the algorithm, the couple had fallen deeply in love.

Both men had lost a woman they loved. Cancer had stolen Chloe from Lyle. The mother of Trey's son, Dez, had abandoned them. As the years rolled by, neither man had demonstrated any interest in searching for a replacement life partner.

Yet, Trey was now deeply in love with a woman who suited him perfectly, and while Lyle marveled at his friend's good fortune, the thought of putting himself out there left him cold.

"What about it?" Lyle asked.

In the barn around him, ranch hands saddled horses while their mounts finished off their breakfasts. The muffled sounds of chewing and muted conversation couldn't calm Lyle's disquiet as an unfamiliar flare of wistfulness hit him.

Jessica's brown eyes held determination. "I signed you up."

Pain shot through his temple. "For a dating app?" What was she thinking?

"It's not just a dating app," Jessica clarified, a smidge defensively. "It offers social and business networking, too."

"So who, exactly, am I supposed to network with?" He focused on screwing the lid on the jar of salve until the urge to grab her shoulders and shake her dissipated.

"Lots of people." Seeing his scowl, she rushed on, quoting the advertising pitch. "It's *the* must-have app for the crème de la crème of Texas society and beyond." The end of her spiel was accompanied by a little flourish of her hand.

Lyle stopped grinding his molars and unclenched his jaw. Obviously, Jessica needed to be reminded that he hadn't been a participating member of society, much less one of its crème-de-la-crème members, since his wife's abrupt death five years earlier.

"Jess!"

"I know. I know." She shook her head, forestalling his admonition. "But I can't bear to think of you alone for the rest of your life."

He couldn't imagine anyone fitting into the life he and Chloe had created for themselves. No doubt Jessica would argue that point. In fact, the town of Royal had several women who would happily become his wife.

Yet, he had no interest in devoting time to developing the sort of intimacy he'd shared with his wife. Relationships took work and the ranch sucked up all his energy.

"Jess…"

"You really deserve to be happy."

"I can't." Lyle was a little shocked by the pain underlying his tone. He and Chloe had spent six glorious years together before he'd lost her. There was no recovering from that. And most days Lyle didn't want to.

"Losing Chloe devastated you." The sympathy in her voice added fuel to his discomfort. "But you have so much love to give. Don't close yourself off."

For a heartbeat, Lyle squeezed his eyes shut. When he opened them again, he had the dejection back under control.

"Delete my account."

"Do you have any idea how hard it is to get accepted?"

He did. Trey was very enthusiastic about the app's potential. Current membership was at six thousand and growing, with another thirty thousand people on the waiting list.

"Delete my account," Lyle repeated.

He had neither the time nor the desire to sift through hundreds of women only to reject them all as unsuitable. He'd already had the great love of his life. Finding another would be impossible and his heart wouldn't let him settle for less than that what he and Chloe had shared. If he needed companionship, he was perfectly capable of finding women who satisfied a temporary need for such.

"But you got matched." Jessica's hopeful expression begged him to be open to her suggestion.

His chest seized. Something close to panic made his throat clench. He didn't want to meet anyone new. Couldn't risk the sudden, unstoppable loss of someone else he loved.

"Doesn't matter," he declared. "Trey said the app's algorithm was sabotaged so the likelihood of the match being viable is nonexistent."

"Still. Aren't you the least bit curious who it might be?"

"No."

He'd never imagined being alone for the rest of his life, but in the years since Chloe's death, he hadn't met a single woman who could replace her in his heart.

"She's awfully pretty," his sister coaxed, her hopeful expression building when he took too long to dissuade her.

Jessica turned her phone screen in his direction, and against his better judgment, Lyle took in a heart-shaped face framed by honey-streaked brown hair and chestnut-brown eyes that sparkled with coquettish glee. An arresting smile curved her full lips and his pulse jerked in response.

He'd barely had a chance to process his reaction when Jessica swiped to the next pic. One glimpse of her lithe body in a red-hot bikini and desire slammed into him like sledgehammer. Sweat broke out all over his body and Lyle resisted the urge to wipe moisture off his forehead. He averted his gaze.

"Nice. Right?"

No matter how attracted he might be to the stunner

he'd been matched to, Lyle preferred meeting women the old-fashioned way. The way he and Chloe had met—organically and in person. This swipe-left-or-right business of evaluating someone based on their looks just so you could hook up was not his idea of romance.

"I mean that red bikini shot is like wow!" Jessica persisted. "Who wouldn't want to get with that?"

"I'm not interested." Which was a big, fat lie, because his hormones were revved up and ready to party. Obviously, his body needed to let off some steam. How long since he'd—

"Really?" His sister tipped her head and peered at him. "Because it looks like you've got a little bit of drool right there…"

Lyle swatted her hand away from his face and scowled. "Delete my account."

Despite what his sister believed, Lyle wasn't completely shut off from the rest of the world. He might not go out of his way to be around people, but that didn't mean he was a confirmed hermit.

Jessica was unfazed by his cranky mood. "I'll give you a couple days to think it over."

Knowing it would do no good to badger her further, Lyle turned the tables. "Why don't you concentrate on your own love life and stop worrying about mine."

The barb worked as he'd hoped. Jessica tossed her head in irritation.

"I'm focused on my career right now." An aspiring chef, Jessica had put herself through the prestigious Auguste Escoffier School of Culinary Arts in Austin,

Texas, and was currently searching for her dream job. "Besides, Camp Up keeps me too busy to date."

Neither Drummond siblings were afraid of hard work, a trait they'd both inherited from their loving dynamo of a working-class single mom. Several years earlier, Jessica had started a glamping business at the ranch and grown it into a thriving enterprise, giving her the money she needed to attend culinary school.

"And I'm focused on the ranch," Lyle said. "I guess neither one of us has time to date. Besides, who would be crazy enough to trust an app with a faulty algorithm?"

"Me," Jessica announced. "I used the 'Surprise Me!' feature in the lifestyle section and met someone who I'm going to swap houses with for the next two weeks."

"Are you out of your mind?"

How could she be so reckless as to put her faith in k!smet's sabotaged operating system?

"Look, I know you love everything about the ranch, but I'm tired of cows and horses and dirt. I want to put on an impractical dress and wear sandals without worrying about getting dirty. I want to go shopping and eat at fancy restaurants. The woman I'm swapping with has a condo in downtown Dallas."

"Who is she?" The last thing he wanted was a stranger living a quarter mile down the driveway. "What do you know about her?"

"She's an entrepreneur like me."

"What else?"

"Her name is Giselle Saito. She runs her own skincare company. A self-confessed workaholic, you two will have lots in common." Seeing that he wasn't convinced, Jessica sighed. "Why are you being like this? Everyone on the app is vetted. She's not an axe murderer."

"You should've talked to me before inviting someone you don't know to stay at the ranch."

"Oh, please." Jessica rolled her eyes. "You've never had an issue with my Camp Up clients and they're all strangers."

"That's different. You're here to supervise them the entire time. With you in Dallas, who's going to keep her out of trouble?"

Unfazed by his annoyance, Jessica sighed like she used to when Lyle grilled her before letting her meet up with her friends. "What do you think is going to happen to her?"

Ranch life was filled with peril. Especially when it came to some clueless newbie. She could get trampled by livestock. Suffocated by falling into a grain bin. Run over by a tractor. Have an allergic reaction to an insect bite. Lyle's imagination ran wild.

"Does she know anything about being on a ranch?"

"Nope. She's a city girl through and through." Jessica beamed at him without a trace of sympathy for the situation she'd put him in. "If you're so worried about what she could get up to, I guess you'll just have keep an eye on her."

"I don't have time to babysit anyone."

"Then assign one of the guys to show her around. She's eager to meet a real live cowboy and there's plenty of those around here." Jessica pointed at a passing figure. "How about Jacob? I'll bet he'd love to show her around."

Hearing the sound of his name, the handsome cowboy shot Jessica a sexy half smile. Lyle glared at his foreman. The cowboy was a little too smooth with the ladies and Lyle didn't want Jessica's guest anywhere near him.

"Are you kidding?" Lyle snapped his head toward the wide barn door, sending Jacob on his way. "These are some of our busiest weeks. We're bringing the cattle to weigh the calves and preg-check the heifers." Not to mention the rest of the regular tasks that needed handling, like checking the fence line and harvesting hay.

"So put her to work."

"No." Irritation blasting through him, Lyle ripped off his hat and raked his fingers through his hair. Slamming the Stetson back on his head, he growled, "Tell her to stay clear of the ranch operations. I do not want to catch a single glimpse of her the entire time she's staying at your house. Got it?"

Jessica tossed her hair, pivoted away and with a huffy tone, said, "Got it."

"Good." For a beat he watched his sister stomp away, and then called after her, "And delete my account."

"Whatever."

Satisfaction flared at her disgruntled tone and just as quickly dimmed. He didn't want to date. Didn't want to fall in love. Didn't want to put his heart in danger ever again. Yet he couldn't ignore the occasional bout of loneliness that assailed him.

Being alone sucked.

But losing someone he loved was an agony he never wanted to revisit.

Giselle Saito dropped her dark glasses into place as her Mini Cooper convertible emerged from the underground parking below her condo building. Three years earlier she'd bought the two-bedroom unit on the twelfth floor, convinced that the location in historic downtown Dallas was her dream home. And it was. Especially when compared to the fifth-floor walk-up she'd lived in when she'd started her eco-conscious, cruelty-free, skin-care brand, Skin by Saito.

Fast-forward three years. These days, the crowded downtown streets and lack of green space had her second-guessing her location. Maybe she needed to settle into the suburbs with a stylish house and a big yard. But her growing business took up all her energy and Giselle had no idea how she'd ever be able to keep up with the nonstop maintenance a house required.

Her smartphone rang as she reached the turnoff to the interstate. Using the car's hands-free option, she answered her sister's call.

"Hey," Giselle said, deftly guiding the convertible into the fast-moving freeway traffic. "What's up?"

"I have news," Gabby declared with her usual dramatic flair. "Let's do lunch."

"Can't." Of course her twin had forgotten Giselle's vacation plans.

"How about dinner then?"

"I'm on my way out of town." Giselle sighed. "I'll

be gone for the next two weeks." She resisted the urge to add *remember*? If Giselle drank a shot every time she used that word during a conversation with her sister, she would need a new liver before the year was out.

"Are you going somewhere glamorous?"

Giselle had already explained to her twin how she was trading spaces with a woman she'd been matched with on the k!smet app. After hearing what happened when the "Surprise me!" option was used at the tech con in Royal, Giselle knew it was the exact thing she needed to do.

Speaking with excruciating patience, Giselle said, "A ranch."

"Oh, right. A ranch." Despite her words, Gabby sounded as if this was the first time she'd heard where her sister was going. "What are you going to do there? I mean, they don't expect you to ride horses and rustle cattle, do they?"

"Of course not." Although Giselle was hoping to get a little taste of ranch life. "I'm just eager to get away from the city and see some stars. Jessica—the woman who owns the house I'm staying at—runs a glamping business and she said—"

"Owns a what kind of business?"

Giselle couldn't blame her sister for sounding confused. She'd had the same reaction when Jessica explained about Camp Up. "Glamping."

"What the hell is glamping?"

"Glamorous camping. You sleep in tents, but there are actual beds with regular sheets and the food is all prepared for you so there's no cooking or chores required." Giselle sounded like an expert as she explained all this, but she'd done her research after Jessica mentioned it.

"That sounds awful."

A typical Gabby reaction. Her fashionista sister's concept of roughing it was a three-star resort. By contrast, Giselle thought the experience sounded like an adventure. The sum total of her own understanding of camping, ranch life and cowboys was from TV and she doubted anything she'd seen was based in reality.

"I think it'll be fun."

"Whatever. So are you really not going to work for two weeks?"

"You know me—of course, I'll be working." For the last ten years Giselle had poured all her time and energy into growing her company. "I'm launching my new line skin-care line for men and there's so much to do. In fact, I thought maybe I'd scope out the cowboys to see if any of them might be model material."

"I thought you already had someone picked out for that. That guy you've been dating. Theo something?"

Giselle clenched the steering wheel as humiliation washed through her. "Thad and I broke up."

"He was too young for you." Gabby spoke with all the superiority of an older sister—older by three minutes. "I knew it wasn't going to last."

"Yes, well…"

Giselle had been flattered when the twenty-six-year-old hottie had asked her out. At the time it had never occurred to her that he'd been more interested in representing her skin-care line than in dating her. She'd invested six months in the relationship before finding out that he only wanted to be with her if she could further his career.

"You should really create a dating profile on k!smet," Gabby suggested, equal parts bossy and supportive. "The men are handsome, successful and rich. Far more desirable than some pretty-boy wannabe model."

"I'm really not interested in—" *getting my heart broken* "—dating anyone right now."

"Fine. More for me."

"You're welcome to them," Giselle declared, wishing her sister the sincerest of good luck. Not that Gabby needed luck. When it came to romance, she could be a bit of a man-eater. Just another way the sisters differed.

Not until the call disconnected did Giselle realize that Gabby had never shared her news. She was on the verge of dialing her sister's number when another call came in. Seeing that it was Jessica Drummond, Giselle's heart gave an excited thump.

"I'm headed towards Royal," Giselle said after they exchanged greetings.

"I'm headed toward downtown Dallas," Jessica countered and there was a smile in her voice.

Since being matched by the k!smet app three weeks earlier, the women had gotten friendly through texts and the occasional chat.

"I hope you like my place." Giselle had stocked the condo with food, booze and miscellaneous sundries. "I left you an assortment of goodies from my product line. And the guest-room closet is full of clothes my sister has designed over the years, so help yourself. Make sure you pamper yourself these next two weeks."

"I feel terrible," Jessica said. "All I left you is a clean house and some meals in the refrigerator. Oh, and my grumpy brother." Jessica gave a self-conscious chuckle. "On second thought, you'd better steer clear of him."

"That sounds ominous. Why is he grumpy?" From the way Jessica had described her brother, Giselle pictured a perpetually scruffy and scowling man dressed in denim and T-shirts. She gathered that he was a workaholic who prioritized the welfare of his ranch above all else.

"He works too much. It makes him antisocial. I try to get him to think of something other than the ranch, but he's just not interested in making an effort."

Giselle sympathized with Jessica's frustrated venting. She had a difficult sibling of her own. "Sounds like he doesn't listen to your advice any more then my sister listens to mine."

"They are both lucky to have such brilliant siblings," Jessica quipped. "And they don't appreciate us at all."

"Exactly." Giselle grinned. She'd liked the other woman from the first.

"Well, you don't need to worry about Lyle. He's so busy with ranch business that you'll never run into him. And believe me when I say that's for the best. He doesn't deserve someone as funny and nice as you."

The comment struck Giselle in the solar plexus. Gabby had always been the more social of the twins. Her sister made friends easily and adored the limelight. Giselle preferred to promote her business over herself.

Which was why in high school she'd started a beauty vlog that attracted thousands of followers.

"That's sweet of you to say," Giselle said, wondering if it was too much to hope that this exchange of homes could develop into a lasting friendship. "Have a great time staying at my place and if do you need anything, just let me know."

"Thanks. Enjoy ranch life. And if you need anything, just ask Rosie. She's Lyle's housekeeper. I left her number on the refrigerator."

"Thanks for everything." And Giselle meant every syllable. While she knew that she been paired with Jessica through the k!smet app's algorithm, she couldn't help feeling like maybe fate had stepped in and done her a solid.

That feeling only increase in strength as she followed the turn-by-turn instructions that guided her through the charming town of Royal, Texas, and put her on the last stretch of road leading to the Royal Cattle Company Ranch. After living in the city all her life, the wide-open spaces filled her with awe. Grass stretched out as far as the eye could see and she suspected that for the next fourteen days, she'd be seeing far more cows than people.

Before embarking on this adventure, she'd wondered how she'd adapt to the countryside. Now, seeing how beautiful everything was, she was absolutely captivated. Not only that, but her tension melted away with each mile she drove. For the first time in ages, the weight of responsibility fell off her shoulders. Giselle knew it was all self-imposed anxiety. She'd been driving herself hard for the last ten years with no end in sight. What was the joke about being your own boss? *I quit my 9-to-5 job so I could work 24/7.* Well, that certainly depicted Giselle's experience.

Even now, with her business flourishing, she struggled to slow down long enough to smell the roses. Part of her feared that if she took her foot off the gas, everything would grind to a screeching halt with no chance of regaining the momentum.

Giselle came back to the present as the navigation guide announced she should prepare to turn in two miles. Her pulse rate increased with excitement. She couldn't wait for her first glimpse of the ranch. As the turnoff neared, she spied the steel gate bearing the name of the Royal Cattle Company and slowed for the turn.

A long, well-maintained road led away from the highway. The sheer size of the ranch became apparent as she drove for nearly a mile before any buildings came into view. Around a curve and over a small rise she glimpsed her destination—a sprawling two-story house. Giselle took her foot off the accelerator, letting the car coast as she goggled at the brick home. From the size of the thing, she guessed that her two-bedroom condo would fit inside four times. And this was going to be her home for the next two weeks.

When a relieved sigh eased out, she realized she'd been a little afraid of what she might be getting herself into. Even though she knew that the k!smet app took on a select group of individuals, part of her head wondered if she was going to be roughing it in some sort of primitive cabin. This was the exact opposite of that.

Rolling to a stop on the circular driveway, Giselle let loose a little squeal of delight. Exiting the car, she advanced toward the front door. The extensive porch held half a dozen rocking chairs, and not one, but two porch swings. She imagined herself relaxing here as the evening cooled and the sky darkened.

Before setting her foot on the steps leading up to the wide planks, she turned around to absorb the view of rolling hills and stands of trees. What would it be like to sit here and take in that amazing scenery every day? Heaven.

In the next moment, she took in the buzzing white noise of a hundred crickets and the wind blowing through the trees. No sirens. No traffic. Giselle filled her lungs with the clean, fresh air, noting the scent of freshly mowed hay, the heavy perfume of the roses filling the garden off to her left and a tantalizing whiff of smoked meat. She loved barbecue and suspected that anything she'd have in Dallas would pale in comparison to the real thing out here.

Standing on the porch, Giselle threw her arms wide and embraced her newest adventure. Although maybe *adventure* wasn't the right word given that Jessica's house was more like a luxury resort than the simple ranch house she'd been picturing.

Giddy with delight, Giselle retraced her steps, popped open the Mini's trunk and wrestled her suitcases onto the driveway. The tiny backseat contained boxes filled with her products, but those she could come back for later. After extending both handles, she marched toward the porch, where she hauled each suitcase up five steps. Only when she stood panting outside the front door did it occur to her that she might've overpacked.

Initially she'd planned on spending the next two weeks capturing an abundance of fun images for her social-media accounts.

However, during the drive, she'd changed her focus. Given that her next product line was for men, she really should promote the products by introducing some rough-and-tumble cowboys in their element.

Just as Jessica had described, the front door had a keyless entry. Giselle pulled out her cell phone and scrolled through her texts until she located the four-digit code Jessica had given her. She keyed in the numbers and then turned the knob to enter.

Giselle caught her breath as the stately front door opened to a spacious foyer, and she wheeled the first of her two suitcases across the threshold. When she'd brought both inside, she closed the door behind her and turned to survey her home for the next two weeks.

Unable to believe her luck, Giselle entered a wide-open living room and stared up at the rough timbers that highlighted the towering vaulted ceiling. Light flooded in through the rows of eight-foot windows on both sides of the long room. To her left, comfortable furniture in leather and velvet was clustered around a massive fireplace adorned with the same fieldstone that covered the exterior.

Obviously, Jessica was doing way better financially than she'd let on. The way the fellow entrepreneur had described her modest glamping business, Giselle had expected a simple, modest home.

The sound of the front door opening behind her was Giselle's first indication that she was no longer alone in the house and she kicked herself for not reengaging the lock. From her years of living in a large, potentially dangerous metropolis, her first reaction to the unknown interloper was panic. Someone had invaded Jessica's house without knocking. Was this something that happened in the country? Were there no boundaries? No civility?

Giselle punched her hand into her purse, scrabbled for a familiar cylinder and pulled out her pepper spray. She'd only had to use it once before, preferring to avoid sketchy situations rather than blindly stumbling into danger. Knowing that the element of surprise worked to her advantage, she held the small canister hidden in the folds of her denim skirt as she swung to face her intruder.

Expecting a shifty, unkempt criminal, she was not prepared for the tall, half-naked god who strolled into view. She'd come to the ranch with a half-formed idea of finding the face of her skin-care line for men among the rugged cowboys she hoped to encounter. But never in a million years did she expect the first hunk she encountered to be this gorgeous.

Giselle gaped in undignified admiration as her gaze toured his defined pecs and drank in the beefy heft of his shoulders. Every chiseled inch of his tanned torso was absolute perfection. This was an oh-so-hot, I-got-all-these-rippling-muscles-from-riding-horses-and-roping-cattle body to die for. She pursed her lips in a breathless whistle. With a mouth this dry, the only sound she could muster was a disbelieving *oh*.

He held a plaid shirt in one hand and a black Stetson in the other. Sweat gleamed on his tanned skin, highlighting the rugged landscape of his tight abs, popping pecs and bulging biceps. His dark hair was damp and spiky, as if he'd doused himself and then whipped away the water with a vigorous headshake.

While she'd been staring in transfixed wonder, his attention had been riveted on the luggage in his foyer, so he'd not yet noticed Giselle's presence. Now, however, his narrowed eyes swept the living room and locked on her. He stopped dead in his tracks and surveyed her in stunned confusion. When their eyes met, time seemed to slow.

Not until that instant had she considered her vacation might benefit from a roll or two in the hay with a sexy cowboy. No doubt a couple weeks of wild, sweaty sex with a man she'd never see again would put Thad right out of her mind.

With his raw masculine strength, he was a fantasy come to life. After finding out she'd be spending the two weeks on a ranch, she'd indulged in a lot of daydreams about cowboys, but they all paled in comparison to the real thing. Giselle felt a rush of giddiness as she developed an instant infatuation with this stranger. This last thought reminded her that she had no idea who this man was, only that he'd barged in uninvited.

He could be a dangerous intruder. On the other hand, would it be so bad if she let someone this hot take advantage of her? Giselle clenched the pepper spray and told her wayward hormones to behave.

"Who are you?" she croaked out, wishing she sounded more forceful.

Her question shattered his immobility. His sculpted lips thinned and he scowled.

"Who am I?" He shook his head, as if in disbelief. "Who the hell are you?"

Either he'd forgotten that he was shirtless or he didn't care. Between his air of command and the aggressive tilt of his head, he looked so sure of himself.

"Well?" he prompted as she continued to ogle him in tongue-tied stupefaction.

"Giselle Saito."

"Well, Giselle Saito, perhaps you can explain to me what you're doing in my house."

Two

Lyle seethed as the woman his sister *claimed* was his k!smet match regarded him with abundant sexual interest. When he'd first entered the house, he'd half wondered if he'd somehow conjured her out of the blue. Ever since Jessica had presented him with her profile pic, he hadn't been able to stop thinking about Giselle's body in the tiny red bikini, her slender curves arranged in a come-and-get-me pose.

"Yo-o-ur…house?" She drew out the first word while eyeing him skeptically.

"Yes."

"But the door unlocked when I put in the code Jessica gave me."

"I don't generally lock my doors during the day."

Her eyes widened in horror. "Aren't you afraid some-one will break in?"

"No."

Lyle regarded the woman, trying to reconcile the flirt in the profile picture with the down-to-earth one stand-ing before him. Today's outfit was a city girl's inter-pretation of cowgirl-chic. A tiered ruffle dress in some sort of denim-looking fabric, cinched with a silver-and-turquoise belt. Instead of cowboy boots, she wore navy wedge peep-toe sandals that added a good four inches to her height and drew attention to her toned calves. She looked feminine and flirty with her long hair styled in soft waves that framed her heart-shaped face.

With her head cocked to one side, she considered the situation for a moment. "Why not?"

"Because this is my ranch."

His answer settled her. All signs of uncertainty van-ished. "That means you're Jessica's brother. Then, this is where I'm supposed to be."

Her confidence irritated him. Obviously, she and his sister had conspired to ambush him. It wasn't a coinci-dence that yesterday Jessica had shown him her profile picture and today she was standing in his living room. Uninvited and unannounced.

Now, he was expected to just welcome her into his house?

"You are mistaken."

"I'm not."

"Enlighten me."

Beneath his anger, something unsettling and unwel-come stirred. Admiration. When he'd initially shown up, she'd been startled and maybe a bit afraid. Now, she confronted him like a woman in charge—she was clear-eyed and confident.

"I've arranged to stay here for the next two weeks."

Ultra-aware of her designer luggage stashed in his entryway and the danger it represented, he countered, "I don't recall agreeing to that."

"You didn't?" Suddenly, she looked worried. "I thought everything was all arranged."

That the pair of them assumed he was going to fall for such an obvious ploy irritated him.

"Is that what my sister told you?"

A line appeared between her brows. "Well, yes."

"How do you know my sister?" he asked, playing dumb to lure her into revealing her scheming ways.

"We connected through the k!smet app." A dimple flashed in her cheek. "We're trading houses."

"Of course, you are," he muttered, sudden weariness washing over him. "You're in the wrong house."

"So Jessica doesn't live here?"

"No."

"Oh."

"Oh?"

"Well, that's a little disappointing."

Heat flared beneath his skin as he read her mind. No doubt she imagined herself parading around his house, flashing skin in the hopes that he'd be overcome by desire. Given the way his thoughts had betrayed him since Jessica had shown him her picture, that might've happened.

Dozens of times in the last twenty-four hours, he'd

caught his thoughts wandering from practical matters to the sexy thrust of her breasts and the provocative jut of her hip. The woman was fucking gorgeous and knew full well the sort of impact she had on men. She seduced the camera with a bold smile, daring the observer to chase her, catch her and claim her.

Lyle shook his head to dispel such dangerous musings. "I'm sure it is."

Giselle looked unfazed by his mocking tone. "Then where does she live?"

"Her home is a half mile farther along the driveway."

"Oh. Okay. Thanks." Giselle started forward, but had only taken three steps before she stopped. "Sorry about the mix-up."

"Sure."

And still, she hesitated. No doubt she hadn't expected to be rebuffed quite so thoroughly and was scrambling for some ploy to keep the conversation going.

"I have things to do, so…." He gestured toward the open front door behind him.

"Of course. I'll get out of your way."

It wasn't until she scooted past, giving him a good six feet of space and banging her hip into the narrow foyer table in the process, that he realized he'd been blocking her path. The way she grabbed her luggage, awkwardly maneuvering the suitcases out the door and banging them down the porch steps to the bright yellow Mini Cooper parked out front, roused a twinge of guilt at how he'd behaved.

Obviously, Jessica was right. He'd turned downright antisocial. The shock of finding his k!smet match ensconced in his house didn't excuse his rudeness. No one could've ever accused him of being a bully. Until now.

"Well, that was a shit show." The caustic opinion came from behind him.

Lyle pivoted toward his mother's best friend, a clean shirt smacking him in the face as he turned. Clawing free of the lavender-scented fabric, Lyle gathered a breath to defend himself. The disapproval in Rosie Masters's keen blue eyes changed his mind.

Their relationship was a complicated one. She had been both his housekeeper and surrogate mother since Tallulah Drummond's fatal car crash seventeen years earlier. Lyle was forever grateful that his mother's BFF had dropped everything to run his house and take care of his much younger sister. Rosie had been a solid presence in his household after the abrupt losses of first his mother and then his wife.

"You don't understand—" he began, sliding his arms into the shirt and fastening the buttons.

"What am I missing?" Rosie countered. "It sounded like she was lost. And instead of being hospitable, you act like she was trespassing."

"She and Jessica—"

"Are trading houses for two weeks. Yes, I know."

Lyle ground his teeth as he realized she'd eavesdropped on the entire conversation without coming to his rescue. He debated whether that put her in the conspirators' camp.

"Which means," Rosie continued, "she's a guest of Royal Cattle Company and should be treated as such."

"She's not a guest," Lyle said, disliking the way Rosie was making him feel defensive.

Why should he feel bad for being upset at finding a stranger in his house? No, not a stranger. The woman from the k!smet app. The one Jessica claimed he'd been matched to. Was that even true? Just because his sister had shown him the woman's profile picture didn't mean they'd actually been matched.

"What would you call her then?"

"She's an interloper." He punched the last word with gusto.

"A what?"

"An interloper. She has no business being here."

Rosie's eyes went wide. "It seems to me that Jessica has every right to do with her house as she chooses."

"Fine." Aware that he'd never win this argument, Lyle set his jaw, unwilling to relent. "But I don't like being manipulated."

"How did you make the leap from Jessica trading homes with that perfectly lovely woman to you being manipulated?"

Initially, he had no intention of explaining himself, but her expression told him she could wait all day for his response.

"Jessica created an account for me on that damn k!smet app and that woman—" he pointed toward the front door "—was the person I matched with."

Rosie regarded him steadily, as if expecting more. When he added nothing, she blew out an impatient breath.

"And?"

"It's a little too coincidental, don't you think?"

"Whose fault is that?"

Lyle regarded his housekeeper in confusion. "Jessica's, obviously."

"You think so?" Rosie let the words hang in the air for a beat, then asked, "You don't think your stubbornness is the reason your sister went to such lengths to introduce to someone who might be perfect for you?"

He wasn't happy with the way his pulse jumped. "She's not."

"And how do you know?" Rosie shook her head in disgust. "According to Jess, she's successful. Intelligent. Beautiful. What's not to like?"

Not one damn thing if Giselle Saito was all the things Rosie described. "For one thing she's a city girl."

"You're not hiring her to work cattle. What does it matter if she's clueless about ranching?"

"It matters."

Chloe hadn't just been his wife, she'd been his partner in the ranch as well. Most days it was like she could read his mind. Even after five years, he still had moments when he'd turn his head to say something to her and was shocked to find himself alone.

"Oh, Lyle." Rosie regarded him in dismay. "Your sister wants you to be happy. She's worried that you're going to wake up one day and regret that you have no one to share your life with."

"She should worry about her own love life and leave mine alone."

"I think your sister is perfectly capable of doing both. Unlike you, who can't seem to focus on anything but this ranch, Jessica runs her glamping business, pursues her culinary career and still manages an active social life. When was the last time you did something fun away from this ranch?"

Lyle opened his mouth to assert that fun activities were better with someone to do them with, and then realized that the declaration made Rosie's point. He hated admitting he was wrong. And it was true that when it came to his personal life, he wasn't good at making it a priority.

That had been different when he and Chloe had been together. Especially in the early days of their marriage, when he'd let things go on the ranch and spent long hours as a blissful newlywed, indulging his wife's every desire. Not that his operation suffered. In the early days after his mother had bought the ranch, they'd developed Royal Cattle Company into a well-oiled machine. Obviously, the ranch functioned better when he focused on all the tiny details, but these days he didn't need to micromanage everything. It was just that doing so helped him stay busy.

"Chloe wouldn't want you to shut yourself off like this."

His housekeeper's quiet words came at him like a charging bull. His dead wife wouldn't approve that he hadn't moved forward with another relationship. Nor would she understand that his fear of opening himself up to loss again overpowered his need for a life partner.

"From your lack of an answer, I will take that as acknowledgment that I'm right and you know it." Rosie turned sympathetic. "Maybe you should be happy that the k!smet app worked as well as it did and just let your-self enjoy the company of someone like Giselle Saito."

Lyle hated how reasonable she sounded while his emotions continued to churn with resentment. "I'm not going to do that."

"Well, fine," she huffed, sounding utterly disap-pointed in his attitude. "I don't know why I thought I could talk sense into you." Rosie shook her head in dis-gust. "But that doesn't excuse you for being rude. You should at least go apologize for that."

"Let me get cleaned up and I'll drop by Jessica's place."

"Wonderful." Rosie nodded in satisfaction at having badgered him into doing the right thing. "Why don't you invite her here for dinner."

Despite her physical appeal, Giselle wasn't his type. Her profile pictures revealed the sort of personality that enjoyed being social. No doubt, she frequented par-ties and events where she could dress up and work the crowd. He tended to avoid fancy shindigs, preferring intimate dinners and meaningful conversation.

"I'm sure Jessica stocked her refrigerator before leav-ing." The last thing Lyle wanted to do was encourage his sister's matchmaking scheme.

"I guess it's a good thing I baked this morning so at least I can put together a care package for you to deliver."

"You do that," Lyle declared, heading toward his bedroom. "I'll drop it off."

"And apologize," Rosie called after him.

"And apologize…to the interloper," he grumbled, in-tending that would be the last time he dealt with Giselle Saito.

* * *

"Stay away from my brother" indeed.

What a rude, insufferable jerk.

The shock of her encounter with Lyle Drummond continued to resonate as Giselle wrestled her luggage back to the Mini, threw everything into the trunk and slammed the lid closed. A glance up at the sky showed the midday sun beaming down on her from a clear blue background. No gray clouds. No flashes of lightning. Which meant the ominous thunder rumbling in her ears was the agitating pounding of her heart.

Her hands shook as she pointed her convertible back to the main road that ran through the ranch. She'd felt so optimistic and buoyant at the start of today's journey. Now, it was like she'd taken a wrong turn into Grumpyville.

Putting distance between herself and Jessica's brother didn't ease her agitation one bit. Not until a cluster of barns appeared to her right, surrounded by pastures dotted with cattle and horses, was Giselle able to recall her earlier excitement.

So what if the unsettling encounter with Lyle was not the welcome she'd anticipated. Just because the tall rancher was as inhospitable as a desert in July didn't mean she had to let it ruin her stay. She'd just make sure she avoided Lyle Drummond. How difficult could that be? Heaven knew she had plenty of work to keep her busy planning next season's ad campaign. And she'd take some stylish photos of herself using her products among the trees that surrounded the stunning ranch house that appeared before her.

As soon as Giselle entered Jessica's home, she noticed all her anxiety melting away. A modern take on a rustic charmer, reclaimed barn wood and timbers gave the spaces a cozy feel. A fieldstone fireplace anchored the great room, while enormous windows let in sunshine and framed stunning vistas.

After poking her head into the master bedroom and admiring yet another stone fireplace and vaulted wood ceiling, Giselle made her way to a large and luxurious guest room that featured a king-size bed, an attached bathroom with a claw-foot tub and an overstuffed reading chair positioned beside French doors that led out to a private deck.

With a muffled squeal of delight, she flopped onto the bed and let herself get swept away by blissful contentment. Seconds later, she bounced up and set about unpacking her suitcases and settling in. Order was important to her. Giselle owed her success to meticulous planning and resolute follow-through. Maybe being goal-driven had hampered her spontaneity, but growing her skin-care business into a multimillion-dollar enterprise by the time she reached thirty had been worth every sacrifice.

But if she let herself go there, Giselle recognized she buried herself in work and neglected her personal life because opening her heart meant risking rejection. She wished she had a tenth of Gabby's confident flamboyance. Her sister had a way of believing everyone adored her. Meanwhile, Giselle defined her value with something she could measure. Financial success and social-media followers offered solid footing for her self-esteem.

Happy hour was approaching as Giselle finished settling in, so she headed into the kitchen to ponder whether to celebrate her first day on the ranch with a red or white. After experiencing the absolute silence of Jessica's isolated house, when a knock sounded on the front door, her heart rate exploded.

Living in a secured building, she wasn't accustomed to people just dropping by. Her nearest neighbors were a retired couple who traveled all the time and a corporate lawyer who worked long hours. Her friends only came over when invited. A tiny voice inside her head reminded her that the ranch was miles and miles from anywhere, and Jessica's house was a long way down a private driveway. Also, it was doubtful that an axe murderer would knock.

All these were excellent points, but Giselle thought she'd feel more confident with a weapon. The first thing she saw was a frying pan. She plucked it off the stove, shocked at the imposing heft of the cast iron, then headed for the door.

She needed both hands to raise the heavy weapon and that left her unable to open the door. Giselle clutched the pan against her chest and wrenched the doorknob. As the door swung open, she positioned the cast-iron skillet in a threatening manner.

Never in a million years had she expected the person who was standing on the front porch. Lyle Drummond looked damn unhappy to be there. He held a basket clutched in one tanned hand. The other rested on his hip, fingers tucked into a front pocket of his jeans. A muscle bunched in his jaw as she studied him in stunned silence.

"What are you planning to do with that?"

Giselle's hands cramped and her arms shook with the effort required to hold the pan suspended in midair.

"Depends." She was proud of her cool, tough-girl tone. "Have you stopped by to run me out of this house, too?"

As she asked this, Giselle shook the six-pound skillet to demonstrate its heft. The maneuver required more exertion than she expected and the grunt that came out of her was woefully unattractive.

"Are you planning to scare me off with your cooking?"

Humor? From Jessica's surly brother? The shock of it made her blood run hot. Abruptly, she recalled the impressive muscles beneath the fabric of his blue shirt and noticed the woodsy scent of pine wafting off his skin. Strange and exhilarating things were happening to her. For a wild second, she was swept up by the insane urge to pluck off his hat, wrap her fingers around his enormous belt buckle and drag him to her.

Her imagination paused at that point. What was she going to do with him then? *Kiss him.* The suggestion whispered through her mind, but she immediately rejected it. Lyle might be hot, but his prickly nature was giving off major stay-back vibes.

"I know you're not going to hit me with that," he continued, one eyebrow darting upward in amused disdain. "It looks like you're having trouble holding it, much less swinging at me."

Truth be told, she hadn't thought beyond trying to look as threatening as possible. "Actually, I was thinking more of dropping it on your foot, because you wouldn't expect that, and then bolting for the back door. I figure between my head start and your broken toe that I might be able to get away."

"You've thought this through."

"I'm a single woman living alone in downtown Dallas. It never hurts to be prepared." While he processed her clever comeback, she used her chin to indicate the basket he was carrying. "Are you going on a picnic?"

"This is for you." He raised the basket. "Rosie—my housekeeper—wasn't sure if Jessica left you anything in the refrigerator so she packed up some brisket and fixings. Plus some stuff she baked earlier today."

"It was nice of you to bring this by."

Giselle told herself not to be disappointed that he was merely running an errand for his housekeeper. This was not a social call, just a practical delivery of food.

Accepting the basket required some shuffling of the heavy skillet. "Tell Rosie thank you."

"I'll do that."

With the welcome gift delivered, Giselle expected him to go. Instead, he remained rooted in place.

"Is there something else?" she asked, noticing an infinitesimal shift in his stoic confidence.

"I also wanted to say that…" His lips pressed into a tight line as he stared at the bridge of her nose. He looked pained, as if a tractor had rolled onto his foot. "I'm sorry about earlier."

Giselle arched an eyebrow. "You don't sound sorry."

Lyle arched an eyebrow back. "How do I sound?"

"Like a ten-year-old boy that's been scolded into apologizing." Seeing surprise flash across his features, she smirked. "Who gave you hell?"

To her intense delight, color flared in his sun-darkened cheeks.

"You don't think I realized I could've handled that better?"

Was she really supposed to believe that the self-righteous Lyle Drummond was suddenly struck by remorse over his earlier rudeness?

"Oh," she declared in a smug tone. "I'm sure you recognized that you were being rude. I just don't think you'll lose any sleep at night because of it. Which makes this the lamest apology ever."

"That's awfully judgmental of you."

Giselle's shoulders rose and fell. "I just call 'em like I see 'em."

"So…" A muscle worked in Lyle's jaw. "Maybe I overreacted."

She wasn't ready to let him off the hook quite yet. "Oh, you totally overreacted." She dropped her voice into a low growl and said, "'Who are you and what are you doing in my house?'"

"I didn't sound like that."

"You did." Giselle gave a decisive nod to dispute his rebuttal. "Didn't Jessica mention she was trading houses with someone?"

"She did." Up until now, Lyle's gaze had visited every part of her face except her eyes. Abruptly, that changed and Giselle found herself mesmerized by the intense glow in the blue depths as he added, "I just didn't realize it would be you."

That statement left her completely bewildered. Whom had he been expecting?

"Look, I'm sure it was a huge shock to find a stranger standing in your living room." This was her meeting him in the middle.

"We don't get a lot of people stopping by the ranch unannounced."

"I'm sure you don't." What was wrong with the female population of town that they didn't pop by for an occasional booty call with this guy? Giselle was convinced if his mouth could be kept busy, that Lyle would be a perfectly acceptable sexual partner. "Although you're not all that far from Royal. Like twenty minutes?"

"About that," Lyle agreed. "But to hear my sister talk, you'd think we were in the middle of nowhere."

Giselle chuckled. "She did make it sound like you're pretty isolated out here." Watching the tension flow out of Lyle's muscles, she relaxed her guard as well. "Did she mention that I've never been on a ranch before?"

"She didn't say much of anything about you."

"Your sister is right. You are grumpy."

His only response was a deep scowl.

"And yet here you are, standing on my front porch." She indicated the basket. "Bringing me food and fumbling your way through a truly terrible apology. It's kinda charming."

With a noncommittal humph, Lyle tugged on his hat brim. "Enjoy the brisket. Rosie is one hell of a cook."

"I was about to open a bottle of wine." Giselle was enjoying their contentious banter, and despite Jessica's warning, she wanted to get to know the enigmatic rancher a whole lot better. "Would you like to come in and join me?"

Lyle studied her for a moment, in silence, then said, "I should probably tell you up front that this—" he pointed from himself to her and back again "—isn't gonna happen."

Shock at his presumption left her head buzzing. The man was insufferable. Unless… Had her earlier thoughts been written all over her face?

"That's not… I'm not…" Heat surged up her neck and exploded in her cheeks. "Excuse me for just trying to be nice."

"Was the invitation just about being nice?" He hit her with a doubtful look. "You don't want anything from me?"

"Well." She balanced the humiliation of asking him for a favor against her pride and decided that she would take one for her business. "I'm interested in learning what you do here."

"This a cattle ranch. We raise cattle."

"Sure. But isn't there's a lot more to it than that?" Giselle offered him her most winning smile. "I'd really like to find out."

"I don't have time to give you a tour."

"It doesn't have to be a tour." She'd dealt with enough difficult men to persist until she got what she wanted. "Put me to work."

His eyes flared at her offer, and then narrowed. "You have zero experience."

Far from being insulted, Giselle plotted her counter-argument. "You'll find I can follow directions."

"Nope."

Frustration bloomed as Giselle watched him turn to go. "With or without your help, I am going to learn about ranching."

"So you're planning to…what? Wander around getting in everyone's way?"

She ignored his sarcasm. "You won't even know I'm there."

He paused. Gravel crunched beneath his heel as he turned back. "Ranching can be dangerous. I don't want you stumbling into trouble."

"I won't."

Lyle shook his head. "You will."

Three

The next time Lyle saw Giselle, she was standing near a paddock fence. It was midmorning, and as he predicted the day before, she'd stumbled into trouble.

At the moment, she was folded over the top rail of that paddock fence, an enticing carrot in her left hand, a camera in her right. She was attempting to lure one of the horses over to her so she could get a picture. The plan wasn't problematic in theory. If a different horse had broken from the herd, Lyle might've gone on with his day. But it wasn't another horse. It was a particular buckskin, and its gaze wasn't locked on the preferred treat, but was aimed at the human offering it.

With a growl, Lyle adjusted his trajectory even as he glanced around to see which of his ranch hands was close enough to rescue her. Their attention was riveted on Giselle as she draped herself over the fence, her arm held straight out. He couldn't blame them. Her take on cowgirl-chic was both impractical and sexy as hell.

On her feet were the most ridiculous pair of sunset-inspired cowboy boots he'd ever seen. Their bright color caught his eye from thirty feet away. She'd paired the boots with denim booty shorts that showed off the toned muscles of her thighs and came a millimeter shy of exposing the intoxicating curve of her firm rear end as she bent over the fence rail.

Holy shit.

Gauging the distance between the mare and Giselle, and then between himself and Giselle, Lyle picked up his pace. The woman was oblivious to her danger as the mare trotted toward her, looking eager and interested. In a flash, the buckskin flattened her ears against her head and lunged straight at Giselle.

With a curse, Lyle dashed the last five feet in a gallant sprint and just managed to wrap his arm around her lower abdomen and pluck Giselle off the fence before the mare reached her. The snap of teeth filled the air as Lyle pivoted, an armful of fragrant, luscious woman clutched against his thundering heart. He might've saved Giselle, but the same could not be said for his hat. The crabby equine had somehow managed to catch the brim and rip it from his head. In his peripheral vision, he saw her drop it to the ground and proceed to stomp it flat.

"Are you okay?" he asked.

"I think so." Shock made her voice husky.

The rasp of it across his nerves awakened something long dormant. He shoved away the feeling, unable to face it.

The press of her exquisite derriere against his lower half sent a Roman candle of lust shooting through him. He was so lost in the sensation that Lyle neglected to set her free after his impromptu rescue. What woke him to their intimate position was the tentative graze of her fingertips across the back of his bare forearm. Despite the heat of the day, goose bumps broke out. As if he's been burned, he dropped her on her feet and backed away.

To his utter dismay, heat exploded in his cheeks.

Damn the woman.

Situations like this were the exact reason why he'd wanted her to stay away.

"What happened? Why did she do that?" Giselle sounded utterly heartbroken.

She looked so shell-shocked that his first impulse was to comfort her. Recognizing that this would play straight into his sister's matchmaking, he vented his frustration at her instead.

"I warned you that things around here are dangerous." He indicated the mare. "This is a good example of what I meant."

"But she seemed so nice as she came toward me."

"You had a carrot."

"I thought when her ears were forward like that—" Giselle gestured toward the horse, who was at that moment demonstrating her fickle nature by looking curious and attentive, only to throw her ears back and shake her head in ornery aggression "—they were happy to see you. And then she just lunged at me like she was possessed."

Damn women and their contrary moods. How was anyone supposed to figure out what was on their mind when they couldn't settle on a single emotion?

"She's a rescue. Probably mistreated."

The mare seemed to understand that they were talking about her because she stepped closer to the fence. She fixed her attention on the carrot Giselle grasped. Ears forward, looking sweet and harmless, the mare reached toward it. Giselle took a step in the mare's direction, arm lifting as if she fully intended on putting herself within reach of the horse again.

Lyle shifted to block her. "Don't."

The mare flung her head back at his sudden movement and backed off a step. Thwarted from her prize, she made her displeasure plain by nosing his hat and then stepping on it once again. Lyle raked his fingers through his sweaty hair and stared at his mauled Stetson. It was lying on the ground, four feet inside the fence, just out of reach.

Giselle noticed his movement. "She took your hat."

"Yep."

"Do you need some help getting it?"

She looked adorably naive as she offered and Lyle shook his head. He climbed the fence, waving off the buckskin. She raced back to the herd, giving him space to fetch his hat and smack it against his thigh to free the worst of the dirt. By the time he'd returned to Giselle's side, the mare had approached once more.

"If she's so dangerous, why do you keep her around?"

"She's one of the finest cutting horses I've ever seen."

"What's a cutting horse?"

The bright curiosity in her eyes was direct and piercing, reflecting none of the come-hither look she'd displayed in her profile pictures. Should he believe that she'd merely been posing for the camera and that being flirtatious and provocative wasn't second nature to her? In fact, although they'd only met three times, he was struggling to reconcile the woman in the pictures with the one standing before him.

Maybe Jessica had warned her that a high-maintenance woman wouldn't appeal to him. That would explain why Giselle seemed less aggressively seductive in person and more thoughtful. Of course, the profile pictures could represent her public image. He kept expecting her to be brash and clueless. By her own admission, she was way out of her element. He'd assumed her curiosity about ranch life was a ploy. Did she expect he would be flattered that she'd shown interest in what he did?

"A horse that's trained to work with cattle."

"Aren't all your horses trained to work with cattle?"

"Cutting horses have specific training. They are useful when we need to separate a cow from the herd."

"Why would you need to do that?"

"A variety of reasons." Lyle realized he was acting the part of tour guide, exactly what he intended to avoid with her. But given her near brush with injury, maybe it was better to show her around and satisfy her curiosity rather than let her blunder into another misadventure. "The animal might be injured and require medical attention. They might need to be tagged or branded. Or it's possible that we're going to make steaks out of them." This last he added out of spite.

Predictably, Giselle's eyes went round with dismay. "Oh, no. You don't really kill them, do you?"

"Where do you think meat comes from? And don't say the supermarket."

"Of course, I know that animals need to be slaughtered to feed us, but that doesn't mean I want to think about happening."

"You wanted to know about ranching. That's the reality of what we do."

As he spoke, Lyle glanced around and noticed his conversation with Giselle was being observed by a half-dozen hands and that they were all grinning broadly at him. One of them even offered an encouraging salute. What the hell?

"You know, I've never been on a horse." Her wistful tone brought his attention back to her. She was peering hopefully up at him from beneath her long dark lashes, but there was no denying the fervent determination in her brown eyes. "I don't suppose there would be any chance of that happening while I'm here?"

She had a disconcerting way of exhibiting resolve and entreaty at the same time. If she'd displayed one or the other, he might've been able to stand his ground. Instead, the contrary combination muddled his reactions. Obviously, she was a woman who was used to getting her own way. No doubt, she thought if she persisted with her goals that he would eventually succumb through sheer exhaustion. Because resisting her was exhausting. Especially when the her lean curves felt so damn good against his body.

A seismic quake built in his midsection and zipped to his extremities, leaving him short of breath and unsteady. Why was he so damn attracted to her? She wasn't the most beautiful woman he'd encountered since Chloe's death. Okay, maybe her banter brightened his mood a little. But her stubbornness and unlimited curiosity was just plain annoying.

Yet there was no denying that something about this woman both infuriated him and kept him coming back for more.

"This isn't a dude ranch," he stated.

"I think you've mentioned that it's a working cattle ranch. What does that have to do with me getting on a horse?"

"I don't have time to teach you how to ride."

"Surely you could recommend someone who could teach me after the workday is over?"

Lyle wondered what he'd done wrong in a past life that fate kept throwing stubborn women at him. His mother, his sister and his housekeeper—all of them were set in their opinions and the very definition of the word *determined*. From the directness of her gaze and the stubborn thrust of her chin, he suspected that Giselle would continue to get into trouble unless he took her in hand.

When he said nothing, she offered further incentive. "I'd be happy to pay. I wouldn't expect someone to do it for free."

No doubt any one of his ranch hands would be delighted to offer lessons regardless of whether they were paid or not. And Lyle should just let one of them take her off his hands. But when he opened his mouth to tell her he'd find someone to teach her how to ride, something else entirely came out.

"Be here tomorrow at eleven. You're going to want to wear jeans." He couldn't stop the hiccup in his pulse as his gaze roamed down her bare thighs. "And sensible boots."

"Thank you, thank you, thank you! You have no idea how much this means to me."

"Just do me a favor and stay clear of ranch operations, won't you?"

He stayed put long enough to obtain her reluctant nod. Feeling only mildly relieved at her concession, he set his hat on his head and walked away before she could talk him into anything else.

Giselle watched Lyle walk off, the odd giddiness undiminished by his absence. In fact, it almost seemed as if her nerve endings sparked with renewed vigor as she processed all that had occurred in the last ten minutes or so.

She wasn't quite sure what to make of Lyle Drummond. In turns, straightforward and complex, gruff and capable of amusement. Unyielding until he compromised. Someone who used both brainpower and physical strength to solve the problems around him.

She'd never been one to get weak in the knees over a man's formidable brawn. And Lyle was immensely formidable. Most of the white-collar professionals she met in Dallas built muscle in a gym setting. They filled out their expensive suits in such a predictable way, but she suspected none of them could keep up with Lyle's all-day workout.

The handsome rancher's raw physical power was an irresistible temptation. Today, when he'd rescued her from the mare's attack, being pinned against his hard body made her ache in all sorts of delicious ways. The wonder of it made her want him to rescue her again and again. He inspired a reckless streak she didn't know she possessed.

Given Jessica's warning, she'd intended to avoid him at all cost. But he kept showing up when she least expected and triggered some perverse character flaw that had been buried in her subconscious until now. Despite knowing she was a guest at the ranch, she couldn't seem to stop aggravating him.

Maybe it would be different if he wasn't so bossy and exasperating. He treated her like an oblivious idiot. Which maybe she was, when it came to all things beyond the bright lights of the Dallas area. But it wasn't like she refused to get a clue. She'd repeatedly stated her interest in learning about the ranch, but he'd rebuffed her every time. She was starting to feel as if she had some sort of communicable disease.

Giselle's gaze went in search of Lyle's tall form and spotted him leading a dark brown horse out of the barn. Her heart gave a funny lurch as he effortlessly stepped into the saddle and whistled for a black-and-white border collie.

Keep your distance from my brother.

Sage advice that she was failing at completely. And really, how hard could it be? It wasn't as if he was everywhere at once. The ranch encompassed thousands of acres. Surely, she could maintain her distance.

With that thought in mind, Giselle wandered around the paddocks and barns, careful to watch her step and keep out of everyone's way. All the activity mystified her. Cowboys were everywhere—walking horses, loading equipment into pickup trucks and moving through paddocks crowded with cattle.

In search of the perfect face to represent her skin-care line, she snapped shot after shot. When she thought she'd captured enough images, Giselle let the camera fall to her side.

Only then did she realize the men were as curious about her as she was about them. The attention was a huge ego boost and she caught herself smiling as heads swiveled in her direction from all sides. Despite the fact that she and Gabby were identical twins, Gabby was known as the pretty one. Giselle had been characterized as smart. Gabby knew how to make everyone fall in love with her. Giselle had always felt dull by comparison. Now, however, as she basked in the limelight, she got why her sister was so confident.

As if thinking about her twin had summoned her, Giselle's phone buzzed. She fumbled it out of her back pocket and swiped to answer her sister's incoming call.

"Your photos of my upcoming line are fantastic. I didn't get to tell you yesterday I got some new stuff for you to try," Gabby announced. "Where are you?"

"A ranch—"

"A what?"

"I swapped—"

"Oh, that's right. Well, you can keep taking pictures just like that. The juxtaposition of my resort wear amid all that rugged landscape is absolutely sublime."

Rugged landscape? Giselle had shot the photos in Jessica's manicured backyard.

"I'm in love, love, love," Gabby continued. "And speaking of love, I think I've found the man of my dreams."

"That's great." Giselle wondered if she'd injected enough enthusiasm into her voice. Her sister had a knack for turning random guys into soul-mate material. "Where'd you two meet?"

"k!smet, of course."

"Of course." Even as Giselle cringed, she reminded herself that Gabby adored all the drama of a new romance and never seemed to suffer the soul-crushing disappointments that came when things didn't work out. She merely moved on to the next delightful encounter and threw herself into that relationship. "I bet he's amazing."

"Well, he's handsome and rich. So, yeah." Gabby's lush chuckle sparked Giselle's envy for all of one second.

"I'm happy for you." And that was one-hundred-percent true. "What does he do?"

"Funny you should ask. He owns a ranch. Isn't that a coincidence?"

"Isn't what a coincidence?"

"He owns a ranch. You're vacationing on a ranch." A pause to let Giselle appreciate the serendipity. "You'll have to tell me all about your experience so I sound smart when we talk."

"Um." She'd been on the ranch less than twenty-four hours and had no clue what went on here. "It's really dark and quiet at night."

"Seriously, Giselle? You've always been the smart one. I can't believe that's all you've got."

"I've been busy taking photos of your resort collection. I haven't started exploring yet." She left out the part where she'd nearly been savaged by a horse and rescued by her own handsome rancher.

"Well, go find some cowboys to talk to and call me back."

"I will."

After bidding goodbye to her sister, Giselle headed for her car. She was eager to download the photos she'd taken and see what might work on her social media. Already the images she'd taken of the sunset the night before had thousands of likes, and she suspected her followers were going to love the pictures of the cowboys as well.

After finding several photos she loved, Giselle cropped and applied her favorite filter before posting them. Almost immediately, the likes began to accumulate. Satisfied by her morning's work, Giselle made lunch and took the salad outside. Sitting on the veranda and staring out over the breathtaking Texas vista, Giselle noticed her foot was waggling.

This relaxing-on-vacation stuff was harder than she expected. It also put into perspective that while Giselle had known she was a workaholic, she didn't understand how deeply rooted it was in her subconscious. Last night she'd spent an hour with a glass of wine in her hand, trying to appreciate the freedom to do nothing at all. Instead, her mind had raced through all the items on her to-do list for the upcoming release of her new men's skin-care line.

At the top of the list was a scouting mission to find a sexy, *real* man—not a model—to represent her new venture. The fingers of her left hand angled the laptop so she could better see the screen. While she'd spotted several handsome men among those she'd photographed today, none of them felt quite right for her campaign. Maybe that was because she couldn't get Lyle Drummond's powerful presence out of her mind.

He was exactly what she'd imagined for her brand. It wasn't just that he was handsome and built. He possessed that special something that made her breath catch and her heart pound. She wasn't sure if it was his aloofness that fascinated her, or his confidence that enthralled her. Perhaps he represented an impossible challenge. What would it take to mellow his bluster and get him to accept her?

Her phone chimed, announcing an incoming text. Expecting it to be work-related, she was pleasantly surprised to see the sender was Rosie Masters, Lyle's housekeeper, inviting her to dinner. She debated her answer for several minutes, wondering if spending more time in Lyle's company was a good idea. In the end, she decided it would be rude to refuse.

Setting aside her unfinished lunch, Giselle set about doing research on Royal Cattle Company. Maybe if she could speak his language, he'd be more inclined to dialogue with her.

Their website had some history on the ranch's origins. Lyle's mother had bought the property after a lottery win and decided to specialize in a very specific sort of cattle. Wagyu was a Japanese beef known for being some of the best-tasting and healthiest beef, with the highest marbling. Giselle poured through the information, growing more impressed with each minute that passed. What a shame that Tallulah Drummond had died without seeing how her son had grown the ranch into a major player in the Wagyu beef industry.

Next, she clicked on the links to the Royal Cattle Company's social media and lost herself in the sumptuous images of Texas rangeland dotted with cattle, cowboys at work and play, and the humorous videos depicting ranching life. She scrutinized the various close-ups of the men, spotting two that might work for her promotional campaign. One in particular sparked her interest. Lively blue-gray eyes glinted in his narrow face. He wore a meticulously trimmed beard, and when she scrolled over his image, a link to his personal social-media account popped up. Jacob Shearling, Royal Cattle Company's foreman and Lyle's right-hand man.

She lingered over images of the two men side by side, appreciating their obvious camaraderie. It made her wish she had a close-knit team of her own. Because she sold her products online, all her employees worked remotely, except for those at the distribution center. When Giselle wasn't overseeing the development of new products, she spent her time dealing with the marketing and promotional aspect of her business.

Giselle was impressed to see that the ranch's page had over a hundred thousand followers. No doubt, that was due to the clever handling of the subjects and the incredible eye of the photographer. She assumed that Jessica was the genius behind the content until she searched for Camp Up and Jessica's personal social-media accounts and saw a completely different and quite distinctive vision.

Jessica posted videos of herself preparing food and photos of her dining experiences at restaurants. On the Camp Up site, there were shots of the various accommodations, but no guests. Based on what she saw, Giselle would never have guessed that Jessica was based in Texas. No sweeping vistas. No cows. No cowboys.

So who was the social-media genius for Royal Cattle Company?

Her next guess was Lyle, but when she found no social media for the man at all, Giselle decided that posting pictures of big-eyed calves with ridiculously long lashes wasn't his jam. She went back through all the photos of him and found one that snagged her interest. It wasn't a particularly sexy shot. He sat on a horse, surveying a pasture of cattle while drinking coffee from a thermos. A successful man appreciating all that he'd achieved.

An untamed longing swelled inside her. Giselle wanted to be beside him in that moment—a companion, a partner. She'd dated her fair share of men, but not one of them sparked anything like this. That she was drawn to a man who found her an annoying pest was just her regular old bad luck. Was it any wonder she'd given up on love?

Four

Lyle entered his house after an exhausting afternoon of chasing down strays and stumbled on his housekeeper fluffing couch pillows. He was looking forward to a shower, a stiff drink and a hearty dinner, in that order.

"It's about time you got back," Rosie said, her tone more acerbic than usual.

"Well, I'm here now."

"So you are." His housekeeper cast a critical eye around the room. "Hurry up and shower."

"I don't smell that bad." Lyle's quip landed like a sack of concrete. He regarded his housekeeper, noticing the way she vibrated with anticipation. "What's going on?"

"I invited Giselle to dinner." Rosie glanced at her watch. "But I forgot that I promised Angie I'd babysit, so you'll have to step in and play host."

"No." Lyle wasn't exactly proud of himself for protesting, but he didn't like being manipulated. "You invited her. You can uninvite her."

"I could, but I'm not going to." Rosie crossed her arms over her chest and stared down her nose at him. "It won't kill you to be sociable."

"Maybe not, but it sure isn't the best way for me to spend my time."

"You can't do paperwork every night."

"You know what it takes to maintain this ranch. If I don't keep updating the records, we aren't gonna have any idea what's going on a month from now."

"Taking one night off won't put you behind." Rosie ejected a frustrated sigh. "It's dinner, Lyle, not a marriage proposal."

While she was right, it occurred to him that if he gave in this time, it would only embolden Rosie and Jessica to push any number of eligible women on him in the future. He might as well put his foot down here and now.

"I will not be cajoled, manipulated or browbeaten into dating anyone. Jessica went too far signing me up for the k!smet app and then trading homes with the woman I matched with. It's too much. I'm perfectly happy as I am. I don't need or want to date anyone."

For a second Rosie seemed taken aback by his vehement declaration. Then, her manner softened, although a steely glint remained in her eyes. "You need a partner to share your life with. What about children? Who are you going to leave the ranch to? Jessica doesn't want it. You're building something amazing here. Your mother would want you to pass her legacy on."

Lyle's gut twisted at Rosie's words. Although his mother had never remarried, Lyle knew she was open to finding someone to spend the rest of her life with and suspected she would've succeeded if fate hadn't intervened. Before winning the lottery, she'd worked so hard to provide for them, and any spare time she had was devoted to her children. After their windfall, she had thrown all her energy into purchasing and creating Royal Cattle Company. Once she'd been accepted as a member of the Texas Cattleman's Club, she'd become more social and several men around town had made their interest in her known.

"Your mother was my best friend and I know she wanted you and Jessica to be happy. She would not want you to be alone."

Having Rosie pull out the your-mom-was-my-best-friend card to defend her opinion was not fair. Lyle ground his teeth to stop resentful words from flowing out. She truly believed she was doing what was best for him. Plus, he owed her for swooping in after Tallulah's death and providing a much-needed point of stability for Jessica while he was dealing with his own grief.

"I'm not alone." They'd debated this topic before and Lyle had disagreed with her every time, but despite how often he'd asserted his opinion, arguing never got him anywhere. And yet, out of pure self-preservation, he persisted. "I have you and Jessica."

"And while we are both wonderful women and you are incredibly lucky to have us—" Rosie paused to let that sink in "—we aren't everything you need."

"I had someone who was everything," he reminded her, his voice a tortured rumble. "And I lost her."

Thinking about moving on from his dead wife left him feeling open and raw. He didn't want to put himself through any of it again. Not the giddy high of falling in love, or the crushing low of holding his wife's hand as she slipped from the world and took his heart with her.

"Chloe's death was devastating," Rosie said, "and I would never suggest that any woman could replace her in your heart. But you can't close yourself off because you think that was your only chance at love."

No. No. No.

He would not let Jessica, Rosie or Giselle get inside his head and make him believe he needed that certain someone who made his life complete. He was doing just fine on his own. He had the ranch to keep him busy and his friends to badger him out of his shell.

Dating was too complicated and he couldn't imagine opening himself up to any woman, but especially not to a woman that had been selected for him by a faulty algorithm.

"Fine. I'll get cleaned up," he said, his tone resentful and obstinate. "I don't suppose you're making me cook as well?"

Rosie beamed as if she'd won. "Just the steaks. Everything else is ready to go for when she gets here."

Lyle groused his way through a shower and shave. He had no idea why he'd done the latter. It wasn't like he was trying to impress Giselle Saito. He was merely going through the motions, like brushing his teeth, rinsing with mouthwash and dousing himself with after-shave.

The fact that he not only smelled great, but also looked good, was made abundantly clear as Rosie offered him a big grin and bolstering thumbs-up. Catching a glimpse of himself in the mirror to the right of the foyer, Lyle snarled at his reflection. He had on the black button-down that Jessica had bought him for Christmas and his faded black jeans. He'd been hoping to come off as a dangerous man to cross, but instead he looked like a dressed-up turkey about to be slaughtered for Thanksgiving dinner.

What had possessed him to agree to playing host at tonight's dinner? He should've just canceled and went ahead with his regular evening's activities. A solo dinner. Several hours updating ranch records on the computer. Bed.

Too late now. The doorbell was ringing. Lyle retreated to the bar cart that held a selection of his favorite whiskeys. The evening promised to test his patience. Taking the edge off would blunt his irritation. While he might not appreciate the lengths Jessica and Rosie had gone to meddle in his personal life, he didn't have to be an overbearing asshole to the woman they foolishly believed they were helping. He would simply set her straight about his disinterest in dating her, or anyone. If she continued to pursue him after that, he wouldn't feel obliged to be as polite.

Two fingers of amber liquid burned their way down his throat as he listened to Rosie greet Giselle. He

poured himself a second drink as his dinner companion appeared.

Tonight she was wearing what had to be her version
of a romantic cowgirl. Yards of gauzy dove-gray ruffles
billowed as she appeared from the foyer. The off-the-
shoulder neckline bared her delicate collarbone, while
the short hem drew his attention to her long, shapely
legs. Tonight's cowboy boots were gray snakeskin. Lyle
clenched his jaw to avoid gaping at her as she closed
in on him.

The instant her personal space touched his, he took
a rapid, involuntary half step backward. Her scent assailed his nostrils, the fresh, light aroma of lemongrass
making his head spin. He was besieged by the urge to
snatch handfuls of the voluminous fabric of her dress
and draw her to him.

She was wearing a tent and he was utterly turned on.
Was it the delicate lines of her shoulders, or the kitten-
ish sweetness of the wavy golden-brown hair framing
her lovely face? She looked so damn happy to see him.
Genuinely, artlessly happy. As if she had no idea this
entire situation was one big setup. Or that he'd been maneuvered with ruthless determination to entertain her.

"Hello," she breathed, reminding him he hadn't
greeted her.

Realizing he was failing as a host, he glanced at
the camera slung over her shoulder and asked, "What's
that for?"

She smiled impishly. "You use it to take pictures."

"I know what a camera is for." Heat flared as he

imagined grazing his lips along her delicate collarbones. "Why did you bring it tonight?"

"I'm trying to document my time on your ranch."

"Why is that?"

"Because I have to feed the machine."

He had no idea what she was talking about. "What machine?"

"The hungry social-media machine that devours content like a ravenous wildebeest."

"What are you taking pictures of?"

"Everything." She lifted the camera to snap a shot of him, but he put out his hand to block the lens.

"Can you be more specific?"

"The cows and horses. Flowers. There are incredible views everywhere I turn." When he remained silent, she added, "It's how I promote my skin-care line. I love to put my products in gorgeous or unique locations. And the contrast between the rugged landscape and self-care products captures people's attention."

At a loss for what to say next, Lyle realized he was failing as a host. "What would you like to drink?"

"What are you drinking?"

"Whiskey."

"May I?" She indicated the tumbler in his hand, drawing his attention to her short nails and neutral manicure.

He handed the drink toward her, not liking the erratic tick of his pulse as their fingers brushed. Or the way his gaze roamed over her as she placed the glass against her rosy lips. She sipped delicately and gave an elegant little cough.

"Nice," she murmured hoarsely. A dimple appeared in one cheek as she handed it back. "I'll take one of those."

He wasn't sure whom he was more annoyed with. Her for being so damn alluring, or himself for his inability to break her spell. How could he be attracted to this woman when he had absolutely no interest in romance? Maybe all the gaslighting being employed by his sister and Rosie was having an effect. In their persistence, they'd succeeded in convincing his subconscious mind that he needed this woman.

"I hope you're not a vegetarian," he said, "because we're having steak for dinner."

"Sounds delicious."

She offered a pleasant smile, not seductive or suggestive in any way. Yet Lyle felt the impact of it in his solar plexus. For a second his breath hitched. Probably a good thing, because she smelled like heaven. He was definitely spending too much time around sweaty ranch hands if Giselle's scent was this captivating.

"Can I give you a hand?"

His voice was gruffer than he intended as he said, "I've got it."

To Lyle's dismay, she didn't take him at his word. Instead, she trailed after him into the kitchen, camera in hand, and watched while he pulled the steaks out of the refrigerator.

"I'll just put these on the grill," he said. "There's a salad in the fridge."

"Looks like the oven is on." Giselle crossed to the enormous range and opened the door. She shot a glance over her shoulder toward Lyle. "Some sort of potato dish."

"Probably my favorite Parmesan mashed potatoes."

"Yum."

While Giselle investigated the contents of his fridge, Lyle slipped outside with the steaks. On the back terrace, Rosie had set the family-size dining table for two, complete with flickering candles, crystal water goblets and a low centerpiece of late-season roses fresh from the garden. Soft jazz poured from a hidden speaker, invoking a relaxing vibe. Lyle scowled as he took in the romantic scene. Giselle followed him outside with the salad and a bottle of pinot noir.

"This was sitting open on the island. I'm guessing it's meant for us to drink with dinner."

Grilling the steaks gave him something to focus on besides Giselle and her damn camera, but Lyle found his attention drawn to her. If his sister's goal had been to present a woman specifically designed to suit him, she'd come up short. Giselle was completely different from Chloe. His wife had been down-to-earth and the least pretentious woman he'd ever met.

She'd been the daughter of a local rancher, and had seamlessly fit into his life and become his perfect partner. Chloe had been utterly devoted to the ranch and his dream of making his mother proud by ensuring Royal Cattle Company's success.

They'd spent long hours discussing breeding stock, distribution and ways of making the ranch profitable. She'd worked side by side with him every day and maintained the database of their herd, leaving him free to manage the day-to-day operations. Royal Cattle Company would not have become a success story without her.

Giselle, by contrast, was a city girl, both in her appearance and her choice of career. No doubt, the mud she'd gathered on her cowboy boots today had been the first bits of dirt she'd ever encountered. What had possessed Jessica and Rosie to imagine a relationship could develop between them?

"Those look amazing," Giselle said, coming to stand beside him as he set the steaks on the grill.

Her arm brushed his. Sizzling heat rushed over his skin.

"How do you like your steak?" he asked, his voice hoarse.

He hoped she'd tell him "well done," because there's no way he could be attracted to her after that.

"I usually order medium rare," she said. "But you'll have to tell me what suits Wagyu beef the best."

"Medium rare is perfect."

He needed to keep a close eye on the steaks to avoid flame-ups, but he couldn't stop his gaze from lingering on the delicate hollows above her collarbone, or the slim column of her neck that just begged to be nibbled on. It took an act of supreme will to tear his eyes away from her.

"These are almost done," he told Giselle.

"I'll go get the potatoes," Giselle offered. "Why don't you pour the wine?"

It wasn't until after he pulled the steaks off the grill that he wondered if Rosie made any of her famous chimichurri sauce. He headed inside in time to see Giselle's hand jerk as her knuckles accidentally came in contact with the upper rack of the oven. She sucked in a sharp breath as she pulled out the potatoes and set them on the stovetop. When she showed no signs of taking care of the burn, Lyle reached for her wrist and tugged her toward the sink. He turned on the tap and ran the water until it was cold, then put her hand beneath it.

Lyle noted her ragged inhale, the jerk of her pulse beneath his fingertip. His own body flickered to life as her thigh grazed his, her long hair stroking across his bare forearm.

"It might not seem like it," she said with a husky laugh, "but I'm not usually in need of rescuing."

"Maybe if you can go a day without risking life and limb, I might believe that."

She placed her palm against his cheek and turned his face until his gaze met hers. "I could do that, but I'm starting to think being saved by you is the best part of my day."

And then she was rising up on her tiptoes and brushing her lips against his cheek. Lyle went perfectly still and half closed his eyes. The fleeting touch sent his heartbeat into overdrive. As if by mutual agreement, the angle of their heads changed, bringing their breath into contact. Lips followed, but it was a tentative brush and retreat that confused Lyle.

She'd started this, so why was she hesitating? From her flirty profile pictures, he expected boldness. She appeared to be a woman who knew what she wanted and went after it. Why was she toying with him? Or was this a clever ploy to make him think the kiss was his idea?

The tempting warmth of her lips called to him. Blood roared in his ears, drowning out all rational thought. He fought his way back from the brink of lust and focused on making a decision. Kiss her or back the hell off. He never got a chance to act one way or another.

Giselle dug her fingers into his shoulder and planted her lips on his. In her eagerness, their teeth bumped. The kiss was an adolescent mishap. An overzealous smooch between clumsy teenagers. Strange how the awkwardness melted Lyle's resistance. Giselle must have noticed the change in his stance, because when she pressed her lips to his a second time, there was more coordination and a hint of curiosity in her kiss.

Curiosity he was happy to indulge. Her tongue flicked out to taste him—not a bold assault but an experimental sweep across his lower lip. Need jolted through him. His muscles vibrated. It took every bit of willpower he possessed not to take over. That didn't stop his imagination from firing tantalizing images through his mind. He saw himself lifting her onto the quartz countertop, stepping between her spread thighs so he could feast on her mouth, her neck, her delightful breasts.

Setting his hands on her hips, he pivoted her, settling her back against the lower cabinet. Sliding one thigh between hers, Lyle pinned her in place. With the tips of his fingers, he whisked aside her hair, then set his mouth on the tender spot where her shoulder joined her neck. He bit down gently and her lips parted on a ragged sigh. The exhalation was sexy as hell. Mouth moving up her neck toward her lips, he imagined her making that sound as he—

He lifted his lips from her soft flesh and shifted his hands from her body to the cool stone on either side of her hips. Breathing heavily, he set his forehead against hers, eyes closed, while he silently cursed himself for being an idiot. She'd maneuvered him perfectly. How the hell was he supposed to act like he wasn't interested after what he'd just done?

Lyle reached over and shut off the water. "The steaks are getting cold. We should probably eat."

All through dinner, Giselle was feeling lighter than air. She hadn't come to the ranch expecting to be knocked so thoroughly off her game. Nor could she explain why Lyle's imposing presence fired her nerve endings. Rough around the edges with a perpetual scowl and surly disposition, he was the furthest thing from the men she met in Dallas.

As an independent woman and a successful entrepreneur, Giselle noticed that combination often intimidated men, leading them to patronize her. Rarely did they meet her on equal footing. Staying on the ranch put her on Lyle's turf. She wasn't used to anyone treating her like a clueless gate-crasher. It made her want to prove herself. And win his approval.

Since she was the one accustomed to being in charge, surrendering control roused uncomfortable feelings. She'd liked it when Lyle had rescued her from the charging mare and fussed over her burned knuckles, but she wasn't used to letting herself be taken care of.

Craving more of that opened her up to potential disappointment and heartache. Allowing herself to be vulnerable was so much harder than acting strong. But something told her if she let down her guard with him, the sex would be mind-blowing.

While erotic images tumbled through her mind, Giselle kept the conversation flowing with questions about Wagyu beef and ranching. She'd gathered enough information from the website to be able to have a good discussion with him. He kept his answers short, playing the part of a good host. Not once did he send a heated glance her way.

By the time they finished carrying the dishes into the kitchen and settled them into the sink, Giselle was wondering if she'd imagined the way he'd seized her by the hips and pressed her against the counter, showing every indication of devouring her.

"Dinner was wonderful," she said, beaming at him to conceal her confusion. Her heart pounded with dizzying intensity against her ribs. "I'd love to reciprocate. I'm not the best cook, but I make a mean charcuterie platter if you were interested in coming by for a drink one of these days."

Exhaling a long breath, Lyle crossed his tree-trunk arms over his massive chest and regarded her somberly. *Uh-oh.* Giselle had seen that look before. She braced for whatever was to come. Her fantasy of winding up in Lyle's bed did not looking promising.

"I'm sorry," Lyle said. "I think I've given you the wrong idea."

She wasn't sure what rattled her more—the kiss or his regret-filled apology. Her gaze locked on his lips. Remembered pleasure cascaded through her. The kiss, she decided. It was definitely the kiss had that had rocked, rattled and rolled her world.

"About what?" Even in her own ears, her voice sounded small and far off.

"This dinner tonight."

Her doubts and fears bloomed as Lyle's obvious discomfort made her cringe. "What about it?"

"Rosie has her heart in the right place, but I'm not really looking to date anyone."

Whoa, date? "Whoa, date?" She had no interest in dating Lyle Drummond. Kissing him, sure. Sex…well, yes. Who wouldn't be interested after what had happened earlier? "It was just a single kiss. Let's not get ahead of ourselves."

Instead of looking relieved, he scowled at her. "If you're trying to play hard to get, it won't work on me."

"I'm not playing anything." If the man wanted brutal honesty, she would give it to him. "God! No wonder Jessica told me to stay away from you."

Lyle's eyes narrowed. "I don't believe you."

"Oh, she did. I'm assuming she wanted to spare me a cringe-worthy conversation like this." Giselle offered him an insincere smile, wishing she'd listened to Jessica instead of following her instincts. "Thank you for explaining your lack of romantic inclinations toward me. It will make our future interactions *way* less awkward."

"I didn't want to mislead you."

A wildfire of humiliation burned through her. "Hold up, cowboy. Don't get ahead of yourself. I mean the kiss was okay…"

"Okay…?"

"Or…" Jeez, what did he want her to say? Mind-blowing? Panty-dropping? She would not give him the satisfaction. "Nice…?"

"Nice?" He frowned. "Just nice?"

The kiss had been nice. Better than nice. Cosmic. A galaxy of shooting stars, each one targeting a cell in her body until she'd transformed into a tingling, sparkling meteor shower.

Before he could point out that she'd gone all swoony in his arms, she suggested, "Maybe you're out of practice."

His eyes flared. "I don't think I am."

It tweaked her funny bone how irritated he sounded. Obviously, Lyle Drummond was way too cocksure. He didn't need to know how much that short, hot kiss had turned her on. She certainly wouldn't want Lyle thinking she was putting the moves on him. Even though she had. She should assure him that she had no plans to do so again.

"It's not like riding a bike, you know," she said. "Your kissing skill get rusty with disuse."

"I've never had any complaints." He practically growled the words.

"Of course not. I mean, who would be rude enough to complain about a kiss being too slobbery or too soft or too hard. Especially after the guy bought her dinner."

Giselle set her hand on her hip and intoned, "'So thanks for the expensive meal and oh, by the way, you suck at kissing.'" She shook her head. "That's just impolite."

Lyle regarded her in bemusement. "I see." But whether or not he did see was up for debate. "So what happens when you are unfortunate enough to be kissed by someone who isn't up to your standards?"

"Depends."

"On?"

"Whether he's worth making an effort to improve." She'd intended her lighthearted tone to indicate she was kidding, but Lyle looked gobsmacked.

"And what, in your eyes, makes him worthy?"

Feeling like she'd ventured into shark-infested waters, Giselle fumbled for an answer. "According to my sister, if the guy is hot or has money to spend on her she's willing to renovate him."

"And according to you?"

Giselle considered her past romances. She chose to date younger men that were less successful than her. They were impressed by her multimillion-dollar skincare line and for a time that muted her insecurities. But relationships between unequal partners never lasted.

"What do you look for in the men you date?" he prompted when she didn't immediately answer.

"I don't have any criteria, exactly." Giselle gulped, suddenly uncomfortable with the turn the conversation had taken. Maybe if she did, she wouldn't keep choosing the wrong guys.

His eyes had grown strangely intent as he stared down at her and she wished she hadn't given so much away. No doubt, he probably thought she was romantically challenged. And he wouldn't be wrong.

"Look," she said. "I was just kidding with all this. The kiss caught me off guard—"

"You kissed me," he pointed out.

Giselle chose to ignore the who'd-done-what-to-whom controversy and continued, "I misread the situation. The candlelight and flowers. Now I realize none of it was your idea. Once I did, I got rattled. Sorry for blurting out the first stupid thing that popped into my mind. The kiss was great." She was close to hyperventilating at the way his facial muscles tightened into stony displeasure. "Really great. You have wonderful technique."

"No, I think you were pretty clear about my need for more practice." His eyes took on a hard, determined glint as he leaned into her space. "You might be right."

If he meant the remark as a threat, he missed the target. Every cell in her body electrified as lightning flashed through her.

"O-o-kay."

A tight smile lifted the corners of his mouth. "But not tonight."

"Of course not. It's late and you want to get to bed." When his eyebrows raised, she realized how her remark could've been interpreted. "I mean you get up really early, after all, and need your sleep. I'll just be heading off." Before she said anything else that got her in trouble, Giselle sidled toward the exit.

Lyle walked her to the front door and looked curious when she paused to face him. "I brought some products from my skin-care line for you to sample."

"For me?" The space between his eyebrows narrowed as he followed her gesture to the entry table, where she'd placed two gift bags filled with her products.

"You and Rosie." Giselle hooked one of the bags and extended it to him. "This one features my soon-to-be-released men's skin-care line."

He glanced at the bag dangling from her finger, examining the contents as if they were poisonous snakes. "I don't use this stuff. I wouldn't even know how."

Something perverse and provocative tickled its way down her spine. "I'm happy to demonstrate their use and explain about the benefits of each product. We'll schedule a spa night."

"I don't think…"

"I'm not hitting on you. This is business." Giselle was back on familiar ground after Lyle's rejection. Ignoring the way his blue eyes had fastened on her lips, she voiced what had been on her mind since arriving. "And it ties into a proposition I have for you."

"What might that be?" His voice held a husky note that made her shiver.

He might not become her vacation fling, but that didn't mean she had to go home empty-handed.

"I'm looking for someone to be the face of Saito for Men. I think you'd be perfect."

Five

When Lyle arrived in the stable yard the next morning for Giselle's promised riding lesson, he found her seated on the ground near where he'd rescued her from the buckskin mare the previous day. Just inside the paddock was a small pile of hay that the same mare was munching on.

Lyle was unsurprised that Giselle continued to underestimate the dangerous situation. No doubt, she believed the mare could be won over with treats and kindness, not understanding that horses weren't pets to be fawned over and indulged. They possessed iron-shod hooves and weighed in at an average of a thousand pounds. No matter how well trained, a horse could spook, rear or buck. Anyone with an ounce of sense in their head would recognize that at any moment something could go drastically wrong.

At least she'd listened to him regarding her clothing. Giselle had on jeans and a plaid Western shirt that had come straight out of Jessica's closet. Worn brown boots and a classic cowboy hat completed the look. For a second, Lyle was jolted by a sense of familiarity. Earlier, Giselle had stood out like a bird of paradise among roses. Now, she fit right in, as if she'd been doing this all her life.

But, of course, it was all an illusion. Giselle was a city girl. Her being here was a lark. She didn't belong on a ranch any more than Lyle was suited to work in an office with a view of downtown Dallas.

"You ready?" he asked, approaching Giselle.

At the sound of his voice, the buckskin mare threw up her head and bared her teeth at him.

Giselle frowned at the horse. "That's so weird. She's been perfectly fine for the last half an hour."

"Tell me you haven't gone near her."

"After what happened earlier, this is as close as I dared get." She indicated the hay. "I put a little of that in, hoping to lure some of the other horses, but she wouldn't let them get near it." She held up the camera. "I wanted to get some shots of the horses, but she kept getting between me and the rest of the group."

"I'm taking time out of my busy day to give you a riding lesson," Lyle said, offering his hand to help her to her feet. "Let's go."

"You're giving me a lesson?"

Lyle resisted a sigh. He should've passed her off to one of his hands like he'd planned and let them explain the intricacies of horsemanship to her, but he couldn't trust any of them to act like professionals around her.

"Everyone else is busy with ranch business."

"And you're not?"

"Do you want to ask questions or get a lesson?"

Eyes widening at his brusque tone, Giselle grabbed his hand and let him haul her up. Lyle ground his teeth at the comfortable warmth of her touch and released her as soon as possible.

"This is Firefly," Lyle declared, leading Giselle toward a short chestnut mare tied in the saddling area. "We usually put kids on her when Jessica is hosting a family."

That engaging dimple appeared in her cheek again. "So you're saying I'm childish?"

"No. That's not what I meant at all." Too late, he realized she was teasing him. The amusement dancing in her eyes made his gut clench. She wasn't flirting with him exactly. It was more the sort of ribbing he received from Jessica. He sighed, determined not to succumb to her antics. "What I'm trying to say is that she's a beginner's horse. Very calm and unflappable. In case you were nervous about riding."

"I'm not."

"It's okay if you are." He'd fully expected her to be skittish around horses after the buckskin mare tried taking her head off. Instead, her entire manner was one of keen enthusiasm. Lyle didn't want to be impressed by how quickly she'd bounced back. Giselle Saito kept confounding his assumptions. "It's just that some people who've never ridden before get nervous their first time."

"That's not me. I've been looking forward to getting on a horse since Jessica and I first connected."

"Well, good."

While Lyle began running a brush over the chestnut mare's glossy coat, Giselle lifted her camera and began taking pictures. His skin prickled as she captured his every move. His discomfort at her keen interest evolved into irritation.

"Look," he began, turning in her direction. "I'm taking time out of my busy schedule to give you a riding lesson. The least you could do is put down the camera and learn how to groom and saddle your mount." As he spoke, he plucked the camera out of her hand and set it on a shelf out of reach.

"You're right." Offering him an apologetic smile, she held out her hand for the brush.

Lyle took a step back as she slipped into the space between his body and the horse's side. His chest tingled where her shoulder had brushed it and he rubbed at the spot as if that would make the sensation vanish.

"Like this?" she asked, whisking the brush over the chestnut mare's cinnamon coat, flicking dust away like a pro.

"Like that. Make sure you get the girth area as well."

He reached around her and indicated Firefly's belly. This put him in close contact with her again and he noted the way she'd furrowed her brow in concentration. She appeared determined to do a good job and he appreciated the way she not only listened to him, but also moved both brush and hand over the horse's flanks and butt, letting the mare get accustomed to Giselle as she worked.

Thanks to Jessica's glamping business, scores of her

clients had received their first experience with a horse on the ranch. Lyle had witnessed any number of them handling horses for the first time and few of them had demonstrated Giselle's level of confidence.

"It seems like you've done this before," he mused, watching her mimic his technique for signaling to Firefly that she was to let Giselle pick up her hoof.

"I haven't." Giselle used a specially designed pick to clean mud and manure from the hoof, carefully avoiding the tender frog as she worked. While he expected a city girl like her to protest that she didn't want to get dirty, Giselle surprised him by showing little squeamishness at the task. "Although I will confess that I watched several days' worth of YouTube videos to get a sense of how to handle a horse. Actually doing it, though, is very different. I don't think I was prepared for how big they are or how fast they can move."

At that moment, Firefly swished her tail and stomped her rear left foot to rid herself of a pesky fly. Giselle started in surprise, placing her palm flat against the horse's side to maintain the distance between them in case the mare decided to step into her space. The wry grin Giselle tossed his way invited him to share in her private amusement and he caught his lips twitching in acknowledgment.

Ruthlessly controlling his body's involuntary reaction to Giselle's nearness, Lyle went about explaining every bit of equipment that went on a horse and the reasons why all of it was useful. Giselle absorbed every word he spoke, nodding periodically to indicate she understood his instructions and warnings.

Given the level of her focus, he probably went into greater detail than he needed to. Once again, he sensed that she was genuinely interested in what he had to tell her. She wasn't pretending to pay attention and didn't seem that her real purpose was to flirt with him. It unsettled him that he'd misread her intentions. How could he be wrong when she and Jessica had contrived to throw them together?

More likely, she was playing a long game, one that would lull him into thinking she had no romantic intentions toward him.

"Now that Firefly is tacked up and ready to go, it's time to get you into the saddle."

The fastest way to get her into the saddle was for her to bend her left knee so he could grab her lower leg and hoist her onto the mare's back. Unfortunately, that move would bring him into close proximity with her, and although he'd done this move a dozen times with other women, somehow when it came to Giselle, he was far too conscious of her shapely form and the subtle floral scent of her hair, which left him wanting to bury his nose in the wavy locks.

"That's a long way up." For the first time, Giselle regarded the chestnut mare with trepidation.

"You'll use the mounting block." He indicated a set of stairs they made available for kids and people that needed help getting into the saddle.

Positioning the mare beside the mounting block, Lyle gestured for Giselle to climb onto the top step. From there, she could easily set her left foot in the stirrup and swing her right leg over the mare's back to settle into the saddle.

Standing atop the stairs, Giselle looked from the horse's back—a scant foot away—to where Lyle waited by the horse's head, gripping the reins to keep the mare in place. "This isn't how a real cowboy mounts." She sounded disappointed.

"What do you know about real cowboys?" he retorted, not realizing his comeback sounded caustic until her eyes widened. He moderated his tone. "It's how a beginner gets on a horse."

She considered this for a silent moment as if trying to decide how to respond, then said, in all seriousness, "Don't you think I should learn the proper way?"

"You can definitely give it a try later. Why don't we do this for now, and then see how you're feeling about it?"

With a nod, Giselle took a hold of the saddle horn and eased herself onto the horse's back. She slid her feet into the stirrups and shifted around a bit to get used to being up there. Once she figured out her balance, she beamed at Lyle.

"What's next?" Giselle asked, her brown eyes sparkling with delight.

He ignored the way his body blazed to life at her charming expression. "You can try walking. Just pick up the reins and squeeze with your legs."

Giselle did as she was told but the mare didn't budge. "What's wrong?"

"Try clucking to her and squeeze a little harder."

"Clucking?"

Lyle made the encouraging sound and Giselle imitated him, at last getting the mare to move forward.

"Where am I going?" she asked, sounding a little anxious as the mare took several steps.

"Head for the corral." He pointed toward the open gate. "You steer by shifting your hand in the direction you want to head. The horse knows to turn when it feels the rein press against its neck."

She experimented as the patient mare trudged along. "Like this?"

"Just like that."

"Now what do I do?" Giselle asked as the mare cleared the gate and entered the corral.

"Just keep walking and getting used to being on her back."

Even as he secured the gate and kept a close eye on her, Lyle noted the attention she was receiving from the ranch hands. Giselle might appear oblivious, but Lyle caught every admiring glance. He shot a thunderous scowl at the assembled cowboys. The silent warning sent them scurrying back to their neglected tasks.

"How long does it take someone to learn to ride?" Giselle asked.

He'd been around a lot of riders and recognized a natural seat when he saw one. With every minute that passed, Giselle gained confidence and relaxed into the mare's rocking stride.

"It depends. Firefly is calm and won't give you any trouble. She's a good horse for beginners. The more comfortable you get in the saddle, the faster you can go, and the more practice you get, the more horse you can handle."

"Can I go faster?"

Lyle doubted she was ready for Firefly's trot, but gave a nod. "Cluck and squeeze," he advised, curious to see if she could get the mare moving.

One of the reasons they put kids on her was Firefly's unflappability. This also meant she was a bit sluggish, preferring a plodding walk to anything faster.

To his immense surprise, not only did Giselle get the mare to jog trot, but she also didn't tense up like most beginning riders did. Instead, she seemed to intuitively understand how to absorb the jarring pace by relaxing her torso.

"This is fun," she exclaimed as the mare jogged past.

"Glad you think so."

"Damn, boss." While Lyle had been focused on Giselle and Firefly, Jacob had come to stand beside him at the fence. As he often did, the foreman held a camera in his hands. He pointed it in Giselle's direction. "Your girl's got some skills. Are you sure she's never done this before?"

"She's not my girl," Lyle corrected, unhappy at the way Jacob had linked them. His ranch hands didn't need to know about Jessica's matchmaking efforts or how the pair had maneuvered to put Giselle into his orbit for the next two weeks. "She's just house-swapping with Jessica. And she claims she's never been on a horse."

"Maybe it was just an excuse to spend time with you?"

Lyle pondered his interaction with her over the last half hour. It could be that Giselle had ridden before and was just pretending that she lacked experience.

"She's not interested in me."

Lyle kept his expression neutral, not wanting to encourage Jacob's curiosity about him and Giselle. Everyone who worked on the ranch knew about Chloe's death five years earlier and they all had probably been waiting for him to move on. He had no idea why they were so interested in his personal life. Sometimes these rough-and-tumble cowboys could be as gossipy as a porch full of old women.

"I don't buy that for a second," Jacob said, his gaze following Giselle with far too much keen speculation. "What I can't figure out is whether you're going to do anything about it."

"I'm not."

Jacob uttered a disbelieving grunt. "Then you wouldn't mind if I take a shot?"

"I would, actually." The declaration came out of nowhere.

His foreman smirked. "That's what I figured."

"What I mean is…" What had he meant?

"No need to explain," Jacob said. "We've all been there a time or two. I'll make sure to pass the word around."

Lyle clamped his lips shut, wishing he'd done so a few seconds sooner. Well, what was done, was done. And it wasn't as if he had to follow through with anything. It shouldn't be all that difficult to keep his hands to himself until she left the ranch two weeks from now.

"You do that."

It took Giselle less than a minute to decide the world looked way better from the back of a horse. No wonder cowboys always looked so relaxed. Who could possibly feel stressed or anxious as their body moved in concert with a horse's swaying gait. In fact, she was so delighted by the experience that Lyle's focused regard no longer rattled her. Her world narrowed to just her and Firefly coming to an understanding.

Time flew by while Giselle absorbed the basics of horsemanship. There was so much to know and Giselle wondered how she could remember it all. Guided by Lyle's deep voice, she learned how to use her legs, as well as her hands, to move the mare in one direction or another. As her confidence increased, she found it easier to urge the horse from a bone-jarring trot into a rocking-chair lope. But when he tried to explain the thing about correct leads, she shook her head with information overload.

By the time an hour had passed, Giselle was completely and irrevocably hooked. How had she lived her entire life without learning how to ride a horse? It was the single coolest thing she'd ever done.

"I think that's enough," Lyle declared, entering the ring and indicating she should come to the middle and stop.

"No," Giselle wailed. "Can't I keep going? I'm just starting to get the hang of it."

"I have things to do."

"Fine." She did as he asked and stopped the mare beside Lyle. "Now what?"

"You dismount," Lyle said, continuing his tutoring. "Swing your left leg over the horse's back, kick your right foot free of the stirrup and drop down."

It sounded easy enough. And, in truth, the maneuver went smoothly for her first time. The problem came when her feet touched the hard earth. The thigh muscles she toned and strengthened in the gym failed to hold her up. Lyle must've been expecting her reaction because as her knees buckled, his arm came around her waist, snuggling her tight against his side. Prevented from becoming a puddle in the dirt, Giselle leaned into his unyielding form, enjoying the steely arm banding her to him. Her already wobbly limbs became even less reliable as his breath kissed her temple.

"Oh, my god," Giselle exclaimed. "What's wrong with me?"

"Riding uses a whole different set of muscles." Was that vindictive amusement in his voice? "You're probably going to be sore for the next couple of days."

Totally worth it.

"You could've warned me." Giselle tipped back her head and scowled up at him. Her heart bumped against her ribs at the warm glow in his cool blue eyes.

"Would it have made a difference?" Lyle's gaze swept her warm cheeks before alighting on her lips. "You were so determined to get on a horse. It'll get easier as the days go on." He arched one bold eyebrow. "Unless you'd like to quit."

"Quit?" she scoffed. "I'm just getting started."

He looked so skeptical that she forced her noodle-like legs to straighten. Despite how much she liked being this close to him, in that moment it was more important to prove she could stand on her own two feet.

From the beginning Lyle let her know he had no patience with women that needed rescuing. Sure, he'd saved her from being attacked by that angry mare and had been quick to lend his support after she dismounted. Then too, he'd tended her burnt knuckles with obvious concern. But that was most likely because he felt responsible for the welfare of everyone on his ranch.

Her theory was proved a moment later, as he released her and stepped back. Luckily, Giselle remained near enough to the horse to grab at the stirrup to stay upright, as her inner thighs screamed in protest.

"Okay, then. Are you ready to untack Firefly and brush her down?"

Wait, there was more? Giselle had been looking forward to escaping to Jessica's house before she made an even bigger fool of herself.

"Sure." Giselle sounded more sure of herself than she was. "Lead the way."

Lyle handed her the reins and headed toward the saddling area, leaving her to bring the mare. She was glad his back was turned, because her legs refused to function properly. It got better as she took a few steps, but Giselle was conscious that she was wobbling along like a toddler with a full diaper. Still, she persisted, and by the time she reached the saddling area, she could lift her feet instead of shuffling through the dirt.

A ruthless half smile tugged at his lips as Lyle walked her through the process of removing the saddle and bridle. Damn the man. He was enjoying her discomfort. Well, it wasn't much different than when she tried a new exercise at the gym. Giselle knew her muscles would appreciate a hot soak when she got back to Jessica's house.

With the mare turned out in the pasture, Lyle tugged on the brim of his hat and strode off.

"Same time tomorrow?" Giselle called after him.

Without turning around, he waved his right hand. Unsure whether to take that as a yes or no, Giselle watched him go. Then, she went in search of her camera. The last time she remembered seeing it was after Lyle had impatiently plucked it from her hand and set it aside.

A thorough search of the area revealed no camera. Perhaps it had been moved somewhere safe. She glanced around for someone to ask and made a beeline for the nearest cowboy.

She noted a cluster of them standing near a corral fence and approached. Several were calling instructions to a lanky teenager trying to toss a lasso over a plastic steer with no legs. The kid was red-faced from exhaustion and frustration. Giselle joined the group, wishing she had her camera to capture the moment.

"Is that as hard as it looks?" Giselle asked the man standing beside her. She studied the boy's technique and tried to make sense of the suggestions being tossed at him.

"It's just a matter of practice. Wanna give it a try?"

"Kinda." She glanced at the man, recognizing Jacob from the ranch's social-media posts. "I'll probably just make an ass out of myself, though."

"No judgment here. Let me show you how it's done."

"I'm Giselle, by the way." She stuck out her right hand.

"Jacob." He offered her a slow, lazy smile as he enfolded her hand into his for a come-hither handshake. "I've seen you around."

"Jessica and I traded homes for a couple weeks."

"Jess said someone would be staying at her place. She didn't mention she'd be so pretty."

"That's probably because we never met." Giselle noticed her cheeks growing warm beneath his intent regard. Oh, this one was a charmer.

From the social-media posts, she knew he was photogenic. Great bone structure and a nose that might've been broken once or twice gave his face character. Charisma oozed when he smiled. Giselle suspected he'd sweet-talked many a woman out of her jeans and into his arms. Giselle herself might've been interested in a rebound hookup if Lyle Drummond hadn't swept into her awareness, his challenging personality taking up residence in her thoughts.

"Come on," Jacob said, pushing away from the fence.

The muscles that had seized up after she'd gotten off the horse felt better with all the walking around she'd been doing. Still, Giselle couldn't help but notice she was strolling with the same rolling gait as the ranch hands as she followed Jacob to the gate that led into the small paddock.

"This is Giselle," he called to the assembled cowboys. "She's going to learn how to work a lasso and show Billy here how it's done."

While the group jeered at poor Billy, Jacob took the rope off the young kid and began demonstrating how to hold the lasso.

"To start out," he said, "you want your loop to be about shoulder height."

Giselle paid careful attention, so when it was her turn, she could imitate him. Tuning out her surroundings, she focused one hundred percent on Jacob's technique.

"The key is to maintain your elbow on the same plane." Jacob showed her both the right way and the wrong way. "What I want you to do is to swing three times and then release." Once again, he demonstrated the technique, then passed her the rope.

She was surprised at the rope's stiffness and how easily it slid through the tiny opening created by a honda knot. This made it easier to maintain the circle as she began to twirl the loop about her head, rotating her wrist in the way that Jacob had shown her.

Giselle tried to imitate him, but struggled to get the hang of a clean release. She watched Jacob demonstrate again and noticed the timing on the release that allowed the loop to fly away and land exactly where he aimed it.

"This is way harder than it looks," Giselle said, shooting Billy a sympathetic grin. At last, she succeeded in landing the rope around one of the steer's horns. Not where it needed to go, but a minor achievement. While her audience cheered, Giselle gathered up the rope and thanked her teacher. "I'll keep practicing."

"You did great for your first time." Jacob's blue-gray eyes sparkled with obvious approval, giving her confidence a much-needed boost. "Before you know it we'll have you doing it from horseback."

"I don't know about that. I'd never ridden a horse before today."

"Really?" His surprise was flattering. "You looked right at home on Firefly."

"It was so much fun, but I have a long way to go." It was then that Giselle recalled why she'd approached the group of men in the first place. "I don't suppose any of you noticed a camera in the saddling area. It isn't where I left it."

Jacob shook his head. "I'll ask around and keep an eye out for it."

"Thanks. I've been taking pictures for my social media and I'd hate to lose them. Speaking of social media, I was really impressed by the images on the Royal Cattle Company account. I don't suppose you're the one who's been taking all the pictures."

"I am."

"You've got a really good eye for what makes an image stand out."

"Thank you."

"Ever thought about doing it professionally?"

"I haven't." Jacob's gaze flicked past her shoulder a second before he tilted his head in flirtatious invitation. "But maybe that's something we could discuss over dinner tonight."

"I—"

A deep voice cut her off before she had a chance to refuse. "She already has plans."

Six

Giselle's head whipped around. She regarded Lyle with confusion. "I do?"

"You do." Damn the woman for drawing him all the way across the stable yard. He'd caught the tail end of her roping lesson and the winning smile she bestowed on Jacob. Instead of feeling relieved that Giselle had found a new target for her romantic inclinations, Lyle was starting to feel a bit surly.

"You changed your mind about spa night." Giselle beamed as she turned to offer an explanation to Jacob, "I'm rolling out a men's skin-care line and offered to show Lyle some of the products."

"Spa night?" Jacob echoed, his voice rich with amusement. "That sounds like a great time. Can I come, too?"

"No."

"The more, the merrier," Giselle said at the same time, appearing oblivious to Lyle's displeasure.

Annoyance flashed, a lightning strike from a clear blue sky. Even though he recognized her ploy, Lyle found himself unwilling to share her.

Lyle turned an icy stare on his foreman. "Ed says there's a problem with the baler. Why don't you go take a look at it?"

"You got it, boss." Jacob offered Lyle a crisp salute and then turned to Giselle. "Maybe tomorrow night—"

"No." Both Giselle and Jacob stared at him. "She's busy. There's a party at the Texas Cattlemen's Club."

"I guess that's my cue to leave." Jacob touched his hat brim. "Catch you later, Giselle."

"I'll bring by some samples for you tomorrow," Giselle called after the foreman, her gaze lingering on his departing form. "This party, do I need to wear something fancy?"

"It's a barn dance."

She nodded. "I'll do some research."

"Stay away from Jacob." His voice was a husky growl.

Giselle's brown eyes were soft with confusion as she regarded him. "Why?"

"He has a very…active social life."

"What does that matter?"

"He's not good boyfriend material."

"He's not…?" She sucked in a giant breath and appeared as if she was silently counting. "You are impossible. I'm not on the prowl for some man to fulfill me. I am perfectly capable of fulfilling myself."

Lyle said nothing, just stood with his hands on his

hips, ignoring the admiration that bloomed at her dia-
tribe. For a woman set on pursuing him, she continued to confound him with her antagonism. Plus, with
her eyes flashing dangerously and angry color in her
cheeks, she was so damn beautiful.

"And I sure as hell don't need rescuing," she insisted,
oblivious to his churning emotions. "Especially not by
you."

"As long as you're on my ranch, you're my responsibility." He refrained from pointing out that she'd needed
him to rescue her and, no doubt, would again.

"I'm not looking for a boyfriend," Giselle declared
through clenched teeth. "I'm looking for someone who
is great at social media."

Somewhat mollified, Lyle asked, "What does that
have to do with Jacob?"

"He's in charge of the ranch's social media."

"We have social media?"

Giselle stared at him in astonishment, her earlier ire
dissipating. "You didn't know?"

"I don't pay much attention to that stuff."

"You should."

Something about Giselle's sly grin worried him.
"Why is that?"

"Let's just say that most of the beefcake showing up
on your accounts is of the two-legged variety."

"Wait… What?"

"You have quite a few sexy cowboys working for
you." Giselle lost her battle with keeping her expression
neutral as Lyle's mouth dropped open. "Oh, don't look
so dismayed. Sex sells everything. Even Wagyu beef."

Lyle shot a narrow-eyed glance in the direction his foreman had departed a short time ago, a growl rumbling in his chest. "By sex you mean…?"

"Gorgeous cowboys." A wicked smile curved her lips. "The social media is quite playful and completely engaging." Giselle's eyes glowed with enthusiasm. "I'm sure that's why your account has over a hundred thousand followers."

The number meant nothing if a bunch of random people probably showed up to view cute pictures of calves and videos of his ranch hands doing stupid dances. "Our social media should be informative, not entertaining."

Giselle rolled her eyes. "It can be both."

"Is it?"

"Um…" Her one-shoulder shrug spoke volumes. "It's more fun than facts. And I should probably mention that I just tried to hire him away from you."

Lyle wasn't sure how to react to Giselle's bit of news. On one hand, he was irritated that she'd tried to poach his foreman. On the other hand, maybe that meant she wasn't personally interested in Jacob.

That the latter filled him with relief worried him.

"He'd miss ranching."

"Maybe." Giselle shot him a smug look. "On the other hand, he didn't give me an immediate no."

To Lyle's dismay, he was less bothered at the thought of losing the Royal Cattle Company foreman than the thought of Giselle working side by side with Jacob day in and day out. Not that he was jealous. More concerned that she'd get swept off her feet by Jacob's charismatic charm and get her heart broken by his fickle nature.

"Seems I should have a word with him," Lyle declared.

"You might want to offer him a raise while you're at it."

Although he didn't appreciate someone advising him on how to handle his employees, in this particular instance, Giselle possessed insight he lacked. He considered her feedback in silence and then nodded. It bothered him to think by neglecting their social-media presence, he'd dropped the ball when it came to ranch operations.

"He's that good?"

"His storytelling is some of the best I've seen." A pregnant pause, and then she added, "Plus, he's positively adorable on-camera."

From the bright glow on Giselle's cheekbones, she appeared to appreciate Jacob's style. Did that mean she preferred it? In most ways, the two men were completely different. Where Lyle was dependable, if a bit too stoic, Jacob could talk the wings off a butterfly.

"Of that, I have no doubt."

"It's a gift, really," Giselle continued, her enthusiasm adding fuel to Lyle's irritation. "He has a knack for knowing just which images and video will invoke whatever mood he's going for while highlighting what's so wonderful about Royal Cattle Company."

"I guess I'll have to check it out."

"You will be blown away, I promise."

She seemed so happy to have convinced him that Lyle noticed his lips moving into a smile. He turned it into a frown instead.

"I was looking for my camera earlier," Giselle said. "I don't suppose you saw it anywhere."

"I didn't. I'll check with the boys. Someone might have moved it somewhere safe."

"Thanks. I guess I'll see you later."

"About that..."

"Are you planning on canceling?"

He really, *really* should. "Skin care and all that is really not my thing."

"It should be every man's thing. A good skin-care routine will keep you looking youthful, saves money over the long run and boosts your confidence."

"Sure." He remained unconvinced, but her enthusiasm was contagious. It wouldn't kill him to spend another evening in her company. "Do you want me to bring anything?"

"Just your open mind." She looked so damn pleased with herself as she flashed him a playful grin. "See you tonight." Then, she was turning away.

Lyle watched her head toward her car, unable to tear his gaze from the delightful swish of her ass. Uneasiness stirred as he recalled his near loss of control the night before. One thing was clear—Giselle Saito was a threat to his peaceful existence. If he wasn't careful, he might find himself under her spell and open to loss all over again.

By the time the knock came on her door signaling Lyle had arrived for spa night, Giselle was a bundle of nervous energy. She'd spent the afternoon cleaning

Jessica's already immaculate house and debating what to wear.

Now, dressed in a bandeau maxi dress in a bright floral from her sister's latest collection, Giselle went to invite Lyle in. Her heart fluttered at the sight of him. He was wearing a blue T-shirt with the ranch's logo that drew attention to his broad, muscular shoulders and the pop of bicep muscles. A shiver raced over her skin as his masculine perfection barreled into her senses. She gathered a breath of him into her lungs. Balsam-and-mint soap, and lavender from whatever fabric softener Rosie used on his clothes. She wanted to bury her face in his neck and breathe him in.

"Welcome to spa night." Her knees were far from steady as she stepped back and gestured him in. "What do you have there?"

A soft grunt rumbled in his chest before he crossed her threshold. "Rosie baked again." He extended a round plastic container to her. "Her famous apple pie."

"Oh, how wonderful." Giselle took the pie and walked toward Jessica's kitchen. She unpacked the dessert and swooned at the scent of warm apples and cinnamon. "This smells amazing. Do you want a slice?"

"I have a lot of paperwork to take care of tonight."

She eyed his crossed arms and rigid stance. "So that's a no to pie?"

"Can we just do this thing?"

"Sure." While Giselle wasn't surprised by his attitude, she'd hoped the fact that he'd agreed to spa night meant he was a little open to what she had planned. "But first I'm going to have some of Rosie's pie. You're sure you won't join me?"

Once he understood that refusing pie wouldn't make his evening any shorter, Lyle gestured for her to cut him a slice. Keeping her smug satisfaction hidden, Giselle set plates and forks on the island and gestured for him to sit.

"This is the best apple pie I've ever tasted," Giselle said, closing her eyes to better enjoy the explosion of sweet, tart and spicy goodness against her tongue. "Rosie is a treasure. How long has she been with you?"

"Seventeen years. She moved in with Jess and me after my mother's fatal car accident. She and my mom were best friends and I needed help with Jess."

"How old were you two?"

"I was twenty-two. Jessica was thirteen."

"A nine-year age difference between siblings is a bit unusual," Giselle ventured, unsure how far she could probe before Lyle shut her down.

"My parents had a complicated relationship." A brief narrowing of his eyes was the only indication that there was more to the story.

"So your dad wasn't around after your mom died?"

"He's not the sort to settle down." Lyle's expression hardened. "He was in and out of the picture before Jessica was born, and after that, entirely out."

"I'm sorry."

"For what? It's not your fault."

Giselle stared at her pie, trying to make sense of the knot in her throat. "Maybe I'm apologizing because I had such a normal family growing up."

"What's normal?"

"My parents are alive and well and they've been married for thirty-five years. I didn't have to step up and take care of my sister before I was capable of taking care of myself."

"At the time I was in charge of getting the ranch up and running. You don't think I was capable of taking care of myself?"

Giselle thought of what she was doing at twenty-two. She had graduated college and was working on her YouTube channel full-time. Money was tight as she poured everything she made into her plans for her own skin-care line.

"I didn't mean it like that," she assured him. "It's just a lot losing a parent, becoming responsible for a thirteen-year-old and trying to run a ranch all at the same time. I know if it happened to me at twenty-two, I wouldn't have been able to cope."

"It was a difficult time." Lyle grew pensive. "But I'd been raised by an amazing mom."

"What was she like?"

"Funny. Kind, but tough. People liked and respected her." Pride shone in Lyle's warm smile. "She worked harder than any person I ever knew."

"Harder than you?" Giselle asked in surprise.

"Definitely. Times were hard after my sister was born. My dad was gone. Mom had to work and take care of us. Luckily, I was old enough that she could leave Jessica with me and pick up part-time hours in the evening to supplement her day job."

"It's really impressive the way you took on so much responsibility."

"It's what the situation required."

Giselle sighed. Here she was trying to give Lyle kudos, and instead of being gracious, he'd returned to his former seriousness.

"What did your mom do?"

"Bartending and waitressing."

"Going from that to ranching is quite a change." Giselle couldn't help but be intrigued.

"She had no idea what she was getting herself into." One corner of his mouth lifted, the half smile turning his face from handsome to breathtaking. "She learned fast, though."

Lyle's fond reflection took the hard edge off his personality and Giselle caught herself captivated by this softer version of him.

"The website mentioned a lottery win helped her buy this place."

"She played every week. It was the only impractical thing she spent money on."

"Not so impractical in the end," Giselle pointed out. "I imagine she'd be pretty proud seeing what a success you've made of Royal Cattle Company."

"Making her proud is what keeps me going every day."

"Whose idea was it to raise Wagyu beef? It's a Japanese thing and that seems a little unusual for Texas."

"When Mom bought the ranch, she wanted to raise something unique and high-quality. The night they got engaged, Dad took Mom to dinner at a fancy place. She had a Wagyu steak and said it was the best meal of her life."

"Sounds like ranching was your mom's dream. Is this what you wanted to do, as well?"

"Ranching is in my blood," Lyle admitted. "My dad's family is involved in the industry. They have a good-size spread in Montana. I spent a summer there when I was ten."

Giselle caught herself slipping beneath the spell of Lyle's deep rich voice and yanked herself back from the brink of a foolish plunge into infatuation. The previous night he'd been clear that he wanted nothing to do with her. Twenty-four hours later he'd agreed to join her for spa night. His change of heart had been unexpected and confusing, leaving her at risk of wanting more than he was willing to give.

She wasn't accustomed to letting her emotions run away with her. Last night's kiss aside, they made no sense as a couple. Not only were they from two completely different worlds, but the only thing they had in common was that they were also both workaholics. Even if they wanted to make it work, their priorities would eventually create conflict.

Yet no amount of caution or common sense kept her pulse from engaging in a strange little flutter as she caught him staring at her lips as she shoveled in the last bit of pie, then pushed away her plate.

"Ready to get started?" she asked in a breathless rush, sliding off the stool as the urge to lean over and kiss him swept her.

"Sure."

His gaze tracked her movements as she fetched a bowl of warm water and a washcloth, then arranged bottles and tubes on the counter beside him. A slightly panicked expression awaited her as she stood beside him once more.

"What is all this?"

"Cleanser. Exfoliant. Moisturizer. Sunscreen." Giselle pointed out each product.

"Soap and water works just fine for me."

Giselle gasped in dismay. "Soap and water is not a skin-care regimen."

"I don't need a skin-care regimen," Lyle grumbled.

"You might not think you do, but it is very important. Your face is the first thing everyone sees."

Lyle's lips shifted into a smirk. "I'm tall. The first thing most people see is my chest."

"But it's through expressions as well as speech that people communicate."

"And you think slathering on a bunch of expensive cream is going to somehow make me communicate better?"

She ignored the spark of mischief in Lyle's blue eyes. "How are you going to feel about yourself forty years from now when you're wrinkled and saggy?"

"Like I've spent the last forty years focusing on things that are important, such as the success of the ranch and keeping my mother's legacy alive."

"I can't argue with that, but if you don't take care of yourself, how can you take care of everything else?"

"Is this the pitch that has made your business so successful?"

"Most of my customers don't need encouragement to take care of themselves. My pitch is based on my dedication to environmental friendliness and the quality of my products."

"You don't just sell people a bill of goods."

"No. I believe in my products and the fact that they're not just good for my customers' skin, but also the environment." She stopped before her passion had her blathering on for the next twenty minutes. "Nothing I've said has changed your mind."

"Not in the least."

For a moment she stared at him, then murmured, "Do you do anything to take care of yourself?"

Lyle didn't look happy at her question, leaving her to wonder if he ever let his guard down and relaxed. Suddenly she wanted nothing more than to see him grin. To glimpse a hint of honest glee in his eyes. Better still, to watch him double over in unrestrained laughter.

Instead, she got a stare of determined steel.

"Of course I do. It's just that I don't have hours and hours to devote to something frivolous like skin care."

"Then what do you do?"

His brows came together. "How do I explain this to you in a way that you'll understand? I don't need to make time for myself."

Giselle understood where he was coming from. Through determination, long hours and a bit of luck, she'd built her company from nothing into a multimillion-dollar operation, forsaking her personal life in the process. It was only recently that she'd realized what that work-life imbalance had cost her.

"Everyone needs to make time for themselves. What do you do for fun?"

Her question left him flat-footed.

"I listen to music."

"Well, that's something."

"While I do paperwork," he added.

Giselle nodded, unsurprised that he prioritized ranch operations over his own well-being. "When was the last time you did nothing?"

A tick began in his left eye. "What do you mean *nothing*?"

"Nothing. No paperwork. No fence mending. No business calls. Just stupid, mindless fun."

"I don't have—"

"Time for stupid mindless fun," Giselle said, finishing for him, letting her exasperation shine through. "Nevertheless, you should make time for skin care. And I'm going to demonstrate how you should go about it."

Seven

"More and more men are realizing that they need to take care of their skin the same way women do." With her crisp delivery, Giselle sounded like a spokesperson in an infomercial.

"This really isn't necessary." Lyle's brain struggled to process what the array of bottles, tubes and jars she'd pulled out could possibly contain. "I'll try them out later."

"Except you won't."

Lyle nodded. "I definitely won't."

"What are you afraid of?"

"Not afraid, just bewildered."

Seeing that her authoritative tone hadn't convinced him, she chose to tease him instead. "So, you're not concerned that you might lose your tough-guy image if anyone learns you're taking care of your skin."

When his gaze landed on her wry smile, his blood heated. What was it about Giselle that she rattled him with a simple look?

"Silly me," she continued. "You're too much of a badass for that to happen."

"Damn straight."

"And a badass wouldn't be caught dead in an exfoliating mask."

"A…what now?"

Giselle pointed to one item amidst the array of products on the counter. "A facial mask."

Still not clear on the concept, Lyle closed his eyes and fortified himself for the coming ordeal. When he opened them again, Giselle was regarding him expectantly.

"I'm going to start by cleansing your skin." She indicated a cluster of bottles.

"I already took care of that when I showered."

The image of long-suffering patience, Giselle said, "The soap you use on your body is not made for your face."

"Soap is soap."

"Cleanser," she corrected firmly, "is what you use on your face. I have several different types here, depending on whether or not your skin is dry or oily." She paused and waited for him to supply an answer, and then frowned as he stared back at her blankly. "So which is it?"

"Usually my skin is dirty from working outside."

She studied his expression, searching for sarcasm, but finding none. She shook her head in amusement, then declared, "I think dry."

He was sitting on a stool with his heels hooked around a rung, his legs forming a *V* that invited her to step between his thighs. Which she now did. The aroma of apples and cinnamon surrounded her, and he recalled how she'd licked the sticky filling off her lips. He gripped his knees hard, successfully avoiding the urge to capture her hips and yank her against him. But as she leaned forward to peer at his face, his willpower gave a rusty shriek and bent a little.

"You have really beautiful skin," he murmured, lifting his hand to brush a strand of hair behind her ear. His thumb skimmed her cheek and the fleeting touch filled him with awe. "Soft and flawless."

Her breath hitched a little as she studied the array of tubes and then chose one. "That's because I take good care of it."

She squirted a little cleanser onto a warm, damp cloth and began working it in circular motions over his cheeks, chin and forehead. A long-dormant need for physical contact awakened at her gentle touch.

"That feels nice."

His simple remark made her smile. Her smile made his heart clench.

"Just wait until I'm done." Her eyes met his, made an impact and shifted away, leaving him short of breath. "You're going to feel like a new man."

She used the opposite end of the damp cloth to remove all traces of the cleanser. While she worked, Lyle considered why he'd agreed to let her do this to him. Plain and simple, watching her with Jacob had pissed him off. Their camaraderie had made him wonder if his foreman's easy charm might be exactly what she needed. So Lyle had swept in and shut it down.

"Once we're done with cleansing, we'll move on to treatment. This can mean any number of things. Toners offer moisture. They can also calm your skin and reduce inflammation. Serums come in a variety of types and target specific skin concerns." Giselle paused and set her hands on her hips, studying his expression. "I'm losing you, aren't I?"

"Would you like for me to explain to you the various best practices of herd management?"

"Point taken. I recommend you exfoliate once a week." Giselle unscrewed the lid off a large jar. A woodsy scent filled the air. At least the stuff smelled manly. "Today we're going to use a bentonite clay mask to remove dirt and oils from your skin."

"And I care about that because?"

"You want to remove built-up dirt and impurities."

"And I can't do that with just plain soap and water?"

Her unforgiving gaze held his for a heartbeat before she dipped her fingers into the jar and began smoothing the goop over his nose and cheeks. "A mask will unclog your pores and improve skin tone."

His nerve endings sparked as her fingers glided over his nose and around his mouth. The close proximity to her. The intoxicating pucker of her mouth as she concentrated on covering every millimeter of his skin. The scent of her. Her hip brushed his inner thigh, setting off a chain reaction through his body. He tensed as he noted a growing tightness in his jeans.

"Are you okay?" Giselle asked, peering at him anxiously.

"Perfectly fine." Although his voice sounded a little rougher than he'd like. "Why?"

"Because you're breathing kinda hard. And you're so keyed up." She studied his face, nibbling her upper lip in concern. "The mask isn't bothering you, is it?"

"Bothering? No." Disturbing, definitely. "I'm just not used to sitting still."

Having Giselle this close was torture. Lyle could no longer trust his hands on his thighs. Instead, he gripped the stool behind him with both hands to keep from snatching her into his arms and revisiting yesterday's all-too-short kiss.

She clicked her tongue. "You just can't relax, can you?"

Not with you standing between my thighs while your fingers glide over my face.

"It's an affliction I inherited from my mother," he said, grinding his teeth while Giselle worked in oblivious concentration, intent on making sure the mask was spread equally over his entire face, giving him all the time in the world to drink her in.

"How long does this stuff have to say on?"

"Until it dries." She stepped back and wiped her hand on a dry towel. "About fifteen minutes."

Was it his imagination or did her breath seem less than steady?

"Is all this really that important?" Somehow, they'd both switched to talking in low, melodic tones, as if this ritual she was performing held some special significance.

"It is. The proper skin-care regime can stop wrinkles and other signs of aging."

"I've never really worried about any of that stuff."

"That's because you're a handsome, desirable man." Humor edged her voice. "I'm sure women will flock to you no matter how old you get."

A statement of fact rather than the sort of over-the-top flattery he sometimes encountered from members of the opposite sex. Lyle recognized that his wealth and position in the community made him a good catch. Many women of his acquaintance had made it clear that they'd be open to pursuing a relationship with him. He was just never sure if they found him as interesting as his money.

"Unfortunately for women," Giselle continued, "we are more desirable when we're young."

"That doesn't seem fair."

"It's not, but it's the world we live in. And my company is a success story because of it."

"I'm sure your company is a success story because of you."

"That's kind of you to say." Color flooded her cheeks, surprising him. For all that she appeared confident, a simple compliment disarmed her.

"I'm not being kind. You remind me of my mother."

First she looked startled, and then pleased. "How so?"

"Smart. Driven. Eternally optimistic. Royal Cattle Company is successful because of her vision and her belief in my abilities."

"I wish my parents had been like that."

A trace of bitterness in her voice snagged Lyle's attention. "They weren't?"

"They're pretty risk-averse. When I told them I intended to start up a skin-care company, they freaked out. They would've preferred me to work for a big corporation that would offer me financial security."

"But you wanted to strike out on your own."

"I've always been fascinated by beauty products, primarily skin care. When I was in high school, I started putting up videos where I would test various creams and serums. By the time I got out of college I had several million followers on various social-media platforms."

"So you knew from an early age that skin care was what you wanted to do?"

"After trying hundreds of products, I started getting more and more interested in what went into them. Eventually I decided to start my own line and I wanted them to be as good for the skin as they were for the environment. All my products are eco-friendly and organic." The same pride Lyle felt when he spoke about the ranch reverberated in her voice.

At last, the mask became a hard shell and Giselle picked up another damp cloth. As she worked to remove the clay, she chatted about her product line, explaining how the various serums and creams would impact his skin's health. Lyle paid no attention to her words, just enjoyed the rise and fall of her voice, appreciating her passion and savoring the enthusiasm that made her beautiful features radiant.

"The next step is moisturizer. This one I would normally recommend you use in the morning and save the night cream for your night-time routine."

"Wait," Lyle protested. "I have to do this twice a day?"

"Of course." She looked amused that he would think otherwise. "Your skin needs moisture and you can't apply moisturizer to a dirty face."

"My face gets dirty while I'm sleeping?"

"Your body produces oils and bacteria all the time. Plus you'll want to remove the night-time products so you can have a fresh surface for your daytime applications."

"This is a lot to keep track of. I'm not sure I'll remember it all."

For a second her expression reflected surprise. "You're actually considering giving this a try?"

To his own shock, Lyle realized that he'd been inspired by her zeal. "If you can give me a simple three-step routine, I will try."

"I can do that." Her voice resonated with barely concealed glee.

If Lyle had known that having a woman's soft fingers massaging cream onto his face would feel this amazing, he would've tried this skin-care stuff a lot sooner. Or maybe it wasn't a woman, but this woman that made the experience so enjoyable. In fact, the application was so pleasant that he wouldn't mind reciprocating.

Maybe she'd even let him spread the lotion over other places on her slim body. He could imagine trailing the fragrant product down her neck and across her chest, to the gentle slope of her breasts, her erect nipples, the ripple of her rib cage and concave slope of her abdomen.

His traitorous hands found their way to her hips without conscious thought directing them there. Her lashes fluttered like a butterfly's wing, generating the faintest of breezes, promising a mammoth shift in his perspective. Already she was close enough for him to kiss, but she inched closer still. He approved.

Since walking in the door, he'd been trying to restrain, derail and ignore his building desire, but she was just so damn appealing. No matter how hard he'd struggled to subdue his longing these last few days, the intoxicating scent of her, the wry curve of her lips, her good-natured bullying, the passion she'd exhibited for her business and her equally strong curiosity about ranching all combined to make her irresistible.

"The last step is sunscreen," she murmured as his arm slid around her waist, drawing her to him. Her voice went all rough and sexy as she added, "But you'll only need that in the morning."

"Maybe to ensure I'm doing it right you can demonstrate this again tomorrow morning?"

Her breath caught on a quiet gasp as she searched his expression. "If that's what it takes."

Her fingers tunneled into his hair as their faces angled, lips grazing, retreating and meeting once more. He hadn't realized how much he wanted this until she leaned into him. Their lips fused, a gentle exploration giving way to something hotter. Electric. Significant.

He stroked his palm up her spine and pressed his fingers into the back of her neck, urging her closer. Her lips were delicious. Delicate and pliant one second, hungry and so damn eager the next.

The part of him that he'd shut down after his wife's death came roaring back to life. He was awake, revitalized, buzzing with energy. He no longer existed in a dull gray world. All around him was brilliant color and rich sensations. His body reacted by drinking it all in. Drinking her in.

He stroked his tongue across her lips, tasting the apple and sugary caramel dessert they'd shared. With a groan, she opened her mouth for him and he delved into its rich, wet depths, eager to devour her. And just as eager to be devoured. As her tongue battled with his, a sexy moan escaped her throat. He swallowed the sound, loving the way she pressed herself against him, hips rolling.

His lungs stopped working and Lyle realized he'd forgotten to breathe. Tearing his lips from her, he growled, "You get me so hard."

She lifted her leg, aligning his erection with the hot seam between her thighs, and pleasure was a bomb detonating in him. Splaying his fingers over her butt, he ground his lower body into hers, letting instinct guide him for several mindless seconds until Giselle whispered in his ear.

"I want to be with you."

Mind blown, he reveled in her admission. "I want that, too."

"Oh, thank, God." Her voice cracked. "I thought it was just me. Wanting you."

Leaning back, he stared at her in amazement. Seeing her raw vulnerability, Lyle cupped her cheek. "How have you missed all the signs?"

"Signs?"

"From the first day when I found you in my house..."
He shook his head. Had she'd really not suspected how
much he wanted her? "I thought you knew."

"So what you're saying is your seduction technique
is to scowl and terrify?" Her laugh grew strangled as
he bunched the fabric of her dress in his hands until he
could slip his fingers beneath the hem and glide them
along her incredibly soft thighs.

He trailed his lips down her neck, finding the wildly
throbbing pulse in her throat. "Were you terrified?"

"Terribly terrified. You're so imposing. All those gorgeous muscles flexing to show off how strong you are."
She stroked his shoulders and murmured appreciative
noises. "And you have no idea how everyone fears your
scowl."

Although she was teasing, Lyle stopped what he was
doing. Worry thickened in his gut. He'd never meant
for her to be scared of him. "Really? Am I that bad?"

She placed her palm against his cheek, the touch
soothing and reassuring. "Of course not. Everybody
knows you're all bark and no bite. Beneath that tough,
rugged exterior is a kind, generous man who would do
anything for someone in need."

Her description slayed him. "Is that really how you
see me?"

"It's how everyone sees you. Every one of your ranch
hands has been singing your praises."

"I guess I'd better deliver steaks and cases of beer to
them as a thank-you for talking me up to you."

"To me? Why would you care what I thought of you?"

He should be glad the woman had no idea how

strongly she affected him. "Because your good opinion matters."

While she processed that, Lyle cupped the backs of her thighs near where her slender legs met her ass. When he thought about all the things he wanted to do to Giselle, near the top on the list was driving his tongue through her sweet center and making her scream as she came. She gasped as his fingertips probed beneath the elastic of her panties, drawing tantalizingly close to the wetness between her thighs. Her hips rocked in a bid to direct him into her scorching heat. Smiling, he lifted her onto the island. She squeaked and shivered.

"Damn, that's cold."

It took Lyle a second to realize she meant the quartz countertop. "Don't worry. I'll warm you up."

While the heat blazing under her skin warmed the stone surface beneath her, Giselle waited for Lyle's next move. He stood between her trembling legs, hands braced on either side of her hips, gaze locked on her lips, his thoughts elsewhere.

"Was this how you expected tonight to go?" he asked, the question sending a flush up her chest and into her cheeks.

Did he see her as some sort of buckle bunny? Giselle frowned. She'd never been any sort of a groupie before. And yet, perhaps that's exactly what she'd become in the last few days.

"I never know what to expect from you." She summoned all her courage. "I was perhaps hoping for—" *desperately craving* "—some really fantastic sex."

Giselle slid her lips into a wry smile to conceal her raging panic as she added, "But I'd settle for one half-way-decent orgasm."

His eyes went wide at her quip. "Oh, you shouldn't have to settle. I'll make sure to give you a whole new definition of the word *fantastic*."

Cocky cowboy.

Her heart bucked like a wild mustang. "Outstanding."

His eyebrows rose. Amusement glinted in his gaze.

Her dress was already bunched about her waist, exposing her bikini underwear. Lyle's blue eyes went molten as he snagged a finger in her neckline. One sharp tug and her bandeau top came to rest at her waist. Had he guessed that she'd left off wearing a bra in the hopes that something exactly like this would happen tonight? Giselle congratulated herself on her wise forethought as he took his time admiring her breasts, first with his eyes and then the tip of one finger.

"Perfection."

That single word, murmured in such appreciation, made her feel safe and cherished. Giselle cupped his cheek and brought her lips to his. The kiss that followed was blistering-hot and made lights explode behind her eyes. She was dizzy and gasping for air by the time his lips left hers. Her lashes lifted in time to catch a wicked gleam in his eye before he dipped his head and kissed her nipple.

Pleasure erupted, spreading shock waves from her breast to her core. She sagged, eyes half-closed, as his tongue swirled around the hard bud. He used the tips of his fingers to caress the underside of her breast. His calloused skin scraped across her smooth flesh. The roughness sent a shower of sparks across her sizzling nerve endings. She was so caught up in each new sensation that when he sucked her nipple into his mouth, she whimpered.

"Everything okay?" His deep voice rumbled against her breastbone, making her quake.

"So good."

"Glad to hear it." His purr skated along her nerve endings, sending ripples of hunger cascading through her. "Lie back."

His command knocked her back on her elbows. In helpless fascination, she watched as he spread her knees wide and stared at the juncture of her thighs, concealed by a delicate strip of satin fabric. To her shock, he bent over and, with his nose a hairbreadth away from her dripping wet core, inhaled deeply.

"You smell so fucking amazing. I can't wait to eat you up."

Her own breath stuttered to a stop at his words, and then wheezed out of her in a ragged cry as he kissed her lightly right above her aching clit. Stars exploded in her head. Her shaking muscles failed, her elbows slid from beneath her and Giselle landed flat on her back with a *whomp*.

"You good?"

She didn't realize she'd closed her eyes until she forced up her lids. Her lashes felt as if they weighed ten pounds each.

"I'm…" Shattered.

"Okay?" He mocked her with a lip twitch as he wrapped his long fingers around her panties and tugged them down her hips.

"Maybe better than that," Giselle agreed, every erogenous zone tingling as she pictured his beautiful mouth coasting down her body.

"Maybe?"

His gaze shifted to the bare flesh he'd exposed. Destroyed by anticipation, she bit down on her trembling fingers, the heat beneath his skin stoking the fire in her belly.

He leaned forward and nuzzled the soft skin of her inner thigh. Inches away, blood pounded in her clit. A frustrated groan tore free of her throat. Why was the man tormenting her like this?

"How about now?" He blew lightly against her most sensitive flesh and goose bumps exploded across her skin.

"I guess." A sob lodged in her throat, nearly strangling her.

Why was she playing his game? All she wanted was for him to thrust his length inside her. Instead, he was teasing her with feather-light kisses and the gentle graze of his fingertips as he stripped off her panties. Her attention sharped suddenly as she noticed that no barrier existed between her most private parts and Lyle's scorching gaze.

Sprawled on the quartz countertop, thighs spread, dress rucked around her middle, she'd never felt so exposed. Lyle stood immobile, his hands on either of her knees, and just stared. She should protest, right? Close her legs in a shy rush. This wasn't like having sex with the lights on. This was a full-on I'm-checking-this-baby-under-the-hood-before-I'm-buying appraisal.

"Lyle?"

"That is the most gorgeous view I've ever seen."

If any other man had declared that about her lady parts, she would've rolled her eyes and put her clothes back on. But something about his intensity made her swoon. A delighted laugh bubbled up, but before it broke free, Lyle moved. Realizing his intent, she gulped.

"Um."

His gaze was molten as it shifted to her face. "Um?"

"I don't usually…" Her whole body writhed with humiliation.

"Don't usually what?"

"Come that way." She closed her eyes, unwilling to see his annoyance or amusement. "I mean I like it, but I can never quite get there." Giselle clamped her lips on the rest of the confession, refusing to divulge just how frustrated her former lovers had become with her inability to deliver a screaming orgasm, or a super low-key quiet one for that matter. "I just don't want you to be disappointed when you go through all that trouble and I can't…you know."

"Trouble?" Lyle narrowed his eyes and sucked in a long breath between clenched teeth. His expression grew intent. "That sounds like a challenge."

She should've expected his reaction. "No. Not a challenge. A warning. The kind of warning label they put on kids toys. Wait. That sounded wrong. Not kids toys, because that would be really creepy. More like 'harmful if swallowed.' Or 'do not operate machinery after ingesting this product.'"

While she babbled, Lyle waited for her nervous energy to burn out.

"You don't need a warning label. You just need someone who knows to handle you with care."

And that did it. She gave herself up to him without a single qualm. "Yes, please."

His breath heated her skin as he ran his nose along the inside of her thigh. She quaked as he pushed her knees outward and spread her legs wide to accommodate the breadth of his shoulders. Her courage almost failed her in the instant before he cleaved through her folds with his tongue and lay waste to her self-possession and what was left of her pride.

She'd never encountered a man with such a clever, creative tongue. He seemed to know exactly what she needed, what drove her crazy. The noises emanating from her throat were something between a whimper and a plea. She lifted her wrist to her mouth and sank her teeth into the flesh as he slid one finger and then two inside her. Giselle had only a moment to enjoy the friction when he curled his fingers and hit the spot only she knew about.

And pow!

She needed to scream out her pleasure, but her tortured lungs failed her. Instead, she panted in shallow gulps of air while waves of raw bliss slammed into her, followed by a stunning realization that he made her come. And not just come, but detonate with the blow-the-roof-off-the-top-of-her-head sort of ecstasy that rocked her world.

She floated back to earth, a feather swept up by a passing tornado. Lifting onto her elbows, a mammoth act of will given that her muscles were the consistency of overcooked spaghetti, Giselle watched as Lyle dropped chaste kisses into the hollow of one hipbone and then the other.

"What. Was. That?" she wheezed.

"That—" one corner of his mouth kicked up in a smug grin "—was an orgasm."

Not like any she'd had before. More like that was his way of ruining her for every other man.

"Okay."

"Just okay?" He didn't look the tiniest bit put out at her unimaginative reply. More like determined. "I'm happy to see if I can do better."

Better?

What could he possibly do to improve?

He'd nearly killed her with pleasure.

"No," she blurted, chest heaving. "No, please. You did great. It was great. Terrific even."

Lyle narrowed his eyes. "I'm not convinced you thought it was all that terrific." Before she had any clue as to what he intended, he grabbed her wrist, raised her to a sitting position and scooped her off the counter. "I need to try again."

Her weight didn't bother him at all as he carried her toward Jessica's guest bedroom. Once inside the room, he set her back on her feet and set about peeling off his clothes. When she stood there watching him in stupe-fied delight, he frowned.

"Strip."

His sharp command made her start. With a crisp salute, she shoved her dress off her hips and kicked it aside. While Lyle dealt with buttons and zippers, boots and socks, she went in search of the condoms she brought just in case. Holding them aloft in triumph, she whirled around and caught sight of the most amazingly perfect and—*OMG!*—hugest erection she'd ever seen.

"Are all those for me?" he teased, sauntering toward her as if they both hadn't been half-crazed with lust ten seconds earlier.

Mouth dry, she nodded. "Sure."

And then, all at once, he stood before her and her world narrowed to a country mile of tanned shoulders, bulging pecs, chiseled abs and his jutting length. She sucked in a breath and appreciated his crisp masculine scent, a concoction that blended the soap he'd used ear-lier and her skin-care products. A little of him, a little of her, mixed together.

While she stood in tongue-tied appreciation, he plucked the condoms out of her numb fingers, sepa-rated one from the bunch, tossed the rest onto the bed and then proceeded to sheathe himself. Giselle allowed herself a few seconds to regret that she hadn't sunk to her knees before him and taken him into her mouth before he swept her into his arms and laid her in the middle of the bed.

"I'd like to take hours learning everything that turns you on," Lyle said as he covered her quivering body with his warm, hard form. Liquid blue flames danced hypnotically in his eyes as he surveyed her parted lips and the agitated rise and fall of her chest. "But I've been thinking about sliding inside you for too long and can't wait."

"Okay."

"Okay again?" With a troubled sigh, he dipped his head and seized one nipple between his strong lips.

Pinned as she was beneath his significant weight, she could only gasp as a vibrant sensation lanced straight to her core. She dug her fingers into his hair as he sucked, licked and nibbled, paying the sort of attention to her breasts that made other parts of her anxious and lonely. Desperately, she rocked her hips and mewled her impatience, needing him to fill her the way he'd promised earlier.

"You were—" the words stalled as he slid a hand between them, fingers parting her to glide through her slippery heat "—in a…hurry."

He dropped slow, tender kisses along her abdomen, his destination becoming more apparent with each dip of his head. "Changed my mind."

"No-o-o-o-o-o."

Since he wasn't heeding her desperate writhing, as the pressure built inside her, Giselle realized if she wanted him inside her, she would have to take matters into her own hands. And by matters, she meant his long, hard erection.

He jerked, his breath coming to a sudden stop when she reached between them and wrapped determined fingers around his velvety length. A satisfied purr rumbled from her throat as his erection pulsed and hardened still further beneath an exploratory caress.

"Foreplay, later," she insisted, while at the same time easing the tips of her fingers over his broad head. Maybe just a little foreplay wouldn't hurt.

"That will make it after-play."

She loved each moan that spilled from his parted lips, every quake that shook his long body as she stroked him. He allowed her two pumps before he pulled her hand away from him and took a second to position himself. Her voice broke on an inarticulate cry of delight as he thrust forward in a single fluid move that joined them together.

"Shit." He ground the word out between clenched teeth. "You're tight."

Giselle had never thought of herself as being particularly small down there, but she'd never had sex with a man as big as Lyle. The feeling of fullness, of being stretched by him, possessed by him, was the headiest sensation she'd ever known. And when he pulled out and rocked forward again, the friction was magic.

"You're massive." She drew up her knees and watched as his pupils expanded until his blue irises nearly disappeared. "I want all of you."

And so he gave her everything he had. The pressure both terrified and exhilarated her. He leaned down and brushed his lips over hers. This changed the angle for his next thrust and together they groaned at the sheer perfection of it.

"Do that again," she pleaded.

"What, this?" He repeated the move, adding a twist that made her gasp.

He'd barely been inside her for a minute and she could already feel an orgasm building in her again. "No one can possibly be this good."

"I can."

His confidence was as sexy as everything else about him and Giselle smiled. "Okay."

The word triggered him. He brought his hand between them and rubbed her clit. Pleasure exploded, quickening her breathing.

"Okay?"

She could only nod as the pressure between her legs spiraled and expanded, driving all thought from her mind. There was only Lyle moving within her, his low murmurs praising her beauty, sweetness, tightness, wetness, hotness. All the while keeping up that amazing loop around her clit. She rocked her hips and groaned, nails sinking into his back as her climax bloomed and expanded.

His mouth crashed over hers as he began drilling into her, chasing her orgasm with one of his own. The dirty, sexy noises he made drove her pleasure higher until she crested and hung suspended while her vision blurred and her brain went completely blank. She drifted down from the high as Lyle collapsed onto her, his lips coasting down her damp neck, tongue flicking out to taste the salty texture beneath her ear.

Once again, she pondered how a man who so thoroughly demonstrated his expertise with a woman's body remained single.

"Are all the women in Royal complete idiots?" she murmured, basking in a postorgasm glow, content inside the circle of Lyle's beefy arms.

"Why?"

"Because you're still single."

He stiffened and then relaxed with a huge sigh. "I'm sure you'll see tomorrow night that there are a surplus of wealthy single men about town."

"Are they as good in bed as you are?"

His chuckle ruffled the hair at her temple. "I don't know. I've never slept with any of them." He slid his fingers into the ticklish spots below her rib cage until she squirmed and protested. "And don't even consider any hands-on comparisons."

"Okay." Her heart gamboled like a frisky fawn at his warning.

"Okay?"

"I'll keep my hands to myself."

"You'll keep your hands on me."

He kissed her hard then, thrusting his tongue past her parted lips in a deep, greedy stroke. She moaned in pleasure at the claiming, unsure what to make of his possessiveness. No man had ever made demands on her like this. She liked it. He made her feel safe and cherished. And maybe that was what she'd been missing all along.

Eight

"Wow," Giselle murmured, gazing around as they strode through the Texas Cattlemen's Club. "This is not at all what I imagined. I was expecting wood paneling. Oil paintings of the founders. A true men's club. Instead, it's bright and welcoming. And inclusive."

Lyle heard the surprise in Giselle voice and recalled his mother's similar reaction. In that moment, it occurred to him how often he compared Giselle to Talullah Drummond. Both women were strong-willed and determined, hard-working and likable. Giselle and his mother both challenged his perceptions, and more and more he found himself opening up to a new way of thinking.

It was a stark contrast to his relationship with Chloe. His wife's nature had been all about compromise rather than confrontation. Instead of disagreeing with him, she'd supported his decisions. While he'd viewed her as his partner, Lyle also recognized that he'd been the one in charge.

Not wanting to question anything about his marriage, he'd been shying away from pondering whether he preferred one woman's style over another. But as he confronted his growing attachment to Giselle, he couldn't ignore what this might mean for his future.

"It's changed a lot in the last twenty years." His palm splayed on her lower back, Lyle guided her through the clubhouse to the stables, where the barn dance was happening. "Once women started to become members in their own right, they began making a lot of the changes you see today. Including a day care."

"How progressive."

Hearing the dry note in her voice, Lyle shot her an arched look. "You're making fun of us, aren't you?"

"A little." Giselle gave a half shrug. "I'm not used to being in such a male-centric environment. In beauty brands, women mostly dominate."

"There's no getting around that Royal is an agricultural community that owes much of its financial success to long hours of hard physical labor."

Lyle took a second to admire the slender lines of Giselle's form encased in a floral halter dress with a handkerchief hem and skin-baring bodice. As diligently as she'd applied herself to learning about ranching, tonight's fashion choice reminded him that she was a city girl who rarely got her hands dirty.

"You know, ever since I arrived, you've gone out of

your way to emphasize how rural Royal is, but in fact, there's a robust technology industry happening here."

Of course, Giselle noticed that he'd been highlighting their different lifestyles. Did she realize that he'd done it to avoid giving in to temptation? A lot of good it had done him. She'd worked her way beneath his defenses with her upbeat tenacity and unstoppable curiosity about the ranch.

"I never imagined you'd fit in on the ranch," he admitted.

She arched an eyebrow at him, a nonverbal *no kidding*. "And now?"

"Well, I haven't had to save your pretty ass lately, so I guess that's something."

"Lyle Drummond, you are a true charmer."

He nodded. "That's what I've been told."

They'd reached the doors that led outside to the large open area behind the clubhouse. A large turquoise pool sparkled in the golden glow of late afternoon. Beyond it were the tennis courts and the large stable where the barn dance party was taking place. Taking Giselle by the hand, Lyle drew her forward.

As they entered the barn, Lyle pointed out the couple of the hour. His best friend, Trey Winters, had texted him a few days earlier to share that his brother, Jericho, and Maggie Del Rio were planning to announce the details of their upcoming engagement party at the barn dance. No doubt, those gathered at the TCC would be buzzing with the news.

"I heard that that there was bad blood between the

engaged couple's families," Giselle said. "How did the feud start?"

Even though Giselle lived in Dallas, Lyle wasn't surprised by the question.

"The way I understand, the Winters and Del Rio families have always been at odds, but things grew really heated a hundred years ago when a woman named Eliza Boudreaux jilted Fernando Del Rio, leaving him at the altar, and married his rival, Teddy Winters, instead."

"That's a way more dramatic story than I was expecting." As they entered the barn, Giselle scanned the partygoers. "So love started the feud and it sounds like love is going to end it." Her tone was so hopeful that Lyle winced.

"For the sake of everyone, I hope that's the case."

Giselle gave his hand a reassuring squeeze. "You don't sound convinced."

"In my experience, love doesn't solve problems."

For a second, Giselle looked like she wanted to argue, but then she said, "I'll have to take your word for it since I've never been in love before."

"Never?"

"Why so surprised? Are you making gender assumptions again? Because I'm a woman I should have fallen in love a dozen times by now?"

"I've stopped making assumptions where you are concerned."

She pondered his remark. "Do you think there's something wrong with me because I haven't been in love? My sister falls in love at the drop of a hat. And falls out of love just as quickly. I don't tend to lead with my emotions quite like that."

Although Lyle had found many women interesting and attractive, he'd fallen in love one time and never expected to again. Or hadn't imagined doing so until lately. But was what Giselle stirred in him something that could survive the obstacles of distance and lifestyle that existed between them?

"Infatuation isn't love," Lyle pointed out.

"That's what I tell her all the time." Giselle gave a nod of vindication. "She thinks I'm too cautious."

"Nothing wrong with being sensible."

"I think the real problem is that I like being in control," she confessed with a self-conscious shrug. "I'm less likely to get hurt that way."

Lyle considered this. "No one wants to get hurt. But sometimes the joy from giving your heart to someone outweighs the grief when things fall apart."

Her eyes latched on to his, a melancholy swirling in their soft brown depths. For a second, she looked so stricken that Lyle regretted his words. Fuck. They were at a party. They were supposed to be having fun, celebrating Maggie and Jericho's engagement, not standing around mourning their romantic struggles.

"Or that's what I've been told, anyway," he added.

The band struck up a familiar tune and on impulse, Lyle tugged at her hand.

"Come on. Let's dance."

"You dance?" Her eyes went wide as he pulled her into the crowd lining up for the Big & Rich song, "Save a Horse (Ride a Cowboy)."

"I do."

He caught himself grinning at her in unrestrained delight as they stomped, sashayed and shuffled along with twenty other couples. He lost himself in the moment. Giselle moving to the music beside him, the folds of her skirt fluttering as she spun, her long hair flowing over her delicate shoulders... She knew all the steps and he had trouble keeping his eyes off her.

For this brief time, he could let himself be swept into the bittersweet fantasy that they were a couple and this would be the first of many events they would attend together.

As the final notes of the song melded into the opening bars of a new melody, Lyle put his arm around Giselle and spun her off her feet. She wrapped both her arms around his neck, a husky laugh breaking free. When he set her back down, they remained in a snug embrace as the song's slower tempo invited the couples to get cozy.

"I never imagined tonight's party would be this much fun," she murmured, her hands gliding along his shoulders, fingers grazing the nape of his neck.

"And I never imagined a city girl would know all the steps." He appreciated the open back of her dress, which allowed him to trace evocative circles on her soft skin.

It took all his considerable willpower to remain with her on the dance floor instead of pulling her into a nearby alcove, running his mouth over her delicate collarbone and nibbling along her long, slender neck.

"I got a little help."

"From?"

"A few of the boys."

When he imagined her dressed in booty shorts and a crop top, her sunset cowboy boots scuffing up dirt in his paddock area while a dozen of horny cowboys taught her the moves she'd used tonight, Lyle wasn't sure if he should thank them or kick some ass.

He must've tensed because she grazed her nose along his jawline. The soft press of her breasts provided a tempting distraction from his dark musings.

"You're wearing my moisturizer." Her voice brimmed with awe. "You actually used my products?"

His heart slammed against his ribs as she beamed at him. He'd forgotten how intoxicating it was to make someone else happy.

"I did."

"I can't believe it."

"You've been such a help around the ranch. What kind of a jerk would I be if I disregarded what you do?"

"But you didn't believe men should bother with something as frivolous as skin care."

"I was…"

"Wrong?"

He ignored her glee and answered, "Short-sighted."

"I'll take that."

The temptation to kiss her smiling lips nearly overwhelmed him, until he realized that they were surrounded by friends, neighbors and acquaintances who would be ravenously curious about the beautiful woman being romanced by the elusive widower from the Royal Cattle Company Ranch.

As the song ended, Lyle spied the two people he wanted Giselle to meet. He drew her off the dance floor and eased through the crowd toward his best friend and the woman who'd captured his heart.

"This is Trey Winters and Misha Law," Lyle said, introducing the couple. "Misha's company developed the k!smet app and Trey is a key investor. Giselle and Jessica used your 'Surprise me!' feature and traded houses for a couple weeks."

"Living on the ranch has been amazing." Giselle shot a smile in Lyle's direction, then added, "Until now, I've been a tried-and-true city girl. Your app has changed my life."

"Oh, how wonderful." Misha beamed. "It's always great to hear positive feedback about the feature." She glanced up at Trey, the adoration in her eyes causing Lyle's heart to spasm.

He was glad someone as wonderful as Misha had cut through Trey's guard and enabled him to trust again. Not only was the tech genius beautiful and brilliant, but she and Trey's eight-year-old son got along great.

"Huh." Trey's eyes narrowed as he took in Lyle's expression.

Lyle bristled at the speculation in his best friend's gaze "What?"

"You look different."

"It's his new skin-care regime," Giselle announced.

Bemused, Trey looked from Giselle to Lyle and back again. "Did you say skin-care regime?"

"I did." The joyful look Giselle sent his way caused his heart to pound. "Lyle has agreed to take better care of himself. And he's starting with his skin."

"You don't say." Trey cocked his head, his gaze falling to where Lyle's hand rested lightly on Giselle's hip.

Lyle scowled at his friend. "I have it on the best advice that it's just as important for men to take care of themselves as women."

"I don't disagree. It's just that you've never…cared before." Trey gave Giselle a long, appraising look. "But I don't think your new glow has anything to do with skin care."

His meaning was so transparent that panic shot through Lyle.

"Don't tell him that," Giselle murmured, squeezing the hand Lyle rested on her hip. "I'm trying to convince him to be the face of my new men's skin-care line, Saito for Men."

"Lyle?" Misha asked, turning an appraising gaze on him. "I can see why you'd choose him."

"At first I thought I'd go with a professional model." Giselle's eyes sparkled as she launched into her explanation. "But since arriving on the Royal Cattle Company Ranch, I've been obsessed with the idea of finding an everyday man, and there's something about cowboys…" The scorching look she shot in Lyle's direction made his lips twitch into an involuntary grin.

"They have their charms," Misha agreed, sending a sizzling glance of her own in Trey's direction. "If you can get past their gruff exterior."

"How long have you and Trey been together?"

While the two women fell to discussing the men in their lives, Trey's gaze clamped onto his best friend.

"It's nice to see you out and about." Trey indicated Giselle. "And it's pretty obvious she's the reason why."

After losing Chloe, Lyle had stepped back from Royal society. She'd been so good in social situations. He'd come to rely on her to ask all the right questions and give all the best answers. No doubt, he'd appeared sullen and withdrawn in the weeks and months following her funeral, when he'd been overwhelmed by loss and had no idea how to express his grief without falling apart.

"I like her."

"Just like?" Trey pitched his voice lower. "The vibe between you on the dance floor made it look more serious than that."

"It's been less than a week and her business and life is in Dallas," Lyle explained just as quietly, unsure how much to reveal about what was going on between him and Giselle.

"So you have no plans to see her after she leaves?" His fellow rancher looked disappointed.

"We haven't talked about it."

Trey ejected an impatient breath. "Don't be an idiot."

"I'm not." Lyle tensed. "I just don't want to rush into anything."

He'd been happy as a husband and excited at the prospect of growing into a family. The abrupt shattering of that dream had left him lost and heartbroken. Never in a million years had he imagined he could have feelings for someone besides Chloe.

Since Giselle had appeared in his life, he'd noticed a gradual shift in his perception. Long-dormant emotions had stirred, making him all too aware that his self-imposed isolation had done more harm than good. But rethinking his solitary life meant making changes he wasn't ready for.

"Sure." Trey didn't sound particularly sympathetic about his friend's plight. "I remember running away after being overwhelmed by my feelings for Misha. Worst decision ever."

"I have no plans to run anywhere."

"No." Trey's voice was thick with disgust. "You're just going to stay put and let her get away."

"Not everyone is as lucky as you and Misha, or Jericho and Maggie," Lyle declared in a lame bid to shift the spotlight off him.

"You say luck." Trey hit his friend with a pointed look. "I say it's a clear example of love conquering all."

Lyle shook his head. "There are some things even love can't overcome."

Several days after the party at the TCC, Giselle woke up alone in Jessica's guest room. She stayed very still, listening for sounds that would indicate Lyle hadn't yet left. Silence. And from the intensity of the sunshine spilling across the wood floors, she suspected he was long gone.

Disappointed that he hadn't stayed for a round of languid, wake-up sex, she curled herself around his pillow. Burying her nose in the cotton fabric, she breathed in his scent. The familiar fragrance filled her with delight. That she'd convinced Lyle to use her men's moisturizer meant she'd had an impact on his life. Although she hadn't given up on him becoming the face of Saito for Men, if he continued to refuse, knowing that Lyle would use her products and think of her was a satisfying victory.

Her muscles protested as she slipped from the bed and headed for the shower. Between ranch chores and all the sex she and Lyle were having, Giselle had never been so physically active. At the end of each day, as she stumbled back to Jessica's house worn out, scratched up and filthy from all the hours spent riding fences, practicing her roping, feeding livestock and any of a hundred different things that came up, Giselle wondered what she was trying so hard to prove.

That she could handle anything Lyle threw at her? She didn't need to be ankle-deep in manure to demonstrate her spunk. It amused her to surprise him, though. He struck her as someone who assumed he had all the answers. Especially when it came to her.

After a hot shower to ease the stiffness in her muscles, Giselle headed to the barn. Whenever she had a spare moment, she spent time with the mare who'd tried to attack her that first day. Thanks to all the hours Giselle had devoted to grooming her, feeding her treats and crooning to her in low, soothing tones, Giselle had won the mare's trust. The progress was thrilling and Giselle fell a little more in love every day.

"She's come a long way," Jacob remarked, coming to stand beside Giselle as she watched the buckskin return to the herd of horses grazing in the pasture.

Giselle smiled. "So have I."

Her time on the ranch made her real life in Dallas feel

like a distant memory. These days she was just as busy, but something about the ever-changing daily activities, the interaction with all the hands and an abundance of crisp, clean air made her feel so alive. Of course, she could also attribute her fresh perspective to the stoic mountain of beefcake she was with day and night.

"You're turning into quite a rancher."

"I don't know about that, but at least I look like I fit in." Giselle indicated her dusty jeans, worn boots and graphic T-shirt. "It's hard to believe that before coming here I'd never been near a horse much less ridden one."

"And now you're keeping up with the veterans." Jacob's approving grin roused feeling of acceptance and camaraderie. "Even your roping is getting better."

"It's coming along a lot slower than my riding skills."

"You'll get there."

"Not fast enough." Swept by a sudden bout of melancholy, Giselle bit down hard on her lower lip. "I only have five days left."

Noticing her distress, Jacob said, "I think everyone here would be happier if you never left at all."

"I wish…" Giselle was afraid to say what was in her heart. She hadn't expected to fall in love with ranch life or to find herself swept into a romance with a sexy cowboy. "I wish I could stay."

"Then you should."

Giselle chuckled. "Jessica will want her house back."

"You could stay at the main house."

With her cheeks on fire, Giselle mumbled, "Oh, that's not… I mean, I couldn't."

"Not only do I think you could," Jacob stated, "I think you should."

He waggled his eyebrows in a suggestive manner and Giselle smacked his arm, laughing to disguise her discomfort. No doubt, the way she and Lyle had been carrying on they'd been a hot topic of conversation among the cowboys. She resisted the urge to squirm at the memory of Lyle's skillful hands driving her wild the night before, his slow, drugging kisses and just how hard she'd come against his mouth.

"I'm not sure what's going on between us is quite what you think."

"I disagree. It's pretty obvious that you're exactly what the boss needs." Jacob's gaze went past her. All of a sudden, he pushed off the rail and winked. "I better get going. The boss hates it when I don't keep an eye on the boys."

Giselle watched him go, mulling over their conversation. Was she what Lyle needed? Sexually, yes. But what about the rest of it. She knew next to nothing about ranching. Surely, Lyle wanted a wife who could share his workload and his bed?

"What were you and Jacob talking about?"

Her thoughts had been so loud that she hadn't noticed Lyle's approach. "You." Her answer popped out automatically.

"What about me?" he drawled, his voice low and sexy.

She shot him a sideways glance. A warm glow flickered in his blue eyes as his gaze drifted over her features. Quivering with longing, she stepped close enough to detect the scent of pine mingling with the comforting aromas of horse and hay.

Determined to keep things light and uncomplicated between them, Giselle said, "He wanted to know if I'd convinced you to model for me."

"You haven't." His hungry smile tempered the rejection. "But don't give up trying."

"He thought you might change your mind if I could persuade you." Giselle fluttered her lashes at him. "Just how badly I want you."

His voice dropped to a raw growl as he asked, "How badly do you want me?"

"So, so badly." Raising her chin, she exposed her face and let him glimpse her need. "Bad enough to beg."

As her palm coasted upward along his thigh and over the rigid length behind his zipper, he sucked in a sharp breath.

"Fuck." The curse groaned out of him. "You don't have to beg me for anything."

"But if I want to?" Her voice was a husky purr.

"I'll never tell you no."

An inferno flared behind her big silver belt buckle as Lyle grabbed a handful of her shirt and tugged her toward him. He slid one large palm over her butt cheek and squeezed hard enough that the hunger raging between her thighs made her reckless.

She lifted on tiptoe and placed her lips near his ear. "Then please, please take me now, fast and hard."

Lyle's eyes blazed at her whispered request. His biceps flexed, drawing her closer. A second later, wolf whistles shattered the erotic bubble enclosing them and he set her free with an impatient curse. Three riders passed by. Noticing their broad grins, Giselle gave a hoarse laugh. Although they'd been caught like this several times, she hadn't yet grown accustomed to the way desire left her oblivious to everything but her hunger for Lyle.

"I guess I should get back to work," Giselle murmured, her emotions split between chagrin and regret. "The Camp Up site won't set itself up."

Jessica had booked a last-minute glamping group consisting of three couples and asked Lyle to host. When he'd grumbled about it to Giselle, she'd offered to help him with the guests, eager to see what glamping was all about.

That afternoon, she was taking a load of supplies out to the site to get everything ready for the guests arriving the following day. In Jessica's absence, Rosie was making the food and Lyle would guide the guests on a trail ride to the site. Giselle was in charge of keeping the food and beverages flowing and of making sure the glampers had everything they needed for a relaxing stay.

"Want some help?" Something about the way he asked the question made goose bumps break out on Giselle's arms.

"I would."

The first time Lyle had shown her the site, they'd traveled on horseback, following the same hour-long circuitous route around the lake that the glampers would travel. This provide plenty of time for the guests to enjoy the sights and decompress. Today, however,

Lyle and Giselle took a more direct route, navigable by ATVs, that took fifteen minutes.

The supplies included fresh bed linens, comfy pillows and throws, towels, snacks and beverages that they would chill in the solar-powered coolers. In addition, Giselle had created gift baskets filled with her skincare products for each of the couples. Making the beds and filling the permanent tents with all the comforts of home took several hours, but the end result was a picture-perfect success.

"So this is glamping," Giselle murmured, spinning in a slow circle to take in the cozy camp. "I can't wait to spend the night here."

"I think you're going to get your wish sooner than you think."

As if to punctuate his statement, thunder boomed overhead. The loud clap vibrated through her, stirring something primeval and wild. Giselle peered up through the trees, noticing the ominous clouds looming over them.

"If it's going to rain, shouldn't we get back?"

"No time. The storm is right on top of us." He grabbed her hand and pulled her away from the main camp, toward the isolated tent they'd chosen as their home away from home while they watched over Jessica's guests.

The early evening darkened dramatically as the rain began. The icy drops started coming at irregular intervals, but by the time they reached the tent, Giselle was drenched. Stumbling out of the storm, gasping and laughing, she and Lyle stared wide-eyed at each other as lightning lit up the sky, followed by a loud, sinister rumble.

"You're soaked," Lyle declared, his gaze taking in the way her hair was plastered to her face and shirt clung to her chest. "Take off your clothes and wrap yourself in this."

He plucked a fleece blanket off the bed and handed it to her. Then, he set about lighting the candles that were on the tables, dresser and floor. Soon, two dozen flames flickered, pushing back the darkness. By the time he'd lit the last one, Giselle had stripped off everything and draped her clothes over a chair to dry.

"You're soaked, too," she pointed out, taking in the way his damp T-shirt clung to his solid torso. "You should strip. We can share the blanket."

She opened her arms wide, flashing her naked body at him for half a second. It was long enough. He ripped his shirt over his head. Boot, socks, jeans and underwear made a puddle on the floor. Naked, he stalked in her direction.

"Wait," she cried, laughing as she backpedaled. "You need to hang up your clothes or they won't dry."

"Later."

While Giselle had never been bothered by storms, she also had never experienced one with only the thin protection of a canvas tent around her. Overpowered by the need to seek comfort within the circle of Lyle's powerful arms, Giselle erased the distance between them, wondering if he'd welcome her in this vulnerable state or try to diminish her fears with practicality. Once again, she opened her arms and his chilled body stepped into the warm cocoon. Squawking as her warm flesh came into contact with his frigid skin, she tried to reverse direction and escape, but his hands gripped her hips, keeping her snug against him, trapping his rock-hard erection between them.

"You're freezing," she protested, squirming to free herself.

"So warm me up."

His mouth covered hers, fingers tangling in her hair. Giselle was on fire as his tongue slid into her mouth and then they were groping, kissing, sucking and stutter-stepping their way toward the enormous bed. By the time they reached the mattress, Giselle no longer needed the blanket for warmth. Lyle's endless muscles radiated enough body heat to melt glaciers.

Somehow, they landed on the bed with Lyle on his back and Giselle straddling him. His erection tapped against her backside as she leaned down to kiss his lips, teasing them with gentle nibbling and tantalizing suction. She reached her right hand behind her and stroked his length, loving the way his breath hitched at the contact.

Of course, they were perfectly safe in the tent. It had obviously been constructed to weather all kinds of storms. They were safe and secure, but elemental energy swirling around them was making her horny as hell.

"I wasn't planning on this happening," she murmured, raking her teeth over his stubbled chin. "So...no condoms. We are going to have to get a little creative."

"I'm down for creativity." He had her breasts in his

hands and was kneading evocatively. "In fact, why don't you scoot up here and ride my face so we can get started."

A shocked laugh broke out of her. "Do what?"

"Save a horse. Ride a cowboy."

"I don't think that's what the song was referring to."

He arched an eyebrow and Giselle was left second-guessing her opinion. After some scooching and shuffling, they settled with her facing away from him on her knees, his jutting erection within arms' reach.

"Are you ready for this?" he asked.

"Hell yes."

She was just about to reach for him when his mouth fastened on to her, tongue flicking against her clit while he hooked a finger inside her, hitting that spot.

Thunder rolled through Giselle and her knees on either side of his head began shaking, throwing her balance askew. But she didn't need a clear head to stay upright—she had Lyle's fingers clenched around her hip to steady her, his hard chest to rest her hands on, his mouth an anchor point for her spinning senses.

Arousal pulsed, moving through her like an ocean wave. He was making her feel so good. She wanted to reciprocate. Taking his erection in her hand, she lowered her lips and wrapped them around the head.

Lyle's hips came off the mattress. "What the—"

Smiling, she drew her tongue around him in a slow circle and sucked gently. More incoherent words spill from Lyle so she kept going, taking more of him in, using her tongue to drive him crazy. And then his mouth was on her again and they were driving each other crazy. The struggle to concentrate was real, but the excitement of what she was doing to Lyle heightened her pleasure. Once she could focus again, she went to town on Lyle in earnest. He stroked his fingertips along her spine and thighs while his hips pumped.

"I'm so close."

She smiled as she took him even closer and then he was coming, his hoarse shout the most beautiful sound she'd ever heard. She'd done that for him, brought him to a place where he was shaking and panting, calling her name and telling her how amazing she was.

Afterward, she settled beside him, one thigh thrown over his, her cheek on his chest. His racing heart drowned out the sound of the rain drumming on the canvas above them.

They were alone out here, cut off from the rest of the ranch by a torrential downpour. Snug and cozy in this large tent with its massive bed, covered in freshly laundered sheets that she and Lyle had smoothed and tucked into place. Candlelight bathed them in a golden glow as the lightning flashes grew less frequent and the growling thunder faded into the distance.

Four more nights after this one. Four more chances to make love with Lyle and be held in his arms. Four more nights to figure out if this was a vacation fling or the beginning of the rest of her life. Four more nights...

Nine

Lyle wasn't at all surprised to approach the main camping area and see that Giselle had everything in hand. She'd demonstrated over and over that she wasn't a frivolous city girl and he was running out of excuses why he hadn't opened up to her about his growing feelings. He straight-up wanted her to stay with him. Not that he expected her to give up her company any more than he could abandon the ranch. Maybe they could find a compromise. She could visit on the weekends. He could drive up a couple nights during the week.

Or was he getting ahead of himself? Was it a mistake to assume his feelings were reciprocated?

Giselle had come to the ranch to get to know him. And while she'd seemed happy to work beside him these past few days, ranching life wasn't for everyone. Was he ready to trust his heart to a woman who would eventually knock the dirt off her boots and get back to civilization?

Their guests dismounted and followed his instructions to hook up their mounts to the tether line stretched between two trees. While he settled the horses, Giselle approached their guests with bottles of water and indicated the snacks set up for them.

While the couples explored the tents and gushed over the amenities, Giselle approached him.

"How did the ride go?" she asked, her gaze lingering on his lips.

He slipped his fingers over the curve of her hip and drew her against his body. His lips glided down her neck as he murmured, "It went fine."

"Lyle," she breathed in protest, even as she plastered her lithe form against him. Snaking her arm around his waist, Giselle gave his butt a provocative squeeze. "We have guests. I don't think we're supposed to be making out in front of them."

Screw that.

"They're Jessica's guests and I don't give a damn what they see." His teeth nipped at her earlobe, causing her to gasp. "Or what they hear later tonight."

"We can't… You can't mean to…" She gave a strangled squeak as he eased one leg between her thighs, applying the perfect amount of pressure to her clit. His reward was a sexy roll of her hips. Her gaze grew heavy and languid as she murmured, "I guess you do."

"You can try to be quiet." He smirked down at her,

admiring the flush staining her cheeks. "But you already know I love a challenge."

She swallowed visibly, but anticipation kindled in her soft brown eyes. "I should probably go see if anyone needs anything."

"You do that. I'll feed the horses and then come find you."

She worked her lower lip between her teeth for several seconds before shifting back to hosting mode. Noticing the tightness in his jeans, Lyle gave his head a rueful shake. He doubted he would ever again spend a night at this camp again without thinking about Giselle.

Or repair a fence. Bale hay. Feed the horses. Grill a steak. Use his shower. Sleep in his bed.

In fact, it might be faster to list all the things that wouldn't remind him of her.

Which compounded the need for him to make a decision. Only four nights remained of their time together. After that she would be headed back to Dallas, returning to her regular life, leaving him behind.

He recoiled at the thought of returning to the dull void she'd pulled him out of. Giselle had come to mean a great deal to him in a very short period of time. That he had an algorithm to thank for pairing them was almost as annoying as the way Jessica, Rosie and Giselle had conspired to push him out of his comfort zone and into a full-on romance.

He'd never been good at accepting that someone else's opinion might be better than his, but then, he'd never actively sabotaged himself by being a stubborn idiot, either. What was he supposed to do with these feelings that he was having for Giselle? His head told him to appreciate their time together and walk away before he grew too attached. But the rest of his body hated to let her go.

While the guests went swimming in the lake, enjoyed cocktails and eventually ate dinner, Giselle and Lyle worked together to ensure the couples had a stellar visit. Giselle kept the drinks flowing and organized the side dishes Rosie had prepared to accompany the Wagyu steaks Lyle was grilling. The sun had dipped below the horizon by the time the meal was done and Giselle had finished cleaning up.

Solar-powered lights, strung between the trees around the firepit, winked on as Giselle made sure their guests knew where to find snacks and beverages. Done with catering to everyone else's needs, Lyle was impatient to get Giselle to himself. He drew her away from the main camp and toward the tent they'd shared the night before. She followed him in silence and he wondered if she'd worn herself out entertaining the glampers.

He needn't have worried. They'd no more stepped inside the tent when Giselle tugged on his sleeve. The instant he turned to her, she sprang up, latched her arms around his neck and half climbed him in an effort to place her lips on his. Her eagerness was exciting and sexy as hell. A total turn-on. He slid his hands into place just below her sweet ass and lifted her into the perfect position to drive both of them crazy. They groaned in unison.

"Clothes," she protested. "Clothes."

"Too many."

"So many."

Lyle had taken to wearing T-shirts around Giselle for faster access. He had the fabric stripped over his head in half a second. Giselle's shirt was less user-friendly, with a dozen buttons from her neck to her waist. Together they fumbled it open, before going to work on belt buckles and zippers. Whatever finesse that age and experience had granted him, Giselle's frantic greed turned Lyle into a bumbling teenager.

Her breasts squished delightfully against his chest, the points hardening as her gyrating hips drove his erection into nearly painful hardness. With a moan, she sucked his lower lip into her mouth, clamped her teeth and gave the tender flesh a tug just shy of pain. Lyle felt the nip in every nerve ending.

He was fast on his way to losing his mind when she dug her fingers into his scalp and murmured, "Please, Lyle, please. Make me yours."

"Wait." Shuddering, he pushed her to arm's length and gulped air into his lungs to steady himself. "Slow down. I want to look at you."

"You've seen me." Her dark brown eyes sharpened with hungry need as she ogled his bare torso.

"I can't get enough." He stroked her bra straps down her arm, grinding his teeth as he glimpsed her rosy nipples peeking through the sheer black lace. "Are you trying to kill me with this lingerie?"

"Would you prefer something else?" She cocked her head. "White cotton granny panties?"

Damn if his erection didn't twitch in eager approval. "Sweetheart, you could wear feed sacks and I'd be turned on."

She shuddered delicately. "Too scratchy."

Lyle bent down to press a kiss to each nipple before dropping to his knees before her. She cradled his head while he unfastened her bra and tossed it aside. Then he was sliding his hands between her soft skin and her jeans to ease them—and the matching black panties—down her legs.

He almost yielded to the urge to take her right there on the soft rug beside the bed. Instead, he gritted his teeth and swept her into his arms. The mattress gave beneath their combined weight, and then he was kissing her, caressing her and trying to rid himself of his own clothes at the same time. His jeans only made it partway down his thighs before she snagged a condom and tore it open. Moments later, he was sheathed in latex and driving into her sweet heat.

In the afterglow of their lovemaking, Giselle snuggled beside him and fell asleep. Lyle lay listening to her deep, even breathing and tried to picture himself a week from now. Alone. Aching with need. Miserable. Facing what had been obvious to everyone else, Lyle admitted he wasn't built to be alone. He might've refused to acknowledge this for the last five years in an effort to protect himself, but that heifer had escaped the pasture and it was too late to shut the gate.

The question he now had to answer was, what the hell was he going to do about it?

With only days left of her ranch vacation, Giselle was at the barn, spending time with Honey. The more Giselle handled the mare, the more the buckskin mellowed. Since the mare had taken a strong dislike to Lyle, Giselle only took her out when he was occupied elsewhere. Today he'd gone to Trey's ranch and wasn't planning on being back until late afternoon.

Over the last little while, Giselle had noticed two things. First, Lyle seemed to enjoy spending both his days and nights with her. Second, she was happier than she'd ever been in her life.

Unsure what this meant for the days, weeks and months to come when she returned to Dallas, Giselle decided to enjoy the delirious haze of sexual satisfaction while it lasted and ignore the confusing emotions that left her giddy and gobsmacked.

When her phone began to ring, Giselle's pulse jerked, but the caller wasn't the Drummond she'd been expecting.

"Thanks for helping me out with the glamping trip," Jessica said. "Everything go okay?"

"I think so. Everyone seemed to enjoy themselves."

"And my brother behaved himself?"

"Yep. He's been good." *Very* good. Giselle released an awkward chuckle.

"So you two are getting along?"

Heat suffused Giselle as she recalled the romantic nights she'd spent with Lyle in the huge tent. She'd tried to be quiet, but it wasn't always possible with Lyle's clever tongue and skillful hands doing such dirty, delicious things to her body.

"We are."

"How well?"

Unsure what Jessica was trying to get at, Giselle said,

"He's been giving me riding lessons and letting me help with fence mending and other chores."

"Oh."

"You sound surprised."

"I guess…" Jessica hesitated for a moment, and then quickly said, "And you like him."

Giselle's stomach clenched at the concern in Jessica's voice. "Sure."

"Then I should probably tell you something. Or maybe I should say warn you about something. I would've mentioned it sooner if I had any idea the two of you would be spending so much time together."

"Really," Giselle began, unsure if she was ready to hear something that might change a casual fling into something more meaningful. "You don't need to…"

"Since I know my brother won't say anything," Jessica continued in her somber tone, "I should mention that Lyle lost his wife five years ago and he's never really recovered."

"I had no idea." Emotional minefield dead ahead.

"He doesn't usually talk about her."

"I imagine it's a very painful subject for him."

"They were the most compatible couple I've ever known."

Giselle tried not to imagine Lyle standing before an altar, watching the love of his life come toward him in a gorgeous lace wedding dress, but there it was, a fully rendered snapshot of the couple's idyllic moment.

"The only struggle they had were when they decided to start a family," Jessica continued, oblivious to the impact of her story. "That's when they discovered she had cancer. By the time she was diagnosed, it had spread too far."

"How awful," Giselle murmured. "First losing your mom, and then his wife."

"I just wanted you to be aware in case someone mentions Chloe and you didn't know who that was."

"I appreciate that. I wouldn't want to say something that would upset him."

That Lyle might still be grieving his dead wife shouldn't have bothered her. Or maybe it was the fact that he'd never spoken to Giselle about her. Did it even make sense that this upset her? She'd come to the Royal Cattle Company Ranch to enjoy a bit of casual fun after which she would return to Dallas and Lyle would stay in Royal.

"I mean it would be great if you two became friends," Jessica said. "Lyle could use someone besides Trey, Rosie and me to talk to. I think he's afraid to be seen as anything less than completely capable and in charge so he doesn't share anything that might be seen as a weakness."

Giselle felt that description was a little too close to her own situation "That makes sense. He has a lot of people counting on him."

"Yes, he's always been like that. Or that's how I remember him being. It got worse after Mom died and he had to take over not just running the ranch, but also dealing with his baby sister."

"From what I understand, she was quite the handful," Giselle teased, rubbing at her chest to ease its tightness. This glimpse into Lyle's pain awakened a need to comfort, but she suspected that he wouldn't appreciate that his sister had shared something so intimate about his past.

"Hell on wheels," Jessica agreed. "But he was always there for me whenever I needed anything. He's the one that encouraged me to attend culinary school when I think he would've preferred if I helped him manage the ranch."

Giselle sighed. "It must be great having a sibling that had your back."

"What about your sister? Aren't you close?"

"Mostly. She's outgoing and bold. I tend to be more introspective and overthink everything. Some days I don't know where I got the courage to actually start my business. I guess it was something I was incredibly passionate about, otherwise I might still be analyzing markets and designing my skin-care line."

"Your skin-care line is amazing. Thank you for leaving some of it for me to try. I swear I've look five years younger in just a few applications."

"I'm delighted to hear that. I think it's better than some of the more expensive lines and I'm not just saying that because it's my product."

"I believe that. Your passion comes through loud and clear. You and my brother have a lot in common on that score. He can go on and on about Wagyu beef. And its benefits. I'm sure he went on and on about it over dinner."

"I think you're underestimating him. We've talked about a lot more than just ranching."

"You don't say. Like what?"

"My skin-care line." Giselle paused, then added, "I'm starting a new line for men and I asked your brother if he wanted to model for me."

A stunned silence came from the other end of the call. Giselle might've been amused if she hadn't been so disappointed by his swift and immediate refusal.

"You didn't."

"I did. He's really handsome and I think his rugged masculinity would really appeal to my buyers. I imagine women flocking to buy up the entire line for their significant other."

"What did he say?"

Giselle ejected a resigned sigh. "Exactly what you'd expect him to say."

"No?"

"Ding, ding, ding."

"Oh, I wish I'd been there to see the look on his face when you asked."

"He doesn't realize how attractive he is." And that was just another thing about Lyle that Giselle found endearing.

Jessica groaned. "I swear, the only thing my brother recognizes as attractive are his cattle."

"I'm going to tell him you said that."

"Go ahead. It isn't as if I haven't voiced my opinion to him a hundred times already. He really needs to find someone to date." Jessica sounded determined to butt into her brother's personal life. "That's why I'm so excited about k!smet."

Jessica's declaration caught Giselle off guard. She wanted to tell Lyle's sister to back off. If anyone was going to take the handsome widower off the market, it would be her. But what if he wasn't ready to get serious? What if she was the only one who'd fallen?

Wait…she'd fallen?

Hell yes, she had.

"How does he feel about it?" Giselle asked, feeling a little sick.

"Well, I can tell you there's one woman he found really attractive."

"Oh."

Breathing heavily, Giselle tried to make herself believe this was for the best. Between his lingering attachment to his dead wife and his sister trying to find him a new one, wanting more than a sexy fling with Lyle would end badly for her.

"The problem is I don't know if she's really his type," Jessica continued, blessedly oblivious to Giselle's inner turmoil. "I mean she's not at all like Chloe. I don't know if ranching would be her thing. But maybe what he needs is his complete opposite to encourage him to try new things. When he meets her he'll see how amazing she is. Then I can brag that I found the perfect woman for him."

"I see," Giselle muttered crossly. "Interfering in someone's love life…what could possibly go wrong?"

Ten

Lyle was on his way into town to check on a feed order when his sister called. After spending most of the day with Trey, he was startled by how impatient he was to see Giselle. When was the last time a few hours apart from a woman made him hungry for her company? He thought back to his marriage and wasn't sure the same gnawing ache had filled him when Chloe wasn't around. What was it about Giselle that was different?

Maybe he'd isolated himself for so long that the idea of being alone filled him with dread. Or maybe everything about the ranch was so new to Giselle that her curiosity and enthusiasm rekindled his own delight. It didn't help that the sex was crazy hot. He couldn't get enough of her.

"So I know you didn't want to have anything to do

with the woman you matched with on k!smet," Jessica began, her voice straining with an effort to contain her excitement.

"And yet you decided to meddle, anyway," he said, wondering what mischief his sister was cooking up now.

"I couldn't help it," his sister continued. "She's perfect for you."

"How do you figure?"

He hadn't forgotten that his sister and Giselle were conspiring against him, but over the last few days, he'd started to think maybe Jessica had done him a favor. He never would've met Giselle if his sister hadn't signed him up for an account on the k!smet app. Not that he believed a piece of technology—however sophisticated— could find his perfect match. It was ridiculous to think that an algorithm knew better than his heart.

"She's beautiful and successful."

"I meet women like that all the time, but that doesn't mean we're right for each other."

"She's sophisticated and interesting. A city girl."

"You, of all people, know what it's like living here." Lyle paused and let that sink in, then added, "Seems like you couldn't wait to escape for the bright lights of Dallas."

"Sure, but she's interested in giving ranch life a try."

"The key word is *try*."

Too soon, Jessica and Giselle were swapping homes once more and neither he nor Giselle had initiated a conversation about what came next for them. In his lifetime, Lyle had stared down charging bulls, escaped encounters with rattlesnakes and been knocked unconscious by a horse, but when it came down to it, none of that alarmed him the way Giselle vanishing out of his life forever did.

"You know that all I want you to be is happy," Jess said, sounding worried. "Right?"

"You're messing in things that aren't any of your business," he grumbled, feeling bad as soon as the words were out. As much as he hated being pushed out of his comfort zone, sometimes he was just too stubborn for his own good. "I appreciate that you're worried about me," he lied. "But why don't you just focus on your future and leave me to mine."

"I am focused on my future," she replied. "In fact, I interviewed for a personal-chef gig this week and I think I'm going to get it."

"That's great." He knew how much Jessica wanted her career to take off and hoped this would be the big break she deserved.

"But all of my future success pales in comparison to how much I want you to find the perfect someone that you can spend the rest of your life with."

While Lyle knew his sister meant well, his heart seized at her words. In Chloe, he'd found that perfect someone. And lost her. Did he dare risk history repeating itself?

Alarm bells clanged in Lyle's head. Yet, he couldn't deny that something was happening between him and Giselle.

The way her smile was the best part of his day. The mind-blowing sex. There was no ignoring the mutual attraction. The app had gotten that much right. But attraction wasn't love. He'd been attracted to several women since his wife's death and had slept with a number of them. But none of those encounters left him wanting more.

The same could not be said for Giselle. He was obsessed. Obsessed. Obsessed. The word banged away in his subconscious. He couldn't seem to get enough of her. For over a week, she'd ridden shotgun in his truck, worked hard without complaint, taken up more room on his king-size bed than a pack of mastiffs.

"Jess, I know you mean well, but can you focus on your career and leave my personal life to me."

"I would be happy to do that if you would demonstrate that you actually have a personal life."

Lyle slowly counted to ten to keep from delivering a sharp retort. "I love you. Butt out."

"I love you, too," Jess said. "And never!"

After the call ended, he pondered the old, worn-out debate. If his sister sensed that he might be ready to love again, she would be relentless.

Love. Had he really just used that word? Was it even possible he could go there again? Love. Marriage. A family? He'd accepted that it wasn't meant to be.

Or so it seemed until Jess flashed Giselle's profile pictures at him. But was she ready for a future with him? Sure, she was intelligent, entertaining and downright gorgeous, but she was also a city girl. Perhaps she'd been working so hard because she knew her time on the ranch was limited.

Less than two weeks earlier, he'd been convinced he would have nothing in common with a city girl. His opinion had seemed correct that first day, when she sashayed around the ranch in a designer version of what a cowgirl would wear. It had been ridiculous to imagine she could possibly survive all the rotten chores he'd thrown at her. But she had and tackled still more. Once she'd gotten the hang of something, she'd been happy to complete even the smelliest, dirtiest tasks. She'd done things Jess flat refused to do.

It was past time to show her how much he appreciated her. Maybe she'd like to meet him in town for dinner. He dialed her number.

"Howdy, cowboy," Giselle said by way of greeting. "Are you on your way back?"

"Actually, I'm headed to Royal."

"Oh."

"Oh?"

"I've missed you."

The admission wrapped around his heart like a well-thrown lasso and pulled tight. With three words, this woman had trussed him up all nice and neat, ready to be branded. He thought about her Skin by Saito logo and imagined it burned into his ass.

"Maybe you'd like to come meet me?" Lyle shook off all thoughts of rope and being tied up. "You've been a big help around the ranch lately, but I thought you might be eager for a little civilization."

"Actually," she murmured, "I'm perfectly happy right here."

"I see." His grip tightened on the steering wheel as he processed her words. Was she happy enough to stick around? "Then I guess you're not interested in a romantic dinner."

"A romantic dinner?" Her tone changed to bright enthusiasm. "With you? How could I refuse?"

Giselle was exiting the Rancher's Daughter, an upscale fashion boutique on Main Street, when she spied Lyle making his way toward the main square. They'd agreed to meet in front of the Eatery. Lyle had let her pick the restaurant for their romantic dinner and she'd chosen it after reading a glowing review. Her stomach flip-flopped as she tracked his progress, but it wasn't hunger that caused the sensation. Or not the sort that could be satisfied by eclectic food pairings. Only Lyle satisfied her appetite. She was utterly, completely mad for the handsome rancher.

And she was getting the sense that he might be smitten as well.

Or at least she had been until her conversation with Jessica spawned a tiny, niggling worry in the back of her mind. If Lyle wanted to be with her and only her, would he be chatting with the woman he'd matched with on k!smet?

On the other hand, was it fair to expect him to read her mind? He had no idea that she wanted to explore a relationship with him. She'd really only come to the realization herself. In her fear of moving too fast, the man assumed he was free to explore other options.

The only way to know for sure what he wanted was to have a conversation with Lyle and lay her cards on the table. And where better to have that cards-on-the-table conversation than in a public place, where she'd be less likely to freak-out cry when he told her he didn't feel the same.

Giselle conceded that she was letting her relationship demons get the better of her, but then she noticed Lyle's progress had been interrupted by a dark-haired woman in a bright pink blouse and a short denim skirt. He looked delighted to see her—delighted in a way that Giselle thought was reserved for her and her alone. An instant later, Lyle caught the woman in his arms and kissed her soundly. Giselle stared in horrified shock as the man she was falling in love with showed her a side of himself she never imagined existed.

Before the embrace ended, Giselle pivoted and walked in the opposite direction. In order to get to her car, she would have to go past Lyle and his lady friend. He would see her, would know she'd observed him. Them. Kissing.

In a panic, head spinning, heart pounding, she raced down the street, all the while praying she'd escaped unnoticed. Normally, her daily routine involved a four-mile run on her treadmill. She liked pushing herself. Today, she was barely able to speed-walk half a block before she ran out of breath. Dodging around the first corner she came to, Giselle doubled over and gasped for breath.

Why was she such an idiot? Of course, Lyle would have other women in his life. Women he turned to for comfort and sex and companionship. Just because she was falling for him didn't mean anything similar was happening in his mind. No doubt, she was just a convenient hookup. After all, she'd pretty much thrown herself at him. What man didn't enjoy that?

By the time Giselle took the long way around and reached her yellow Mini, she'd compressed her misery and shoved it into the box where she buried the rest of her romantic missteps. Her phone dinged as she started the engine, but she couldn't bring herself to check the message. Lyle was probably at the restaurant, wondering what was keeping her. Leaving him hanging chafed at her, but she couldn't pretend to be okay, or summon an excuse for standing him up.

She needed time and space to recover before she could face him. A month or twenty might get her to a place where she didn't feel smashed into a million pieces. Her phone buzzed twice more during the drive back to the ranch. Her heart clanged like an alarm bell in the ominous silence that followed. Twenty minutes had never felt so endless.

At last, she arrived at Jessica's house and parked. While her whole body ached from bottling up her emotions, the drive had given her time to order her thoughts and make some decisions.

I'm at here at the Eatery, Lyle texted. Are you running late?

I'm not coming.

Is something wrong? Did something happen?

Tears threatened. Giselle blinked repeatedly to drive them back.

She would not be mad or sad. Her insides were not

twisted up with humiliation. Her entire being was not a tangled, jangled mishmash of anguished disappointment. She was fine. Perfectly fine.

You mean besides seeing you kiss another woman?

Damn her traitorous thumbs.

You saw that?

The whole damn town saw it!!

Perhaps she'd exaggerated that a bit.

I thought that other woman was you. She looked exactly like you.

A ridiculous explanation. No. More like an excuse. Unless…

Exactly?

Exactly!

Like it was me, but not me.

She noticed she wasn't breathing as three blinking dots appeared and blinked and blinked. She was on the verge of passing out when his answer appeared.

Exactly like you, but not you.

But you thought it was me.

Obviously! I don't go around kissing random women.

But you did. Because the woman you kissed wasn't me.

But she could've been your twin.

Understanding penetrated the anxiety and disappointment buzzing in her overwrought brain.

That's probably because she is my twin.

You have a twin? An identical twin?

Giselle sent a thumbs-up emoji.
Where are you? Lyle asked.

Jessica's.

I'm on my way.

If the situation had involved any other man, Giselle knew she would be laughing at the mix-up. But seeing Lyle with his arms around not just another woman, but her sister. Watching him kiss the preferred twin, the twin with three times as many social-media followers, the twin with a knack for getting any man she wanted.

Something disturbing and terrifying broke open inside Giselle as she opened her contacts and dialed her sister's number.

"Oh, my god, you'll never guess what happened," Gabby said excitedly, her energy level off the charts.

Giselle's spirits, by contrast, were flat and lifeless. "You ran into a gorgeous cowboy on the street and he kissed you."

"How did you know that?" Gabby's excitement dimmed slightly.

"Because I saw him do it."

"You saw us? Wait, you're in Royal?"

"I've been staying at a ranch a few miles out of town."

"What a coincidence."

Coincidence? What did Gabby mean by that?

"What are you doing in Royal?" Giselle asked.

"My k!smet match lives here. I came to meet him."

Relief flooded Giselle at that news. What was wrong with her? Of course, Lyle mistook Gabby for her. It made perfect sense. The sisters had sometimes been confused for one another. Their personalities were very different, but they looked identical. It didn't hurt any less that he'd kissed Gabby, but at least it hadn't happened deliberately.

"He owns a ranch near Royal," Gabby said, her words bringing Giselle back from the brink of full-blown dread.

"I wouldn't have thought you'd be interested in dating someone whose entire life is a ranch."

"Normally, I wouldn't. But this guy…" Gabby made an appreciative noise. "This guy is freaking gorgeous."

"I'd expect nothing less for you," Giselle murmured.

"And it's not like they have regular cows. They raise that fancy beef with the weird name."

Giselle realized her roller-coaster ride of emotions wasn't over quite yet. "Wagyu beef?" she offered, praying her assumption was wrong.

"That's it."

"And your match is Lyle Drummond?"

Gabby sounded delighted. "How did you know?"

Giselle's brain exploded, scattering all coherent thought.

Lyle had arranged to meet Gabby even as he was sleeping with Giselle? He'd acted all surprised and confused when she'd confronted him about kissing the woman she now knew was her sister. This whole time he'd been chatting up Gabby while Giselle had been falling for him. What sort of man did something like that? Played with the hearts of two women, two sisters…twin sisters? Was he harboring a twin sex fantasy? Giselle shuddered. That was just wrong.

"Giselle." Her sister's voice pierced the white-water rush of accusations raging in Giselle's mind. "How do you know who Lyle Drummond is?"

"Because I've been staying at his ranch for the last almost two weeks." Giselle's stomach twisted, driving bile into her throat. "He and I have been…"

Shit. She couldn't say it out loud.

"You've been what?" Gabby demanded, her tone sharpening. When Giselle didn't immediately answer, her sister snapped, "You and he have been what, Giselle?"

"Sleeping together, okay?"

Dead silence on the other end of the call.

Giselle doubled over, planting her face in her lap as all hope ceased to exist.

"You've been sleeping with my k!smet match?"

"I didn't know. Honestly, do you seriously think that if I had any idea you and Lyle had been matched that I would've gotten within a hundred feet of him?"

"No. Of course not." Gabby sounded confused and regretful. "It's so weird, though. We've been chatting for the last ten days and it seemed like he was really into me. And it's not like he didn't know what I looked like. You and I are twins. Did he mistake you for me?"

Gabby's suggestion squeezed Giselle's heart into a pea-sized nugget. A life spent being overlooked in favor of her older, flamboyant sister had left Giselle haunted by an inferiority complex. She'd coped by achieving measurable results with her beauty brand. Her financial success had given her confidence a much-needed boost. But she hadn't experienced true peace until she'd glimpsed her reflection in Lyle's blue eyes.

"I don't know." She could barely get the words out past the lump in her throat.

While she and Lyle had been working side by side, soaking up each other's company, engaging in the best sex of her life, he had been...what? Hedging his bets? Trying to decide which of the Saito sisters he liked better?

"He told me all about the ranch," Gabby said. "And about losing his wife five years earlier. How he's tired of being alone and how he's ready to start dating again."

Every word coming out of Gabby's mouth left Gisele feeling like an idiot. Lyle hadn't shared anything about

his wife with Giselle. It was Jessica who'd shared what
had happened. With her, Lyle had discussed his plans
for the ranch and stuff about his mom and sister.

Maybe despite her deepening feelings for Lyle, all
they had going for them was sexual chemistry. Deep
down, she didn't believe that. They'd made a meaningful connection. Hadn't they?

"So are you into this guy?"

Giselle had an immediate and vehement answer to
her sister's question. "Very."

"I suppose I should back off then."

"Do you even need to ask?"

"I was just…" For the first time Gabby sounded un-
certain.

"What?" Giselle demanded. "Are you really asking
if it's okay to keep seeing Lyle even though you know
how I feel about him?"

"No. Of course not." Gabby might put herself first
most of the time, but she wasn't heartless. "But what
if he doesn't want you the same way you want him?"

"I don't know that he does or doesn't."

What this declaration meant for her future, Giselle
didn't know. She'd been fooled before. It wasn't outside
the realm of possibility that she'd misread the situation
between her and Lyle. Now that she knew he'd been
talking to Gabby, what was she supposed to want? Lyle
had awakened something inside her she hadn't known
existed. She'd been on the verge of putting herself out
there, asking if he wanted to pursue a relationship.

Now what?

Giselle hadn't come to the ranch to fall in love. Or to face a decision that would affect the rest of her life. "And I won't know until I ask him."

Eleven

On the drive back to the ranch, Lyle replayed the moments leading up to the kiss. Giselle's twin looked exactly like her, but there'd been subtle differences as well. Her hair had been darker and styled differently. She'd been wearing a lot more makeup than what he was used to seeing on Giselle. Her hot pink blouse had not come out of Jessica's closet.

Yet none of that had given him pause, because she'd looked delighted to see him.

She'd recognized him.

Obviously, she was in on whatever scheme Giselle had in mind. Was that why Giselle hadn't told him she had an identical twin? He already knew she'd conspired with his sister to infiltrate his life. Was it so hard to imagine that she and her sister might be up to something, too?

He stopped his truck outside his sister's home and took the porch steps two at a time. Giselle must've been waiting for him because the door opened before his knuckles reached the wood. They stared at each other across the threshold, both of them breathing hard.

"What's going on with you and your sister?" he demanded, determined to confront her scheming.

Her eyebrows drew together at his ominous tone. "Going on?" she echoed. "Going on? What's that supposed to mean?"

"Your twin sister just happens to show up in Royal and pretends to be you. What game are you playing?"

Giselle gaped at him in bemusement. "She wasn't pretending to be me."

"No? She sure acted like you."

"How did she act?"

"Like she was glad to see me." His voice slowed as her frown deepened.

"Of course, she was glad to see you. A smoking-hot cowboy swept her into his arms and kissed her silly."

It was clear that Giselle was jealous and Lyle felt damn good about that. "You think I'm smoking hot?"

"Duh. Even before you started using my products you were gorgeous."

Lyle's ire cooled. "Are we fighting because I accidentally kissed the identical twin sister I didn't know you had?"

"We're not fighting. Not exactly."

"It feels like a fight."

"I'm freaked out. Freaking out is not fighting."

"I understand, but kissing her was an honest mistake."

"And I've accepted that. I don't blame you for what happened. I mean if you had a twin and I ran into him in town, I'd probably kiss him, too."

"Fuck that," he growled, rage flaring at the thought of Giselle anywhere near another man's lips.

"But that's not what's bothering me."

"Then, perhaps you can tell me why you're upset." Lyle wasn't sure how, but he'd suddenly gone from playing offense to defending himself against…what, exactly?

Giselle crossed her arms in front of her, squeezing her elbows as if she needed to hold herself in check. "It's all the other stuff."

"Other stuff?" Her sudden ferocity confused him. "I have no idea what other stuff you're talking about."

"Oh, my god."

"Giselle." A catastrophic event was happening, but Lyle found himself completely in the dark. "I need you to explain to me what's actually going on."

"I know we're not exclusive or anything."

"We're not?" He tried for a weightless tone and failed. She'd just confirmed his suspicions about her eagerness to return to her life in Dallas.

"But it wasn't until I found out that you've been communicating with my sister the whole time you and I have been…" She shuddered and stared past his shoulder into whatever hellish landscape had opened up around them.

"How could I communicate with someone I've never met?"

"Because you matched on k!smet."

"No." The word came out harsher than he intended.

"*We* matched on k!smet." He moved his hand back and forth between them. "That's why you came to stay at Jessica's house."

Giselle blinked at him in dismay.

"No. Jessica and I were a match by the 'Surprise me!' function on the lifestyle section. You and Gabby matched as a dating couple."

"No." Lyle shook his head. "You and I…"

Giselle's brown eyes were filled with anguish as she fanned her fingers, giving him jazz hands. "Surprise!"

And then, it was as if all the inconsistencies that had been nagging at him about her suddenly fell into place. "Shit."

"I know. What a mess. I mean if it had been anyone but Gabby, I might've been able to get past it, but the things you and my sister shared…"

"Wait." Lyle was doing his best to keep stay calm and reasonable. "I never spoke to your sister before today."

"It's pointless to lie to me. I *know*."

Lyle ripped his hat off his head and ran his fingers through his hair. "Know what?"

"That you've told my sister about your wife and what she meant to you." Giselle's voice broke. "And you haven't said anything at all to me. I automatically assumed that it might be too painful for you to talk about, but now I realize I wasn't the one you wanted to share your story with."

"I haven't spoken with anyone about Chloe." He closed his eyes as a familiar ache shot through his chest. Too late, he saw it had been a mistake to avoid having such an emotional conversation with Giselle.

"Then how did Gabby know everything about her?"

"I really don't know." And then it hit him. No, it slammed into him. Hard. A one-ton bull that left him flat on his back, seeing stars. "Dammit. Jessica."

Giselle exhaled a ragged breath. "She mentioned that you'd matched with a woman and that she might be perfect for you."

"And that person was your sister?"

"I guess."

Everything had been going so great between them. Why had fate placed Giselle's twin sister in his path?

"Then it was Jessica, pretending to be me, who has been chatting with your sister." Lyle paused to see how she'd react to that. "Because I damn well know that I haven't been anywhere near a dating app."

"So you weren't talking to my sister."

"No."

"But you saw her profile picture on k!smet."

Lyle nodded.

"So when I showed up you thought I was your match."

"I did."

"And you didn't say anything to me about it?"

"I didn't…" Without warning, the ground was crumbling beneath his feet. "Because you didn't mention it."

"And why did you think I didn't?"

"The day before I'd been pretty adamant with Jessica that I wanted her to delete my account. When you showed up, I thought you two had conspired to make me change my mind."

She shook her head. "Let me get this straight—for

the last two weeks, you were under the impression that I was a not just manipulative, but desperate as well?"

The pit into which he was sliding was lined with spikes and no handholds appeared to stop his descent.

"Once I got to know you, I realized you were nothing of the kind."

"Well, I'm glad we cleared the air." Giselle straightened her spine and gave him the sort of smile meant to appease overbearing bosses and demanding customers. "Sorry if I overreacted."

"We both did." Lyle's uneasiness remained unabated as he peered at her. "Are we okay?"

"Sure." But from her tense body language, the misunderstanding had changed everything.

"We missed dinner. I'm sure Rosie would be happy to whip something up for us."

"It's nice of you to offer, but I'm going to pass. I'm leaving the day after tomorrow and should probably pack and clean before Jessica comes home."

Lyle recognized a brush-off when he heard one. He'd never imagined that the closeness building between them this last week was as fragile as a soap bubble.

"Are you still planning on joining us for the roundup tomorrow?" he asked.

"Of course. I mean, I'm excited to be going. Who knows when or if I'll ever get the chance to do something that cool ever again."

Her words recalled his doubts about their divergent lifestyles. She appeared ready to leave the ranch and never look back. Was this a new development? Or what she'd planned all along?

"See you tomorrow then."

A second later Lyle was alone on the porch, staring at the closed front door. Several heartbeats passed before he headed back to his truck. As soon as he settled behind the wheel, he sent a text to his sister.

Did you delete that k!smet app account like I asked?

Her reply came just as he arrived at the barn to check on the preparations for the next day's cattle drive.

Why?

Because I just ran into the woman you showed me a picture of and she seem to know a lot about me.

She's nice right?

Lyle knew Jessica would love the whole mixed-up story about the Saito twins and how the "Surprise me!" function had stirred up more trouble. But being smack dab in the middle of the vexing situation left him too ornery to share.

Stop meddling, Lyle texted back. And delete that damn app!!!!!

Fine. But I was just trying to help.

I told you I wasn't interested in dating anyone.

You can't stay alone forever.

Lyle stared at his sister's words and noticed something unbearable happening in his chest. After his wife's death, he'd coped with his loss by making the ranch his priority. And then Giselle had arrived with her clueless enthusiasm and eager curiosity about ranch life. Before he knew what had happened, the void around his heart began to collapse.

The result was like being awakened from a sound sleep by a deluge of ice water. He was no longer comfortably numb. Instead, every nerve roared to agonizing awareness. Instinct urged him to retreat. But the chaos came from within. He had nowhere to run. Nowhere to escape to. He had to confront the need for her stirring inside himself.

I don't want to stay alone forever.

Coming to grips with his feelings for Giselle revealed that he hadn't rejected love because his heart remained tied to Chloe. Five years of numbing himself with work had kept him from realizing that he could go on without her. He just hadn't figured out that guilt was preventing him from doing so.

Giselle stood with her back against the front door, barely breathing until she heard Lyle's engine fire up. Disappointment surged as the sound of his truck faded. Alone once more, she opened the front door and looked in the direction Lyle had gone.

What had she just done?

Freaked out. That's what.

She'd let her insecurities drive her into overreacting. At first, she'd been in shock. Seeing Lyle kiss another woman—the intimate, joyful way he'd kissed her all those times—had left her feeling forgotten and inadequate. And just the wrong everything.

Not the right size. Not pretty enough. Too smart. Socially awkward. The list went on and on.

And maybe it wasn't even the kiss that had shaken her, but the joy on his face in the moment before he'd swept a woman who wasn't her into his arms. The rational side of her recognized that he had merely been a victim of their twin-ness. How many times had she and Gabby switched places and no one had been the wiser? But she was also gutted by the fact that the k!smet app had matched Lyle and Gabby.

Surprise me!

Well, Giselle had certainly been surprised.

And what about the fact that for the last two weeks, he'd been under the impression that she'd deliberately shown up on the ranch to seduce him into falling for her? Could she even blame him when she'd thrown herself at him over and over?

But they'd had fun. At some point he'd forgiven her and Jessica for tricking him and let himself explore their connection. Yet she couldn't shake that he hadn't been honest with her. Why hadn't he confronted her about lying to him? The situation could've been straightened out right from the start.

She was tired of confusing and perplexing circumstances. Why couldn't she just have straightforward and up-front? She and Lyle were definitely into each other.

But was it a real bond? He'd slept with her thinking she was Gabby, his perfect match.

When he had a chance to think clearly about it, would he choose her sister? Because it wouldn't be the first time a boy she liked preferred Gabby. If she lost Lyle to her twin, she'd reinvent her entire life in Seattle or Boise.

She couldn't even lay the chaos at Gabby's feet. People gravitated toward her. She was fun and upbeat, bold and engaging. Gabby was a gorgeous butterfly. Giselle was a lowly caterpillar. Despite the fact that they were identical in face and form, Gabby would always shine brighter.

But was an incandescent star what Lyle needed to be happy? Even as the question formed, Giselle realized she was getting ahead of herself. It was quite possible that he wasn't looking for anything more than a distraction with her or with Gabby.

Which was all she'd been wanting before she slept with him. A fun vacation fling. No strings attached. When had a series of fantastic sexual encounters morphed into a desire to dive into a full-on relationship, complete with rings and vows?

Just the thought of it sent a queer little shiver up her spine. She rubbed at the goose bumps that had broken out on her skin. This was madness. She couldn't possibly be thinking of Lyle in terms of marriage. That was a crazy, incredible leap given that they'd only known each other for two weeks. Such impulsiveness was in Gabby's wheelhouse, not hers.

Giselle gave her head a vigorous shake to disrupt the

crazy thoughts swirling through her brain. What was wrong with her? She'd slept with a guy a couple dozen times. Why was she mentally fitting him for a tux?

How had she gotten here? And why was it so hard to walk away?

At a little after seven in the morning, Lyle sat atop his favorite dark bay gelding, watching his crew of six get their shit together. Today they were moving heifers and calves from their summer pasture to the closer one they used for fall. That meant gathering around two hundred head and driving them across a creek and keeping them organized along a mile of highway, before easing them through a wooded area to a lush pasture nearer the main part of the ranch.

It was going to be a long, miserable day.

He hadn't slept much the night before. In a ridiculously short time he'd grown accustomed to Giselle's soft form snuggled against his in bed, her light snores the sweetest white noise he'd ever fallen asleep to. When his mind hadn't replayed the encounter with Gabby, he'd reviewed his argument with Giselle and the crazy scenario where an algorithm had matched him with her twin sister.

As if she'd been summoned from his thoughts, her ridiculous yellow convertible pulled into the busy paddock yard. From the moment he'd first spotted the tiny vehicle, Lyle had made assumptions about the woman who drove it. Wrong assumptions, as it turned out.

Exiting the car, Giselle waved at the various cowboys that hailed her. Emotion swelled, tightening his chest at her friendly smile and relaxed stride. Little showed of the fashionable city girl who'd arrived almost two weeks earlier. Today, Giselle wore dusty chaps over her jeans, a blue striped button-down shirt and a kerchief tied around her neck. Beneath a brown felt hat, her long caramel hair trailed down her back in a neat braid.

"When she first asked you to teach her to ride, I bet you never imagined she'd be herding cattle with us." Jacob had ridden up beside him and sat staring at Giselle.

Lyle couldn't tear his eyes away. "Nope."

"I'm glad you believe she can do this."

"She's worked really hard. And the dogs will do a lot of the work. Just stick close by her and she'll be fine."

"Me?" Jacob looked surprised, no doubt because Lyle had chased his foreman away from Giselle at every opportunity. "She's your girlfriend."

"She's not."

Jacob seemed to find something amusing in Lyle's grim answer. "She turned you down?"

"I never asked."

"Why the hell not? She's the package. Smart, beautiful, funny. What's not to love?"

Lyle shot a dark look at his foreman. "Don't you have something you should be doing besides jawing the morning away with me?"

"Probably, but it's way more fun to list all the ways you've screwed up the best thing that's happened to you in years."

"I don't pay you to have fun." His dark tone didn't faze the other man one bit.

Jacob had worked for Royal Cattle Company since Tallulah hired him right out of high school. He'd worked his way up from ranch hand to foreman and had been there through Lyle's good days and worst nightmares. He'd kept the ranch running while Lyle dealt with the grief from losing his mom and wife, and sometimes was as bad as Jessica and Rosie when it came to poking his nose into his employer's love life.

"What the hell is she doing with that mare?"

Heart thundering, Lyle watched as Giselle led the buckskin mare out of the barn.

"Giselle asked me if she could ride Honey today," Jacob said, showing a grave lack of concern where Giselle and that crazy mare were concerned.

"Honey?" Lyle snarled.

"That's what Giselle's been calling her. She says it's both her color and her personality." Jacob paused to sigh. "That woman is adorable."

Eyeing Jacob's infatuated grin, Lyle realized something had happened while he'd been falling for Giselle. She'd not only captured his heart, but also woven herself into the fabric of the ranch. All the riding, roping and pitching in with chores had made the city girl one of them.

"You've been letting her handle the mare?"

Jacob gave an easy nod. "Sure."

"Even though she's dangerous."

"She isn't anymore." At last Jacob seemed to register his boss's anxiety. "Hey, don't worry. Giselle has done wonders with her. Honey is a completely new horse."

"I don't want Giselle riding her." Lyle couldn't tear

his eyes away from the pair. This woman had become so damn important to him, he couldn't bear it if anything happened to her. "She could get hurt."

"She won't."

"You don't know that."

"Giselle has been on her several times," Jacob admitted, his expression filled with pride. "She even did a little cutting with her the other day."

Lyle's mood turned savage at his foreman's reckless disregard for Giselle's safety. "Have you lost your mind?"

"Giselle did great. I'm telling you, she's a natural. And that mare took really good care of her. You should've seen it." The respect in Jacob's voice only exacerbated Lyle's displeasure.

"Get Harvey ready for her," Lyle snapped, nudging his bay forward. "I want to head out in ten minutes."

"Sure, boss."

Lyle turned his bay and sent him in Giselle's direction. When he drew within earshot, he said, "Unsaddle her and put her back. You'll ride Harvey today."

Giselle shifted to put herself between him and the horse. "Why?"

"She's dangerous." Lyle would've swung down off his gelding and snatched Giselle to safety, but he noticed that the mare seemed relatively calm and didn't want to spook her into acting out. "Did you forget the way she attacked you?"

"Don't worry. She's fine."

To Lyle's intense shock, Giselle grabbed the bridle on either side of the buckskin's nose and planted a kiss on the satiny flesh between the wide nostrils. The mare stood in placid stillness and happily accepted the affection.

"See?" Giselle shot a meaningful glance his way. "I don't think it was me she went after."

His breath caught as the mare nuzzled against Giselle's neck, her square teeth mere millimeters from the carotid artery pulsing beneath Giselle's delicate skin.

"What do you mean?"

"I think it was you that she struck out at."

"Me? Why?"

"You said she was abused." Giselle laughed as the mare nudged her off balance. "I'm guessing that it was a man who hurt her."

"I've spent hour and hours with her and she's never once tried to bite or kick me. I've been gentle and kind with her and she's just as docile as can be." Giselle's warm brown eyes turned to him in an earnest plea. "Will you let me ride her today? It's my last chance before I leave the ranch. Please?"

"No." He hated to disappoint her, but he'd feel even worse if something happened to her under his watch. "You'll ride Harvey." As if summoned by his words, one of the hands strode over, leading a placid gray gelding. He directed his next words to the cowboy. "Untack the mare and put her back."

"Sure thing."

Before the mare could be led away, Giselle gave her a hug. After flashing a dirty look at Lyle, she took Harvey's reins and mounted. That was another thing she'd mastered in the last two weeks. No more using a mounting block to get herself into the saddle. She looked like every other rider on his ranch as she swung her right leg over the horse's back.

Without saying another word to Lyle, Giselle went to join the cluster of cowboys as they headed out. He watched her go, his chest tight, and wondered if he should've just given in and let her ride the mare. It was apparent that Giselle's riding had steadily improved thanks to the hours and hours she'd spent in the saddle. Had he really been afraid for her safety, or was he acting like a jealous bastard because Jacob knew she'd been handling the mare and Lyle hadn't?

Jealous bastard.

He'd discovered the best version of himself with Giselle and without her he'd become an insecure jerk who blamed everyone else for the mistakes he'd made.

That would not do. He had to convince her to take a chance on him. On them. Being gloriously happy for the rest of his life depended on having her by his side.

Twelve

After the heifers and calves were settled into their new pasture, Giselle dismounted from Harvey and led him into the barn to unsaddle him. Despite her still burning irritation over not being allowed to ride Honey one last time, she made certain to give the gray gelding a good brushing and spoil him with several treats. Her mood brightened as she returned Harvey to the paddock and spied Honey trotting up to her with an eager whinny.

Sorrow was a rock in her chest as she fed the mare carrots and murmured goodbye. In some ways, she was just as upset about leaving Honey as she was to part from Lyle. For one thing, the mare had been nothing but sweet to her, offering equine hugs and horsey kisses. In contrast, her connection to Lyle had gone from perfection to problematic with the k!smet revelations.

With the carrots consumed and the mare's neck dampened by her tears, Giselle finally exited the paddock. Earlier, she'd bid farewell to the ranch hands she'd gotten to know these last two weeks. Honey had been her last goodbye.

Her spirits were about as low as they could get as Giselle headed toward her car. Before she reached it, Jacob called her name and she spun around. In his hands, he held the camera that she'd misplaced early on in her visit.

"You found my camera," she exclaimed, delighted that the expensive piece of equipment had reappeared.

"I know you were hoping to have some photos of ranch life for your social media, so I took a few."

"Thanks, Jacob." She resisted the urge to kiss his cheek. Even though she refused to glance at Lyle all the way across the yard, she sensed him moving in her direction like an ominous storm. "You and the guys have really made me feel welcome. I can't begin to tell you how much I appreciate that."

"Enough to give us a lifetime supply of your men's skin-care line?"

The boldness of his request, coming out of nowhere like that, shocked a laugh out of her. "So you like my products." Pleasure suffused her.

"Are you kidding?" He hooked his thumbs into his belt and slouched. "Just because we're sweaty and grimy all day doesn't mean we don't wanna look good and smell pretty for our womenfolk."

"My apologies for making assumptions." Glancing to the side, she noticed Lyle's gaze fixed on her as he approached. Her chest ached as she returned her attention to Jacob. "If you ever want a career change, don't forget about my offer."

"You'll be my first call." Noticing her sudden nervousness, Jacob glanced over his shoulder and saw Lyle's approach. To her shock, he leaned forward and kissed her cheek, then whispered, "We're going to miss you around here. Don't be a stranger."

"I won't," she called as he walked off. Drawing a deep breath into her lungs, Giselle braced for this final conversation with Lyle.

Hungry blue eyes roamed over her. "You did great today."

She resisted the pull of longing and gripped her camera until her knuckles ached. How many times over the last two weeks had she made excuses to put her body in contact with his? Today, she wanted nothing more than to keep her distance.

The sexual chemistry between them was as predictable as the sun rising in the east and she didn't trust herself to resist the crazy explosive hunger that robbed her of logic and common sense every time he touched her. No man had ever made her weak in the knees before. She thought that was some sort of ridiculous exaggeration made up to sell romance novels. But Lyle made her breathless and dizzy and hot in all the right places.

"Thanks," she said, "it was loads of fun." Unsure what to say next, she held up the camera. "Jacob brought my camera back. He said he found it and took a few pictures. Wasn't that nice of him?"

"Nice." Lyle gave the camera a cursory glance before dismissing it. "Look, about earlier. Sorry I was so rough with you about riding Honey."

"I understand." She'd had eight hours and numerous miles to get over her annoyance.

"It wasn't about your abilities."

"You were worried about me being out there with a horse you didn't trust." As much as she'd wanted to ride Honey, the mare had never been tested on a roundup and Harvey was a veteran.

"You've come a long way in a really short period of time." His features softened and her heart gave a happy trill. "I was really impressed."

"Not so much the city girl anymore, am I?"

"Oh, you're still a city girl," he teased, but from his somber gaze, she could tell his heart wasn't in it. "It's just that you fit in with us here, too."

The praise was so unexpected and so appreciated that a lump formed in her throat. "That's nice of you."

"I'm not being nice." He stepped into her space, slid his hand over her hip and lowered his head. "Giselle…."

With a vigorous headshake, she sidestepped. "I really should get back to Jessica's and pack. I want to get back to Dallas as soon as possible. I've neglected my business too long as it is." Her body cried in misery as he let her move beyond his reach.

"You're leaving today?" He sounded so stunned that butterflies erupted in her stomach.

"That was the plan all along. Two weeks on a ranch and then back to my real life."

"I thought you were staying until tomorrow." His

mouth flattened at her flippant tone. "I thought we could have dinner and talk."

"I think we've said all there is to say." She clamped down on the hope that flared at his invitation.

"Please, can we clear the air? I don't want to say goodbye like this." Seeing that she wasn't persuaded, Lyle's tone softened. "I don't want to say goodbye at all."

Her heart urged her to believe that everything would work out if she could just ignore the facts exposed in the last twenty-four hours.

When she didn't speak right away, Lyle continued, "Doesn't what happened between us these last two weeks demonstrate that we're good together?"

They were good together and Giselle decided she owed him the truth. "Yesterday when we met for dinner, I was going to tell you that I wanted to keep seeing you." Hearing his breath hitch, she hardened her resolve and kept going. "But then you kissed Gabby and I found out…" Her throat tightened. "The k!smet app matched you with my sister. Not with me."

"It's a stupid dating app with a faulty algorithm." Lyle's voice roughened, scraping across her best intentions, making her shiver. "It doesn't know anything about our hearts."

"Our hearts? You and I have been living in a sex-fueled fantasy for the last two weeks." The effort it took to mislead him was sapping all her strength. "I will never forget what we had, but let's be real, it was all a huge misunderstanding. You thought I was meant for you. I wasn't." Giselle gasped air into her tortured lungs to finish. "I want to be in a relationship where I feel safe."

"And you don't think you can be safe with me." A statement, not a question.

"Maybe before what I found out yesterday. Now, I'll always be wondering what if." She wanted to lose herself in the protective circle of his arms and believe that she was the woman for him, but maybe she was just the one who helped him realize he needed someone. "Take my sister on a date."

Lyle's eyebrows crashed together. "Not happening."

"k!smet matched you."

"You can't seriously think your sister is better for me than you."

She ignored the way his skepticism made hope flare. "You won't know until you try."

"I know now." Lyle stared at her for a long minute while a muscle worked in his jaw. "Nothing I say will change your mind, will it?"

With her throat too tight for speech, Giselle shook her head and spun away. Even though she doubted he'd chase after her, when she reached her car and settled behind the wheel, she was crushed to find him on his way back to work.

And just like that, it was over.

Giselle let the tears come as she drove back to Jessica's house. An unfamiliar vehicle was in the driveway and she spent a minute dabbing at her wet cheeks before exiting the car. She let herself into the house and spied a tall woman with sultry curves and shoulder-length brown hair standing in the kitchen.

"Jessica?"

Lyle's sister glanced up from her phone and stared at Giselle in shock. "Gabby? What are you doing here?"

Gabby? Was everyone going to mistake her for her twin?

"I'm Giselle."

"What?" Jessica shook her head. "I thought your name was Gabby?"

"She's my twin."

"Your identical twin?" At first Jessica seemed intrigued and then amused. "Oh, wow. Does Lyle know...?"

"That he matched with my twin sister on k!smet?" Giselle couldn't summon the energy to be angry at Jessica. "He does now."

Jessica winced. "So for two weeks he thought you were Gabby?"

Giselle responded with a sharp nod. "And he thought you and I had set him up."

"This is wild. I had no idea. I never saw your picture. Your profile photo is your business logo. And Gabby's user name is Gabby S. No wonder he's so annoyed with me."

"He's not the only one."

Jessica took one look at Giselle's expression and her eyes went wide. "You, too? Why?"

"Because you've been pretending to be him and talking to Gabby the whole time I was here. She showed up in Royal yesterday and Lyle thought she was me and kissed her."

"No!" Jessica didn't have the decency to hide her glee. "Wait. Why did he kiss your sister? He hasn't had any communication with her." When Giselle shot her a dark glower, Jessica clapped her hand over her mouth. "You and Lyle? This is too perfect."

"There's nothing perfect about us." Not anymore. "We had some fun, but it's over now and I'm heading back to Dallas. Tonight."

"Don't leave. I came back early so we could hang out and share house-swapping stories."

"I can't stay." To Giselle's dismay, tears flooded her eyes. Sucking in a shaky breath, she silently cursed.

"You're upset." Jessica pulled a bottle of pinot noir out of the wine fridge and dug in a drawer for the opener. "Have a glass of wine and tell me everything that happened. Then I'm going to find my brother and kick his ass."

"You don't need to do that." Giselle found herself seated at the island with a glass in her hand and Jessica's sympathetic expression encouraging her to bare her soul. "It's not Lyle's fault. I'm the one to blame in all this. When I found out everything that's been going on, I freaked out. We were never meant to be."

"Why would you say that?"

"Because he matched with Gabby on the k!smet app."

"Only because your profile isn't on the dating side. And what does it matter if he matched with your sister? It's you he's interested in."

"I'm not sure that's true."

"Trust me, the only thing my brother knows about your sister is how she looks. And when you really think about it, the case could be made for your sister being my dating match because I'm the one who created Lyle's profile."

Giselle appreciated how hard Jessica was working to make her feel better, but she couldn't jump through any more what-if hoops. The fact remained that Lyle never would've given her a second look if he hadn't believed she was his k!smet match. That's why he'd developed an affinity for her.

"You don't have to go back to Dallas right away." Jessica seemed to be trying for casual, but lines of tension bracketed her mouth. "You could stay here with me a little longer."

The offer stirred the sorrow Giselle had been trying to push down. "I can't. This was a two-week house swap." She'd never imagined how comfortable she'd feel on the ranch or how much she'd dreaded leaving. "I've got work and…"

Nothing. Absolutely nothing except work waited for her in Dallas.

"Ah." Jessica looked crestfallen. "Maybe with a little more time together you and Lyle could work things out."

Not once had they talked about the future and no matter how well they were getting along, she was merely his gateway to love, the woman who'd broken through his shell of indifference.

"We had fun, but even without all the k!smet drama, it has nowhere to go."

"Are you sure?"

Giselle's heart gave a painful squeeze as she thought about Lyle's profile being up on the k!smet app and what that might mean for his romantic future. "I'm sure."

Jessica winced at whatever Giselle's expression revealed. "My brother's not a guy who messes around. He never would've started up with you on a whim."

While she doubted Lyle had been celibate since his wife's death, she suspected that he hadn't indulged in the sort of extended sex romp they'd been enjoying. She'd lost track of all the places they'd done it, or how often he'd made her come. But wanting to believe it was more than just a memorable fling didn't mean Lyle wanted more.

"It's no use. My life is in Dallas. That's where I belong." Or so she kept reminding herself even as she fantasized about a life with Lyle. "Lyle needs someone whose lifestyle is similar to his own. He and I are polar opposites when it comes to our careers and living situations. I'm a city girl. He's country boy. Not only is there a geographic separation, there's an ideological one as well."

"I get it. You don't want to give up what you have in Dallas and obviously Lyle is tied to the ranch."

Even as Giselle nodded, she pondered what she was there for her in Dallas. Granted, her family lived there and it was where she'd established her business, but her shipping operations were in California. The only thing stopping her from moving to Royal was fear.

Lyle was staring into the empty comfort of a whiskey when Jessica barged into his house to read him the riot act. "I know what you're going to say. She went back to Dallas. What isn't clear is why you're mad at me about it."

Jessica glowered in frustration. "So your answer to not losing someone you're crazy about is to let them walk out of your life? Does that make any sense?"

It didn't. "She lives in Dallas. Her company is there. My life is Royal Cattle Company. What did you expect would happen?"

Her expression said it all. Jessica wouldn't be happy until he admitted that they could make it work despite the distance.

"I thought maybe you two could act like adults and admit you have feelings for each other."

"We've barely known each other two weeks."

"Lame." Jessica snorted in derision. "You both fell and fell hard."

Lyle acknowledged that truth with a pang. From the moment she'd answered her door wielding a cast-iron skillet she could scarcely lift, he'd been hooked. The ache in his chest expanded to include his entire torso.

"Sure, fine," he said. "But it doesn't make sense for us to continue when there's no chance—"

"You don't know that," Jessica interrupted.

"We come from completely different worlds." Shame twisted in his gut at the feeble excuse. "Look what happened between Mom and Dad. He craved life on the road. She wanted stability for her family."

"Dad is a selfish jerk," Jessica declared hotly. "Using their failed relationship to push Giselle away is a cop-out and you know it."

He did know it, but for a long time he'd retreated from stressful emotions and taken comfort in isolation. "I asked her to stay for dinner so we could talk and she refused."

"Stop being like this. Don't shut down and close yourself off. Don't let what happened with Chloe prevent you from loving someone else."

Lyle flinched away from remembered pain. In an instant, he was back in the past, disconnected from the joy of newly-discovered love. He could only wallow in his panic and fear as Giselle told him it was over.

"It's not that easy."

"Easy." His sister regarded him in disgust. "That's the problem with you. When you met Chloe, there was never a question that you would get married and have the perfect life. And maybe that's why you chose her. After watching Mom and Dad's messed-up relationship, you picked a girl with a ranching background who wanted the same things you did. And it worked out. But there's no reason why a relationship has to be perfect to be amazing. It can also be heartbreaking, exhausting and frustrating."

"You're not selling this correctly." Lyle's lips twitched into a sad half smile.

"It can also be magical, wonderful and life-changing." Jessica grabbed her brother's arm and gave it a rough shake. "I want you to be happy. Giselle could make you happy. Don't let her get away."

Pain lanced through him. "I already have."

"Then I guess things are gonna get more difficult for you." In that instant, Jessica sounded so like their mom. Talullah Drummond had been the best at tough love. Emphasis on the tough. Emphasis on the love.

"How do you figure?" Lyle couldn't imagine his heart becoming any more battered and bruised.

"If you'd confessed how you feel about her right away, you two might've been able to laugh at what happened and written off the entire incident as a comedy of errors."

"There was nothing particularly funny about it."

"Oh, come on." Mischief glinted in his sister's brown eyes. "You and I match twin sisters on k!smet and you end up falling for the wrong one? Or the right one."

With his emotions in turmoil, it was hard to see the humor. "You do realize this is all your fault. None of this would've happened if you hadn't set me up on that damned app."

Jessica's eyes widened at his biting accusation. "Sure, whatever. I'm to blame for the mix-up, but you are the one who messed up with Giselle."

"Whatever." Blaming his sister was so much easier than admitting he'd screwed up by letting Giselle believe she wasn't everything he could ever want or need in a lover and a partner.

"Plus, if you told me sooner that you were into the woman I'd house-swapped with, I wouldn't have felt driven to fix you up with Gabby."

"So it comes back to all this being my fault."

"Oh, Lyle." Jessica patted him on the arm without a trace of sympathy in her manner. "Doesn't it always?"

Jess had a point. If he hadn't been so caught up in keeping his heart safe, he might've been able to give Giselle the reassurance she needed. Instead, he'd kept his mouth shut and let a fantastic woman get away.

"I'm just not good at talking about my feelings."

"You don't have to be good at it," Jessica assured him, demonstrating more of that tough love. "You just have to be willing to try."

He couldn't help but agree that his relationship with Chloe had been uncomplicated from the second they met. They'd dated, fallen in love and gotten married without any drama. Her family had loved him. Jess had loved Chloe. Maybe he hadn't been all that good at telling her how he felt, but his mother had always said that it wasn't what a man said that a woman should listen to, but she should watch how he acted.

And with Giselle, he'd acted like an idiot. Today, he'd let her drive away instead of tossing her over his shoulder and carrying her straight to his bed, where he could spend however long it took to prove she was the only woman he wanted or needed.

"I screwed up," Lyle admitted.

"Of course, you did," Jessica replied with all the smug superiority of a younger sister.

"When she told me she wanted to feel safe in a relationship, I should've told her that I would take care of her."

"And that you love her."

"And that I love her. I guess I'd better go fix it."

Jessica beamed at him. "I'll text you her address and the code to get into her building."

Thirteen

Giselle walked into her downtown Dallas condo and registered a distinct absence of relief at being home once more. Usually, after she'd been gone for more than a few nights, she couldn't wait to settle back into her familiar routine. But that was before she'd spent two weeks on Lyle's ranch. Now, despair was the only thing riding Giselle's shoulders as she lugged her suitcases into her beautifully decorated bedroom.

This was it. This was her future. The rest of her life loomed before her, a meaningless, solitary existence devoid of blissful companionship, great sex and adorable livestock. Giselle set her fist against the pain in her chest as her heart clenched. For a second she could only stand beside her bed and wait for the agony to subside.

She'd made a huge mistake when she'd let humiliation and fear goad her into pushing away Lyle. Then, she'd compounded the error by running. A sensible woman would've given the man a chance to change her mind. She'd realized her stupidity about ten minutes outside of Royal. At that point, she hadn't fully committed to her journey. She could've gone back, could've apologized for being such an idiot, but having dug a deep hole, she chose instead to fling herself into it.

With her luggage put away and a load of laundry started, Giselle sat down at her computer to check her email. As she churned through her bloated inbox, the last two weeks at a ranch outside Royal, Texas became like a wonderful dream. Of course, there was proof that it had been all too real plastered all over her social media. With more images to come. Grabbing her camera, she settled into her home office and plugged in the camera to start the download.

While the transfer happened, she scrolled through the photos she'd captured on her smartphone, deleting duplicates and tagging her favorites to edit later. Then, she turned to the videos. She smiled as she scrolled past cavorting calves, running horses and exhibitions of serious roping skills.

Giselle paused at a video of Lyle approaching on horseback, one finger hovering over the delete button. She remembered that bright fall day. The dark bay gelding had ambled along a dusty trail, his rider surveying the activity buzzing around him. Beside the horse trotted Blink, one of the black-and-white border collies they used for herding. For some weird reason she happened to be recording in slow motion. Now, the video played out, giving her abundant time to admire the way his body languidly rocked in response to his horse's relaxed gait. She got a whopping five seconds of breath-stealing video before his roaming gaze found her. His slow, crooked smile and the joy in his eyes at the sight of her had made her hands jerk. The video shifted, showing sky, then grass, then nothing.

After setting aside her phone, Giselle got up to make a snack, hoping it was low blood sugar that was making her feel weepy and out of sorts. When she returned to her computer with a plate of cheese and grapes, she noticed the images were still downloading. Why was the process taking so long? She was amazed to see hundreds of photos and dozens of videos capturing all aspects of ranch life. How was all this possible when she'd misplaced the camera on her second day at the ranch?

As soon as she began sifting through the photos, she recognized the photographer. Many of the shots had been staged, but most were candid shots of cowboys doing what they did best. Shockingly, there were also images of her. Riding. From her first tentative ride to her final gallop. Roping. The moment captured when she'd successfully dropped the lasso around the neck of the plastic steer. Her obvious delight then made her throat ache now.

The pain only intensified as she encountered photos of Lyle. She scrolled through dozens, all taken at different times. In most of them, his handsome face wore its customary solemn expression. She shook her head as she scrolled. And then there were the photos of her and Lyle, laughing together, his eyes intent as he leaned toward her. The chemistry between them was on full display. She traced her lips, remembering his kisses, and found herself smiling.

Next, she turned to the videos. Giselle was trying to decide which one to watch first when she arrived at the last one recorded. Spying Jacob's smiling face filling the screen, she clicked on it.

"Hey, Giselle," he began with a sly smile. "By now you'll probably guess where your camera has been for the last week and a half. I just wanted to let you know that it was Lyle's idea to shoot photos and videos of you to post on your social media. I was the one who got carried away with all the rest." He paused and grew somber. "Lyle has a hard time letting anyone new in, but I watched him open up to you. The connection you two share has changed his life. Don't put Royal Cattle Company in your rearview mirror for good. He's going to miss you. We all will."

She'd let doubt and anxiety push her into a stupid decision. Leaving the ranch so abruptly had been an act of cowardice. Lyle hadn't broken her heart. She hadn't given him the chance. She'd let her insecurities get the better of her. The question now became whether or not Lyle would forgive her.

Giselle sprang to her feet and raced from the room. Even though the fastest way to resolve the situation was a phone call, this was a conversation she needed to have in person.

Purse in hand, she jerked open her front door and would've barreled through if the way hadn't been blocked by a wall of muscle. Lyle!

Her breath hitched.

"What are you doing here?" This wasn't the first thing she wanted to say to him, but his presence in her hallway threw her off her game. "How did you get here?"

"My truck brought me." A smile ghosted across his lips at her impatient hiss. "As to what I'm doing here, I hated the way we left things."

"But how did you get in?"

Lyle scooped her off her feet with a wicked smile. "Don't you think you're focusing on the wrong things right now?"

"Sure. You're right."

Tossing her purse in the direction of the entry-hall table, she wrapped her arms around his neck and breathed him in. Lyle was here. In Dallas. In her condo. Joy exploded inside her, dispelling the misery of the last twenty-four hours.

"Jessica gave me the security code." He carried her into her living room, and stood looking at the view of downtown afforded by the floor-to-ceiling windows. "I hope it's okay."

"Perfectly okay," Giselle said, setting her hand against his cheek, loving that he'd driven to Dallas to be with her. "And your timing is perfect. Five minutes later and we would've missed each other."

He settled on the couch with her on his lap and made sure she stayed there with one arm locked around her back and the other pinning her thighs.

"It's late." He nuzzled her neck, his lips tracing a line of fire from her earlobe to her collarbone. "Where were you headed?"

She threaded her fingers through his dark hair. "Back to the ranch."

"You were?" He pressed a kiss to the hollow of her throat. "Why? Did you forget something?"

"I forgot to tell you how much I love you." When Lyle went perfectly still beneath her, Giselle rushed on before she could doubt herself again. "And that I can't imagine the rest of my life without you."

"Giselle." The rough throb in his voice raised goose bumps all over her body.

"I'm sure it seems fast," she declared, wondering if she'd freaked him out. "After all, we've only known each other two weeks."

"Sweetheart." Lyle snared her chin and turned her face so she had to meet his gaze. There was reassurance there, but also a trace of remorse. "I came here tonight to tell you that I love you. I've known for several days but I let my pride keep me silent. I didn't want to admit that Jessica and Rosie and…oh, hell, everyone from my friends to the ranch hands was right. You are what has been missing in my life."

The most beautiful words in the world were coming out of Lyle's mouth and Giselle could scarcely believe what she was hearing. "You love me?"

Lyle's answer was a deep, hungry kiss, filled with equal parts tenderness and passion. Giselle responded with a strangled cry that contained joy and awe. They were both breathing hard when he lifted his lips and kissed the tip of her nose.

"How could you doubt it?"

"Well…" She peered at him through her lashes. "You did kiss my sister."

"Your twin sister," he growled. "And only because I thought she was you."

She was only half-teasing as she asked, "What if it happens again."

"It won't." No man had ever sounded so convincing. "Now that I know there's two of you, I won't make the same mistake again." He leaned his forehead against hers. "And just so you know, I knew instantly that there was something wrong."

Giselle cuddled against his chest. "But the k!smet app—"

"No more about that damned app," he warned, fingers tightening on her. "You are the one I chose and you're the only woman I'll ever want for the rest of my life."

"Good, because you're the only man I want to spend the rest of my life with."

He skimmed his fingertips along her spine with mesmerizing slowness. "So we're on the same page."

While his caresses demonstrated the same delicious sensuality as always, she detected a slight hesitation in his tone. Was the ever-confident Lyle Drummond worried that she didn't want to give up her life in the city to live permanently with him on the ranch? This hint of vulnerability triggered a need to protect him.

"We are." Giselle guided her lips into the soft skin behind his ear and murmured, "In fact, I've decided to start looking for some commercial space in Royal."

"You are?" There was a smile in Lyle's voice. "So you're moving to Royal?"

"Even closer." She shot him an overly innocent smile. "Jessica invited me to move in with her."

Lyle's eyes widened. He obviously hadn't expected that answer. "The hell she did. You're moving in with me and that's final."

"Okay."

One dark eyebrow rose. "Just okay?"

Giselle captured his face between her palms and planted a quick, firm kiss on his lips. "Haven't you realized yet that being with you is the only place for me?"

"I do now." The kiss that followed was deep and hot and sweet. "I love you."

"I love you, too. Now, take me to bed so we can get this love fest started for reals."

"Damn straight."

And so he did.

Lyle stood on the outskirts of all the frenetic activity taking place on the ranch, his gaze tracking a fireball of energy with honey-brown waves trailing down her back and his favorite sunset-inspired boots on her feet. Today, instead of booty shorts, she was wearing a short, cream-colored dress with long puffy sleeves.

It was hard to believe that three months had gone by since she'd charmed her way into his life. Twelve amazing weeks where he'd smiled more and worried less. Where his future plans included romantic getaways, candlelit dinners and serious conversations about marriage and kids.

He was ridiculously happy, outrageously obsessed with his good fortune. The hard times he'd known in the

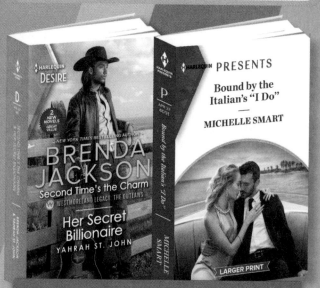

Get Free Books
In Just 3 Easy Steps

Are you an avid reader searching for more books?
The **Harlequin Reader Service** might be for you! We'd love to send
you up to **4 free books** just for trying it out. Just write **"YES"** on the
Free Books Voucher Card and we'll send your free books and a gift,
altogether worth over $20.

Step 1: Choose your Books

Try *Harlequin® Desire* and get 2 books featuring the worlds of the
American elite with juicy plot twists, delicious sensuality and intriguing
scandal.

Try *Harlequin Presents® Larger-Print* and get 2 books featuring the
glamorous lives of royals and billionaires in a world of exotic locations,
where passion knows no bounds.

Or *TRY BOTH!*

Step 2: Return your completed Free Books Voucher Card

Step 3: Receive your books and continue reading!

Your free books are **completely free**, even the shipping! If you continue
with your subscription, you can look forward to curated monthly
shipments of brand-new books from your selected series, always at a
discount off the cover price! Plus you can cancel any time.

Don't miss out, reply today! Over $20 FREE value.

Free Books Voucher Card

YES! I love reading, please send me more books from the series I'd like to explore and a free gift from each series I select.

More books are just 3 steps away!

Just write in "**YES**" on the dotted line below then select your series and return this Books Voucher today and we'll send your free books & a gift asap!

▶▶▶ YES ◀◀◀

Choose your books:

☐ **Harlequin Desire®**
225/326 CTI GRT3

☐ **Harlequin Presents® Larger-Print**
176/376 CTI GRT3

☐ **BOTH**
225/326 & 176/376 CTI G295

FIRST NAME

LAST NAME

ADDRESS

APT.#

CITY

STATE/PROV.

ZIP/POSTAL CODE

EMAIL ☐ Please check this box if you would like to receive newsletters and promotional emails from Harlequin Enterprises ULC and its affiliates. You can unsubscribe anytime.

HD/HP-1123-OM_123ST

past gave him a greater appreciation of his current joy. Most mornings he woke with her beside him in bed and wondered how he'd coped with his loneliness. Nothing felt as good as having her near. Unless it was watching her succeed and thrive, whether in her business or in the ever-increasing horsemanship skill.

"Stop scowling," Giselle told him as she strode past him on her way to the tables loaded down with gift bags filled with samples for the soon-to-be-arriving guests. She had on a headset provided by the party planner and was checking on a dozen last-minute details.

"I can't." Lyle followed in her wake, unsure if she'd been talking to him.

She tossed him a look over her shoulder. "Why not?"

"I'm going through withdrawal," he complained, his long strides enabling him to catch her easily.

Giselle had decided the ranch would be the perfect place for the Saito for Men launch party. An enormous tent had been set up, large enough to hold damn near the entire town of Royal, plus a significant number of beauty influencers. She'd been eating, breathing and sleeping the event for nearly a month and no one was more excited than Lyle that the day had finally arrived. In five hours, the launch would be hailed as a massive success and the woman he loved would be glowing with euphoria.

"Withdrawal from what?" She made sure the helpers handing out the bags knew where extras were being kept, and then she moved to check on the catering staff.

"You."

She turned an amused gaze on him. "Impossible.

I've been on the ranch all day and all night for the past week."

"Sure." He took her free hand and ran his thumb across her knuckles. "But you've been so busy getting ready for this party that you haven't had a time for us."

"Once this line launches today, I promise work will go back to normal." For just a second, she let him glimpse her weariness and anxiety. "So much is riding on today."

"Today's launch is going to be a complete success," Lyle assured her, giving her hand a quick squeeze.

"I hope so. Of course, it would help a lot if my spokesmodel charmed some of the influencers I invited to the party." She'd stopped beside an enormous banner featuring the man she'd chosen to represent the Saito for Men product line.

Casting a glance at the banner, Lyle said, "I don't think he's happy to be on display."

"Perhaps I need to remind him that I vetoed everyone's suggestion that he attend the party sans shirt."

He grimaced. "Thanks for that."

Giselle turned to face him. Stepping into his space, she snaked her arm around his waist, and offered him a tender smile. "You are going to be amazing today. Wait until everyone gets a look at you. You're going to become an instant celebrity."

For weeks now Giselle and her team had been promoting the event, letting everyone know they would be live streaming on social media. At the same time, the new product line would become available on the website and Giselle was hoping all the planning and hard work would pay off.

"You know perfectly well that's not why I did this," Lyle said, dusting kisses across her knuckles.

"I know." Giselle shivered as he turned her hand over and brushed his lips against the pulse thrumming madly in her wrist. "You did it because you love me."

"It's the only reason I'd be willing to make a fool of myself in front of strangers."

"You won't make a fool of yourself. In fact, if anyone should be regretting that you agreed to be the face of Saito for Men it should be me."

Her pique caught him off guard. "Why's that?"

"Up until now, I've had you all to myself." She frowned up at him. "Now, millions of women will want you."

"Billions could want me," he assured her. "But all I'll ever want is you."

She threaded her fingers through his hair and lifted onto her toes. Their lips came together in a loving kiss that turned hungry and hot in an instant. As with every time they came together, she became his everything and sent his hormones into overdrive. It wasn't until Giselle gave a start and broke away that he recalled where they were and what today was about.

Giselle keyed her mic. "Yes, I'm here." She was breathing hard from their kiss as she listened to the voice coming over the headset. "Tell them we'll start in ten minutes. I'm on my way." Blowing Lyle a kiss, she headed toward the backstage area.

As he watched her go, body humming with desire, Lyle once again congratulated himself for being right all along. The k!smet app had been wrong to match him and Gabby. No algorithm could understand what he needed. While he and Giselle weren't an obvious pairing on paper, she was perfect for him. Her sassy sweetness had charmed the hell out of his ranch hands. Her kindness and patience had tamed the meanest mare on the ranch. Her determination had enabled her to master roping and riding. But it was her loving heart and passionate nature that had brought him back to life.

As Giselle took to the stage to welcome everyone and share a little bit about her company, she was definitely in her element. From his vantage point in the wings, Lyle stared at her in wonder. Radiant. Charming. Confident. The assembled guests were eating out of her hand.

"I'd like to introduce to you the owner of Royal Cattle Company, where our large event is taking place today." Giselle swept her arm in his direction, his cue to join her on stage. "Lyle Drummond."

He stepped onto the low platform and waved self-consciously at the roaring crowd. He picked out many of his friends and neighbors, and wondered what sort of ribbing he would take in the weeks to come for his decision to become a brand ambassador for a beauty product. Then, seeing Giselle's beaming smile, he reveled in her joy at their partnership.

"As you've probably noticed from the banners scattered around the tent, Lyle is also the face of Saito for Men. I chose him because he's handsome." She sent a saucy glance his way. "But also to demonstrate that every man can benefit from a good skin-care regimen."

Keeping her speech informative, but concise, Giselle pointed out her commitment to eco-friendliness and touched on the benefits of a daily routine before handing off the mic to Lyle so he could share his experience with Saito for Men, from resisting the need for a skin-care regimen to noticing a difference since using the products.

As he finished with his testimonial, Lyle reached over and took Giselle's hand. "One last thing before we end today's presentation. I hope she doesn't mind if I tell all of you how wonderful this woman is and how important she's become to me." Oblivious to everything but the love expanding his chest, Lyle smiled down at her. "In fact, I'm madly in love with her and…hoping that she'll agree to spend the rest of her life with me."

There was a beat of silence while everyone absorbed the news, including Giselle, who pressed her hands to her face as he dropped to one knee. The tent erupted.

"Really?" Her murmured question was lost beneath the cheers and applause coming from the two hundred guests.

"Really." Taking out a ring, Lyle spoke clearly into the mic. "Giselle Saito. I love you with all my heart and everything I am. Will you marry me?"

The air around them sparked with anticipation as Giselle stared at him in wonder. Proposing in such a public way had been a huge risk and Lyle couldn't deny the relief that swept through him as she nodded. He slid the diamond ring onto her left hand and got to his feet to pull her into his arms and kiss her.

"I adore you," he murmured against her lips. "I want us to spend the rest of our lives together."

Tears shimmered in her brown eyes. "That's what I want, too."

Hand in hand, they turned to face their cheering guests.

* * * * *

Stacey Kennedy is a *USA TODAY* bestselling author who writes romances full of heat, heart and happily-ever-afters. Stacey lives with her husband and two children in southwestern Ontario. Most days, you'll find her enjoying the outdoors or venturing into the forest with her horse, Clementine. Stacey's just as happy curled up indoors, where she writes surrounded by her lazy dogs. She believes that sexy books about hot cowboys can fix any bad day. But wine and chocolate help, too.

Books by Stacey Kennedy

Harlequin Desire

Devil's Bluffs

Most Eligible Cowboy
Stranded with a Cowboy

Texas Cattleman's Club: Diamonds & Dating Apps

The Trouble with an Heir

Visit the Author Profile page
at Harlequin.com for more titles.

You can also find Stacey Kennedy on Facebook, along with other Harlequin Desire authors, at Facebook.com/HarlequinDesireAuthors!

Dear Reader,

If you love fast-paced stories, laugh-out-loud moments,
heart-squeezing emotion and sizzling chemistry, then
you've come to the right place!

The Trouble with an Heir is my first story in the Texas
Cattleman Club's world, where glamping business
owner Jessica Drummond is chasing down her dreams
of becoming a chef. When she finally gets her first big
gig for an engagement party, filling in for a maternity
leave, it's make-or-break time for her reputation. Only
problem? One person stands in her way—devastatingly
handsome CEO, and designer for the party, Marcus
Winters, who has plans of his own. Regardless, she's not
going to let any man—even a criminally good-looking
one—derail her momentum.

To pull off the grandest party the Texas Cattleman Club
has ever seen, Jessica and Marcus forge a truce, determined
to bring two feuding families together, but an undeniable
attraction also bubbles beneath the surface. And when
Marcus enlists Jessica's help to archive his family's
heirlooms, love letters that should have remained hidden
are found. With romance swirling in the air, and lust burning
just as hot, they fall prey to their mutual attraction, and the
cellar becomes their secret rendezvous spot. But that's
not all that's heating up in Royal, Texas—a discovery in
the archives soon unearths a dark secret.

And even Jessica and Marcus may get caught in the cross
fire...

To stay up-to-date on upcoming releases and sales,
subscribe to my mailing list at www.staceykennedy.com.
To stay in touch, follow me on Instagram and TikTok
@staceykennedybooks and on Facebook at
authorstaceykennedy. I love new friends!

Happy reading!

Stacey

THE TROUBLE WITH AN HEIR

Stacey Kennedy

For everyone brave enough to
live life on their own terms!

One

Marcus Winters entered the Texas Cattleman's Club, a timely single-story building constructed of dark stone and wood, originally an old-world men's club built around 1910. His dress shoes clicked against the wood flooring as he rebuttoned his suit jacket, passing the day care on the left of the entryway. He continued down the hallway, striding by hunting trophies and historical artifacts on the paneled walls. The rich scent of cedar fighting against the warm aroma of leather.

Marcus recalled when the club held more of an old boys' club feel. After a renovation several years back, the Texas Cattleman's Club moved into modern times with brighter colors, more lighting seeping in from the larger windows and higher ceilings.

As he entered the great room, he discovered his soon-to-be sister-in-law, and owner of MaggieInk, Maggie Del Rio, discussing details about her upcoming engagement party to the catering staff.

Maggie held elegance and grace that couldn't be bought with her long black shiny hair and stunning dark brown eyes. His brother Jericho had found himself a beautiful partner.

Marcus froze a moment, letting reality sink in. Maggie Del Rio would soon be his *sister-in-law*. A month ago, he wouldn't have put a dime on an engagement between the Winters and the Del Rio families.

The century-old feud running between the families was as deep as the roots in the Davy Crockett National Forest. A feud that began in 1920 when Marcus's great-grandmother Eliza Boudreaux left Fernando Del Rio at the altar for Marcus's great-grandfather Teddy Winters. A hot scandal at the time, and the bitterness of that shame had remained unfaltering until Marcus's brother Jericho was matched with Maggie Del Rio on the dating app k!smet, the hottest new trend in Royal, Texas.

More than once, Marcus had questioned his brother's sanity, but love was a fickle thing. Jericho had proposed to Maggie after only two weeks, remaining steadfast in his decision to marry a woman belonging to a family that had been deemed the enemy, and their love single-handedly extinguished the red-hot fire that had burned between the families for years.

For that reason, and regardless of the layer of tension simmering in the room, Marcus would support his brother in his decision, letting bygones be bygones in the name of happiness.

His sole focus now, after his brother had asked him to oversee the design of the engagement party, was to ensure the party happening in three days exceeded the couple's dreams.

Spotting Jericho, his older brother by three years—and shorter by three inches, something Marcus never forgot to mention—standing in the center of the room, he headed for that way. His brother was overlooking the single table that showed the direction of Marcus's idea with scrutiny, and Marcus grinned. He wouldn't expect his older brother to make this too easy on him.

A rising star in the architect world with his eco-friendly firm, RoyalGreen Architects LLS, Jericho knew a thing or two about quality of work. Seeing as Marcus was CEO of a luxury goods line, Fresh by Winters, he, along with his team, was honored to lead the design elements for the engagement party.

Settling in next to Jericho, Marcus shoved his hands into his pants pockets. "You're not scowling. That must be a good sign."

Jericho laughed. He glanced sidelong, his brown eyes—a Winters trait—softening, as he ran a hand over his omnipresent facial scruff. "I like what I'm seeing."

Marcus nodded in thanks, studying the romantic table with white linens, pink and white roses and dark greenery, matched with crystal and gold accents. For the last week, he'd gone back and forth over ideas presented to him by his team. Through elimination, they'd combed through the Fresh by Winters Fall Guide, until they were confident in the design for the party. The premise was Jane Austen meets the modern world, or so a member on his team told him. Admittedly, romance was not his strong point. "I'm glad you're pleased," he told his brother.

"Thanks again for taking the reins on this," Jericho said, honest sincerity in his voice.

Marcus snorted. "No thanks needed. I would've been offended if you hadn't asked me." Though he also understood why Jericho brought family into the planning. He had no doubt his brother and Maggie were trying to make both families feel involved in hopes to mend the feud.

Jericho smiled, cupping Marcus's shoulder. "Let me talk to Maggie and get her opinion on this in case she wants to make any changes."

"Of course," Marcus replied, restraining the tension in his voice. He still hoped the party went off without anyone resulting to violence. His brother was a staunch supporter of his closest friends and family, and Marcus would do his best to ensure nothing ruined his celebration with Maggie, including dragging out anyone who started trouble.

With a final nod, Jericho headed for his soon-to-be wife smiling at him with damn stars in her eyes. A pain of envy hit Marcus's chest. Jericho hadn't been the only one to sign up to the dating app. Entering his thirties now, Marcus was making a shift in his life. The first, to partner with the one business he never thought he'd partner with—his family's manufacturing business, Winters Industries.

He'd preferred to do things on his terms and stand on his own two feet. He was the first to break away from the family business and chose his own path years ago.

But partnering with the family business now gave him the means to launch a more accessible version of his luxury goods line. His focus was to get top-of-the-line furniture, bedding, lighting and window treatments into more houses across the country. Winters Industries could make that happen.

A ding from his pocket had Marcus reaching for his cell phone. When he lifted his phone, finding a marketing report, a sultry voice across the room said, "Yes, I have some major concerns. I don't get the overall design. The entire feel clashes with the menu I've planned."

Interest piqued over who thought his work was subpar, he looked toward the voice, but the woman was standing behind a large plant, talking to Maggie and his brother.

That husky voice continued, "I'd like to know who thought this mix of materials and elements was a good idea, because it's not. It's a terrible idea."

Determined to defend his choices, he stepped around the plant to face off with her, but the words on his tongue vanished, his body awakening swiftly at the beauty staring back at him. It became instantly clear that sultry voice belonged to an even sultrier woman with curves for days.

Tall, she looked around six feet, with legs that went on and on, ending at sexy black heels. Her chestnut shoulder-length hair fell in waves around her face and her sculpted lips made his thoughts turn dirty fast. Though her eyes were what stopped his lungs from getting in any air. Pure fire simmered in her brown eyes. Fire that intrigued, captivated...*aroused*.

Obviously aware he'd been listening to her conversation, she blinked at him. "Can I help you or is eavesdropping a normal habit for you?"

Maggie covered her mouth, her shoulders shaking with her silent laughter.

Jericho didn't even attempt to hide his laugh and chuckled freely.

Marcus narrowed his eyes on the stunning beauty. "Marcus Winters," he said, offering his hand, curious *who* the hell this woman was. "The man behind the design."

Anyone else he'd met before would have blushed in embarrassment. Even casting their gaze down under his fierce examination.

Apparently, not this woman.

She lifted her chin and returned his handshake with a firm grip. "Jessica Drummond, the chef, and the woman who hates your design."

Maggie burst out laughing. "Well, that's one way for an introduction to happen." She looked between them and then held her hands up in surrender. "I'm so not getting in the middle of this. You both have great ideas. I can't wait to see what you come up with."

Jericho nodded agreement. "I'm with Maggie. I'm not getting anywhere near this." He strode away with his fiancée, his laughter following him.

The traitor.

Marcus didn't dare look away from the woman challenging him with her stare. He would've bet she was part of the Del Rio family for how she treated him, but her last name declared she wasn't.

An intensity Marcus hadn't quite felt before crackled in the air as he lifted an eyebrow at her. "What exactly don't you like about my design, Ms. Drummond?"

"Well, Mr. Winters, the fact that you completely ignored my menu," she said, eyes narrowed on him.

"I didn't think it important to take your menu into consideration," he stated firmly.

She snorted, folding her arms. "Of course you didn't, and that was your first wrong move."

Hot or not, he frowned at her. "The design elements are on point. This idea wasn't dreamed up in a day, Ms. Drummond. My team and I have worked on this for a week. Maggie is pleased. Jericho is pleased. Get on board with the design."

Apparently what he said was the wrong thing. Her eyes narrowed into slits. "Marcus Winters," she said slowly. "CEO of Fresh by Winters, right?"

"That's right," he said firmly to prove his point. "I did not create a multimillion-dollar company from the ground up by coming up with—" he used his fingers as quotation marks "—terrible ideas."

"Good for you," she shot back. "I hate to break it to you, but this is what this is." She waved out to his mock-up table. "It's like I'm walking into IKEA and seeing a fake dining room they've set up. Sure, it's nice, but the overall design falls flat because it doesn't take into account that you're creating a *mood*. If the mood of the venue doesn't match the mood of the food, then what do you have?"

His frown deepened. "Did you just compare my line to IKEA?"

"I actually like IKEA. Great products for a good value," she said. "And what I mean is, what you have is a mediocre engagement party that no one will talk about ever again."

He slowly shook his head, stuck on certain things she'd said. "So what I have is a mediocre, expensive line that is less appealing than a furniture store where you put together your own furniture?"

She shrugged. "Food is an experience. It's a journey. From the beginning to the end. I have planned out every single thing from the appetizer to the wine to the main course. All of these things are special. And you have not paid attention to any of it."

He lifted an eyebrow at her. "I didn't think I had to pay attention to anyone else but my idea for the party."

She held his gaze and then snorted. "I do understand that you're likely used to getting your own way, but the menu and your ideas simply don't jibe. I also know you have a famous name and don't have to worry about how the world sees you, but my name means something to me, as does my work, and I refuse to watch this party drown because you can't see past your failures."

Marcus was…without words. He couldn't decide if he was impressed by her or pissed off.

He gave her another long look over, reassessing. He could count on one hand the amount of people who pushed back at him, who weren't dazzled by his family's money and who weren't intimated or charmed by him. And all those people he could count were his family.

Who was Jessica Drummond?

Crossing his arms, he considered his choices. On one

hand, he wanted to refuse her ideas simply due to push-back. On the other hand, he couldn't deny the sparks charging the air between them. Delicious intense sparks that he wanted to play with a little.

Over the years, he had dated, only casually, but he had signed up to k!smet in hopes of meeting a woman that would shake up his world like Maggie shook up Jericho's life. The app had yet to match him.

Maybe he didn't need k!smet after all.

This woman, holding his gaze like an equal, telling him off like no one had done so since he was a child, made him take notice. This woman whose sculpted lips drew his eye. This woman that made him lose his damn breath by one look at her. Yeah, she was his type, and then some.

He didn't want a woman to always agree with him. He craved a woman that challenged him.

Wanting to know more about this woman staring him down and calling him out with her demands, he offered, "You hate what I've done, then you've got until tomorrow morning to prove it to me and show me your ideas."

Her eyes widened before she quickly regained her composure. "You're willing to change the vision of the party?"

"No," he corrected. "But if you have ways to improve the party, we can find ways to integrate your ideas."

She paused, surprise glinting in her pretty eyes. "Good," she finally said, exhaling deeply, lowering her shoulders. "As long as you're open to my ideas, then we won't have a problem." With the same fire he'd seen moments ago, she added, "I've been hired by the Del Rio family, and I intend to make sure this party is talked about for years."

Marcus couldn't help himself. He took a step forward, getting a little closer, testing the waters. "You'll hear no arguments from me about that."

She visibly swallowed, her cheeks turning slightly pink as her eyes searched his. His gaze fell to her lips. A mouth that currently wasn't saying a single word.

Good. He wasn't the only one made speechless today.

With a grin he suspected looked salacious, he said, "Come by my design studio at Fresh by Winters at eleven fifteen and we can go over your ideas." He cocked his head, lifting an eyebrow at her. "Do you know the building?"

She cleared her throat but didn't step away from him. "Downtown on the corner, right?"

"That's it." Needing to get a further read on whatever was happening between them, he offered his hand again. As she slid her slender fingers across his, he added, "I look forward to our meeting tomorrow."

She licked her lips, dragging her fingers against his longer than necessary. "Try and be open-minded, Marcus."

Her last dig should annoy him, but he couldn't fight the heat flooding him as she practically purred his name. Oh, hell, yeah, there was something special about this woman.

Marcus grinned as she strode away, his gaze falling to her heart-shaped ass hugged by her skirt.

Apparently, she wanted a game, and he was more than willing to play, all to find out if this woman would become his new enemy…or if she was something else entirely.

Two

The following morning, standing in the chef's kitchen in her rustic ranch-style house, Jessica finished placing the silver food cover over the four plates of breakfast. On the menu this morning were ricotta hotcakes with maple bacon, roasted vine tomatoes and arugula, a dish that would have made her favorite teacher at the Auguste Escoffier School of Culinary Arts in Austin proud.

She picked up her steaming cup of coffee and took a slow, small sip, standing in front of the farmhouse sink, located on her brother, Lyle's ranch. The sun shone over the lake and ducks floated along the peaceful water, bringing warmth to her chest. She'd spent the most on her kitchen when designing her house. From the banked appliances, at eye level, and a brass pot holder over the long island for entertaining, the space was meant to impress. And it impressed her every day. It helped that the white subway tile, along with the white cabinets, was bright and welcoming to get her day started.

But she couldn't shake meeting Marcus yesterday. He'd stayed there on her mind all night long, leaving her sleep restless. She knew his type—all sexy charm that probably had panties dropping whenever he grinned. Perhaps that was why she met his charm head-on, instead of ignoring his type like she usually did.

She realized her mistake yesterday when she'd opened her big mouth and her words fell out. *Marcus Winters.* The second he'd said his name, she considered backpedaling about coming down so hard on him.

Marcus belonged to the other prominent family, aside from the Del Rios, who had weight in Royal, Texas. Though, knowing his CEO type of personality, she knew he wouldn't be swayed with polite smiles and soft words, and she needed to convince him to change his design.

She had one shot at proving to both the Winterses and the Del Rios that she was a new chef worth looking at. If all Jessica needed to do to get her name out there was play nice with the cocky Marcus to get her on his side, so be it. Besides, if she could win him over, she would gain his respect and that could gain her his professional contacts.

Doesn't hurt that he's gorgeous too... She promptly ignored the thought that slithered through her mind, and turned to her brother, Lyle, standing behind her.

With a frown, he asked the same question he'd been asking for days. "You sure you're not taking on too much?"

Jessica carefully picked up the tray, giving him a beaming smile. "Whatever do you mean? Running a glamping business, cooking for the guests and filling in for the Del Rios' family's chef for an engagement party seems like too much?"

Lyle narrowed his blue eyes, giving her a dry look. "Hilarious." He took the tray out of her hands. "I'm serious, Jess. You're only one person."

"But I've got big dreams, and with big dreams come big responsibilities." She grinned.

He scoffed. "You are not Spider-Man."

"How do you know?" she asked lightly.

Wanting to put distance between her and this conversation, she made her way through her house, soon stepping outside. Her glamping business, Camp Up, had never been the dream, but it had been her way of achieving the dream. It financed her ability to go to culinary school instead of asking Lyle for the money. When she'd graduated from culinary school, she'd had two options: move to the big city or work in one of the small diners for crap money. At the time, neither of those options sounded appealing, so instead she'd sharpened her skills with various dietary requirements and varying numbers of glamping guests. She'd never expected the company to take off like it had, and she was proud of her little business.

As she exited her house, she smiled under the morning sun. Fall had descended on Royal, bringing rich colors and fallen leaves, and all her favorite things: leggings, sweaters and apple caramel lattes.

She headed down the porch steps of the house, made

of stone and wood accents. It had been the original house on the ranch her late mother, Tallulah, bought after a lottery windfall. She'd named the ranch the Royal Cattle Co., and specialized in raising Wagyu beef.

The ranch was her brother's now. Lyle built his own house a mile from hers.

"Jessica," her brother grumbled behind her.

She nearly rolled her eyes but stopped herself. Lyle loved her, and was the best kind of brother: protective, kind and supportive. Hell, even she felt the exhaustion hanging on her lately.

She finally reached the ATV and turned to him, as Lyle carefully carried the tray down the porch steps. "I know you're worried about me, but honestly, I'm okay." She took the tray from him and set it on the back of the ATV, where he'd built a bin to keep the food safe. "Besides, I've got Rosie helping for lunch and dinner and snacks. I can handle breakfast."

Lyle frowned, crossing his arms. "Just don't over-exert yourself."

"I won't," she said, nudging her shoulder into his. "Geesh, I'm thirty years old. When will you quit it with the big-brother act?"

He grumbled something incoherent, shoving his hands into his pockets.

"He'll never quit hovering over you. He loves you too much," Giselle said, the front door shutting behind her.

Jessica smiled at her new friend, Giselle Saito, soon to be Giselle Drummond. Giselle had gone to the bathroom the moment she and Lyle entered the house, obviously giving her brother time to grill Jessica.

A quick look at Lyle revealed his shining eyes. Eyes that reminded Jessica so much of her late mother whenever he looked so happy. Because that's just how their mother had been before she died. A ray of sunshine that never let hard times bring her down. She'd worked harder than anyone Jessica had ever known. Even after winning the lottery she worked hard to have a successful cattle ranch. Jessica liked to think she inherited her mom's strong work ethic.

Her chest radiated with heat as she watched her brother and friend's love blossom before her eyes. She was delighted for them, even wished her mother was still alive to see Lyle living for love, instead of living to work at the ranch. And her mom would've laughed knowing Lyle and Giselle fell in love when Jessica and Giselle blindly switched houses for a vacation at the same time as Jess was trying to set up Lyle on the k!smet app—unknowingly with Giselle's twin.

Seeing her two favorite people hopelessly in love, and after Lyle already lost his late wife, Chloe, made the world a little brighter lately. Especially when things hadn't been so easy for them. Not when their mother died when Jessica was only thirteen years old, and Lyle, being nine years older than Jessica, had taken over raising her, with the help of their mom's best friend, Rosie Masters. Rosie moved in after Tallulah's death and helped with Jess while Lyle worked the ranch.

Things were getting easier, and Jessica only hoped this new brightness continued into her business life too. She'd worry about her personal life later, when it made sense to bring someone into her world. Being raised by a single mom taught her to stand on her own two feet. And after two semi-serious relationships in her past flopped, leaving her emotionally grappling to recover, she made the decision to put her life before anyone else's. She wanted to find love, just not right now.

Regardless, she pointed at Giselle. "Don't you dare side with him on this. He's being a mother hen."

"Take that back," Lyle growled. "I am not a mother hen."

"I'll take it back when you stop helicopter parenting me," she said, moving to the front of the ATV. "Like I've said for days now—I. Am. Fine." She drew in a big deep breath before adding quickly, "Even if I'm just filling in for a maternity leave, this is a dream come true. I'm a legit chef."

Not that she wasn't loving how she spent her days. Camp Up had a near perfect rating on Airbnb and Google. She was making enough money to no longer live paycheck to paycheck, but her glamping business was the side hustle. The job she did until she could hire enough staff to take over, and until she made a name for herself with catering jobs, so when she became a full-time chef she'd make good money to support herself.

After seeing her mother struggle in life, she refused to follow that path, and she didn't want to count on a lottery windfall coming to her rescue. Her brother and Giselle were both millionaires, but that was their money. Jess wanted to earn her own success, like they both did—Lyle with the ranch and Giselle with her skincare line.

"Experience is important," said Lyle, breaking into

her thoughts. He pulled Giselle against him after she trotted down the porch steps. "Just keep doing what you're doing." Which had consisted of picking up some private dinners and events for the wealthy residents of Royal and getting some catering experience. "The dream will happen."

Giselle wrapped an arm around Lyle's waist and added, "I bet the engagement party for the Del Rio family will put you on the radar."

"Let's hope so," Jessica agreed, sliding into the ATV. Truth was, it was make-or-break time for her reputation. Both the Winterses and the Del Rios were rich beyond measure, and while she was not, and would never be like them, considering her bank account had all of $500 in it, she could cook for them. And they had the money to pay her what she deserved and adding their name on her résumé would only benefit her. "Though there's been a bit of a snag in that department."

"Oh?" Giselle asked, eyes wide.

"Two words," Jessica said. "Marcus Winters."

Lyle scratched at his temple. "Trey's brother?" Trey was Marcus's older brother, and Lyle's close friend.

Jessica nodded. "He's the one designing the party, and he's doing a piss-poor job of it too."

Knowing Jessica as well as Jessica knew herself, Lyle's brows rose. "Please tell me you didn't say that to him."

"I used...*nice* words," Jessica replied with a laugh. "But I also can't let his idea continue. It's my reputation on the line here, and the elements of his design look like every other engagement party out there. It's boring, basic and falls flat. There's no flow of ideas, no journey from the moment you walk in until you take the last bite of the meal. No sense of an experience or adventure or a special moment shared. Just...*stuff*."

This time Giselle's brow rose. "You're going to bat with him over the design he came up with?"

"No man—" even a criminally good-looking one like Marcus Winters "—will derail my momentum." She *finally* got a big gig that would help her stand out. Her dreams were right there; she could almost taste them. "I'm going to meet him at his design studio to go over things this morning."

Giselle's mouth twitched. "Now that is a meeting where I'd love to be a fly on the wall."

"Oh, hush, it'll be fine," Jessica said, waving her friend off. "He's the brother of the groom. I have to play nice."

"Yeah, no one's buying that, sis," Lyle stated, even though pride shone in his eyes. "You're not going to give Marcus Winters a hard time, are you?"

Jessica grinned, blinking innocently. "Of course I am." She hit the gas on the ATV and drove off down the laneway, hearing the laughter behind her fading. Sure, she had to tread a careful line to stay on his good side so he didn't tarnish her name, but she'd do whatever she had to do to show she was right about the design.

The tires crunched against light brown and orange fallen leaves as she headed through the forest, the woodsy aroma infusing the air.

Thanksgiving was just around the corner, and a few families were coming to stay to celebrate the holiday, with Jessica offering a mini photo shoot with one of the old tractors on the property and a local photographer. If the campers were pleased, she'd look into doing the same for the winter campers that came over Christmas to icefish on the lake.

Within a few minutes, she exited the forest, staying along the main path that worked itself along the lake, and arrived at the first campsite.

In total, there were ten sites along the lake's edge, but they were far enough apart to give the campers privacy, and far enough away from Lyle's cattle that he couldn't complain. Each site had a canvas tent upon a wooden platform, with two Adirondack chairs out front and a firepit.

At campsite #1, the firepit was still smoking from the night before. The leaves crunched beneath her suede boots as she exited the ATV and grabbed the tray off the back. She dressed casually for her meeting with Marcus, wearing black leggings with a long white button-up, beneath a light gray cardigan. The guests were nowhere in sight, and the closer she got, the more she heard the moaning. She slowed, tiptoeing toward the tent, and hurried to leave the tray of breakfast on the wooden platform.

Another low moan had her spinning on her heels and walking away as quietly and as quickly as possible, not to disturb them.

She smiled, returning to the ATV and swiftly driving off toward the next site.

Sex, followed by breakfast, seemed like a great morning to her. Until she reminded herself that morning sex wouldn't lead to her dreams coming true.

After her morning chores were done at Camp Up, Jessica arrived at Fresh by Winters ten minutes early. Located in the heart of downtown Royal, Marcus's design studio was as modern of a building as Jessica had ever seen in the town. Cars drove past behind her on the two-lane road, the chilly breeze fluttering the awning of the shop next door. The storefront was floor-to-ceiling glass walls, with cherrywood and metal accents. A metal sign to the right of the single door read Fresh by Winters.

The sudden weight of whom she was going up against squeezed her throat tight. Marcus had power and wealth and the ability to crush her. She owned a little glamping business that only recently started making her feel like she could breath financially.

No! You are Jessica Drummond, kick-ass chef.

She forced a big deep breath and lifted her chin, entering the business with enough fake confidence she was sure she could fool anyone into believing she had this under control.

A receptionist sat behind a live-edge reception desk. She was pretty with big blue eyes and shiny blond hair—because of course she was. Jessica doubted Marcus ever surrounded himself with anything but pretty, shiny things. "Welcome to Fresh by Winters. How can I help you?" she asked.

Jessica smiled. "Jessica Drummond here to see Marcus Winters."

"Ah, yes, come on back, Jessica," the receptionist said, leaving her chair and heading down the hallway.

The receptionist entered the first door on the right and then proceeded to pour a glass of water. "Please let me know if you need anything else."

"Thanks," Jessica said, accepting the glass and then taking her seat at the meeting room table.

The room itself had her taking a big, long sip. The type of wealth the Winters and Del Rio families had was nothing she'd ever encountered before. The space was modern, with more glass walls and big, bright windows, and even the air seemed humidified, lacking the dryness most office spaces had. The office chair beneath her was more comfortable than her chair in her living room.

She set her water back down, telling herself *again* that she belonged there. Sure, she was a classically trained chef, but she'd never planned a party the scale of the engagement party. Her reputation was on the line now, and all she had to do was get this hunk of a CEO to see that they could do so much better and bring more life to the design and then they could get things back on track.

A firm plan.

Until those dark eyes that had made her restless last night again locked onto hers as Marcus approached through the hallway. She swallowed the butterflies fluttering in her belly and shoved them far...far...down.

No man had a right to look that good in a suit. Especially one that she should want nothing to do with. The Del Rio family had been good to her, giving her a chance at her dream job and setting into the motion all the right steps toward seeing her dreams come true.

The feud between the families meant that Marcus was off-limits. Right?

Regardless, she couldn't take her eyes off him or stop the fluttering in her chest. Somehow Marcus was polished and rough all at once, with dimples. *Dimples!* And a scruffy beard that told her he wasn't nearly as stuffy as his suit suggested. She had no doubt there was plenty of hard muscle beneath those fancy clothes.

Off-limits or not, Marcus Winters was a walking fantasy.

He removed his jacket and rolled up the sleeves of his white dress shirt, revealing muscular forearms, a look of casualness she suspected was precisely planned. But the slight curve of his full lips indicated he was armed and ready to challenge her like he had yesterday, and he would enjoy it.

She straightened her back the moment he entered the meeting room. "Hello, Marcus," she said to him.

His slight smile widened. "Good morning, Jessica." He took the seat next to her, turning his chair to face her, crossing an ankle over his knee.

Any guard against those butterflies shattered at the low vibration of his voice as he drew out her name on his tongue. A tongue that she suddenly wondered too much about.

Well aware that he was winning at throwing her off her game, she smiled sensually back. Two could most definitely play this game. "Thank you again for meeting with me."

"It's my absolute pleasure." He grinned.

Pleasure sounded a little too naughty. She cleared her throat, her frustration growing that she didn't hate any of his game. "I've brought my ideas with me if you're still open to hearing them."

"I'm all ears," he said, resting an elbow on the table. "Tell me everything I've got so wrong."

She grabbed the folder from her tote bag and opened it on the table. "To start, if you'd read my menu you'd see it clashes against your romantic summer design."

"Oh?" He arched an eyebrow. "What's the menu?"

She took out the menu plan she'd printed off last night, handing the cardstock to him. "Dinner starts with an appetizer of heirloom beet salad with Monforte feta, toasted almonds and dill vinaigrette. The main course is sesame-and-hoisin-glazed beef short ribs with potato puree and pickled red onion, with a vegetarian option of herb and potato gnocchi with mushrooms, blue cheese and crispy sage. Followed by desert of vanilla bean cheesecake with sweet-and-sour cherries and smoked maple bourbon ice cream. All served with sauvignon blanc for white and pinot noir for red."

He studied the menu, then looked to her with a frown. "These dishes won't go with my design elements?"

"Sure, it'll be fine with it, since your goods line is beautiful," she stated, holding his stare firmly. She only had one chance to get this right. One chance to ensure her name came with rave reviews. "But the vibe is also basic and boring. Is that what you want?"

His frown deepened. "No." He offered her the menu. "Explain what you mean by *vibe*."

"Take restaurants, for example," she said. "When you go to a diner, you expect quick, casual food. It's not only the food that gives you that impression, it's the setting, the furniture, even the waiter and waitresses uniforms. Now take a five-star restaurant where you feel like you walked right into a Tuscany winery. You'd immediately know you're going to get fantastic wine, fettunta and potato tortelli. You look at the waiters and waitresses and see them wearing fancier uniforms, you know you're going to get quality food geared toward wine pairings. That's the vibe, the feel. And as a chef, you want your customers to feel like they are dining in Tuscany from the moment they walk in until they leave. It's an experience. It's an adventure. It's bringing food to life."

He made a noise in the back of his throat and then leaned back in his chair. "All right. What, of my design, would you change, then?"

She grabbed the next piece of paper from her folder and offered him the design she'd drawn up last night with colored pencils. "Think less romantic summer and more rustic meets winery. Instead of light-colored flowers, with crystal and gold, we should go with dark, rich flowers, paired with dark pink roses. Small tea lights, as well as candle votives. Rich greenery filling up the middle space of the table."

He studied her design, then glanced at her through his thick lashes that most women would die for. "Only one table?"

She nodded and chose her words carefully. "From everything I know about the Winters and Del Rio families, this party is bringing together two feuding families.

What better way to begin to unite them than sitting everyone together." She paused to let that sink in before adding, "If you keep things separate, you're not really helping your brother and Maggie achieve the peace they are looking to create. The vibe needs to be about uniting your families, but to do so, you have to acknowledge the past. And the history of your families isn't like a lovely stroll through a park in the summer. It's like a dark forbidden romance, bold and powerful. That's Jericho and Maggie. That's my menu. And *that's* the vibe we're looking for."

"Some fair points," he stated, tapping his fingers against the table.

She liked that part of her redesign most. Seeing he was unconvinced, she drew from her life. "I come from a very close family. If this was my engagement party, I'd want everyone that I love at the same table, sharing laughter, stories and food. So, instead of playing into the feud, I think you should play into two families coming together as one."

He hesitated and then surprised her by what he said next. "You're right, a table should have all those things."

For a moment, a veil dropped and she realized Marcus had probably never sat at a table like that.

But the veil snapped up just as quick as it fell. "Did you draw this with colored pencils?" he asked, amusement lightening his voice.

Like she needed a reminder she wasn't in the same tax bracket as him. "I don't have a computer program that I could use, so this was the next best thing. I wanted to make sure you saw my vision."

A pause. Then, "I happen to respect resourcefulness."

He almost sounded impressed, but she couldn't be sure. "Does that mean you like what I've done?"

"Possibly," he said, staring at her with what looked like a mix of curiosity and confusion.

Refusing to drop her stare, she picked at her fingernail beneath the table, forcing her leg to stop its bouncing. The silence became...*heavy*. Unable to stand it any longer, she said, "I know we only have two days to change the design. I'm not even sure if we could get the flowers—"

"We can get what we need," he interjected. "That's not a problem."

She supposed when you had money you could get anything you wanted whenever you needed it. She envied that about rich people. If she'd been wealthier, she'd own a restaurant by now and be head chef, making enough money to pay all her bills and her staff and to travel a little, with a good amount in her savings. Plus keep her glamping business going, all to see the happy faces of her campers. "So, then, you're on board with the plan?"

"Depends," he said, handing her the design back. "Is there anything but the vibe that you're not happy with?"

She paused to consider it carefully, but eventually shook her head. "Honestly, I think the rest is great. The timing of the events is perfect. The wine, beers and hard liquor at the bar is on point. My only issue was with the vibe we're creating and matching it with the menu to give both families an experience they'll never forget. Something new that these two feuding families have never had."

He arched an eyebrow. "A dinner together, sharing laughter, stories and food?"

"Exactly," she said with a firm nod.

Silence fell between them again, but this time, it felt different. The energy between them felt like it was shifting. A moment where she suddenly felt like she was looking at Marcus the man, not the CEO, not the charmer that always got his way. "Before I agree to anything, tell me—why is it so important to you that we get the vibe right?"

She had no plans on revealing anything too personal, but she needed him to understand what was on the line. "To be perfectly honestly with you, it's because this is my career-defining moment. I have waited to work for a prominent family that would give me a leg up in my industry and this is my moment to put my name out into the culinary world. So, yes, my most important focus is making this night perfect for Maggie and Jericho, but I need to pull off a party that everyone in Royal is talking about, so people hear who Jessica Drummond is and that name means outstanding quality and a meaningful experience."

He watched her closely for a moment and then rose. "Let's get lunch."

She stared up at him as he shoved his hands into his pockets—a formidable, commanding presence—and she swallowed back the extra moisture in her mouth. "Lunch?" she repeated.

"Mmm-hmm," he said with a nod. "You said that res-

taurants get vibes right, so show me what you mean."
Like a switch being flipped, all the intensity in his expression faded back to his charming grin. "Besides, you're a chef, right? Isn't food your thing?"

She got his game. She could only imagine how many women melted under all that heat he oozed. But like hell would she be one of them. She had a job to do, and that job didn't include doing him. She rose, meeting his challenge. Moving directly into his space, she said, "Lunch sounds great." And just to knock him off his high horse, she added, "Let's hope you can keep up." She strode away, hearing his low chuckle behind her.

A sensual chuckle that sent a shiver sliding down her body, warming places Marcus Winters had no business warming.

Three

A short walk later, Marcus held the door open at The Eatery, a hot spot in the main square, surrounded by country buildings, shops and restaurants. Colorful art decorated the walls of the bright space, and knowing Jessica's culinary talents, he assumed she'd appreciate the eclectic food pairings.

"Table for two?" the hostess asked.

"Please," Jessica replied with a nod.

The aroma of spices and freshly baked bread infused the air as Marcus followed them through the tables. He couldn't fight his gaze from dropping to the curve of Jessica's hips down to her round bottom. His groin tightened and he fought back a groan. *Damn, she's sexy...*

More than her physical appeal, Jessica's drive and heart had impressed him. Her sincerity touched something cold in his chest, making him uncomfortable and curious all at once. She appeared to be the whole package and then some.

And that was the problem.

Jessica came with complications that were currently ringing deafening alarms in his head.

Last night, he'd done his research on her and learned why he'd never met her. She did not run in the elite circles of Royal. Jessica came from a working-class family that only fell into money after a lottery windfall. While, typically, he never cared if anyone came from money, at times the status differences in Royal could cause tension between him and his family. Tension that he didn't want or need. Especially since it brought his hard-ass father down on his head.

As tempting Jessica was, he shoved his hands into his pockets, knowing he had to keep his hands to himself.

He passed the round tables covered with white linens, and the restaurant was as busy as always with people murmuring over their lunch. When the hostess finally sat them by the window overlooking the square, the sun beams brought out the reddish hue in Jessica's hair as she sat in her chair, the leg scraping against the floor. Her brown eyes now had hints of gold as they carefully regarded him before turning to the approaching waitress.

After a quick study of the menu, Jessica snapped it closed and ordered the spicy mustard greens, yuzu ceviche with a glass of Godello. He ordered the pork katsu, pear and bock choy, pairing it with a glass of pinot noir as Jessica had suggested.

Once their drinks were set in front of them, Jessica shifted away from the small talk they'd been carrying on and asked, "So, the vibe…?"

He finished his sip of the dry wine tasting of dark cherries and currants, then he repeated, "The vibe." He watched her closely and found his curiosity growing. "You said food is an experience that should be shared with laughter and stories. What did you mean by that?"

She sipped her wine and then asked, "Have you ever wondered why coffee shops are cozy, with dim lighting and comfortable seating?"

"No," he answered honestly.

"It's because the space creates a warm, intimate place for conversation. The scenery gives a person the right feeling to relax and enjoy, while talking over baked goods and specialty coffees. Believe me, the design isn't by accident."

"I suppose that makes sense," he said, glancing around at the bright space. "This restaurant doesn't give an intimate vibe at all, so what are they looking for?"

She studied the room. "This space is bright, colorful, and the food seeks to wow." She met his gaze again. "What that tells me as a chef is the restaurant is catering to the business-minded community. I suspect most of the customers who come here are having business meetings over lunch and dinner." She drew in a big deep breath and glanced around. "Though I imagine this is a hot spot for the younger crowd on the weekends. Especially the artsy types—they'd appreciate the unusual pairings of food and the unique cocktails on the menu."

He took in all of what she'd said, but he only focused on one point. "Are you suggesting that I'm trying to impress you?"

"Possibly." She shrugged. "I don't know you."

And why did he suddenly feel like he wanted to change that? "Fair point," he said, shoving the thought away. He took another sip of his wine, letting the rich flavor sit a little longer on his tongue before swallowing. "What about stories, then?"

Eyes squinting, lit with an inner glow, she asked, "You want to share stories?"

He nodded. "It is part of the *vibe*, as you say."

A fork clanged against a plate at the table behind him, but nothing could distract him from the challenge staring back at him. His mouth quirked slightly as she asked, "In the spirit of sharing stories, when I was first hired by the Del Rio family, Maggie told me about the feud between your two families. She also showed me a painting of a stunning diamond necklace, the very one that your great-grandmother apparently stole."

He set his wineglass down. "You're well versed on the theft from the museum in Paris?"

"I am now," she explained, dragging her finger along the stem of her wineglass. "After Maggie told me about what happened between your families, and being a self-proclaimed history buff myself, I read articles and books about the crime."

"Alleged crime," he corrected.

She laughed softly. "Right, alleged."

A waitress strode by with two plates, the spicy scent

making his stomach tighten in hunger before he returned his focus onto Jessica. "Why does a crime that supposedly happened back in 1920s interest you?"

Another shrug. "Like I said, getting the vibe right at any party means understanding the families you're working for. The history between your families is what I drew inspiration from when I came up with my ideas." She paused as a laughing couple passed their table. "I've heard Maggie's side of things. What's yours?"

"I think all of it is nonsense," he answered flatly.

She took a sip of her wine, studying him with clever eyes. "What is nonsense? The feud between two predominant Royal families? The missing priceless diamond, ruby and emerald necklace? The possible cat burglary by your great-grandmother Eliza?"

He snorted. "All of it."

She cocked her head. "You don't think it's possible Eliza could have pulled it off?"

"No." He'd heard the story over and over again, and he knew the truth was likely somewhere between the Del Rio family's and Winters family's versions. "I think history has a way of romancing a sad story."

"What story is that?"

"That my great-grandmother—who was born to a modest New Orleans family—was nearly ruined by the Del Rio family. I suspect that the Del Rio family was behind getting Eliza's name as the thief on the tongue of every member of Texas high society. The last thing they would have wanted was a penniless woman to marry

Fernando. What better way to get her out of the way than create a grand story of stealing a family heirloom."

Jessica watched him closely, the side of her mouth curving. "What's your take on why she married your great-grandfather, then?"

He'd wondered this himself. Repeatedly. He always came to the same conclusion. "Because he was the only one who stood by her side when others cast her out. At the time, she'd been likely devastated. He'd been her rock. Of course they'd fall in love during such a turbulent experience."

Jessica narrowed her eyes, nibbling her lip. "That's interesting."

Marcus's gaze fell to her teeth digging into her bottom lip. He bet he could make her bite down harder, if only he could get his hands on her... He slowly shook his head, clearing his thoughts. "Interesting how?"

"You're the only one I've spoken to who has that opinion," she said.

At that, he grinned. "Then I'm the only smart person you have spoken to."

She laughed softly, a sound as warm as the afternoon sun. "Cocky much?"

"Always." He grinned, unapologetic.

He thought she might get a stiffened back, but she did the opposite—she leaned forward a little closer. A tempting treat that he nearly reacted to, if the waitress hadn't returned to their table then, setting their meals in front of them.

"See," she said, gesturing to her table.

He glanced down at his plate. "I see gorgeous, high-quality plates and silverware from our summer line."

Again, she laughed, dragging his gaze up to meet hers. Her eyes danced. "Of course you'd take me somewhere you supplied the goods."

He winked. "I'm not the only one that should be impressed here."

She smirked. "Consider me impressed by the dinnerware, but what are you feeling right now?"

A little turned on. Very intrigued. He sat back in his chair and considered the question. His pride wanted to deny she was right, but oddly he wasn't thinking about his pride right now. "I feel impressed."

"By the food?"

"Yes."

"Like you're looking at something new and fresh?"

"Yes."

"Relaxed by the wine?"

"Yes."

"Bright and energized, ready to get back to your day?"

"Yes."

She gave a knowing smile. "Would you have that same feeling if you went to a dimly lit Italian restaurant where there were candles lit on the tables?"

He chuckled, shaking his head, knowing he'd feel like he was on a date, not a casual lunch. "All right, point proven." Stomach rumbling, he picked up his fork and the flavor of the pork exploded on his tongue in a single bite. "I admit it," he continued after he chewed. "I'm seeing the importance of getting the vibe right and why you were so adamant about the design change."

She snorted. "Other than the design being totally wrong?"

He set his fork back down, leaning back in his chair. "Do you ever not say what crosses your mind?"

"Both a positive and a negative trait, or so I've heard."

He couldn't help himself but admit, "Put you around the right people, I bet your lack of filter would be very amusing."

A child began fussing and crying a few tables over, drawing her gaze, until those smoldering eyes met his again. "My brother would agree with you there."

Before yesterday, he'd never heard the name Jessica Drummond, but he would never have stepped out from under his father's hold if he hadn't been resourceful. A few phone calls and an internet search had helped him learn a lot. "Lyle, that's your brother, right?"

Halfway to placing a forkful of food in her mouth, she stilled. "Yes. Do you know him?"

He shook his head. "Not personally, though I've met him a couple times through Trey."

Lyle and Trey were close friends. Still, she paused, a long, *long* study. She finally asked, "Did you look into me?"

"Of course I did," he said, which narrowed her eyes into slits. "I needed to see who I was up against."

Prepared to go to battle, he held her gaze, but it occurred to him then that she came as ready to play as she did yesterday. "What did you learn about me?"

"That we both have lost our mothers," he answered, reaching for his fork again. "Though my mother passed away when I was four, just shortly after the birth of my sister Tiffany. While your mother passed away when you were thirteen."

Her eyes softened. "I'm sorry, Marcus. That's so young to lose your mother."

"Thirteen is not that much older," he countered.

"No, it's not," she said quietly.

He felt the connection of loss sit heavy between them, something he'd never felt with anyone other than his family. The loss of his mother had been so great and it had changed his entire family's dynamic. Thankfully his dad remarried. Camille was wonderful. She not only kept the family together, she showered all the kids with an abundance of love. When his mother passed away, Marcus's relationship with his father deteriorated. But Camille managed to keep his father's temper in check. Marcus loved Camille and his stepsister, Alisha, and was grateful to have them in his life. While he was close with his brothers and sisters, he knew the death of their mother changed all of them in some way. He couldn't help but wonder how the death of her mother changed Jessica. "I also learned that you're smart and savvy," he added, "one hell of an entrepreneur and a chef, and all of that told me that I needed to stay on my toes."

He wasn't sure what he expected, but damn did he enjoy it when she leaned forward and leveled him with a firm look. "Am I a worthy opponent, then?"

Mirroring her stance, he rested his arms against the table, leaning in as close as he could get. Damn did he want to ignore the fire between them, but it was tangible, almost as if he could reach out and touch the power of it. "You might be one better."

"What's that?" she breathed.

He let his gaze roam over her kissable lips. "Smarter than me."

Jessica was well aware of Marcus's type. All charm. All gorgeousness. All things she'd had in the past with men where the relationships went nowhere but the trash. Where they took up too much of her mental bandwidth, leaving her focusing on them instead of her career.

Not this time around.

And yet, she couldn't stop thinking about what he said.

Smarter than me.

His reply stunned her stupid. Men like Marcus didn't surprise her. They didn't give credit where credit was due. They were arrogant, opinionated and always thought their ideas were right.

The warm, spicy aroma seeping from the kitchen kept trying to invade her nostrils, but she couldn't ignore the sharp woodsy scent of Marcus's cologne. Keeping her legs crossed beneath the table, she squeezed her thighs together against the heat settling low in her body at his penetrating stare, sexy grin and confidence.

Oh, this was a bad, *bad* idea!

Marcus most certainly should not land on her to-do list. She owed so much to the Del Rio family, and while they were coming together out of the love of Maggie and Jericho, she doubted they'd take too kindly to her getting involved with the enemy.

Ignore him...ignore him...ignore him!

Setting her fork down on her empty plate, her palate

singing in joy at the spices lingering on her tongue, she studied the dinnerware and did think the design was elegant, fresh and beautiful.

Obviously, she'd judged him wrong.

When she'd seen what he came up with for the party, she figured he knew nothing about design, but apparently he knew a lot about a good, stunning product. "Can I ask how Fresh by Winters came about?" She gestured to the plate in front of her. "I admit I was surprised to learn that you owned the company yourself, and it wasn't a division of your family's manufacturing company."

A slow grin rose to his sculpted face. "Who's checking into who now?"

Of course she'd done a little digging last night about who Marcus was as a man and a business owner, but he didn't need to know that. "I think everyone in Royal knows about your family."

"Maybe," he said with a wink that had no business being so sexy. "But I doubt many people know about me, not personally anyway."

"What don't they know about you?" she asked before she regretted getting so personal.

His long pause had her thinking he wouldn't answer, but he surprised her...*again.* "That I was the first of my siblings to forge my own way in life. I didn't glide on the coattails of the family business. I needed Royal to know I am not the same man as my father."

The answer was so raw, honest and real, she sat stunned for a moment.

Admittedly, she didn't have the best assumptions of men. She caught her last boyfriend in three lies. The third one had been his last strike. The boyfriend before that was as closed up as a clam. She didn't want to admit it to herself, but his openness was refreshing. "I have heard your father is pretty cutthroat when it comes to business."

"He's a shark," Marcus said dryly. "He's also prone to hold grudges."

"The feud?" she offered.

"That's one example," he agreed with a nod. "I could tell you numerous others. We just don't see eye to eye. Never have, and I suspect we never will."

She remained stumped by his frankness, and her heart opened a little to him. Cold father, dead mother...tragic. "You opened your business to stand on your own two feet, then?"

"Exactly, and that worked until recently," he admitted. "Now, in my thirties, it made sense to join forces with Winters Industries to take my company to the next level. But I would not have done that without my company being successful first. I wouldn't have given my father that satisfaction."

She studied him carefully, wondering why he was telling her this. She figured the answer would probably get her into trouble with the Del Rios. And whatever *this* was, this slight intensity she could feel simmering between them was not something that she needed to put on her plate right now. Getting her name out in Royal high society was so close she could almost touch it. Nothing would distract her now.

Not even those kissable lips, those piercing eyes that promised hours of pleasure, and that muscular body that'd feel so damn good against her...

No!

She shook the thoughts away, thinking over what he'd told her so far, and sipped her wine, tasting the oaky hints before returning her glass to the table. "I respect your choice to go out on your own. I'm not sure many people would have done the same."

"Likely not," he said. "The hard road is often a deterrent for most people."

She smiled, an honest smile, one she had not expected to give him today. "I can relate to that."

They finished their meal with easier conversation of discussing the schedule for the engagement party.

Once their waitress came and took their plates away, they settled up the bill, with Jessica paying her share, something that Marcus seemed to hate, yet also didn't make a fuss about it. She didn't want to admit it, especially to herself, but Marcus was kind of a likable guy.

And hot. So, so hot.

All things she promptly ignored. *Again.*

Marcus finished off the rest of his wine and then sighed heavily. "All right, let's talk shop," he said. "Those ideas of yours."

"Those fabulous, brilliant ideas of mine," she offered.

He chuckled. "Yes, those." A pause, his head cocking. "But I also think I can do one better than what you've presented to me."

She frowned. And here she was kinda liking him. "Really?"

He nodded. "A couple years ago we came out with a line that I think will suit what you're looking for."

It occurred to her then that he was only appeasing

her. Sure, he'd take her ideas into account, but the last call was his and his only.

Before she could speak up, he tapped his fingers against the table. "My only concern here is seeing my brother happy."

She countered, "My only concern is that this party is talked about all over town, so I get my name out there."

"Good," he said, rising. "I'll get on a call with the florist, Corryna and the party equipment company to see what they can do about the table."

She tucked her chair under the table. "You can really change things that fast? The party is in three days."

He nodded. "Jericho is a Winters. I am a Winters. I'll get it done."

"Wonderful." She smiled, and took out her Camp Up business card, offering it to him. "That's my cell on there. Feel free to call or text if anything comes up, or if we need to discuss planning at all."

Marcus slid the card into his front pocket. "I'll shoot you a text later so you've got my number."

Once again, he gave that charming grin. But there was more of a punch behind it now. More of an intensity in his gaze.

To put an end to that, and drawing the line very clear, she said, "I would prefer if you use my number sparingly."

Both brows rose. "Oh, and why is that?"

"You're a Winters, and right now, I'm working for the Del Rio family. I am loyal to them."

The side of his mouth curved. "You're pulling out the feud card even when you're not part of either family?"

"Yes," she countered adamantly. "Whether you like it or not, there is a feud between your families, and I am firmly on their side."

He paused for a long moment, his eyes searching hers, when suddenly, he took the last step to erase the distance. His body *this* close to hers, the air feeling charged between them. "I bet I could bring you over to the dark side."

Her core heated and she felt the warmth creep along her cheeks. She should step away, but she also figured this was some power play where he was trying to win.

Refusing to let him, and holding her ground, she took the final step between them, their bodies nearly touching, the energy sizzling in the small space that separated them. "Should I expect to receive the new design ideas?" she asked with a purr.

His gaze roamed over her lips and then met her eyes again, his pupils dilated with dark desire. "Should I text you with any changes once I've given your menu a thorough review?"

She narrowed her eyes and restrained her curses.

Two could play at this game, and while she was the one to turn away, she also brushed herself against him, feeling every single bit of hardness. His low quiet groan was her sweet reward.

Four

Three days later, and the evening of the party, Marcus couldn't get Jessica out of his head. He'd respected her choice and only texted when needed, but he'd been ready to crawl out of his skin. Sure, he wanted to date. Hell, he'd joined k!smet for that reason, but the woman needed to make sense, and Jessica did not. She was employed by the Del Rio family and the last thing he wanted was to make things awkward with his brother, fraternizing with Del Rio family staff. More importantly, it didn't make sense to pursue a woman who ran in different circles in Royal. He needed a woman to fit perfectly into his life, not create more problems for him.

But none of that seemed to matter. He thought about her every morning, every night and during his workday. He thought of that hot energy pinging between them, the sexy challenge in her eyes, and her smart mind and sharp tongue. And that ass—he couldn't stop thinking about that.

An hour away from the guests arriving to celebrate his brother and Maggie, Marcus entered Texas Cattleman's Club, discovering Jessica had been right about something else too.

Her concept for the party was flawless. The room smelled rich, like a mulled wine he'd tasted once. Dark flowers of shades of burgundy, red and light pink with dark greenery filled the space, and those color choices made the space feel sexy, yet sophisticated. The line he had considered fit her new concept perfectly. The rustic stoneware plates and matte silverware paired perfectly with the long single live-edge table with bench seating. Together, he and Jessica had created something that most definitely would get talked about inside Royal's inner elite.

Del Rio staff were busy at their stations, tending to the bar, ensuring every place setting was perfect, the live band tuning their instruments, the kitchen staff bringing in fresh ingredients in boxes. But Jessica was nowhere to be found.

Marcus rolled his shoulders, his suit jacket feeling a little too tight. He loosened his black tie slightly and turned to one of the servers who walked by carrying wine bottles. "Have you seen the chef?" he asked.

"She's down in the wine cellar," he replied.

Marcus gave a nod of thanks and headed that way, trotting down the steps, well aware they only had a short time before Jericho and Maggie would arrive, then the venue would fill with their loved ones. Marcus crossed his fingers everyone behaved tonight and a fight didn't break out. There was a tentative peace, but Marcus had doubts it would last.

When he reached the end of the hallway, he entered the wine cellar.

Then he found *her*, and he restrained a groan.

He'd expected to find her in a chef uniform, not looking like she was ready to tear the town apart and make it hers. She wore a long fitted black dress with high heels, and a slit up the side, revealing smooth silky skin, and he froze. He had plans tonight. None of those involved getting her naked in only those heels, but he decided that needed to change. All the reasons he needed to stay away from her suddenly seemed incomparable to the need coursing through him. For days, he'd thought of her. For days, he pleasured himself thinking of her. For days, he nearly grabbed his phone all to hear that sensual voice. And those days not seeing her had only built the intensity between them.

Intensity he no longer wanted to ignore. Intensity that had his limbs trembling. Intensity that stole all the logical thoughts out of his damn head.

"Jessica," he said. Even he heard the desire in his voice.

She placed the bottle she'd been looking at back down and turned. Her eyes slightly widened as she gave him a slow once-over, her gaze raking over his all-black suit and tie. Her eyes became hooded and his cock went from soft to hard so fast, he grunted. She wore dark, smoky makeup around her eyes and red lipstick. Her gaze had gone directly to his crotch and held there, like she knew exactly what she did to him. Like she *wanted* him, just as much, even if none of this made any sense. Even if *they* didn't make sense.

Suddenly, her eyes lifted, her smile pure sex. "Better be careful, Marcus, you're drooling."

He lifted an eyebrow at her. "Want to come wipe my mouth?"

A pinkish hue crept along her cheeks as she dragged her finger along her bare arm.

Good. He wasn't the only one driven mad these past days.

Fighting against himself to move closer, to take her into his arms, and to satisfy the hell out of them both, he remained rooted to the spot. "You are a vision, Jessica. I have no words to describe how beautiful you look."

Her lips parted. "You could try." A challenge he heard loud and clear.

"I could," he told her, barely hanging on to his control. "Would you want me to?" Her permission, that's all that held him back at the door.

She began walking toward him. "Yes."

Acting on pure instinct drawing him forward, he slammed the door behind him. To ensure no one interrupted what he planned to do next, he grabbed the chair in the corner, placing it under the handle to ensure no one got into the cellar.

By the time he turned to her, she had nearly reached him. He met her halfway, his hands on her face a moment later and his mouth sealing over hers. Her floral scent invaded him, and she tasted of sweet sin.

Spinning her around, he sent her back against the wine rack, dragging his mouth from hers to kiss her neck. He squeezed her breast over the top of her dress, and her greedy moan nearly undid him.

"Condom?" she gasped.

With frantic hands, he hurriedly grabbed his wallet from his back pocket, while she opened his belt buckle and pants and then shoved those down, along with his boxer briefs, exposing his cock. He was so damn hard as he ripped open the condom and quickly sheathed himself.

She lifted her leg, wrapping it around his hip, as he slipped his hand between her legs, moving her panties aside, finding her sensitive skin drenched. He groaned, caressing his fingers gently against her silky arousal, wishing he had the time to play. How he'd love to taste her, to make her lose her mind with need, to watch her arch into the pleasure, but one look into her half-lidded eyes and he knew what she needed, and that wasn't soft lovemaking.

He slid his soaked fingers along her bare thigh, gripping her bottom. His other hand grasping the base of his cock, priming himself at her entrance. Locked in her lust-filled gaze, he entered her, slowly, inch by inch. His eyes fluttered shut against the pleasure of her tight inner walls stroking him.

"Marcus," she breathed.

He devoured his name on her tongue, sealing his mouth over hers. Careful not to touch her hair and displace it, he squeezed her bottom, slowly withdrawing, and she clamped against him, as if begging to hold them there. Again, he pushed forward, until his movements were easier and she accepted him. Her soft moans, all for him, were all he heard. Her tight heat, warm skin, his sanctuary.

But he had a point to prove. And gentleness was not going to prove it.

Sliding his hand toward her hip, he pinned her to the wine shelf, and gripping her tight, fueled by this unexplainable desire for her, he unleashed himself with hard thrusts, tightening his sac with each. She began moving with him, and they found their rhythm together, while the wine bottles rattled behind her with each thrust.

Lost in the pleasure, he thrust harder, faster, drinking in her moans until she gasped and went silent, her lips frozen against his. He lifted his head and found her chin tipped up, her eyes closed tight, any moan she had stuck in her throat as her climax hit her. Her leg, hooked onto his arm, began trembling—the hottest thing he'd ever seen—and her soaked, hot sex became a vise of his cock.

Watching her unravel stole his control as she came apart around him. His thrusts turned desperate, his groans uncontrolled as heat rushed up his spine, freezing him in the intensity of his orgasm.

Then her hoarse, throaty moan of pure satisfaction, matched with her sex milking him, sent him over the edge. With a growl, he thrust forward, bucking and jerking against her, spilling his seed into the condom.

All he knew, all he felt, was *her*, and it was sweet perfection.

Until the sounds of satisfaction shifted to their deep breathing.

With shock at what they'd done replacing the insatiable desire, he pressed a soft kiss to her neck, feeling her hammering pulse against his lips. "Did that properly portray how beautiful I think you are?" he asked.

She laughed and parted her lips. Then clicking of heels against the stone floor sounded outside the door in the hallway.

Maggie called, "Jessica."

"Shit!" She shoved him away, hurrying to wiggle her dress down, and wiped the sides of her lips, removing her smeared lipstick.

Marcus had pants rezipped nearly as fast. He turned away, wiping the lipstick he knew was on his mouth, pretending to be examining the wine bottles, as Jessica moved the chair aside and opened the wine cellar's door.

"Oh, hi, Maggie," she said breezily, as if she hadn't just fell apart in Marcus's arms. "My gosh, don't you look stunning."

"Thanks," Maggie said. Then she froze. "Marcus, what are—"

Jessica held up two bottles of wine. "He was helping me pick the perfect wine for you and Jericho tonight. We went with these."

Marcus glanced their way, finding his future sister-in-law wearing a fitted burgundy velvet dress with thin straps and a diamond teardrop pendant necklace, and he put on his winning smile he used while in "networking" mode to expand his impact in the design world. "Good evening, Maggie. Jessica is right, you look stunning."

Maggie smiled. "Thanks. You two clean up nice too." Though beneath that smile was red-hot curiosity.

Before she could make any assumptions, Marcus asked, "Is Jericho here too?"

Maggie nodded. "He's upstairs." Then she glanced between them. "I came down to find you to tell you how amazing everything looks. You two pulled off something that I could not even have dreamed up."

Aware of Jessica's precarious situation, and even knowing she wanted to do it on her own, he couldn't help but let her shine tonight. "This was all Jessica," he told Maggie, shoving his hands in his pockets, doing his best not to show his heart was still hammering. "I simply did all the planning and organizing."

Jessica set the wine bottles down and rolled her eyes. "Don't listen to him. We both worked very hard to make this night perfect for you and Jericho."

"Well, thank you," Maggie said, touching her hand to her heart. "We're really grateful."

"There you all are," Jericho said gruffly, stepping into the doorway. To his future wife, he said, "You're needed upstairs for a moment. The photographer has some things to run over with you."

"Okay, no problem at all," Maggie replied, but then headed for Jessica. "Truly, thank you." She gave her a meaningful hug and then offered the same to Marcus. "Tonight is just perfect."

Jessica beamed. "You're welcome."

Maggie took Jericho's outstretched hand as Jericho gave a thumbs-up. "Nice work, the both of you."

"Thank you." Jessica smiled.

Marcus inclined his head in thanks.

Once their footsteps faded down the hallway, and silence greeted them, Jessica's smile fell and she turned to him. "I cannot believe we just did that," she said quietly, moving toward him. "What in the hell were we thinking?"

"That we wanted to rip each other's clothes off," he said simply with a grin.

Looking everywhere but at him, she ignored his making light of the situation and shook her head firmly. "That can never happen again. We had an itch, we scratched it, but that's it. Never again."

Yeah, she'd apparently had the same itch that he'd been suffering for days. He wanted to agree with her now. He knew they *had* to not let that happen again. He wasn't even sure what in the hell he'd been thinking. But a problem arose.

Even after he *just* had her, he wanted her again. Her eyes held a satisfaction he'd never seen before, and he could get hooked on that look alone.

Before he could speak any of his thoughts, she added, "I don't want to do anything that would jeopardize my name as a chef." She came to stand in front of him, giving him a firm, unyielding look. "I don't have what you have—a legacy behind my name. I'm working to make that happen. I won't let you take that from me."

His mind told him: "Yes, I understand." His mouth opened and he said, "Your determination to prove yourself is sexy as hell."

"Marcus," she snapped.

He bristled. His mind cleared to the realization that

he could put her in jeopardy if a relationship between them began and failed. He had his family name and the power behind it. She would always be seen as Marcus Winters's ex-girlfriend. Of course he got that. "I would never stand in the way of you creating a legacy," he told her firmly.

"Thank you," she said with a long, heavy sigh. "I'm glad we understand each other." She headed for the door toward the loud footsteps above indicating the guests were arriving.

He ran a hand through his hair. What the fuck was wrong with him? And why did this feel like it was anything but over?

A few hours later, the band lit up the dance floor, playing a classic from George Strait when Jessica took a long, *long* drink of her wine, settling against the hard marble top of the bar with a sigh. Laughter and chatter mixed in with the music as the aroma of the scented candles mingled with the rich floral scents. Half-drank and empty glasses were scattered among the tables, while the two families either danced together or remained at the table.

All throughout the evening, her mind kept wanting to drift back to the wine cellar with Marcus, but she refused to go there. She'd never done anything like that before. This man held some serious magic, and she wanted the spell broken. She couldn't let herself forget that too much was on the line.

Something she was reminded of when she'd changed back into her dress after slipping into her chef uniform to blow everyone's mind with her dishes. Now, being all said and done, pride nearly burst out of her—the party was gorgeous, the couple of the moment were beaming on the dance floor, and the food was a hit. She'd received praise not only from the Del Rio family, but also the Winters family.

Maybe it was partly from the mind-blowing orgasm she'd had, but she'd never felt happier. And that felt... *good*.

She'd wanted this for so long. To bring people together with food. To see all the smiles. To hear all the praise over the food. And the fact that both families were enjoying themselves, and no one was throwing punches, she called tonight a huge win.

She sipped the fine, dark red wine, tasting hints of black cherry as she watched a few barefooted women dancing together like no one was watching. No matter how much she tried, she couldn't ignore the little pang in her heart alongside the happiness sliding through her. She bet none of them knew just how lucky they were to have each other. She'd always wanted a big family and hoped one day she would create what she never had—a big family sitting around a table to enjoy the meals she created.

But she stuffed that little bit of longing away before it got any bigger in her heart. She had wonderful memories of her mother, and she had Lyle, Giselle and Rosie.

The music suddenly quieted, and silence soon fell over the crowd as Marcus's father, Joseph Winters, approached the stage and was handed the microphone. Maggie's father, Fernando Del Rio III, a tall, imposing man with dark hair, tousled with gray streaks, and a beard, had already said his toast before dessert. Jessica had been wondering how they decided which of the patriarchs went first for the speeches. Until Maggie had told her that they drew a straw to determine who spoke first.

With his gorgeous wife, Camille, a toned, fit woman in her early sixties with long, curly black hair, standing next him, Joseph looked like a man who had everything. In his late fifties, a little shorter than Marcus, he was handsome with blue eyes, shaggy blond hair and neatly trimmed beard, both peppered with gray. Jessica could see a lot of Marcus in his father as Joseph lifted his glass half-filled with scotch. "We are thrilled to celebrate Jericho and Maggie tonight," he said. "Family is *everything.*"

Jessica held her breath, as his voice deepened at *everything.* She had no doubt there was nothing Joseph Winters wouldn't do to protect his family's name, or the members in his family. While that made him scary in Jessica's book, at least Joseph was in his children's lives, which was more than she could say for her dad.

Joseph's imposing stare fell to Jericho. "My heartfelt congratulations to my son and his beautiful fiancée on your engagement. What a blessing that you have found one another. I think I speak for the entire Winters family when I say, we are beyond delighted to soon have Maggie join our family too. Let's raise a glass to the happy couple!"

Audible exhales followed, as everyone clanged glasses, wishing the couple well.

Jessica sighed with the unexpected release of tension from her shoulders that the speeches were over, and no one had said anything that would have led to bloodshed. While both families were behaving for their loved ones, there was taut tension simmering in the room that felt like it could snap at any moment.

The families kept saying the feud was over, but was it? After so many years could the betrayal be forgotten so quickly?

As Joseph left the stage, taking Maggie into an embrace and shaking Jericho's hand, the band shifted tunes and began playing "Your Song" by Elton John, and as the singer's sweet voice filled the air, couples took to the dance floor.

Ready to head back to the kitchen to give her kitchen staff praise for the stellar job tonight, she drained the rest of her wine when laughter caught her attention. Looking to her right, she found two women, early twenties, staring at a couple on the dance floor.

"Look at them," the brunette snickered.

"Not a k!smet match from what I heard," the redhead said. "But it sure looks like something is happening there."

The brunette giggled. "They are practically all over each other."

Jessica followed their gazes, finding a lean and athletic woman with slightly curly shoulder-length hair and brown eyes she'd seen before. Marcus's eyes. The woman was dancing with Preston Del Rio, Maggie's younger brother. Jessica instantly understood all the whispers. Sparks were flying between the two as they held each other close—too close and intimate for things to only be friendly—and Tiffany Winters was laughing as Preston spun her around the dance floor.

Jessica released the longest sigh of her life. All eyes on Tiffany and Preston meant no eyes were on her and Marcus, and the electricity humming between them, all night long. She kept trying to pretend nothing happened in that wine cellar, but even she couldn't shake the feel of Marcus's kiss, his touch, his tongue, his scent, his low groans and his spectacular cock.

Again, she sighed, shaking her head, clearing those thoughts away. *Bad idea, Jess, bad idea!*

Regardless, no matter how she tried, she felt the stare she'd been feeling since she left the wine cellar burning her skin. She glanced Marcus's way as he stood with his other brother, Trey, and Trey's eight-year-old son, Dez. Trey and Marcus shared similar features—dark brown eyes and black hair, same muscular build, only Trey was missing Marcus's dimple, and magnetic pull.

Though one look into Marcus's intense stare and she immediately regretted looking his way. He watched her closely, and as if that was the only invitation he needed, he approached.

Shit! She still couldn't believe what they'd done, but then again, she'd been thinking about him for days. She'd slid her hand between her thighs, more than once, imagining him touching her in all the ways he had in the wine cellar until she came apart.

It did not make sense.

Nothing about any of this made sense—most of all her reckless behavior—but all she knew when she turned and saw him standing there staring at her with dark desire was that something inside her snapped, and in that void, an urgent need replaced it.

Even now, after some time to cool down and think about it, she didn't regret their hot moment, but it couldn't happen again.

She only had herself to look out for her. With her dreams right there, she couldn't let a fling get in the way of that. And a fling was all Marcus could ever be—he was a Winters after all, and she was a Drummond.

She wouldn't damage her career for sex. Even if that sex was the hottest of her life.

With that annoyingly sexy smirk, he slid up to the bar. "Scotch on the rocks, please," he said to the bartender.

After the bartender served up his drink, Marcus took a long sip, leaning an elbow against the bar, staring out at the dance floor. His gaze settled on the dancing couple that everyone else was looking at too.

Jessica knew that *look*. She'd seen it a thousand times on Lyle's face. "That's your sister, right?" she asked.

A nod. "Younger sister, Tiffany."

His lips pursed as the song ended and the older couples began leaving the dance floor, while the beat picked up to a fast song and the younger crowd filled the floor. Then he visibly stiffened, and a quick look to the source declared why.

Preston was leaning in and whispering something in Tiffany's ear. She smiled and nodded, and then slid her arm in his and they headed out the door that led to the grounds.

Seeing the scowl on Marcus's face, she asked, "Do you plan on going after her?"

Marcus snorted a laugh, the ice clinking in his glass as he swirled the scotch around. "Yeah, right, Tiffany would hand me my balls if I ever did that. She can handle herself, but it doesn't mean I don't worry."

Jessica's heart squeezed. Hot, and loving to his family. Was her job really that important? She shook her head, erasing that idea immediately. "I'm impressed you can actually control yourself. My older brother doesn't possess that skill."

Marcus lifted a brow. "He's protective?"

She smiled and nodded. "While annoying at times, it comes from a good place, and I'm sure Tiffany feels the same way too."

Marcus didn't comment on that, watching his sister leave through the door. He took another sip of his drink before he turned to face her fully. Any tension now faded off his face, replaced by a heated grin. "And how are you? Feeling good?"

"Of course I am," she said, lifting her chin, refusing to let him steer the conversation to a place she didn't want to go. "We nailed this party and then some."

He leaned in, the scent of his woodsy cologne becoming overwhelmingly delicious, as he winked. "Nailed each other too."

She elbowed him. Hard. Of course—and annoyingly—this only made him chuckle. "Stop it," she told him seriously. Glancing around, she was more than relieved to find no one looking their way. "Forget all about that."

His grin turned wicked, telling her their moment of weakness—and temporary insanity—was exactly what he was thinking about right now.

Under all that heat he was throwing her way, her nipples puckered, yearning pooling low in her body, tempting her to squeeze her thighs together for a little friction. She clamped down the urge to smile back. *No. No way. Not happening again.* She hadn't worked this hard to let it get washed down the drain because she was lusting over some guy.

Sex was a temporary rush. Her career would last her a lifetime.

Her reputation mattered more than her lust. She'd had her taste, and while it was a fine taste indeed, she felt her life meeting a crossroads. This was her time to flourish in her career. And no matter how good he was with his mouth…his hands…his cock…

Dammit!

She bit the inside of her cheek, forcing the thoughts away. Seeing that he didn't look like he was ready to keep things *friendly*, she asked, with pity for her aching feet, "How long do you think everyone will last tonight?"

"Knowing the Winters and Del Rio families, a challenge has been laid out now to see who will last the longest." He paused, arching an eyebrow. "My guess, this party will rage on until the wee hours."

She wanted to cry for her poor feet. Instead, she snorted. "Why don't you all just do a dick-measuring contest and get it over with?"

Marcus barked a loud laugh and lifted his glass. "I'm

game. As you well know, I'd certainty win that competition."

"Oh, my God, stop," she said, slapping his arm, feeling the heat rise to her cheeks. Before he could get her in any trouble, she left him standing at the bar chuckling. Because she did need to go and give her staff the praise they deserved. And to find some flats for her feet. But most of all, she needed to get far away from him because Marcus was right.

He would win.

Five

Seated near the window in a brown leather chair at the Texas Cattleman's Club, Marcus ran a finger around the rim of his glass, staring out the window watching a tree's branches dance in the breeze. Three long days had passed. Three days of thinking about Jessica. Three days of hearing her sensual moans in his head. Three days of craving her. Three days was too damn long, and Marcus had enough of sitting around and not using every advantage he had to see her again. Yeah, he got spending more time with her was a terrible idea, but not seeing her was terrible too.

The situation was precarious for her, and he couldn't ignore that. She was making her way in the world. Damn, did he respect her for it, and he understood that being with him publicly could hurt her professionally if the relationship failed. While the connection could also give her a leg up, he respected her more that she didn't want it.

He couldn't change her mind, that was for sure, so he did one better—he found a loophole with an offer of friendship.

He wasn't sure how she went from a woman who insulted and challenged him at every turn to a woman he wanted to be near, but here they were. Sure, the idea of being friends with a woman was new to him and the thought of not touching her again made his skin crawl, but if it didn't make sense to have a relationship now, he'd settle for a friendship. That wasn't crossing any dangerous lines that could endanger her career.

"The engagement party impressed me."

Marcus was drawn from his thoughts at his father's praise, and he met Joseph's gaze again. "Thank you." He sipped his scotch, relishing the smoky taste hitting his tongue, the alcohol the only thing going to get him through this sit-down with his father.

The clubhouse was quiet this afternoon. Only a couple of servers getting ready for the busy evening ahead, but every so often, a member would come by and talk to them, doing whatever networking they thought would help them. Marcus understood the importance of networking, so he didn't hold it against anyone.

Though tightness hit his chest the moment he walked through the TCC's doors. The only time he came to the clubhouse and enjoyed it was for parties. He'd never fit in here quite like the rest of his family. He'd also never seen eye to eye with his father, likely because he'd never wanted to blindly follow in his father's footsteps, and while his father had accepted Marcus's choice to go out on his own, tension lingered. But Marcus knew his decision also laid the groundwork for his siblings to follow their own dreams. "The credit for the party's success belongs not only to me but to the Del Rio chef too."

His father rolled his eyes. "Of course the Del Rios hired an unknown. They're only too lucky she did a decent job."

Marcus nearly snorted. His father wasn't hiding that he already thought her beneath him because she wasn't *in* with the Royal elite.

Staring at his father now, Marcus knew he wouldn't want Jessica to meet him either. His father would only pass judgment on her for being middle-class. But the thought only reminded Marcus that being with Jessica wouldn't be easy. And dammit, he wanted easy. He had enough of a strained relationship with his father. He didn't want to mirror that with a woman, but he also couldn't get her out of his head.

His father continued. "What's the chef's name again?"

Though Marcus didn't want this conversation to go downhill before it even got started. "Her name is Jessica Drummond," he explained, trying to keep his emotions off his face.

His father read right through him. "A friend of yours?"

Marcus slowly shook his head. "I only met her a few days before the party to discuss meshing her ideas with mine. Her brother, Lyle, is a friend of Trey's. Lyle is a Wagyu cattle rancher here in Royal." To remind his father of his earlier praise, he added, "Like you said, our combined efforts paid off."

His father took a long, slow sip of his bourbon before setting his glass back down, giving a look Marcus had seen a thousand times growing up—disdain darkened his features. "How does she know the Del Rio family?"

"They hired her on as the chef for the party because their usual chef is on maternity leave."

"Ah, so she's a cook?"

A job Joseph Winters scrunched his nose at. "She's a classically trained chef, but she also owns a glamping business, Camp Up."

His father arched an eyebrow. "Glamping?"

"It's like camping, but more comfortable. Better food. Better bed. Permanent tent, etcetera."

Joseph looked baffled. "Strange."

"A lucrative business, actually," Marcus countered, hearing his voice hardening. "It's an impressive company."

"How lucrative can it be?"

Marcus fought the narrowing of his eyes and failed. "Not every business needs to make multimillions to call it a success." His back straightened and teeth ground before he added, "She's made one business successful, and clearly, she's got more talents as a chef and even in design. Give her time and I'd say it all will be quite lucrative."

His father's brows shot up. He leaned back in his seat, giving his typical stern look. "Defensive again, and she's not even a friend?"

"I'd like her to be," Marcus countered, sticking it

to his dad like he always did. Probably why their relationship was more strained than the ones between his father and his brothers and sisters. He never stayed quiet. "She's a smart, strong woman. I'd consider myself lucky to know her."

Joseph leaned forward, his gaze turning intense. "Don't forget who you are, Marcus, and what you represent. Choose your friends wisely."

A thousand things rested on Marcus's tongue. None of which he planned to say, because he hadn't come here to fight with his father. There was no changing his father's horrible opinions. All his father would see was a woman whose family didn't go back generations and didn't run in the social circles that his father deemed acceptable.

At Marcus's heavy silence, his father added, "Though I suppose if she's not from the Del Rio family that's a step up. Somehow, we've managed to get through all this relatively unscathed. I'm trying for Jericho's sake but I can't let my guard down completely with the Del Rios, no matter how I try. The feud is ingrained in my DNA."

"Jericho is happy," Marcus retorted in his brother's defense, letting the matter with Jessica go, feeling oddly protective over her in a similar way he felt with Tiffany. "Not much matters above that."

Marcus understood his dad's attitude. The feud between the families had run so deep for so long that it was entangled in his father's blood. While everyone was on their best behavior for the party, and was handling the engagement with grace, Marcus knew the peace was being held together by a very thin—easily broken—line.

Joseph finished the remainder of his drink and then slid his glass to the middle of the table. "All right, Marcus, you called me here. What is it you want to ask me?"

Marcus was unsurprised his father knew a question was coming. Until Jericho's engagement party, he rarely came to the clubhouse, always sticking out like a sore thumb. The one who didn't belong, no matter how much he tried growing up to fit into the Texas Cattleman's Club.

Now thirty years old, he didn't care to fit into the mold his father wanted. And he called this meeting for one purpose only—he needed a good reason for Jessica to want to spend more time with him. "Now that we're forming a partnership to produce a line, I'd like to propose something you've been hesitant to agree to."

His father laughed dryly, staring hard through thick lashes. "You want into the archives?"

Of course his father guessed the request. "In the name of business, I would like to get in there," Marcus countered. His father had never let him into the old wine cellar that held his family's history, belongings and possible secrets, no matter how many times he'd asked. Marcus understood why—his father kept the past in the past. Camille once told Marcus how Joseph was heartbroken after his mom died. He locked the door and never went back because the memories were too much. Knowing how fascinated Jessica had been about his family's rich history, he suspected she wouldn't turn down the offer to get a look, and that was his *in* to seeing her again. "When—" He stopped short of saying: *when Jessica offered her ideas*, not to get her name back on his father's tongue so he could demean it. "When we planned the engagement party, we took inspiration from our families' history. That gave me an idea." In fact, Jessica gave him the idea, but his father didn't need to know that, or he'd likely shut Marcus down for that very reason. "What if we launch a collection of luxury goods, inspired by vintage Winters family heirlooms? You saw at the party how drawing inspiration from our family came together. I can use this same inspiration to create a line that will appeal to a greater market. But to do so, I need to see the heirlooms."

His father paused, running a hand across his jaw. "It's not a terrible idea," he eventually said. "This design is currently hot in the market?"

When Marcus first got into design, his father treated his business venture similar to as if Marcus brought shame to his family. The only time his opinion changed was when Marcus took the company public and he, alongside his company, was featured in *Forbes* magazine. "Modern vintage will always be a hot market."

His father watched Marcus closely, and Marcus held his gaze back firmly, something he learned a necessity by the age of eight years old. His father hated weakness. And Marcus knew he was a stronger, better man than his father would ever be, because Marcus did not hold the judgments his father did. Sometimes Marcus wondered why his father was harder on him.

"You've got my blessing." His father took out a set of keys from his pocket and slid one of the keys off, offering it to Marcus. "Show me the designs when you have them. Run anything you find by me."

"Understood," Marcus agreed, accepting the key. Marcus couldn't wait to get Jessica in on this, since it was her ideas that inspired this new line. And it was his way to get to know this woman invading his thoughts a little more. What his father didn't know wouldn't hurt him.

Within minutes of leaving their table, they had said their goodbyes, with the same hard handshake his father always gave, and Marcus was on the road in his black Ferrari Spider.

As the car hugged the road, the hum of the engine filling the silence, heavy weight pressed against his shoulders. His father was giving him access that he'd long wanted, but he needed to prove that trust wasn't misplaced. And he needed to give his father ideas that knocked the new line out of the park.

Twenty minutes later, along a quiet stretch of the road, he was driving up the driveway of his late grand-mother's estate, a two-story mansion that was over seven thousand square feet with a European design—in need of repairs but still beautiful.

As he parked in the driveway, he was reminded of his love of the home, a part of his family's history. The grand house had two wings centered by a beautifully lit foyer with double front doors with sidelights. His sister loved old things more than anyone in his family, and Marcus suspected his late grandmother knew she'd be the one to restore the property to its former glory.

He hurried out and trotted up the porch steps. Then he knocked once and found it unlocked, so he opened it and called, "Alisha?"

"In the dining room," his sister yelled.

He shut the door behind him and then followed her voice down the hall. Greeted by silence, he entered the large dining room, finding his sister standing on a ladder and painting the trim around the crown molding. "Hey," he said.

She finished the edge, then set her paintbrush back into the bucket, heading down the ladder. "I wasn't expecting a visit," she said, her large brown eyes sparkling. She had shoulder-length, naturally curly black hair that she had pulled back in half braids.

Alisha was technically his stepsister, becoming family when Joseph married her mom, Camille, but she never felt like anything to Marcus but his true sister. The one person in his family that he trusted the most, and the one person who truly got him. "I'm going to blow your mind," he told her with a smile.

"With what?" she asked, placing the container on a cardboard box at the foot of the ladder.

"Dad's given me access to the archives."

"No!" she exclaimed, her eyes wide.

"It's true," he said, and then quickly filled her in on his drink with their father and what his plan was with the new line.

"Well, that's surprising," Alisha finally said when he finished. "I can't believe Dad finally agreed."

"Not so surprising if he thinks he'll make money off it."

Alisha laughed, her nose scrunching. "True. Honestly, though, I have no idea why you want to get in the wine cellar." They headed into the newly renovated white chef's kitchen with pops of dark blue offered by the appliances and accessories. "It's probably an absolute mess like the rest of the house has been."

"It won't be that bad," Marcus said.

"Wanna bet?" Alisha laughed dryly.

Using the key his dad gave him, Marcus unlocked the door next to the large pantry, which led to a small staircase. He flicked on the lights and headed down.

Alisha followed Marcus and then groaned at the musky smell. The large space was full of heirlooms from top to bottom, some covered with old sheets, others out in the open. Wine bottles covered in dust were in rows around the room, and there was barely walking room. "All right, so it's a mess."

"Told you," Alisha said, glancing back at him with a frown. "Between my antique store, and renovations, I can't help you down here, but I want to hear if you find anything interesting."

Marcus was so damn proud of Alisha's store, Odds & Ends. She was doing so well for herself, and with restoring the family home. "That's all right," he said. "I've got just the person in mind who can help with this. We'll catalog everything we find."

"Is that person Chef Jessica?" Alisha waggled her eyebrows. "I saw the way you were looking at her at the party." Then she grinned. "And the way she was trying her best to ignore you."

He immediately turned around, heading back up the basement steps. "I'm not talking about this with you." Mainly because he didn't want this to go anywhere. He wanted to get to know Jessica better, and he knew the only way to do that was to protect her, so that in no way would anyone in Royal think they were dating.

"Why? Because she's woven a spell over you?"

"No, because some things don't need to be shared with a nosy sister, and there is nothing going on between us anyway." He reached the foyer again, turning back to his sister. "We're just friends. She's the reason I even thought about the idea for this line. And as her friend, I think she'll enjoy looking through all the heirlooms with me."

Alisha lifted her eyebrows. Then she burst out laughing. "Yeah, right, Marcus. Sure, let's go with that."

He didn't smile back. "Friends, Alisha, that's all we can be. Please don't make anything more out of this. And don't mention Jessica helping to anyone, especially Dad."

He wasn't sure if it was his expression or his tone or the words he used, but Alisha's smile faded. She nodded softly. "I look forward to meeting her, then."

"You'll like her," he told his sister. Then he kissed her cheek. "I'll be back soon."

And just as his hand wrapped around the door handle, Alisha said, "This is the first time I've ever seen you be so protective over anyone else but our family."

He opened the door, glanced over his shoulder and smiled. "Maybe I'm growing as a person."

She didn't smile back. She said, deadly serious, "Or maybe Jessica is someone worth protecting."

Not having a reply, he shut the door behind him and trotted back down the steps with Alisha's words echoing in his ears.

* * *

Late in the afternoon, Jessica lounged in luxury, blissfully happy beneath the hot sun, regardless that she needed a light sweater to combat the chill in the air. The Del Rio homestead was out of her league in every which way, but she went with the flow, clanging her glass with Maggie's, then drinking the glass of char- donnay she never could afford herself.

For the last couple of hours, they sat beneath an ivy- covered pergola and at a wrought iron table in chairs covered with cream-colored cushions. "I can't thank you enough for lunch," she said to Maggie, who sat across from her in a chair near the edge of the pool.

"I'm just glad to spoil you," Maggie said. "Lasagna is the only thing I know how to cook well, so I'm happy it didn't disappoint."

"Disappoint?" Jessica said, rubbing her bloated stom- ach. "I'm still drooling."

Maggie clapped her hands. "Oh, I'm just so happy!"

Jessica wasn't about to tell her the noodles were over- cooked, the meat was dry and it needed more spices and salt. But she liked being spoiled. Rosie often baked, but Jessica usually shared the mouthwatering creations with Lyle and Giselle. Lyle tried every so often to cook but the only thing he was good at was grilling meat. While he did it well, she always had to make the sides. Just the gesture of making a meal all for her was enough to warm her belly.

"I know this is absolutely none of my business," Maggie said after taking a long sip of her wine, "so if you don't want to talk about it, just tell me to stuff it.

But is there something going on between you and Jericho's brother Marcus?"

Jessica schooled her expression into neutral. Good God, did Maggie guess correctly that they did more than look for wine in the wine cellar? "We worked together for your party," she replied, as innocently as possible.

Maggie's eyebrows rose. "Is that all that's going on between you?"

Jessica searched Maggie's eyes for any hint that she knew the truth, and she figured lying would get nowhere good. "We...we..."

Maggie burst out laughing. "I take it that it's complicated?"

Jessica breathed a sigh of relief and nodded. "It's all very new, and while I'm not really looking to date, there is some chemistry there, and I'm not really sure what's happening, to be honest." Even she still couldn't wrap her head around her time with him in the wine cellar. Or the fact that she couldn't forget about the best sex of her life or him. He'd invaded every thought in her mind, so bad that she nearly almost texted him three times over the passing days.

Until she reminded herself that her mother had likely been in this very spot. She'd picked the man, and in the end, that man left her broke with two kids to raise on her own. Jessica refused to let that circle repeat itself.

This time, she had to choose herself, and not allow anything to derail her professional momentum.

Maggie cocked her head. "But you like him?"

"I can't really answer that," Jessica said with a shrug. "I don't even know him." Which, of course, sent heat to her cheeks. She'd slept with him. She knew things about him that most people didn't. Like when he climaxed, he groaned so deep and intense it sent goose bumps, even now, down her arms. "So that's where I'm at. Right now, absolutely nothing is going on between us."

Maggie's expression pinched, her eyes searching Jessica's intently. "Listen, I know better than anyone that this feud between my family and the Winters can make things very complicated. I just don't want you to think you can't see Marcus because you have ties to my family."

"But it is a fact that I can't ignore either," Jessica countered. "Yes, everyone is being tolerant because they want to see you and Jericho happy, but I don't want to push everyone's patience."

Maggie gave a small smile. "Can I give you a little piece of advice?"

Jessica nodded. "Sure."

"Maybe just wait," Maggie offered, as a bird landed next them on the patio, picking at something in the patio stones. "Let things settle down after the engagement party. I know my parents were very impressed with you at the party. You never know, it could lead to a job offer." Maggie stared at the bird for a moment before looking at Jessica again. "Both Jericho and I know very well that sometimes you just need to let the air breathe so this feud doesn't burn us all to the ground."

"Sound advice," Jessica said with a smile. "And honestly, I really have no intention of dating anyone right now, so the point is moot. There is legit nothing going on there at all."

"I remember saying that," Maggie said with a laugh. "Now look at me." She lifted her hand, showing off her sparkling diamond. "Though, just a word of warning, if you change your mind and start dating Marcus, just know it'll get heavy fast. There's something incredible about the Winters men. One kiss, and it's game over."

Jessica believed that. She couldn't stop thinking about Marcus's passionate kisses. They lingered on her skin like a memory that would never leave. "True or not, I've got a lot on my plate. Men just complicate things."

"Take it from me," Maggie said, her eyes twinkling. "Sometimes, no matter how much you want to control it, fate just swoops in and you have to go along for the ride."

Jessica didn't know how to answer that, so she smiled instead.

Maggie lifted her wineglass to her mouth and then froze halfway. "Marcus!" she exclaimed.

Jessica's breath caught in her throat. She forced herself to stay neutral and turned to discover Marcus striding toward them. Heat slid low in her body at the sight.

Dear God...

In a three-piece suit, with a navy blue tie, she suddenly had the urge to rip all those perfectly fitted clothes off his muscular body.

"What a surprise," Maggie said, bouncing in her seat. "We weren't expecting you."

"Sorry to show up unannounced," Marcus said. He leaned down and kissed Maggie's cheek.

A bit of affection that Jessica could tell surprised Maggie in a nice way, and Jessica couldn't fight her smile. His kindness to her, when the rest of the family seemed a little tense about the families blending, was a definite sweet side she liked.

As he leaned away, Maggie said, "You are most welcome whenever you like."

"Thank you." He smiled.

Then he turned that smile, and it became *hot*, as he gazed into her eyes. "Hello, Jessica."

"Hi, Marcus," she said, giving her most proper smile.

Marcus took in the empty plates and the nearly empty wineglasses. "I see you've been enjoying your day."

"It's Jessica's day off," Maggie explained, "and I wanted to spoil her a little with lunch for helping us pull off such an amazing party."

"Ah," Marcus said, and winked at Jessica. "She does deserve to be spoiled."

Why did that sound sexual? It shouldn't have. But coming from those sculpted lips, with that low voice, anything he said sounded equivalent to: *sex now!*

A wickedly hot shiver slid low in her body. She laughed, lifting her chin, refusing to let her blush creep up to her cheeks. "I appreciate being spoiled," she said to Maggie. "It's been lovely."

Maggie grinned, looking between them, a telling sign they weren't fooling anyone that nothing had gone on between them. Thankfully she changed the subject, "Have you come to see Jericho?" she asked Marcus. "I'm afraid he's not here."

Marcus shook his head, shoving his hands into his pockets. "Actually, I've come to see Jessica."

Which, of course, drew her gaze to his crotch. She

cleared her throat, narrowing her eyes on him. Was he doing this on purpose? Just to tease her? To make this hard for her? "How did you know I was here?" she asked, narrowing her eyes on him.

Just as he'd done before when she challenged him, he grinned. "Your brother told me."

The reply was so unexpected she blinked. "You went to my house?"

He nodded. "Something has come up that I thought you might be interested in taking part in."

"Okay, what's that?" she asked, preparing herself for him to say something inappropriate.

Again, he surprised. "All your great ideas at the party to use our families' history to create the vibe inspired me. For a new line I'm creating, I've been given access to go through my family's archives, and since you've got a talent in design, plus are a history buff, I wondered if you'd be interested in helping me archive the documents and family heirlooms at my late grandmother's house. I could use your input."

There was so much to unpack she took a moment to process. She'd inspired him? He wanted her input? But the one thing that stood out was he wanted to spend more time with her. Maybe she wasn't the only one who couldn't stop thinking about that *wine cellar*. Or fighting to find a way to forget all about it.

Before she could reply, he added, "It's not for the faint of heart. It's a mess in the cellar, but I could use the help, if you're interested."

Just as she parted her lips, someone called from inside the house, "Maggie, your cell phone is ringing."

"Sorry," Maggie said, rising. "Let me go grab that."

When she vanished inside, Jessica turned to Marcus, and he grinned, all the heat he'd been hiding suddenly spreading across his features. "I promise I'll keep my hands to myself while we work." Leaning down, he stared into her eyes before his gaze roamed over her lips. "Unless you ask me not to."

Heat flushed through her, her traitorous nipples puckering, and she swore by the widening of his grin, he knew it too.

Not letting him get one up on her, she rose, telling her body to stuff it. For days she'd been thinking of him, imagining them together again, but maybe that was where she'd gone wrong. She'd decidedly shut him out of her life, leaving the fantasy and all that heat lingering between them. Maybe all she needed was to put Marcus into the friend zone. Maybe all she had to do was spend more time with him and then his true colors would show and she'd see some great flaw that would extinguish all the heat. Then she could forget all about Marcus Winters. "Sounds fun. When do we start?"

"Tonight, if you're up to it," he said. "I can pick you up at seven."

"Oh, I'm always up for it," she said before she immediately realized what she'd said.

Marcus caught on immediately. He leaned closer, bringing all that intensity within her reach, and lowered his voice. "And that's exactly why I like you."

A clearing of a throat had them both glancing behind them to a smiling Maggie. "That was Jericho," she said, watching them *very* carefully. "I have to go meet him.

I'd apologize for breaking our lunch date off early, but I'm thinking you might have other plans."

"I'm going to help Marcus archive some family heirlooms," Jessica replied. And to put this matter to bed for good, she shrugged as nonchalantly as she could muster. "What else are friends for?"

Maggie looked between them and failed to hide her laugher. "Okay, right." She turned, her shoulders shaking as she waved. "See you later, you two."

Jessica cursed beneath her breath, glancing at Marcus, who grinned proudly. "Did you just publicly friend zone me?" he asked.

"Yes," she said adamant. "Got it?"

His grin turned wicked. "All clear."

"Good. See you later." But as she turned away, feeling his intense stare burning into her back, she realized her mistake.

She'd just laid a challenge at his feet.

Six

Later that evening, surrounded by a quiet house, as Alisha was working late at the antique shop, Marcus sneezed, pulling the photo album off the bottom of the tea wagon. Rolled-up rugs, antiques, furniture and trunks sat atop dusty floorboards. The air smelled of dust, mold and damp wood. Spider webs drifted off the beams and straddled old rocking chairs and coat stands.

After he picked up Jessica at home and arrived at his late grandmother's house, they got right to work, making a spreadsheet and using their cell phones to catalog the heirlooms.

They worked in slight darkness for a while, given the inadequate lighting from the bare bulb in the cellar, but they'd managed to pull down an old curtain off the large circular widow, allowing the moonlight to add further light into the dusty space. Surrounded by flickering candles, in the right-side corner of the cellar, Marcus sat on the wingback chair he'd seen in a painting of his grandparents down in the library, and he opened the photo album.

"Eliza was such a beautiful woman," Jessica said, over Marcus's shoulder.

She wasn't wrong. Marcus studied the sweetness in Eliza's eyes, her fine features. "She was stunning in every sense of the word," he agreed, flipping through the photographs of the lives belonging to his great-grandparents, the two people that forged the way for his and his entire family's lives. "Her fashion alone—" consisting of luxurious dresses of lace and rich fabrics "—is the perfect type of inspiration I need for the new design."

"You've got that right," she said, awe in her voice, as she pulled items out of a vintage wardrobe. "I wish I had a reason to get all dressed up like they did back in the 1920s. I mean, come on, look at this." She pulled out a dress with lace. "You cannot find flapper dresses like this anymore, at least not ones this beautiful." She held it out in front of her. "Ivory silk and chiffon. This dress is to die for."

Marcus disagreed. Jessica wearing that dress was the prettiest thing he'd ever seen, but saying that aloud wouldn't keep him in the friend zone she'd placed him into. Not that he didn't agree for now that was exactly where he needed to stay. "Eliza definitely knew how to garner attention." Something he made a mental note of for his design elements.

"No wonder she had men fighting over her." Jessica

hung the dress from the wardrobe's door and took a picture before she set the dress back inside. Then she headed to the small table with the laptop on top and cataloged the find, using Airdrop to transfer the photograph of the dress into the spreadsheet.

So far this evening they'd cataloged two dozen items, and they only made a tiny dent in one corner of the cellar. Looking around, Marcus knew they had weeks of work ahead of them. He was glad for the time with her so he could dig a bit deeper into why this woman was so damn unforgettable.

"What exactly are you looking to find in here for your new line?" she asked, pulling another dress from the wardrobe.

"Take that mirror for an example." He gestured to the large gold mirror he'd cataloged earlier that brought an idea instantly. "That's not something you'd find in any store right now."

She moved in next to him, studying the mirror, with the dress slung over her arm. "True, but a mirror like this must suit a house. The only house I can think of that would suit a mirror this grand is the one I'm standing in."

"Agreed," he countered, inclining his head. "That's where I come in. We'll take something vintage but put a modern twist on it, so that piece could be brought into any house across the country."

She cocked her head, brows tugging together. "What would you do with this mirror to make it more modern?"

He understood her doubt, but his talents lay in seeing through an item to make it sellable in today's market.

"For starters, I'd make the mirror smaller to fit over an entry wall table or a sink, and I'd offer it in gold, silver and white finishing. Vintage chic is a very hot market right now."

"Okay, yeah," she said, face brightening. "I can totally picture how that would look in an entryway." She turned to him and smiled. "Pretty."

He nodded, appreciating the sparkle in her eyes. "Basically, that's what my company entails. I help bring beauty and comfort into houses, giving a family the feel of the home they want."

She watched him a moment, then smiled softly. "That's a sweet sentiment, Marcus. There's nothing more important than creating a safe, warm home."

He nodded in agreement.

She held his gaze for a moment, her eyes searching his for an answer to the obvious question on her mind. Until she broke away, hanging the dress on the wardrobe's door and taking a picture. "Can I ask you a personal question?"

"Of course." He flipped the page to a family photograph, where he didn't know who was whom besides Eliza. Her side of the family, he guessed.

She slid the dress back onto the rod. "How did you get into this line of work, instead of going into your family's manufacturing business?"

He flipped another page, finding a baby whom he suspected was his grandmother. "Because that's the logical route?"

"For most people, yeah."

Closing the photo album, he answered, "I'd say I'm

not like most people, but that's too cliché so I can't bring myself to say it."

She laughed, reaching for a crystal vase and lifting it to the candlelight, and the light shimmered throughout the room. "Was that the only reason, though? You wanted to stand apart from your family?"

"I suppose that had a lot to do with it," he said, taking note of that vase and how it curved in a way very similar to Jessica's curves. "I always wanted to carve my own path in life and not ride on my father's coattails."

"I can respect that," she said immediately. "It says a lot about you that you could have had a wealthy life handed to you and you chose hard work instead."

"Or, in my father's eyes, I'm just the pain-in-the-ass son who has to be difficult."

She smiled, setting the vase down and returning to the wardrobe. "What I said is way better."

He agreed with a nod. Curious over her, he asked, "Are you still working for the Del Rios?"

She shook her head. "Their chef came back early from maternity leave. I get the feeling that if something came up, they would reach out, but how many more parties will they have? They have nothing else for me to do."

"Does that disappoint you?"

"A little," she said. "Being a chef fills me with so much joy."

"The glamping business doesn't do that?"

"It does, in a way, it's just different, I guess." She paused, clearly thinking over her feelings on the matter. "The glamping business had made sense at the time. It hadn't been done here in Royal, and I knew that worked in my favor. Besides, it paid for cooking school and I got to practice on the guests, so there is that part. But then I just started feeling unfulfilled. I'm proud of Camp Up. It's successful and I got it there. But lately, I've been itching to work on a larger scale. Reach more clients. Create experiences for more people. Touch lives in a way that I simply can't with Camp Up."

"That could still happen," he offered. "I, out of anyone, know how scary it is to take that leap into something that could either take off or bury you."

She gave a knowing smile. "Yes, but that leap is not as gigantic when you have a family name where everyone wants to work with you."

He understood why she kept circling back to that, but… "Or it makes the task that much harder because everyone in Royal knows that you're opening a company that displeases the head of the Winters family."

She stilled. "Is that what happened?"

He nodded. "In the beginning, most of my clients were out of state, where no one knew my family. It wasn't until the last couple years that clients connected to my father began working with me."

She watched him a little closely, seemed to be re-assessing him. "I guess you're right. Maybe someday I'll decide to take that big leap, but with Thanksgiving and Christmas coming up, it won't happen anytime soon." She gave a slight shrug. "Maybe after that I can see how things are and if it makes sense to hire staff to cover my role."

Holding her gaze, he hoped she believed him as he

said, "I have no doubt in my mind that you can achieve anything you put your mind to."

Her smile was a little more honest now. "Thanks, Marcus."

"You're welcome."

She turned away then headed toward the wardrobe and knelt down, opening the drawers. Marcus couldn't look away. He liked her. Not only was she sexy, but she had a good heart, with big dreams, and the oddest feeling filled him that he wanted to be around to see those come true.

"Oh, what's this?" She reached into the drawer and then set it on the ground before reaching back inside.

Marcus rose, moving to her side, the floorboards creaking beneath him. "What is it?"

By the time he reached her, she had opened a small wooden box set on the floor in front of her. "They're letters, I think." As she pulled one out, it looked like it had been read a thousand times. "Marcus," she gasped. "You are never going to believe what this is." She offered him the letter.

My Dearest Eliza...
My heart is breaking without you. Not a day passes that I don't wish you were here in my arms. I don't understand why you've left or what has come between us.

Whatever you think, or whatever has been told to you about how I feel, believe me when I say the only thing that matters is my love for you.

The necklace does not matter. You are the only

*priceless jewel in my life. Do not marry Teddy
Winters. You know where you belong. Come back
to me.*
Yours forever,
Fernando

"Holy shit," Marcus muttered when he stopped reading. Glancing at Jessica, he suspected his eyes were as wide as hers. "Did we just find Fernando's love letters to Eliza?"

She blinked. "I think we did."

Seated on the floorboards, ignoring the creatures she could hear scattering about in the cellar but couldn't see, she finished reading her sixth love letter that was never meant for her eyes. She could barely swallow, her throat tight with emotion. And it wasn't just Fernando's letters. Eliza's letters to Fernando were also there. Who knew how Eliza got those back.

Eliza's and Fernando's hearts bled on these letters. And none of it made any sense.

"This is heartbreaking, don't you think?" she asked, turning to Marcus, sitting across from her. The love letters surrounded them on the floor. Hundreds of them, and Eliza had kept them all. To her death.

Marcus folded the last letter Jessica had handed him, placing it back into the envelope and in the wooden box. "Heartbreaking, how?"

She waved out to the declarations of love before them. "That Eliza and Fernando didn't end up together." At the rising of his eyebrows, she hastily added, "Okay,

I know that means you wouldn't be here, and that's terrible and all, but they were so in love."

He looked out at the letters and nodded. "From their writing, it does sound like they were madly in love."

"I can't even with these," she said, placing a hand on her chest, feeling the rapid beat of her heart. "The way they talked to each other was so beautiful. And look at their penmanship!"

Marcus laughed. "You're a fan of penmanship?"

"When it looks as fancy as this—" she handed him another letter "—yes."

"It is lovely," he agreed. "Mine looks like chicken scratch."

"I'm not even very good at cursive," she said, picking up another letter. She read for a moment, still not understanding how people this in love didn't end up together. "They're just so honest, so open, so willing to be each other's everything. Listen to this. *You are the sun, the moon, and every star in the sky, Eliza. My life only shines when you're with me.*"

Marcus's finger suddenly brushed against her cheek, and she glanced up, discovering he'd brushed away a tear she hadn't realized was there.

"Oh, I'm sorry," she said, moving the letter away from her, ensuring she didn't damage it.

His gaze held hers, unwavering, as he pulled his hand away. "Don't be sorry. These letters are bleeding emotion. It's hard not to get affected."

Not allowing herself to turn into a big sloppy mess, she drew in a big, long breath. "I never knew love like this growing up," she explained. "My mom had my brother and me, and then she worked her ass off to support us. For as long as I can remember, I always wondered if love like this was real—" she lifted the letter "—if love like this was possible."

He studied Fernando's tight handwriting. "I'm not sure love like this can withstand time, or if it's simply an intense, fleeting moment. As you know, Eliza and Fernando did not have a happily-ever-after."

"It doesn't matter," she said, wiping another tear. They wouldn't quit no matter how much she wanted them to stop. "You can feel the emotion in these letters. The love poured into the ink. It doesn't matter what went wrong after, this love was true at the moment, and that's the sweetest damn thing I have ever seen."

He inclined his head in agreement. Then his gaze turned inquisitive, a hundred questions filling his gaze. He finally asked, "Can I ask you a personal question?"

She shrugged. "I asked you one. It's only fair you ask me."

He gazed solely at her. "You never mentioned your father. Why is that?"

"Because he's not in the picture."

"Do you talk to him?"

She shook her head. "My dad competed on the rodeo circuit when Lyle was young. He was completely out of the picture after I was born. You'd think when my mom passed away that he'd come back to take care of us, but he didn't, he stayed on his family's large spread out in Montana. My brother raised me, with no help from him. Rosie, my mom's best friend, stepped up and moved in with us. She looked after me while Lyle worked the ranch. Lyle hung out with me every chance he could."

"Brave of your brother."

She nodded. "More than you know. Poor guy thought he needed to talk to me about periods and sex."

Marcus laughed. "Did he?"

"He tried his best," she said, smiling at the memories of watching her brother squirm through uncomfortable conversations. Lyle was the whole reason she didn't hate men altogether. Lyle showed her the difference between a weak man and a strong man, and she learned a long time ago to not let her father hurt her life any more than he had with being absent on Father's Day and daughter dances. Though, with such an incredible mother and Lyle filling in, she never missed the man that didn't want to be in their lives. "I'll never forget that day. He came home with all these pamphlets he must have picked up at the doctor's office. Really, looking back on it, he was just the sweetest. But, obviously, at the time, I was horrified that my big brother was trying to talk to me about women stuff. He could've had Rosie do it, but he never took the easy way out."

"Good for him," Marcus said.

"Yeah, he's pretty great," she agreed with a nod. "He ended up looking more embarrassed than I did by the end. He didn't talk about that stuff again until he found out I had a boyfriend in high school. One day after school, he picked me up and drove me to the doctor's office so I could get birth control pills."

Marcus cocked his head. "No questions asked?"

She shook her head, laughing. "I think he was too

afraid to ask anything. I got my prescription and a referral to a gynecologist, and Rosie answered all my questions about sex. I think Lyle was just thanking his lucky stars at this point that I had someone else to talk to."

Marcus chuckled. Until his smile faded and softness reached his expression. "I get it now, though. You don't talk about your dad because he holds no weight in your life. You've got your brother."

"Yeah, he's pretty extraordinary." She pressed her fingers against the letters around her, wondering if it was Eliza's and Fernando's emotions coursing into her, but being around Marcus felt good. It occurred to her then that talking to him was easy, as easy as it was with Lyle. Only difference was Marcus was a really great listener, where Lyle got all protective when something emotional happened to her. "Just recently Lyle became engaged to Giselle, after Giselle and I traded houses for two weeks using k!smet's Surprise Me! function."

"I heard Trey mentioning something about that," Marcus said. "That must have been an adjustment for you."

"Hardly," she replied swiftly. "When Giselle and I met, we became instant friends. I couldn't be happier for them." She told him about signing Lyle up on k!smet at the same time as she and Giselle traded homes, and the accidental mix-up of Lyle thinking Giselle was really there as a potential girlfriend.

Surprise glistened in his eyes. "It sounds like a rom-com."

"It was," she answered with a shrug. "And they got their happily-ever-after."

"You're good to them," he said.

She smiled, and suddenly felt like Marcus would fit very neatly into her inner circle of friends. She knew Lyle would like him. There was no denying it—Marcus was a good man. And she started wondering why she'd been so adamant to shut a good person out of her life. "They're good to me so I call us even."

Marcus laughed softly, reached for another letter and read a moment before he broke the silence again. "Fernando sure had a way with words. Listen to this. *My love, I long for you. To touch the soft strands of your hair. To feel your tender kiss across my lips. I forget all my worries when I'm with you. I am half the man when you're not near.*" He read the words again, like he was cementing them into his memory. His gaze suddenly lifted, chest suddenly heaving. "You're not the only one, you know. I don't know this love either."

She was more stunned by the emotion raging in his eyes than his admission. Emotion that suddenly wrapped around her, holding her tight. Because there was longing in his gaze, to feel loved, just like his great-grandmother had been, and his yearning battered at her guards. "Never?"

"Not like this," he murmured, staring at her like she had answers he was looking for. "Never like this."

A long tender moment passed between them, one that was warm, curious and filled with possibility. All things Jessica had never felt before and, suddenly, were all the things that she wanted. Maybe it was the love letters, but her heart reached out to Marcus, and she felt his tender caress back.

The same feeling that she endured when she saw him in the wine cellar at the engagement party overwhelmed her. It was like all the logic in her mind shut off, and it became just the two of them, yearning for each other in a way that couldn't be explained, but was happening regardless.

And now that feeling grew tenfold. Because she had had him before. She'd felt his touch, his kiss and his desire, and the power of this unexplainable connection between them was a living, pulsing thing in the space.

Something that she couldn't ignore anymore. Something that wouldn't be pushed aside to ensure dreams came true. Something as consuming as it was urgent. Something that told her that somehow everything would work out as long as they let it.

Needing to taste that sweetness of the magic they created for herself, she leaned in, cupping his face, and pressed her mouth to his. The second his lips touched hers, she felt the remainder of her guards and all the reasons to stop this between them fade away.

His kiss was potent. His touch all-consuming. And she wanted *more*.

Before long, and in between kisses that grew deeper and more heated as they continued, their clothes were gone, and Marcus had found a blanket to lay down on the floor. The love letters were next to them, almost as if they had power, containing a spell to break through barriers and bring hearts together.

He laid her before him, his fingers sliding down her breast, circling her nipple until his tongue traveled lower to her rib cage. "What's this tattoo symbolize?" he asked.

"Daisies were my mom's favorite flower."

He brushed a finger over one little bud, and then the other that was a bit larger. "You and your brother."

She nodded, needing that touch to go farther down her body.

Like he heard her request, his finger continued its dance downward while he licked and sucked on her nipple. He switched breasts at the same time he stroked her slit and then brought her arousal up to her clit, working the bud until she was arching off the blanket, needing more than his finger.

"Please," she managed.

"Please more?" he murmured.

She grinned, cupping his face. "Please you."

His answering smile had her squeezing her thighs, desperate to ease the ache.

After he'd grabbed a condom from his wallet, she took it from him, carefully opening the package.

She pushed on his chest, and he obliged her, lying back where she had been. She took his thick cock into her grip and stroked velvet over steel. He groaned, thrusting up into her hands, so she played a while. Until she had him moaning, and she couldn't take it anymore. She sheathed him, his gaze burning for...*her*, as she climbed atop him, straddling his waist. His hands came to her thighs, traveling all the way up until he gripped her hips tight.

Atop him, she marveled at his flexing muscles and strength, as she lowered herself down onto him, their moans mirroring each other. Pressing her hands against his chest, she moved, slowly at first, growing faster and harder.

Until he was moving with her, and then they were moving together, in perfect sync, bringing hot pleasure.

And when she came, trembling and falling over the edge, he went with her.

Seven

One week had flown by, and after all those days of treasure hunting and documenting the finds in the cellar, Marcus was full of ideas for his new line, and Jessica felt just as productive.

While she was tempted to spend another Friday night in the wine cellar, as it'd become a secret rendezvous spot that they had put to good use—multiple times—a phone call from Giselle after dinner changed her mind. And as Jessica set her wineglass into the dishwasher, after a long game of Catan and a couple glasses of wine, she still hadn't quite figured out what possessed her to shoot Marcus a text asking him to join games night with Giselle and Lyle. Other than the fact that it seemed like the right thing to do.

Standing in her kitchen, she looked over her shoulder, finding Lyle and Marcus sitting across from each other on the couches in the living room, drinking beers. The aroma of banana bread baking in the oven came from the scented candle on her kitchen island. Though the longer she watched her brother and Marcus talk easily, it became clear then, *that's* why she invited him—it felt right to include him in her inner circle, and he fit right in like he'd always belonged. Her first impression of Marcus had him pegged for a rich, arrogant, bossy jerk, but he wasn't that.

In fact, he was so far from that. And as much as she tried to fight it, she liked him, far more than simply friends with benefits. As each day passed, it became harder and harder to not think that Marcus was worth the risk. He was open and honest, and didn't hide behind the power of his family. He was good and kind. He'd understood the loss of her mother in a way no one but Lyle ever had. He was determined and brave. And being around him inspired her, lifted her and made her feel…*happy*. Like life would be easier because he'd bear the weight of how hard it could be sometimes.

While she knew she couldn't just dive in and let all her guards down, she could also feel those guards were growing weaker and weaker with every kiss, every laugh, every long conversation they shared.

"You've been withholding some juicy gossip from me."

Drawn away from her thoughts, Jessica spun Giselle, who promptly tugged her down the hallway. She gasped, "Hey, what are you—"

Once Marcus's and Lyle's voices quieted with the distance, Giselle released Jessica's hand and promptly folded her arms, narrowing her eyes. "You are so full of it, you know that, right? Here you had me totally believing that you two were just friends and you were helping a friend with the heirlooms."

Jessica had talked to Giselle at least every other day on the telephone, and texted if they were too busy to talk, but Jessica just hadn't told Giselle *everything*. Some things needed to be told in person.

Before Jessica could defend herself, Giselle added, with eyes dancing, "I have no doubt that hunk is helping you out with something, and it ain't heirlooms."

Jessica burst out laughing. "Giselle!"

Her friend's gaze only narrowed farther. "Girl, tell me everything, and leave nothing out."

Jessica peeked back into the living room, finding Marcus and Lyle had turned on the sports rerun, and they were talking sports. "Okay, come on." She took Giselle's hand and tugged her into the bedroom, suddenly feeling like this was exactly what she needed to do. Talk this all out with her good friend. She was so glad Giselle was now part of her life.

She shut the door behind them and then moved to her queen-size bed with light gray tufted upholstered headboard. "There isn't much to tell, except the part where he's been lighting my life on fire for a week now."

Giselle smacked Jessica's arm. "That is so much to tell. So… Are you dating?"

"No."

Giselle frowned. "You're not dating?"

Jessica shook her head, adamant. "We're not dating.

I'd say we're building a friendship, while also being unable to keep our hands off each other."

The mattress bounced beneath Jessica as Giselle pulled her legs up. "If that's the case, why aren't you dating?"

"It's just not the right time to do anything but casual," Jessica explained, snatching a pillow and hugging it in her lap. "I have so much going on, and focusing mainly on my career, I don't have the time to add a relationship in there too."

"Fair," Giselle said. "But it seems to be happening anyway."

Of course Giselle would tell it like it was—that's why Jessica loved her fiercely after such a short time. "Maybe that's true, but he hasn't said anything either about being exclusive or anything, so I think we're both in this place where we're letting things fall where they fall, you know. Just enjoying each other."

Giselle watched Jessica closely before offering, "I mean, there is nothing wrong with that. Sometimes casual is a good thing, but just so you know, I really like him. He seems like such a great guy."

Jessica nodded. "He is a really great guy."

Giselle tilted her head to the side. "So, it's not a no to dating him, it's more of a not-right-now kind of thing."

"At first, I had shut down the idea because I don't want anything to get in the way of the momentum I've created workwise, but I can't help that I'm catching some feelings there." She drew in a big deep breath. "But I also can't ignore that I need to keep my head on straight about this. What if another job comes up, then I'm working a ton to make it happen? I'd have to choose between a relationship and the job I've been dreaming about, so for now, keeping things casual is better." Her mother was proof enough of the importance of standing on your own two feet. Her dreams came above all else. "Besides, why mess with something when it's so damn good."

Giselle's eyes sparkled. "It's *that* good with him, huh?"

"Giselle," Jessica said slowly. "I don't think I can even put into words how good sex with him is."

Learning forward, eagerness on her face, Giselle said, "Try."

Jessica laughed, but she did her best to explain how hot their nights had been together. And the more she talked, the more words were easier to find. She hadn't realized her heart needed some serious dishing with Giselle, because once that floodgate opened, her feelings poured out between them.

"Wow," Giselle breathed, when Jessica finally stopped speaking. "Just wow."

"I think I've been saying that every single night," Jessica said with a laugh. But the knowing look in Giselle's gaze told Jessica she understood completely where Jessica was coming from.

Being that her lover was Lyle, Jessica cringed and rose, wrapping her arms around Giselle. "There, you have all the tea. Satisfied?"

Giselle leaned away, laughing. "Yes, and maybe we should schedule in some coffee dates so you can keep me up to date on all this hot sex."

"As long as it involves brownies or cake, I'm in," Jessica said, following Giselle out of the bedroom and back into the living room, where Marcus was no longer on the couch. She found him standing out on her back deck. "Did you scare him away?" she asked her brother.

Giselle took a seat next to Lyle, sliding tight against him. "I wouldn't be surprised," she mused.

Lyle snorted. "He took a call." He glanced between Giselle and Jessica and said firmly, "I've got no problems with him."

"Now *that* is amazing," Giselle said with wide eyes, pressing her hand to her heart. "I think that might be the first time you've ever actually liked someone Jess has brought home." Turning to face Jess, she added, "Jess, he's told me about all your horrible dates before."

"This is not a date," Jessica interjected. "I only invited him to games night with us. That's a big difference."

Both her brother and Giselle stared at her like she was totally full of it.

"What?" Jessica asked, folding her arms. "I'm serious."

Giselle smiled at Lyle. "She's in denial."

"I see that," Lyle agreed.

Jessica rolled her eyes at them and then she caught Marcus's eye. He waved her to join him outside.

Leaving the judgmental—probably right—stares behind her, she hurried out the patio door and into the chilly night, just as Marcus was ending the call. "Everything okay?" she asked, wrapping her arms around herself to stay warm.

A nod. "I was actually waiting for that call." He slid his cell back into his pocket. "Tomorrow, there's an early Halloween charity ball going on in Dallas for the Children's Cancer Center. Interested in joining me?"

She nibbled her lip. "What kind of ball are we talking about?"

"From what my sister tells me, there will be artisanal cocktails, choice hors d'oeuvres and a soirée-style dinner prepared by a star chef."

Her cheeks warmed, and she was suddenly reminded how different their lives truly were. "While all of that sounds amazing, it also sounds like definitely something I cannot afford."

"This is my treat," he said immediately. "It's for charity, and like I said, it's a really great cause."

Hesitant to accept, she nibbled her lip harder.

He chuckled, taking her hand into his strong grip and tugging her into him, in a move that seemed to be feeling more natural the more he did it this past week. "If it makes you feel any better, it's not my personal money that pays for charities. It comes from the business. Think of it as Fresh by Winters is donating to a great cause. Does that make you feel any better?"

"Sort of," she said. "Do I even want to know the cost of the plate?"

"Charity," he reminded her, dropping his eye level to hers. "It's all for charity." Taking her into his arms, a declaration he knew Giselle and Lyle were probably watching, but she couldn't seem to care, he added, "Every year, funds are allocated for charity, so instead of thinking of it as I'm paying your way, think of it as I'd be donating these funds anyway, so why not come and enjoy yourself?"

She let go the remainder of her hesitation. "Okay,

you're right, I'm being silly. It's amazing that you give to charities, and thank you, I'd love to join you."

"Balls are more about networking with the rich," he said, seriously, "and are part of being in business, so when I can do that but it's also supporting a good cause, then everyone benefits."

"It's an entire world I know nothing about," she said with a laugh. "But just so I know, how fancy is the Halloween party?"

"It's fancy, but you don't have to worry about your costume, I've got you covered. I'm sending you something over tomorrow afternoon."

A million ideas crossed her mind, but it also occurred to her then how long it had been since anyone surprised her with anything. Even the boyfriends she dated in the past didn't go out of their way to plan something *for* her. She melted a little into his arms. "Any hints at what I'm wearing?"

"No hints but wear your hair up." He grabbed the strand of hair by her face and stroked it. "In one of those low bun things."

"Low bun things?" She smiled. "Is that the technical term?"

He scooped her up in his arms, lifting her up. "Smart-ass." He turned her away from the window, and the possible eyes on them, and then got a firm grip on her butt. "Good thing I really like this ass."

She was beginning to really like that he did too.

The following night, and after the drive to Dallas, Marcus sat in the car, admiring the grand, historic hotel in the downtown core. Built in 1920s, the hotel was the perfect space for their Halloween costumes tonight.

Drawn to the sensual energy next to him, Marcus glanced as Jessica clipped the silver diamond hair clip into the side of her hair that fit well with the 1920s ivory flapper dress that she'd fallen so in love with. He'd seen the hair clip in one of the photographs of Eliza, and one night in the cellar, he'd found it. He'd taken the dress to the cleaners, and had it freshened up, and while the dress was a little snug on Jessica, it was snug in all the right places. And Marcus suddenly wondered what the hell he was thinking sending the dress to her today, when all he wanted to do now was rip it off her.

"Ready?" she asked.

He blinked, realizing he'd been staring at her cleavage. "Almost." He reached back into the back seat and grabbed a dark gray fedora hat and slid it on. "Now I'm ready."

She fanned herself. "Oh my, how will I control myself tonight?"

"I'm hoping you don't," he told her seriously, giving a grin he knew looked salacious by the way her eyes flicked with desire.

He opened his car door, and she opened hers by the time he got there, so he offered his hand. When she rose, he caught her blush. One he was growing rather found of, but more than anything, he liked having her by his side. He enjoyed her company, her strength, her... *comfort*. He shut the door and offered her his hand. "All right, doll face, let's go dance the night away."

She twined her fingers with his. "Keep calling me

doll face, in that fedora, and you might get your wish of lack of control tonight."

He chuckled, counting on that holding true.

They headed through the double doors of the hotel, bustling with plain-dressed guests and other ball partygoers dressed in costumes. Greeters guided their way toward the ballroom, and when they entered, he was impressed.

Ghoulish lighting and projection-mapped ghosts and bats covered the walls, with decorative cobwebs, fake bones and gravestones and skulls littering the ground. They even had a smoking cauldron, with a woman dressed as a witch stirring the cauldron. And a live band was currently playing Michael Jackson's "Thriller."

"Marcus."

Glancing left, he found Alisha wearing a pirate costume that showed off too much skin. He leaned down to Jessica. "My sister has beckoned us. We will now be at her mercy all night long."

Jessica's deep red painted lips spread into a smile. "Is all your family coming tonight?"

"Everyone but my father and Camille, I imagine."

Alisha finally reached them, and Marcus was surprised when she took Jessica into a hug first, instead of him. Apparently, Jessica had made a very good impression since they'd been spending time at the house.

"It's good to see you again," Alisha said, leaning away to give Jessica a long once-over. "You look absolutely stunning in that dress."

"Thanks," Jessica replied with a smile. "You look pretty damn fine yourself."

Alisha grinned, gesturing to Marcus. "I bet my brother hates everything about my dress."

"Wrong. I love the dress," he corrected. "I just don't like that it's on you."

"Which, of course, means it's the *perfect* dress," Alisha said with a wink. She took Jessica's hand, tugging her out of Marcus's reach. "Come on, you've got to meet everyone else."

Marcus followed through the sea of tables to near the dance floor and smiled. He couldn't remember a time that Alisha liked any of the women he had been seeing as much. He got that. He couldn't remember enjoying anyone as much as he'd been enjoying Jessica. The sex was the best of his life, and it occurred to him then she made him feel a mix of content and happy.

When they turned the corner, his family appeared, all sitting on white leather couches hugging a long glass rectangular table. Trey dressed as Gomez from the Addams Family and his girlfriend, Misha was Morticia—and Maggie and Jericho were vampires.

The moment Maggie noticed Jessica, she jumped up. "Jessica! Come sit, we've got Halloween margaritas on the way."

Marcus chuckled as Alisha, Misha and Maggie stole Jessica away, but he liked it—Jessica just...*fit*.

Now ignored, Trey and Jericho rose from the couch, coming to stand with Marcus.

"First date?" Trey asked, offering a beer from the pail filled with ice.

"Not exactly," Marcus explained. Then corrected,

"Sort of a second date, I guess, but since we both are not calling this dating, then I suppose, it's no date at all."

Trey snorted a laugh, obviously getting Marcus's meaning that he and Jessica were friends with benefits.

"Maggie likes her a lot," Jericho said, sounding muffled with his fake fangs. "Whatever you do, don't make a mess out of this or I'll be hearing about it."

"And I'll have Lyle on my case. Don't screw up," Trey added.

"I'll try my best," Marcus said with a laugh.

The waitress arrived to the table then, with glowing green margaritas and black salt on the rim. Jessica smiled his way, and he followed his brothers to the couches set around the table, and they all clanged glasses to a fun night ahead.

The margarita drinking soon turned into wine drinking during dinner that Jessica was praising with every bite. Before dessert, Marcus called and booked hotel rooms for the night. The booze was going down easy, and no one was driving home tonight.

When dinner wrapped up, he leaned over to Jessica. "I need to go and schmooze for a bit. Are you all right here?"

Alisha waved him off. "She's fine. Go and do your thing."

Jessica just laughed, but nodded. "I'm good. Schmooze away."

"All right," he said, sliding his fingers across her bare shoulder, loving the heat filling her gaze. "I won't be long."

"Be long," Alisha said, shooing him.

He shook his head at his sister, but couldn't fight the way his chest warmed at how his family welcomed her. The trouble was no matter how many times he told himself this couldn't be more than sex, it felt like so much more than that. He liked Jessica's fiery personality at first, but the more time he spent with her, the more he enjoyed everything about her. He couldn't help but wonder where they'd end up if he pushed against her guards to keep things causal.

Trey called his name, so with a final look at Jessica laughing with Alisha, Misha and Maggie, he, alongside his brothers, worked the room.

Charity functions were important for keeping building relationships tight and meeting new people in the city. But the more time he spent with others, the more this odd sensation of missing Jessica filled him. And he never missed anyone.

When he finally returned to the couches after finishing networking for the night, Jessica was nowhere in sight. He passed through the decorated tables, with black feather centerpieces and spiderwebs covering the tables, with a smoke machine creating fog at his feet. He scanned over the bar, until he quickly found her following his sister toward the dance floor, garnering stares of other men around her.

He understood why—she was seduction on heels— but he knew things they didn't. He knew how well she listened, the solid advice she gave, how she could make a man feel like he could achieve anything with her support next to him, and that she was the type of woman that made a man want to better himself to deserve her.

His world narrowed on her, and he waited until she walked by, unknowing he was standing there off to the side. Then he snatched up her hand. She jerked her gaze to his in surprise, but he didn't pause, tugging her toward the single bathroom.

Once he had the door closed, he pressed her against it, thrusting his knee between her legs, pinning her right where he wanted her. With a grin, he locked the door.

Jessica's eyes were huge. "Your sister!" she exclaimed.

Dropping his mouth close to hers, he murmured, "I've had enough of sharing you for one night. I'd like a little of you all to myself."

Before she could respond, he dropped to one knee and ran his hands up her thighs, taking the dress with him. There was nothing slow and easy about his movements. He craved her. He wanted her taste to stay on his tongue for the rest of the night, her scent to linger all around him. He hooked her leg over his shoulder, sliding her panties out of his way, and then he nestled his head between her legs. Her husky moans brushed across his flesh as he sucked, licked, swirled her clit until she threaded her fingers into his hair.

More...

More...

More...

He heard every plea in her taut body.

He never let up, or slowed, or gave her a chance to feel anything but pleasure, and soon, her legs began trembling.

Only then did he slide one finger, and then another into her drenched heat.

A few, hard, well-planned thrusts later, and she was riding his face to completion, and he was riding the high alongside her.

She tasted of heaven and of something feeling wholly made for him.

When her moans quieted and trembles eased, he backed away, pressing a soft kiss on her inner thigh. He dragged her panties back into position, and with a final kiss atop the silk, he rose, expecting to find a satisfied woman staring back at him.

He did find that, but he also found something more: *hunger*.

A loud grunt was yanked from his chest as he was pushed back against the sink, and she had his belt undone a moment later, his cock freed from his pants. He barely had time to catch up before she was on her knees, taking him deep into her mouth.

He groaned, his eyes rolling into the back of his head as he gripped the edge of the sink. Another groan ripped from his throat as she began gliding her mouth over him, with her hand following behind, stroking him with determination. He understood immediately the need to possess, to claim, as the same desire filling her had filled him earlier.

This was no tease, no playful embrace. She wanted to taste him, and he was happy to oblige.

Especially when she twirled her tongue like…*that*. "Fucking hell," he moaned.

Forcing himself, he barely managed to drop his head to see her bobbing on his cock before heat and intensity rushed over him as her hand tightened, pumping him hard and fast.

Grunt after grunt escaped him with little control over anything as he gripped her nape, guiding her to go faster.

The moment she did, pleasure overtook him, and he thrust his hips, until he was sputtering against her tongue, satisfied down to his bones.

When he could manage it, he glanced down, finding her grinning up at him. "And here I thought I was going to blow your mind tonight," he told her seriously, fighting to catch his breath.

She grinned. "You did. I just returned the favor."

"You know," he said, dragging his thumb across her bottom lip, "I have never been happier that you told me my idea was terrible than this very moment."

She laughed softly, accepting his help up. "I can do it again if you want."

Staring into the playful strength of her eyes, he wondered if she might be the most unexpected surprise of all. "After *that*," he said with a laugh, "you can do any damn thing you want."

Eight

The following three days were spent returning to a routine, with all the heat from the Halloween party seemingly following Jessica whenever Marcus was around. Not that she minded any; things between them seemed to only get hotter...and *sweeter*.

Marcus had stayed busy turning the heirlooms into new modern ideas for the new line, and Jessica was back to cooking for the glamping guests. Thanksgiving was coming up quick, and Christmas wasn't that far out, but with the next two months booked solid, she was focusing heavily on the menu and events to keep the guests happy and entertained for their stay in the coming weeks.

Though her evenings were spent with Marcus in the cellar, sorting through the memories and heirlooms of his family. Not a day had passed that wasn't thrilling in that cellar, in and out of clothes. The sex continued to remain off-the-charts fantastic, and she loved sifting through treasures.

As the days had passed, she and Marcus were moving closer and closer to relationship territory, and she wasn't fighting that idea anymore.

Her heart was leading her into his arms, and she couldn't seem to tell herself that was a bad idea anymore.

Pushing that aside for now, like she continued to do until the conversation came up naturally, she stayed lost in all the heirlooms encompassing her. Surrounded once again by the lit jar candles, bringing a pine scent battling the mildew, she reached into the trunk. The first find revealed a box of gold-edged plates, with a decorative border. A gorgeous set that she suspected was as old as the feud itself. After setting the box down, she counted the plates before taking a photograph to document the dinnerware, and then cataloging them into the spreadsheet that was now hundreds of lines long.

Every day came a new item, a new surprise, and she was envious of Alisha, who planned to bring a lot of this old furniture and household goods back to life, as she restored the old house to its original beauty. Whatever Alisha didn't keep, and if the other family members passed, she planned to sell the items at her antique store to help fund renovations at the house. Jessica had seen a few pieces she planned to scoop up if she could.

"Jessica, come see this."

At Marcus's rushed words, she hurried to the other

side of the cellar, stepping over a dead moth on the floorboards. She found him near another large wardrobe, with fluted side moldings, ending in volutes at the top and bottom. He'd moved it slightly out from the wall. "Is something behind there?" she asked.

"Yeah, help me move the wardrobe out more," he said, just as rushed as before. "It looks like a secret door."

Helping move it with all her might, the old, heavy cabinet scraped across the wooden floor as they pushed the wardrobe out enough to open the door behind it. The door was thin, with an antique brass lock, a skeleton key obviously needed to open it.

Marcus slid back there. "It's locked." He slipped out from behind the wardrobe. "Should I break it open?"

"Yes," she said immediately.

He laughed, giving a knowing look. "You didn't even pause."

"Why would I?" she countered, ignoring the scampering feet running along the floorboards behind her. "A secret door means secret things. I want to know— no, *need*—to know what's behind that door."

"You and me both," he agreed. "I saw some tools over there." Leaving her staring at the secret door in wonderment, he headed over to where Jessica had been and fetched a toolbox from another trunk.

When he returned, he grabbed out a couple of screwdrivers. "Hopefully Alisha doesn't ring my neck for breaking this open."

"I'm sure she'll forgive you if there is something really cool in there." Though as he assaulted the lock until the door popped open, she cringed, hating break-

ing anything if she could help it. A bit of habit of being
raised by a single mom. Nothing got thrown out, especially food, and if something could be fixed, they
always fixed it. But she stopped cringing when she remembered they both had the money to fix that door
and replace the lock.

Screwdrivers in hand, Marcus entered the tiny room
and, a moment later, he cursed.

The moment she followed him into the cramped
space she understood completely.

In the thin room, cobwebs covered the shelves lining all three walls, but on the middle shelf there was a
large velvet black box.

A box that Marcus had clearly opened.

A box that contained a diamond-and-gemstone necklace of unfathomable value—a piece Jessica would recognize anywhere. One she'd seen on the painting in the
Del Rio house.

"Oh, shit," she gasped, hands covering her mouth.
"Please tell me that's not..."

"It's exactly what you think it is," Marcus replied
through clenched teeth. He set the screwdrivers down
on the shelf next to him and picked up something beside the necklace.

She tried to peek around his shoulder, but the room
was too little, and his shoulders were too wide.

"It's a letter," he said, turning to her.

She hurried back out into the open space and took
a seat on one of the closed trunks, while he sat on the
wingback chair. He set the necklace in the velvet box
on the small table next to him beside the laptop.

Having no idea what to even say, she sat silent, until he looked away from the necklace to her. "I wish I knew what to say right now," she told him, seriously.

He snorted. "I'm not sure there is anything to say other than…fuck."

She couldn't help it; a small laugh escaped her. The feud between the families had been raging red-hot for a century. All over *this* necklace. The Del Rio necklace that was in the Winterses' cellar. "I just don't understand how this can be."

"Neither do I," Marcus said, carving a hand through his styled hair. "And I have no idea what the hell to do about it either." He scowled at the necklace. "Why is this here? How was this not found before?"

"You said that your father wouldn't let anyone up here," Jessica said. "Could he have maybe known?"

"About the necklace?"

She didn't want to think the worst of Marcus's father, but history, and his cold personality, declared when it came to his family, he would do what he needed to do to protect them and his family's name. "You said he was always adamant about you not looking down here."

"That was more about looking into the past," Marcus explained, running a hand across the back of his neck. "The only reason he let me up here now is because he liked my idea and is a smart businessman."

"How can you be so sure?" she asked.

"Because he never would have left this necklace here if he knew about it," Marcus said adamantly. "He's too proud of our family name. He would have taken it and destroyed it to ensure that the truth never came out."

Jessica stared at the necklace, not even wanting to touch it. "He'd destroy something worth this much money?"

Marcus held her gaze, dead serious. "To protect the family, yes."

She swallowed at the intensity on his face. "What are you going to do now, then?" She wouldn't have blamed him if he kept this from the public. It did make his family look terrible. The scandal it would cause was head spinning even to her, and she wasn't a part of the family.

"I don't know, but I know this affects more than just our family's name. This would affect Trey's investment in k!smet, Maggie and Jericho's relationship, and any future business between the families," he said, softly, still rubbing at his neck. "Peace has *just* been made between the families." He pointed to the necklace. "This will obliterate that."

"I'd say that maybe they'll understand," she offered. "But I really don't think that's the case."

"They won't understand," Marcus agreed. "Not after my family has ruthlessly denied the theft ever happened. Not after the hatred that exists between our families."

Jessica wrapped her arms around herself, staring at the gorgeous sparkling necklace, and then glanced at the letter in his hand. "What does the letter say?"

Marcus glanced at his hands. "I'm almost afraid to open it."

Spotting the tightness in his eyes, Jessica moved to him and offered her hand. "I'll read it."

His head lifted, revealing dark eyes drenched in concern. "We read this letter, and everything will change."

Even she felt the weight of that awareness. She couldn't really explain the heaviness suddenly surrounding her, the feeling that if they learned what that letter contained, even her life would be affected, but that heaviness was there, regardless. "True, but the answer could be the one thing everyone needs to hear too. Maybe there's a good reason this necklace is here, hidden away. An explanation that makes sense out of everything."

Marcus glanced back down and sighed heavily. "Let's hope there is." He offered her the letter.

She gently opened the envelope and grabbed out the folded note. She scanned the gorgeous cursive once... twice...until she couldn't deny the truth of what was written. Meeting Marcus's emotion-filled eyes, she said, "The letter reads, *I don't expect forgiveness. I don't even expect anyone to understand why I did what I did. But, to whoever finds the greatest mistake I ever made, I am truly sorry.*" She paused to note Marcus's pale complexion and then forced her voice past her dry throat. "It's signed, *Eliza.*"

Marcus thrust his hands in his hair and rose. "There's no denying it now."

Her heart reached for his at the slowness in his voice. "No denying what?"

He finally turned, met her gaze, giving a long, *long* sigh. "My great-grandmother was a jewel thief."

"Please tell me this is joke," said Alisha, holding on to her stomach as she stared upon the necklace on the kitchen island.

Marcus breathed a sigh of relief that his sister had

come home on time, instead of working late at her shop. On the countertop was a paper grocery bag with food half spilling out after Alisha had knocked it over when Marcus had hit her with the news.

They stood around the necklace, the one place in the house that wasn't in shambles from the renovation. "I wish I could tell you this is anything but real." He felt ready to climb out of his skin, a thousand questions swirling in his mind. He ran a hand across his tired eyes that seemed to grow heavier as the time went on. "What do we do now? Hell, what is the right thing to do?" He looked to his sister, then to Jessica. "Expose this, or put necklace and this letter back in that hidden room and lock it up tight, pretending we didn't see it?"

"Don't ask me," Jessica replied, slowly shaking her head. "Since I'm not a Winters, and still can't believe I'm looking at the stolen necklace, I am of absolute no help here, and have no opinion on how you should handle this."

"We have to give it back to the Del Rio family," Alisha said without pause, staring at the necklace like just touching it might be burn her. She finally lifted her gaze to Marcus and added, "The day Eliza stole that necklace she created a war. A war we need to end. We have to right this wrong, Marcus."

"I feel that's the way we should go too," he replied. "But Dad won't like this. In fact, he'll vehemently disapprove of bringing this mystery to light." Marcus knew in their father's eyes, they should bury this necklace and forget all about it, but doing that sat wrong in Marcus's gut. Because his brothers and sisters were not Eliza's mistakes. They were better than this.

"You're right, he'll hate this because it makes our family look bad," Alisha agreed with a nod. "But you also don't have to warn him."

Marcus paused and considered. "That could backfire," he finally said, "but I don't really feel like I have a choice. If I warn him, he'll find a way to destroy this necklace and the truth." Because nothing should ever tarnish the Winters name. While Marcus valued his name, he also wasn't his father. He could not look at himself in the mirror if he didn't return the necklace to the Del Rio family, and he knew to right this wrong, the truth had to come out.

He'd considered this from every angle, always coming back to the same conclusion. "I agree, this necklace belongs to the Del Rio family." Looking at Jessica, he added, "It's the right thing to do."

She nodded slowly. "It is."

Marcus knew he was glaring at the necklace, and he didn't withhold it. For as long as he could remember, his father had drilled into his head that his great-grandmother could never have done something so terrible. But she had. Her letter, with handwriting he'd seen before, was all the proof he needed.

He liked to think Eliza's apology had been real, and she'd regretted her decision, but it didn't change the fact that her terrible actions had sent a rippling effect over the family for years. The only way to forgive her was to return the necklace to its rightful place.

"One thing I know for certain," Alisha said, breaking the heavy silence in the room, "is we need to keep this letter a secret. I refuse to let our great-grandmother's name be besmirched."

"Won't her name get ruined anyway?" Jessica asked gently. "The necklace is here, in her house."

"It's a valid point," Marcus interjected, "but does she not deserve to have her name besmirched for what she's done?" He threw out the question.

Alisha stared up at Marcus with pleading eyes. "She's not here to defend herself."

Marcus glanced to Jessica, wanting her input. She shrugged. "I'm with your sister on this one. You even said yourself that you felt like the Del Rio family treated her terribly because she wasn't wealthy. Who knows what happened back then. Who knows how horrible they were to her."

He couldn't help but lift an eyebrow at her. "You think it's all right to steal?"

"Lord, no, of course not," she said with a laugh. "But I believe in karma. And without knowing what was done to her, I wouldn't drag her name through the mud. Alisha's right—Eliza is not here to speak for herself, so as her family, you should protect her."

Marcus paused to consider. Protecting his family always came first, but he wouldn't protect anyone at a cost of not doing the right thing.

He rose, moving to the window, staring out into the dark night, spotting the shadows of the trees waving in the breeze. He saw the logic in what they were offering. The way to right this wrong was to get the necklace back to the Del Rio family, but it would change nothing and hurt everything if Eliza's letter came out.

He ran a hand across his eyes again. The one thing he knew for certain was he had to ensure this was handled with the greatest care.

Turning back to the others, he asked, "What if I deliver the necklace to the sheriff and the Royal Police Department, and tell them that the package was left here at the house? That when I came to go through the cellar, I found it, which is not necessarily lying. I did find the necklace here."

Jessica cocked her head. "Are there security cameras here?"

He shook his head. "The house was never equipped with them."

"Which will change once I get this place looking like it should be protected with security," Alisha said. Then she heaved a long sigh. "That said, I think that idea could work. If there's no way to trace a package by surveillance or anything like that, it's a believable story."

"And it is close to the truth," Jessica said. "Which I think is important."

Marcus agreed with a nod. A world of heaviness sank down on his shoulders. He moved to the kitchen table, attempting to roll it away, and failed miserably. Leaning against the back of the chair, he said, "With the peace between the families, along with the business and moneymaking potential that the new peace affords, as well as Jericho and Maggie's relationship, we have to tread on very delicate ground while we deal with this."

"Especially because of Maggie and Jericho," Jessica

added. "I can't even imagine how this will be for them once everything comes out."

Marcus noted her pinching at her throat and worrying her bottom lip. His chest tightened as he moved to her, taking her hand atop the counter, not caring if Alisha was there. "You're right, this won't be easy for them, but hopefully, the fact that I'm bringing it forward will show the Del Rios that we are not Eliza. That we are better and honest, and with Jericho and Maggie getting married, that we are loyal to creating peace between the families."

Jessica drew in a long breath before blowing it out slowly. "Okay, just being the devil's advocate here to prepare ourselves, but this could go the other way. The Del Rio family could feel vindicated that their version of the story was correct, and then, in turn, it could create more hatred."

"It could," Marcus agreed in total agreement. "And I'm not writing that off as a possibility, but this necklace has plagued our family, creating deep rifts here in Royal. The only way to mend those wounds is to expose the truth."

Jessica's gaze flitted around the room, finally landing back on Marcus, her stare steady. "We need to warn Maggie and Jericho. While yes, this affects all of you, it most certainly will disrupt their lives. We need to warn them, so they have a solid front against the shitstorm coming their way." He couldn't help but love how she had mingled herself so deep into their lives so fast that she was considering this her problem as well. He squeezed her hand tight. Her firm grip back made that tension in his chest ease.

"I agree," Alisha said, obviously not realizing the moment between them. "Marcus, tell Jericho."

Marcus nodded.

"I'd like to tell Maggie, if possible," Jessica asked. "We've grown closer since the engagement party. I think she'll appreciate it coming from me."

"Of course, that makes sense." Marcus inclined his head, hoping his firm grip displayed his appreciation that she was there with him. "Let's stick to the same story—I arrived at the house and found a package had been slipped through the mail slot, and that package contained the necklace. The envelope had my name on it, so I opened it."

Alisha blew out a long breath and glanced up at the ceiling like she was praying. "You know I'm not good at lying."

"We're not necessarily lying," said Jessica. "We're protecting your family's name. Besides, don't forget that Eliza did this, not us. We're just cleaning up her mess, and we're doing it for Maggie and Jericho, to ensure their happiness isn't tainted by someone else's wrongdoings." She looked between Marcus and Alisha, her eyes filled with that same fire that originally drew Marcus to her. "We all know what will happen if it comes out that Eliza actually stole the necklace. The feud will be red-hot again, with no chance of overcoming this, and the people who will suffer most are Maggie and Jericho. For them, we have to do this."

His vision narrowed on her. Sexy. Brave. Loyal.

Smart. She was the whole damn package. And he wasn't sure how he got so lucky that she'd come into his life.

Though the moment the thought passed through his mind, another one quickly followed. *Will this affect us?* Jessica's only thought was on Jericho and Maggie, but Marcus was well aware that Jessica had been worried about being connected to him, when she was connected to the Del Rio family too. He couldn't pinpoint it exactly, but he had a terrible feeling in his gut that this affected his life as much as Jericho's.

He shoved the thought away with a huff.

First thing first, he needed to get the necklace into the right hands. The rest he could figure out later. "I wholeheartedly agree with you." Forcing himself to glance away from Jessica's strength, he looked to his sister, who frowned at him. "Jericho and Maggie will be done if the Del Rio family knows the truth," he told Alisha. "Beyond the monetary reasons we need these families to stay together, peace has been a good thing for everyone. I refuse for the peace to shatter now."

Alisha blew out the breath she held and said, dead serious, "You might not have a choice, brother."

Nine

Jessica arrived at the Courtyard Shops with her heart rate racing. Standing out on the curb, she spotted Maggie through the window of her shop, MaggieInk, and she hoped what followed wouldn't affect their friendship. She liked Maggie, and appreciated their growing friendship. She didn't want to lose her, and she couldn't fight the tightness in her chest telling her that this necklace was going to change everything.

After a big breath for bravery, she entered the storefront to a mess of dark-colored water in glasses full of used paint brushes. Obviously, she'd interrupted Maggie cleaning up after one of the paint nights she hosted. She was met by an aroma of paint thinner, oils and solvents that all would amount to a headache if she stayed here too long.

Maggie's eyes brightened as she caught Jessica's arrival. "Hey, Jess. I wasn't expecting a visit."

"Sorry for not calling first." The door chimed closed as she shut it, and then she met Maggie halfway, exchanging a quick hug. "I hope I'm not interrupting you."

"Nah, it's fine," Maggie said. "What's up?"

Having absolutely no idea how to broach this subject, she said, "I need to talk to you about something... sensitive."

"Okay," Maggie drawled, worry heavy in her dark eyes, as she waved out to the two plastic chairs in front of the wooden easels. "Is everything okay?"

"I'm afraid it's not." Jessica plopped down into the chair, while Maggie took the other. "It's so bad, in fact, that I don't even know how to tell you."

Maggie pressed her hand to her heart. "Is Jericho okay?"

"Yes, yes, he's totally fine," Jessica said, and suddenly realized Maggie's thoughts had taken her to a dark place that Jessica never intended. With a big sigh, she sputtered, "Marcus has the stolen necklace in his possession."

Maggie blinked. "What stolen necklace?"

"*The* necklace," Jessica said slowly. "The stolen Del Rio necklace."

"No." Maggie shot up from her chair, her skin ashen, eyes wide with an emotion Jessica couldn't name. "That's impossible."

Jessica's insides were quivering under the strain on Maggie's face as she rose, but she stayed back, giving Maggie room to breathe while the weight of all this must have hit her hard. "I'm sorry, Maggie, but it's true. He's got it now at Alisha's house."

Maggie took a step back, her hand returning to her heart like she was trying to keep it inside her chest. "Oh, my God, Jessica, this is so, so bad."

"I know," Jessica said, running a shaky hand through her hair.

Maggie moved to the storefront's window and stared out into the dark, clear night, hugging herself tight. "We just have peace between the families," she said, more to herself than to Jessica it seemed.

After a long moment, she finally turned to Jessica again; some color had returned to her cheeks. "This necklace could very well obliterate that," she said.

"Maybe not," Jessica offered in hope. "Maybe it will close the book on this feud for good. The necklace can be returned to its rightful place."

Maggie pinched the skin at her throat before she turned back to the window, staring out for the longest minute of Jessica's life.

When she finally returned to Jessica, she took her hand, pulling her back to the chairs. "Tell me everything," said Maggie, after taking her seat. "How did he get the necklace?"

Jessica froze. She hated lying. It went against everything she believed in. But as she stared at Maggie, she realized that no matter how much she liked her growing friendship with Maggie, her loyalty lay with Marcus, a revelation even to herself. His happiness mattered. His future mattered. He was protecting his family, and she would do the same.

Besides, she agreed with Marcus and Alisha that the truth would ruin the Winterses' name, so she ate her guilt, returned to her seat and withheld the parts of the story that would do no one good to hear.

By the time she finished, Maggie was rubbing her eyebrow. "Does Marcus have any idea who delivered the necklace to him?"

Jessica shook her head. "The house doesn't have any security cameras. He found the envelope when he arrived at the house. Someone put it through the mail slot."

"That's a shame," Maggie said, picking up a few of the used paintbrushes and dropping them into the glass of murky water.

"It is a shame," Jessica agreed, "but now the necklace has appeared and this feud can come to an end."

The upbeat song playing from the speakers broke through the silence as Maggie tilted her head to the side, pursing her lips. Then, "One thing I don't get is the necklace doesn't belong to the Winters family. It belongs to my family. So, why would they deliver the necklace to him and not us?"

Jessica did the only thing she could do and shrugged. "Who knows?" Speaking the truth now, she said, "Maybe because they knew Marcus would do the right thing." Because he *had* done the right thing. And she really, *really* liked that about him. That even knowing his father wouldn't like how he was protecting his family, he was doing so in the way that mattered to him, and making things right by returning the necklace.

She'd never respected him more.

Maggie's brows rose. "What do you mean by Marcus would do the right thing?"

"Marcus is the only one who stands apart from his family," Jessica offered, her lungs expanding to their fullest with her deep breath. "He acts for himself, not on behalf of his father, or his family. From what I've seen, Marcus is the most supportive of you and Jericho, so he definitely seems like the logical choice to me. He is honorable." It felt so good to say those words aloud, like an acknowledgment she hadn't known she needed to say.

Maggie titled her head to the other side and considered.

Jessica shrugged. "It's just a thought, but maybe the necklace was delivered to him because they knew he wouldn't destroy it." She shifted against her chair, and told Maggie sincerely, "Maybe they know him personally and know his character—and that Marcus would want the truth to come out."

Maggie's eyes narrowed in concentration until she finally nodded. "It's fair to say that the patriarchs of either family would likely destroy the necklace to ensure their particular family didn't look bad in the public eye." Her brow wrinkled as she wrapped her arms around herself, her expression tightening with every breath. "I'm not even sure what Jericho would have done if he'd been the one who got the necklace." She finally sighed dejectedly, her shoulders slumping. "Marcus does seem like the logical choice to make sure the truth wasn't buried."

The music she had streaming in the shop changed

to something a little funkier as Jessica took Maggie's hand again and held on tight. "It's going to be okay," she promised, believing that to be true. "No matter what, Jericho loves you, and you love him, and because of that, all this will find a way to resolve itself."

Maggie smiled. It looked forced. "I'm sure it will, and I'm glad you told me. Marcus is very lucky to have you."

Emotion hit Jessica's throat and squeezed tight. He did have her, and she firmly believed that now. She was as invested in all this as his family. It occurred to her then that she wasn't exactly sure when that happened. When she crossed the lines from just sex to a person who cared what happened not only to Marcus but also his family.

Not sure what to say, she smiled.

Maggie returned the tight squeeze of her hand. "He's going to need you, because Jessica, this… This is really fucking bad. You've just met both families. This anger runs deep."

Jessica did the only thing she could do. She nodded and then she hugged Maggie tight, a million thoughts weighing on her mind.

Turbulent thoughts that wouldn't fade. Even after she left Maggie's shop, and she went home to take a long shower and grab a quick dinner, she still felt just as unsettled about it all. Because the ground beneath her felt rocky in ways she had said she didn't want. She'd planned for her only focus to be on her career.

Right now, she wasn't thinking about her career, she was thinking about Marcus and the hellish nightmare that had been placed at his feet. She was thinking about Maggie and Jericho, who didn't deserve any of this.

Most of all, she was thinking about how the only thing she wanted was to be holding tight on to Marcus.

Which was why when Marcus's text arrived right after she put her dirty plate in the dishwasher, her heart skipped a beat: Meet at my place in 30 min?

She fired a text back: I'll be there.

A half an hour later, she was cleared through security and drove through the gated community of Pine Valley. She followed his directions, passing the clubhouse and pool, and the entrance for the eighteen-hole golf course and continued along until she reached the bend in the road, and arrived at Marcus's house.

Turning off the road, she drove up the long driveway slowly, taking in the view of his house. Considering Marcus drove a Ferrari, she thought his house would be equally as excessive, but his home surprised her.

While the cost of houses in this gated community would be in the millions, his house wasn't outlandish. A mix of white stucco and stone, the grandest thing about the house was its gorgeously manicured gardens surrounding the front. Which told her something about Marcus—he didn't always unnecessarily splurge or show off his wealth, but spoiled himself sometimes on things like his car, and she respected that. Considering what his grandmother's house looked like, he lived in a modest house for what he could afford. Which, oddly, made her feel comfortable. With Marcus's family, it was easy to feel like an outsider considering she didn't come from money, but at his home and with Marcus, she realized she didn't feel like that at all.

Once she reached the house, she parked next to Marcus's car, and was out a moment later, hurrying to the front.

She knocked on the dark wood door, and it opened a moment later to a very tired Marcus. Dark circles rested beneath his eyes. His hair was disheveled, a telling sign that he'd been running his hands through his hair all night. One look into his pained eyes, and she did what she'd been wanting to do since she left him. She wrapped herself around him, holding him tight.

"Hi," she said, her cheek resting against the warmth of his chest.

"Hey," he said, pressing a kiss to the top of her head.

He held on for a long time. When he finally did lean away, he gave a small smile. "I needed that," he said.

She smiled. "I did too."

She stepped farther into the house, entering the two-story foyer, greeted by a gorgeous double-iron staircase. "Your house is so beautiful."

"Thanks," he said, shutting the door behind her. "I'm rather partial to it."

Eying the beautiful paintings decorating the walls that probably cost more than she made in a year, she followed him into the great room. She tried hard not to get too hung up on what things cost because Marcus told her once he bought art as investments.

Through the back wall of floor-to-ceiling windows, she saw the flicker of a burning fire.

"Would you like a glass of wine?" he asked, walking ahead of her.

"After the day we had, I could probably use the whole bottle, but since I'm driving, a glass will have to do."

She thought that might garner a laugh, but the fact that he didn't react, his shoulders remaining stiff, told her whatever happened with Jericho wasn't good.

She silently waited near the back of the couch as he fetched them both a glass of wine and then she followed him outside into the backyard. A TV was hung high on the wall of the house, with a bar and a grill off to the right side.

She took a seat on one of the big, comfortable couches, sensing the tension rippling off him. "How did it go with Jericho?" she asked.

Marcus finished his long sip of wine. "He was shocked," he finally answered, "just like I'm guessing Maggie was."

Jessica nodded. "*Shocked* is the right word, but she handled it well. I think she's just worried how this will all unfold."

"Jericho too," Marcus said, placing his drink on the glass coffee table. He leaned his elbows on his knees, leveling her with a hard look. "Let's hope both families handle it like they have."

"Agreed," Jessica said with a nod, curling her legs up underneath her. "What's going to happen now?"

He drew in a big, deep breath and blew it out slowly. "Sheriff Nathan Battle is on his way here to take my statement."

She froze, midway to taking a sip of her wine. "Now?"

Marcus lifted an eyebrow at her. "Didn't we agree going to the police was the right thing to do?"

"Yes, of course," Jessica said. She simply didn't expect to be there. She'd thought Alisha would have been there. Maggie or Jericho. Anyone but her, a nonmember of their family.

Her thoughts must have registered on her face, since Marcus asked, "Do you not want to be here?"

She shook her head, cursing herself for not shutting the emotions of her face. "If you need me to be here, I'll be here. I guess I'm just surprised you didn't want someone from your family here."

"The second my family gets involved emotions will run heated," Marcus explained dryly. "I need…"

His longing gaze tugged at her heart. It occurred to her then that she didn't need to make sense out of her growing feelings for him. Because what she felt for him was the one thing this situation with his family wasn't… easy. "You need me here."

He looked to his feet for a moment and then haunted eyes met hers. "Yeah, Jessica, I need you here."

"Then I'm here."

When the knock came at the front door and Marcus opened the door to Sheriff Nathan Battle, he found an imposing man, dressed in a brown uniform, his gun holstered to his hip. Slightly shorter than Marcus, the sheriff looked about ten years older, and could have passed for a member of the Winters family with his close-cropped dark brown hair and dark brown eyes. Marcus didn't know the sheriff well, but knew he lived on the

Battlelands Ranch, just west of town, along with his wife, Amanda, who owned one of the diners in town.

"Thanks for coming," Marcus said, shutting the door behind the sheriff. "Sorry it's so late."

"It's no problem," the sheriff replied. "I admit that I was very surprised to get your call."

Marcus acknowledged the sheriff's thought with a nod. "Please come in. I'll explain." His chest tightened at both his shame that his great-grandmother could do and lie about such a thing, and that he had to withhold the letter's existence from the police to protect his family.

The sheriff followed Marcus into the living room, which was set next to the open-concept kitchen.

As they rounded the corner, and Jessica appeared, Marcus said, "Sheriff, this is Jessica Drummond. Jessica owns the glamping company, Camp Up, here in town."

The sheriff tipped his cowboy hat. "Good to meet you, ma'am. My wife was telling me about your company, and how great it is."

Jessica gave a small smile. "I'm glad she had good things to say."

Marcus understood the slight tension he could feel emanating off her. He didn't feel like smiling either. "Would you like anything to drink?" he asked the sheriff.

"Nah, I'm all right," Nathan said, gesturing to the couch. "How about we talk about why you called me here."

Right to business, then. Marcus took a seat next to Jessica on the couch, moving aside a couple of the colorful pillows. He craved to reach over and take her hand.

Instead of leaning into what his instincts were yelling at him to do, he said, "I take it you've heard about the long-standing feud between the Winters and the Del Rio families."

Nathan nodded. "I'm aware, yes."

"Are you also aware of the apparent theft in Paris of the Del Rio family necklace back in the 1920s? It was on display at a museum."

The sheriff cocked his head. "That story has been around town for as long as I can remember."

"It's not a story any longer," Marcus said. "I have the necklace."

Nathan froze, staring at Marcus for a long moment. "Are you sure it's the Del Rio necklace?" he eventually asked.

Marcus nodded. "Without a doubt in my mind."

Nathan watched Marcus closely, tapping his boot against the floor, until he pulled a notepad from the pocket of his shirt. His eyes sharpened. "Tell me everything from the moment you discovered the necklace."

Marcus looked to the stack of magazines on his coffee table, drawing in a deep breath. Withholding the letter's existence went against every one of his instincts, but he refused to let what Eliza had done hurt his brothers and sisters, when none of them deserved any of this. To protect them, and Jericho and Maggie's happiness, he would take this truth to his grave. And after meeting with Jericho, he dug a small hole at Eliza's grave and buried the note there with her, for her to burden the shame. He had placed flowers atop and turned away from her. One day he'd forgive her. That day was not today.

Doing what he had to do, he looked the sheriff in the eye and told as much truth as he could.

The sheriff made notes while Marcus caught him up, leaving out Eliza's letter from the story and implanting the package being delivered to the house through the mail slot. "There are no security cameras on the property of your late grandmother's house?" he finally asked once Marcus was finished.

"I'm afraid not," Marcus replied. "The house has been empty for years. My sister, Alisha has only recently begun renovations."

"All right." Nathan made another note. He lifted his gaze and stared hard at Marcus for a long moment. Then, "Have you received any unknown phone calls? Odd interactions with anyone?"

Marcus shook his head. "Not at all." All true, but the guilt rode him just the same. None of this was his mess. Eliza had done this, and it ripped him to shreds that he had to withhold the truth or watch his family's lives be ruined.

After scribbling a few more notes, Nathan asked, "Would you mind if I checked your phone records, just in case you missed a call?"

"Of course not," Marcus said, trying to be as transparent as he possibly could, knowing nothing would be found anyway. "Whatever you need, you've got."

"Good," Nathan said, scraping a hand against his jaw. Studying his notepad, he inhaled a long, deep breath and then let it out slowly. "I have heard, as I'm sure the whole town has heard, about the stolen necklace. The word on the street is it was your great-grandmother who stole the piece."

Marcus inclined his head in agreement. "That's the story the Del Rios tell. My family disagrees." He pressed his toes into the area rug on the floor, waiting for Nathan to ask the one question that Marcus didn't want to answer.

Blessedly, likely because his great-grandmother was long dead, the sheriff went a different route. "Do you have any idea who left the package at an empty house?" he asked.

Marcus could have kissed Nathan for the way he worded the question. "I can honestly say I have no idea or why they wouldn't deliver to the Del Rio family directly."

Jessica piped up then. "Just an idea," she said, her voice strong and steady, "but what if they were hanging on to the necklace to keep the feud going, but when Jericho and Maggie became engaged, they realized it was pointless to hold on to the necklace and the guilt overtook them."

"It's possible," the sheriff said after a moment of thought.

Marcus could have kissed her too for planting an alternative idea. One that, like anything in Royal, would spread like wildfire.

The sheriff tapped his pen against his notebook. "We'll definitely do an investigation and see what we can get from that." He closed his notepad and slid it, along with his pen, back into his pocket. "Do you still have the envelope that the necklace came in?"

Marcus nodded. "I can get you that." His phone beeped in his pocket, but he ignored the email that had come through.

"We'll dust it for prints and see if that brings any leads," Nathan said.

"Great," Marcus said, knowing the only prints on the envelope were his. Ready to have this conversation done and over with, he asked, "What will happen from here?"

Nathan adjusted his holster, shifting on the couch cushion. "I'm afraid this needs to be transferred to the Texas DPS, CID."

Marcus exchanged a look with Jessica, who shrugged. Looking back to the sheriff, he asked, "Which is?"

"Texas Department of Public Safety, Criminal Investigations Department," Nathan explained. "This falls under their jurisdiction." He rose, resting a hand on his gun. "Do you have the necklace in your possession now?"

Marcus and Jessica rose too, moving around the coffee table, and Marcus shook his head. "No, it's in safekeeping for the time being. I've called an emergency meeting at the TCC for tomorrow morning at ten. I've invited both the Winters and the Del Rio families to join. I don't want to hand over the necklace until both families have seen proof of its existence."

Nathan studied Marcus with a steely look. "Tempers will flare."

Marcus snorted, shoving his hands into his pockets.

"They'll flare more if I don't show proof of the necklace."

Nathan pondered and then nodded agreement. "I'll come to the meeting tomorrow and will arrange for a few officers to join me, just in case there is any trouble between the families."

Marcus got the feeling *a few* meant enough to handle the Texas-size fight that could very well take place tomorrow. "I appreciate anything you can do to keep the peace tomorrow, Sheriff."

"We'll support you through this, Marcus." Nathan headed for the front door and glanced back. "Call me if anything develops between now and tomorrow, or if you're contacted again." He offered Marcus his hand.

Marcus clasped the man's hand tight. "I will, thank you."

Before he left through the door, Nathan's gaze met Jessica's over Marcus's shoulder. "Have a good night, miss."

"Thanks. You too." Jessica smiled.

With a final goodbye, Marcus shut the door behind the sheriff, watched through the window as Nathan got in his car, then turned back to Jessica, who watched him carefully.

"You did good," she said.

"None of that felt good," he told her seriously. "I lied to law enforcement."

"It's a lie that hurts no one," she said, walking closer. "And only protects your family when none of you caused this." She took his hands in hers, lacing their fingers together, and suddenly all her warmth felt like exactly what he needed. "Don't forget, Marcus, that Eliza did this. You shouldn't all continue to suffer." With a grin that didn't look all too innocent, she tugged him forward.

He arched an eyebrow at her. "What are you up to?"

Her grin widened. "You're going to show me where your bedroom is, and then we're going to make this shit day way, *way* better."

"Considering my day, that's a difficult task." Even he heard the thickness of his voice.

She walked backward, her cheeks filling with beautiful color. "Good thing I'm up for the challenge."

The playful heat shining in her eyes tightened his groin. She squeaked as he gathered her in his arms and scooped her up, placing her over his shoulder. She laughed as he grabbed a fistful of her ass.

In a few long, purposeful strides, he tossed her on the couch, the cushions squishing beneath her. "Too bad I can't wait for the bedroom," he told her, as she laughed.

But when she cupped his face and claimed his mouth with a hot, wicked kiss, he knew that this was only a temporary fix because he couldn't shake the feeling that tomorrow everything was going to change.

Not just for his family.

But for him and Jessica too.

Ten

Jessica woke the next morning with the feeling that she wasn't alone. She opened her eyes, the room a blur, until she blinked a couple of times, discovering she lay in a bed with light gray sheets and a darker gray duvet. The wall behind the bed was a black-slate accent wall, and the rest of the walls were a light, warm gray. Contemporary dark furniture decorated the room, with a light oak wooden floor and an area rug beneath the bed.

With her mind clearing of sleep, she turned over and immediately smiled. Until she caught Marcus's conflicted stare on her.

It all came back to her in an instant. Last night, once she got into his king-size bed, she never got out of it. And waking there next to him seemed like something that should have sounded some inner alarm, but she couldn't hear that alarm any longer.

The space was bright and welcoming, and his gorgeous deep brown eyes were a nice thing to see in the morning. But the strain on his expression reminded her of the task he had ahead of him, and the tension they'd released multiples times last night suddenly engulfed her again.

She scootched closer and rubbed her foot against his. "Good morning," she said.

"Good morning."

While there was warmth flowing into the room from the sunbeams coming through the spaces through the curtains, there was none in his face. Forcing herself to wake up fully, she leaned up a little. "Are you okay?" she asked, already knowing the answer.

His lips pursed. "No, I am not."

Wearing only Marcus's T-shirt that she borrowed from him to sleep in, she sat up and rubbed her eyes, wondering if something had happened while she slept that she didn't know about. "Are you just worried about the meeting today?"

"That, and…everything," he said, lying unnaturally still.

She reached out, gripping his forearm, feeling the strain beneath rigid muscle. "Want to talk about it?"

Holding her stare, he sighed heavily. Then he finally cursed and threw his legs over the side of the bed, putting his back to her.

Every muscle was taut. His posture stiff. Heavy emotions rolled off him, nearly becoming suffocating. And all of it made her hurt for him. Because Marcus did not deserve this weight that Eliza had dumped on him. And for the briefest of moments, Jessica regretted offering up the idea of tying the families' history into the engagement party. If she hadn't, he wouldn't have been inspired to look at the heirlooms, and the necklace wouldn't have been found.

She moved closer against the messy bedsheets and pressed a kiss to his shoulder. When he stayed silent, she ran her hand across hard muscle vibrating beneath her fingers. "How can I help you?" she asked.

Head bowed, he thrust his fingers into his hair. "You can't."

Not believing that for a second, she pressed another to kiss to his shoulder, feeling the tension rippling through him. "Talk to me, Marcus."

He gave an impatient huff. "I'm not even sure what to talk about. Right now, I'm just trying to reconcile all this in my head." He glanced sidelong, his forehead wrinkling. "Today will be hard."

"It'll be hard," she said, "but you'll get through it. You all will."

He snorted. "I love your optimism, I do, but no one is coming out of this okay."

She shifted against the mattress, the bed bouncing beneath her, until she was sitting cross-legged next to him. "Why do you say that?"

His jaw muscles clenched as he bowed his head. "There is a very good chance my father will not talk to me after this."

"That can't be true." Needing to touch him, she placed

a hand on his thigh, wishing she could somehow make this all better for him. "He's your father."

"Don't write that idea off too quickly," he countered. "My father and I have a rocky relationship on a good day. He might not forgive me for not bringing the necklace to him and keeping this private between the family."

She paused, realizing that they both had another thing in common than the passing of their mothers. They didn't have great relationships with their fathers. And Jessica didn't know which one was worse—forcing a relationship or simply ignoring it. "Are you beginning to have second thoughts about calling the meeting?"

Glancing sidelong, he shook his head. "It's the right thing to do. I know this is the only choice, but it doesn't change the fact that after today things are going to change. Whether it be for the better or worse, only time will tell."

She took his hand and squeezed. "If your dad doesn't realize why you're doing what you're doing, then screw him."

He gave a bitter laugh, lifting his brows. "Screw him?"

"Exactly," she said with a firm nod. "From what I've seen, all you've done is made good on the Winters name. If he can't see that, he's simply too blind, and there will be no changing his mind."

Marcus exhaled slowly and then rose. She got a good view of every hard line of his body as he headed for the walk-in closet. In the silence, she realized what she said sounded so easy because she didn't have a relationship with her dad. Love was complicated, she knew that.

When Marcus returned to her, he had a pair of shorts on, but he still wore the anxiety emanating off him.

He went to the bedroom window, pushed the curtains open and stared out the window, arms crossed.

She let the quiet fill the space between them, not even sure what to say to help. She couldn't imagine being in his shoes.

But her heart bled when he finally broke the silence and said, "These are the times I wish my mother was still here. Don't get me wrong. I love Camille and she's been a wonderful stepmom. But she's never been able to get my father to understand me."

Unable to stand the distance between them, knowing exactly how he felt about missing his mom as she'd felt that same feeling many times herself, she slid off the bed and wrapped her arms around his waist. "You think your mom would've known how to deal with this?"

Wrapping himself around her, he nodded. "Maybe. I was young when she passed, but my brothers have told me more about her. About the way she was very good at bringing the family together." He hesitated, placing his chin on her head. "I don't know how I know, but I just know that in a situation like this she'd know how to put all the pieces together, so everything didn't fall apart."

Jessica swallowed the thick emotion crawling up her throat and managed, "You know that because you're her son and you do have memories of her, even if they're hard to recall."

He made a soft noise in the back of his throat and then pressed his lips against the top of her head, holding her tight. "You, of all people, will understand this."

"I do." It occurred to her then that Marcus understood her, and she understood him, in a way she hadn't had with anyone before, all because Lyle never shared this part of himself with her. Deep loss banded them together, and she sensed the binds of her heart tug a little at this revelation, because in this pain, they weren't alone anymore. They had each other.

Locked in the comfort of his arms, she considered all she'd heard, her heart breaking for him. "Even if your dad can't see that you're protecting your family, then you've got your brothers and sisters, who all have your mother in them too, and you have Camille and Alisha too. They will all have your back, no matter what."

"You're right, they will," he said with a heavy sigh. He pressed another kiss to the top of her head and then leaned back, brushing the hair away from her face. "Thank you for listening. You're so good at that. Listening." He slid his thumbs against her cheeks. "I didn't realize how much I needed someone to listen."

She smiled, leaning into his touch. "You don't need to thank me," she said, and then suddenly realized how much she liked this too. How nice it was to have someone lean on her, and to feel like she was needed by someone.

She'd forgotten this part of a relationship. The good parts. Not all the parts that kept her thinking a relationship was a terrible thing and would get in the way of her job. The parts where her heart felt wide open and safe to be 100 percent herself, and to somehow experience life together in a way that made her world better.

Breaking the silence, he asked, "Will you come today to the meeting?"

Her heart tripped at that. Yes, she wanted to support him, but she was hastily reminded that while Marcus made her feel like she belonged, she doubted his father would feel the same way. "Are you sure I'm welcome there?" She moved away, heading back to the bed.

He followed her. "Why wouldn't you be?"

"Because I'm not a part of either family," she reminded him, taking a seat back on the bed.

He stepped between her legs and bent at the waist, placing his hand on either side of her. "I'm telling you you're welcome there, and I want you with me."

She took a few seconds to think all this through, feeling like she didn't belong in that meeting today. She was definitely an outsider. But one look into his pained gaze changed everything. "I'm not sure how much I can help you, but I'll stand by you if that's what you want."

"It's not what I want. It's what I *need*." He pressed his lips against hers, but he backed away before the kiss could heat up. "We better go shower and get ready. Being late will only make things worse."

She nodded.

He pulled away, taking the heat of his body with him, and headed for the shower. She stared after him, her heart squeezing harder with every step he took. The emotions oozing from Marcus seemed more than only worry about the day ahead. He seemed to be fighting his thoughts. "Marcus," she called.

He looked over his shoulder, his expression downcast.

"You're not alone today. I'm with you," she said.

His chin dipped. "And I'm grateful for it."

Her breath caught in her throat as she watched him

vanish into the bathroom. She suddenly knew, deep in her belly, that Marcus was right—no one was walking out of today okay.

A few minutes before ten o'clock, Marcus arrived at the clubhouse and found Jack Chowdhry waiting outside one of the meeting room doors. Jessica was quiet next to him ever since they left her house after she changed for the meeting. She held his hand tight, and he was glad for it. Though he couldn't shake this feeling that everything that had been good was slipping through his fingers. His mind had spun all night long and it didn't only feel like it was about the meeting.

Pushing the thought aside for now as they approached Jack, Marcus held the briefcase with the necklace firm in his grip. The former CEO of media giant CMG, now officer of the Texas Cattleman's Club, Jack was a few inches shorter than Marcus, with sharp brown eyes, stubble and black hair that had a slight curl.

"Jessica Drummond," Marcus said, gesturing between them, "meet Jack Chowdhry."

Jessica gave a tight smile, offering her hand. "Hi, Jack, it's nice to meet you."

"Likewise," said Jack, returning the handshake. Then he offered his hand to Marcus. "Want to tell me what this is all about?"

Marcus clasped Jack's hand, and explained, "I apologize to have kept you in the dark, but I didn't want word of this getting around until today."

Jack's brows lifted. "You've got me intrigued."

Marcus gave Jessica a quick look. She encouraged

him with a nod, so he turned to Jack. "Before I get into it, because I suspect I won't be able to tell you later, thank you for agreeing to moderate today's meeting, especially on such short notice. You did such a great job moderating the last time the two families got together for Jericho and Maggie's dating agreement." Someone needed to be the sense of reason today, and he hoped Jack could keep the emotions down.

"Of course," Jack said, folding his arms across his chest. "Lay it on me. What is this all about?"

Marcus did just that. He gave a quick rundown of finding the necklace and what would happen today in the meeting.

By the time Marcus finished, Jack was pursing his lips. "I see why you needed me here today."

Marcus agreed with a nod. "I suspect tempers will run hot." Turning to Jessica again with a heavy sigh, he asked her, "Ready?"

She laced her fingers with his again. "Ready."

He didn't share her confidence.

Ready or not, this was happening and there was no stopping any of it. He opened the meeting room door, letting Jessica and Jack go first, and the same tightness hit his chest that had been nearly strangling him all night. He felt like he was walking into the beginning of a war that was going to change everything.

When they entered the room, they were greeted by confused faces.

His family, beyond Jericho, looking baffled to be in the presence of the Del Rio family so soon after the engagement party. A look over at the Del Rio faces revealed the same type of bewilderment, as Maggie looked on, with dark circles under her eyes, a telling sign she'd been sleeping as much as Marcus had.

"You got this," Jessica said, stroking her fingers against his in a move that likely the only one who noticed was him.

He gave her a nod, and then watched as she left his side, moving to Alisha, who stood next to Maggie and Jericho. They had stayed back from the crowd, obviously anticipating the blowup.

Marcus took to the center of the room, realizing that both families were intermingled together. Some were sitting together at the tables. Others standing around. But they were all *together*. He wondered how long that would last.

Before he could say a word, questions were thrown at him.

Until one question cut through all the noise. "Has the wedding been called off?"

"No," Jericho said, stepping away from the group. His firm voice filled the room. "That will *never* happen." He took Maggie's hand, pulled her close like he was ready to fight a war for her...ready to go to war for *them*.

Marcus sighed and ran a hand across the back of his neck. He stopped short of explaining to the crowd when the sheriff, along with half a dozen police officers, entered the room. They all spread out, looking as ready to act as Jericho had.

Marcus gave the sheriff a nod of thanks, but then someone else caught his eye.

Standing next to Camille, his father took in the police officers and then narrowed his eyes on Marcus. "Explain all this, son," he demanded.

Marcus held up his hand, calling for quiet to come over the growing anxiousness of the crowd.

Once the chattering stopped, he told his father, "We'll get to that soon." Turning to Jack behind him, he added, "The floor is yours."

Jack stepped in next to Marcus. He looked from person to person, his expression hard and unyielding. "A revelation will be made today. I expect calmness and order throughout this revelation. If you cannot achieve that, you will be forcibly removed from the meeting by law enforcement."

The sheriff stepped forward and added, "Anyone who lashes out in violence will be taken to jail."

Marcus saw the widening eyes and the shock paling the faces around him, but he was relieved for the rules and the order.

When Jack finally gave him a nod, Marcus placed his briefcase on the small table next to him. "Yesterday, I came into possession of something." He opened his briefcase and pulled out the velvet box and opened it, showing the contents to the crowd.

Audible gasps echoed throughout the room as the necklace sparkled against the overhead lighting. Until those shocked sounds turned into roars.

"You bastards had it," Fernando snarled.

Joseph shot back, "We did not!" Turning to Marcus, he bared his teeth. "Where did you get that?"

Marcus lifted his hand again, until everyone stopped shouting and the room went quiet. Though now there was a ripple of anger simmering throughout the space. "The necklace was delivered to my late grandmother's house. There are no security cameras at the house, so we have no idea who left it. That is all I can tell you right now."

The blowback nearly rocked Marcus back on his heels, as questions fired off at him, and Marcus answered each one as calmly as he could.

"What is this?" a member of the Del Rio family asked. "A publicity stunt concocted to further monetize this new truce?"

Marcus shook his head. "No—"

His father stepped forward and roared as the vein in the middle of his forehead looked a moment away from bursting, "How dare you make such an accusation toward my family!"

Fernando pushed through the crowd, spittle forming in the corners of his mouth. "Or mine." In two long strides, he snatched the box from Marcus. "This necklace belongs to our family."

Jack closed in, a solid force in front of Fernando. "Give me the necklace, Mr. Del Rio."

When Fernando didn't move, the sheriff moved into their space. "That was not a request."

With a curse, Fernando handed over the velvet box to Jack, glaring at anyone who met his gaze.

Jack sighed and then turned the necklace over to the sheriff. "For now, the necklace will stay with the sheriff's department until we can form a plan going forward."

The sheriff placed the necklace in a small safe and locked it. He turned to the families. "The necklace and the criminal theft case are now transferred to the Texas Department of Public Safety, Criminal Investigations Department." He handed the safe to a man in a suit behind him. "Direct all your questions and concerns to Special Agent Daniel Whitlock at the Texas DPS."

Special Agent Whitlock, a man in his midfifties with salt-and-pepper hair, said, "I understand both families are upset, but this case is our top priority, and I will reach out to each one of you to discuss the theft and the rediscovery of the necklace."

The moment his lips shut, the shouting erupted and became near deafening in the space, but one man was not yelling.

Marcus caught his father's eye and spotted the rage burning in their depths, focused solely on him. He glared in return. He would not allow his father to bully him into thinking he'd acted any other way than to protect his family.

The stare-down continued until Fernando snarled at Joseph, "I knew your family stole the necklace."

Joseph scoffed. "You have no proof! Your family could be behind all of this."

Police began walking toward them as Fernando's nostrils flared. "Whatever peace, whatever business that might have happened between our families, is now over."

One uniformed cop took Joseph's arm, tugging him away, as Joseph's skin mottled. "You took the words right out of my mouth, you bastard!"

Marcus's gaze fell to Jericho, who held Maggie as she cried. A hard throb pounded behind his eyes as he turned to Jessica, who lifted her chin, as if she was telling him he wasn't alone.

But he felt very alone when his father pulled himself out of the cop's hold and snapped his fingers at Marcus. "Come with me. Now."

Marcus gestured to Jessica and she hurried to his side. The moment they stepped out into the hallway, his father looked to her with such distaste, Marcus's mouth went sour.

"Not fucking you," he spat at her. "You are no one. Go away."

Marcus growled, "Do it. Talk to her again like that. I dare you." He closed the distance between him and his father, feeling a vein in the middle of his head pulsating.

His father's lips pulled back, baring his teeth.

Marcus planted his feet wide and said very, *very* slowly, "Apologize to her. *Now.*"

"It's okay," Jessica interjected, her voice shaking.

He glanced over his shoulder, finding tears in her eyes. Her skin ashen. Her fingers trembling. "Jessica, don't—"

She shook her head rapidly, her tears beginning to fall. "It's okay... It's okay."

"No," he said, reaching for her. "Don't—"

She turned on her heels and ran for the door.

The air left his lungs like he'd been punched in his chest. It occurred to Marcus in that very moment that he shouldn't have brought her there. Not because he didn't want her next to him. But because his father couldn't only hurt him, he could destroy her.

And he just did.

Eleven

The following evening, Jessica had just finished delivering dinner to the glamping guests when she noticed Marcus's car in front of her house off in the distance. She hadn't seen him since she left him in the hallway in the TCC, hearing him berate his father before she made it out the front doors. He had texted her late last night, obviously after things had quieted down with both families, but she had stayed with Lyle and Giselle, after falling into her friend's arms and crying the night away.

She thought about texting him today, but she needed the day to get her head straight.

When Marcus's father spat those horrible words at her, it was as if all her worries that she didn't fit in with Marcus's family weren't just worries anymore, they were fact.

There was no running from the truth—she wasn't like them.

While Marcus's brothers and sisters accepted her, his father did not and never would. It took her until this morning to realize why that had upset her so much, and it was because of that unwarranted feeling she'd experienced growing up.

The last thing she needed in her life was another dad that didn't want her.

With a thousand things running through her mind on why Marcus had come, she hit the gas on the ATV and the empty tray in the back began banging as she headed through the forest, around the lake.

A few of the guests had checked out earlier, with only two couples left. She had some busy days ahead of her to get the sites ready for the next guests, who'd arrive in a few days, but talking to Marcus had to come first.

When she exited the forest heading down the laneway, the tires crunching against the fallen leaves, she spotted Marcus sitting on her porch steps, head bowed. He wore his business clothes, a telling sign that he'd just come from work.

As she approached, he glanced up and she saw the strain in his stare. Every line of his body looked taut with tension, seemingly a second away from snapping.

She pulled up close to the porch and cut the ATV's ignition. Leaving the tray on the back, she headed for him. "Hi," she said when she reached him.

"Hey," he said softly.

He didn't rise to greet her, or move to kiss her like he normally would, and suddenly not having that seemed all wrong. The world slowed around her as she took the seat next to him on the porch. "I'd ask how things went but, just by looking at you, I think I know."

He glanced sidelong, frowning. "It's about as bad as you can imagine. Peace between the families has been destroyed. Accusations are being thrown around like weapons. Jericho and Maggie are desperately clinging to each other. It's a mess."

Her fingers twitched to reach out to him, but the coldness between them stopped her. She tangled her fingers together on her lap. "How are things with your father?"

A heavy, *heavy* sigh escaped him. "It's about what I expected. He doesn't understand my choices, but he also knows he can't do anything about it."

She hated that yesterday affected her like it had. That Joseph's words cut so deep. But by this afternoon, she let herself off the hook, simply glad that she didn't have a father that could and would hurt her in her life. "I'm sorry for the way he is with you," she said.

Turning to face her, his voice broke. "No, Jessica, I am sorry for how he talked to you."

She gave a small shrug, shifting against the hard, wooden porch step. "Honestly, Marcus, my reaction was less about your father and more about my own. Even though my dad left before I was born, it just felt familiar…the feeling the same…and for whatever reason, it hit me hard."

"Of course it would hit you hard," Marcus countered, a harder edge to his voice. "He never should have talked to you like that. It was despicable. I'm so ashamed that he's my father."

She glanced away, looking at her hands, realizing she was wringing them. She stretched out her clammy fingers, resting them on her thighs. "Your father is who he is and has the views he has. You won't change him. Nothing anyone did could change my father's opinions. But you can change the way you deal with it.

"Yesterday, I reacted, and that's okay because it's honest. But today, I know that to give your father a second thought would give him power that I'd never let him have." Which was how she found peace with her father. He simply did not matter in her life, and she found strength in the ability to not allow his failures to affect her life.

Marcus made an annoyed sound in the back of his throat.

She took a very long look at him. She barely recognized him. Gone was the charming, fully interested man. A barrier had been erected between them that hadn't been there before. A hard wall that she had now realized had been slowly going up since she woke up in his bed yesterday. "Marcus, talk to me."

The despondent look he gave her told her he knew she wasn't talking about his family. He took her hand, but his touch felt...*cold*. "I'm not sure I can ever forgive my father for the way he spoke to you. With me, it's fine. I'm used to it. But not with you. Ever."

She wrapped both of her hands around his to warm the touch between them. "It's done. It's over. Let it go."

"I can't." Bowing his head, he stared down at their held hands. "I wanted you there with me, for the sheriff, for the meeting, all for myself, all to support me because I was leaning on you. But I see now that was selfish of me."

She snorted. "How is that selfish of you?"

"Because you never signed up for this," he said, rubbing this thumb over the back of her hand. "You told me you did not want this. You made a good impression on my father at the party. He would have given you a glowing recommendation. And now…" He appeared to swallow the words like he couldn't bring himself to say them.

The thought hadn't been lost on her either. That everything she had worried about with getting involved with him had suddenly come true. "Yeah, well, you never signed up for this either," she told him dryly. "None of you did. Eliza was the one who stole the necklace, and now you're all paying for that crime."

"We are all paying for her mistake," he said, finally looking at her. His blank look was like a punch to her chest. She held her breath as he added, "But I can't walk away from this shit show. You can."

She watched him closely, saw the tightness around his mouth, the inability to meet her stare for very long, and her heart dropped into her stomach. Because she knew exactly what he meant.

Last night after she cried in Giselle's arms and went to sleep in their spare room, she knew her tears went beyond his father's rejection. She barely slept, tossing and turning all night long, thinking that all of this had become way bigger than her and Marcus.

Considering her ties to the Del Rio family, and the fact that they weren't dating seriously yet, the right thing to do was stop things before she lost not only the good opinion of Joseph Winters but lost the opinion of Fernando Del Rio too.

Because the truth of the matter was, she wasn't a Del Rio and she wasn't a Winters. She was a Drummond, and that meant her name mattered above all else because there was not a rich history behind her name and she didn't have millions in her bank account to keep her safe.

But her heart didn't want to hear any of that.

She sniffed, fighting against the tears welling in her eyes. "I hate this," she admitted, as a tear fell onto his hand holding hers. "I hate all of this."

He squeezed her hand tighter. "I hate my actions over the last couple days." He tucked a finger under her chin, drawing her gaze to his distant stare. "You lied to law enforcement for me. You lied to Maggie. You did all this to protect me."

"You protected me yesterday with your dad," she managed to say through her tight throat.

His gaze fell to their held hands again. "But this shouldn't be about protecting each other. It should be about being happy and caring for each other." He paused to draw in a long deep breath. Then he looked at her again. "I have no idea how this is all going to play out, but history is enough to tell us that it's going to get messy."

She wiped her damp cheek and sniffed. "I know," she agreed softly.

Marcus cursed, looked out toward the lake as leaves

fell from the trees and gave the longest sigh she'd ever heard from him.

When he finally glanced her way again, he rose and cupped her face, intensity burning across his features. "You don't deserve to be involved with this shit, and the way my father talked to you only proved that. You also don't deserve for the Del Rio family not to give you a possible reference you've earned because you are attached to my family."

Her heart rate began increasing, her throat tightening, as she placed her hands atop his. The world began to slowly speed up again as everything felt like it was slipping away. "You don't deserve this either."

His head cocked, eyes searching hers, his chest heaving with his heavy breathing. His hands tightened on her face. "I'm sorry, Jessica. I'm so fucking sorry."

Before she could even think of what to say to stop him, he headed for his car, but then she stopped trying to think of how to keep him there.

Because there were three truths between them that she couldn't ignore even if her heart begged her to.

She had a dream to catch.

He had a mess to clean up.

And those two things could not intermingle.

When Marcus entered Alisha's kitchen after leaving Jessica's house, his mood was dark, soured. He found his brothers and sisters all standing around the kitchen island. Except for Tiffany, who was sitting on a stool, sipping from a glass of water. They all stopped talking when he entered the room.

"You look miserable," Trey commented.

"Feel it too," he said, heading straight for the scotch on the counter. Breaking things off with Jessica wasn't the plan he wanted, until he couldn't even look himself in the mirror this morning. She'd been clear about keeping things casual between them so as not to hurt her reputation, and he'd done just that.

After his father's cruelty to her, Marcus knew his dad would never accept Jessica into the family. Marcus could deal with that. He'd cut ties if he'd have to for his happiness. But he couldn't—and would not—ask her to fall into this mess with him, not when all she'd done was be at his side supporting him and making him happier than he'd ever been in his life.

He had it all. He had the money. The connections. He would be fine. He couldn't live with himself if he'd taken all that from her.

And she did not deserve any of it.

She deserved the world handed to her.

Clenching his jaw, he poured himself a shot and drank it back, embracing the burn down his throat. After pouring another one, he looked at his family.

Jericho lifted his eyebrows, a telling sign that Marcus looked miserable. "Did you talk to Dad?"

He shook his head, leaning against the counter. "I haven't spoken to Dad since the meeting. I was at Jessica's."

"Is she all right?" Alisha asked gently. "I just hate how mean Dad was to her. She totally didn't deserve that."

"You're right—she didn't deserve any of this fucking shit," Marcus agreed. "And it won't happen again."

His sister cocked her head. "What do you mean it won't happen again?"

"I won't be seeing her again," Marcus said simply.

Alisha frowned. "Marcus—"

"Don't," he growled at her. The widening of her eyes had him bowing his head and breathing deep. "Please," he said, and knew his voice sounded near begging. "I don't want to talk about it. That's not why I'm here." He took another long sip of his drink, closing his eyes and wishing the alcohol would wash away the misery drowning him.

None of this felt good, but if it was protecting her from this mess, then he'd bear the weight nearly suffocating him.

A long moment passed until Jericho blessedly asked, "Has anyone talked to Dad?"

"I have," said Tiffany. "I think the finding of the necklace was just a shock and his brain melted a little."

Jericho snorted. "Melted it into a fit of rage?"

Marcus lifted his head to catch Tiffany's nod. "Yeah," she agreed. "He's a bit pissed off."

"Join the club," Trey interjected, leaning against the counter, his arms folded. "What a fucking disaster. I cannot believe there is truth behind the theft of the necklace. I honestly thought this whole time the Del Rio family had made it up to make Eliza look bad."

"You're not the only one," Jericho said.

Marcus set his glass down on the counter and nodded in agreement. "I wish that damned necklace would've stayed gone forever." Though even as he said it, for how all this hellfire rained down on his head, he still knew the best thing to do was bring it forward. He couldn't have buried the truth that the necklace was in fact stolen. It would've eaten him alive.

Jericho grabbed the bottle of scotch and poured himself a shot. Before he downed it, he asked, "What is going to happen now with the necklace?"

Marcus had been on the phone with Special Agent Whitlock before he'd gone to see Jessica. "The special agent told me that the necklace will soon be certified. After that, there will be a high-level negotiation between both families."

Trey shook his head, frowning. "All of this is just unreal. Do any of you have any guesses who or why someone would have delivered the necklace to Grandma's house?"

Everyone shook their head, and as Marcus watched Alisha using her hair to hide her face, he only confirmed he'd done the right thing with Jessica. Alisha and Jessica were good...too good to come anywhere near this mess.

He shifted against the counter, wishing he'd never talked to Alisha about it in the first place, saving her from the guilt he could tell she was fighting. But this was a secret they had to take to their grave. He refused to let Eliza's theft tarnish his family and destroy the livelihood of his sisters and brothers. "It doesn't matter who delivered it, or even why," he finally said, glancing from face to face. "The only thing that matters is salvaging all this for Jericho and Maggie."

"I agree," said Alisha. "Things were going so well

after the engagement party. We've got until the wedding to help smooth this all over."

Jericho slid his shot glass down the counter until it stopped just short of the sink. He snorted. "Do you honestly believe this can be smoothed over?" he asked.

Tiffany shrugged halfheartedly. "It was once before. It can be again."

"Handled correctly, I think we can find our way back from this too," Marcus agreed, taking out his phone and pulling up the article he'd seen. "But first, we need to get on top of this. This morning I woke up to an article printed in the newspaper saying this is a publicity stunt because we're coming up on the hundredth anniversary of the theft."

Alisha nodded. "I saw that too."

"Yeah, me too," Jericho grumbled. "It doesn't look good on either family."

Trey leaned closer toward the phone. "I haven't seen it. What did it say?" Marcus handed him the phone and he scrolled the article, titled "Royal's greatest scandal is back and as red-hot as ever." Trey finally said with a snort, "The gossipers are going to be all over this."

"They already are," Marcus said.

Trey handed the phone back, and as Marcus tucked it into his pocket, his older brother asked, "Being the devil's advocate here, but what if there is some truth behind the article? We have no idea who delivered the necklace, and at this point, any theory is possible."

"I considered this," Tiffany interjected, spinning the water glass in her hands. "Because honestly after I saw the article I thought there might be some truth to it, but there is a major flaw there."

"What flaw?" Jericho asked.

"Our family loves you too much and Maggie's family loves her too much," Tiffany offered. "We all saw Maggie yesterday. She was devastated. No one in her family would do that to her. And no one in our family would hurt you like that, Jericho, simply to make more money. Not even Dad."

While Marcus knew the truth, he also knew his father would never stoop that low, not to make money. To his kids who never questioned him, Joseph would give them the world and more. The only one he wouldn't was Marcus. And after yesterday's display, Marcus couldn't find it in him to care.

Jericho pondered and then nodded. "It does seem unlikely that anyone would be so cruel to do this to their family member. But then why wouldn't they deliver the necklace when Maggie and I were first matched in k!smet?" He paused, glancing down to his finger tapping against the counter. "The finding of the necklace doesn't bring the family together or make us more money. It's definitely making things challenging for Maggie and me."

Alisha placed a comforting hand on his shoulder. "I'm sorry, Jericho. It's just unfair."

Jericho gave her a small smile, then looked to each one of them before moving on to the next. "I'll tell you all what I told Maggie. We'll be all right," he said slowly. "It never would have worked between us if we weren't up to deal with this feud."

Marcus slapped his hand against the counter and nodded. "Hear, hear. You will be all right because we're going to see this through. Our only goal here is to get this diamond mess put behind us so that the feud ends once and for all."

"I second that," Trey said, slapping his hand against the counter too.

As everyone called out their support, Marcus knew things were on the right track, and his family was solid, but somehow without Jessica, it felt like the warmth in the room was missing. Because suddenly no victory felt like a victory without her, and he didn't know how to reconcile all this. How to protect her from his father, and this mess, while having her where he wanted her…in his arms.

For the first time in his life, Marcus didn't want to conquer and win, he wanted to keep her safe. He wanted *her* dreams to happen. He wanted all of Royal to know the name Jessica Drummond and to see her as he saw her—a force to be reckoned with.

He wanted her to shine.

Done with today, and ready to take a bottle of scotch to bed until sleep stole him away, he finished off his shot and then placed his glass in the dishwasher.

Alisha asked, "When do you plan on talking to Dad?"

Marcus snorted. "When he sees some goddamn sense and stops yelling."

"That might take a while," Trey said with a dry laugh.

"We're not alone in this," Jericho said. "Fernando is being no better. The Del Rio family *is* just as rattled."

Silence settled into the kitchen, until Tiffany asked,

"Do you think she did it?" As all eyes turned to her, she added, "Eliza? Do you think Eliza stole the diamonds?"

Everyone exchanged glances, and then laughter filled the kitchen, as everyone shook their head.

"Not a chance in hell," Trey said. "No way was our great-grandmother a cat burglar."

Marcus caught Alisha's gaze, and she gave him a little smile.

One that told him, no matter that things felt rocky, they were in this together. The secret would stay and die with them.

He forced a smile, hoping it comforted her. "It's been a long day," he said to no one in particular. "If anyone needs me, call." He headed for the door, his footsteps weighted and his body cold.

He reached the foyer and grabbed the door handle, when Alisha called, "Marcus."

Dropping his hand, he sighed. "I don't want to talk about this, Alisha."

Her voice broke. "You're making a huge mistake. Don't walk away from her."

Glancing over his shoulder, he caught his sister's wet eyes. "I love you, Alisha, but I won't destroy her, no matter how much it might hurt me now." He moved to her—the one person that truly understood him other than Jessica—and he pressed a kiss to her cheek. "Please, leave this alone."

And this time, as he reached for the door, she let him.

Twelve

The passing week that went by had been the slowest of Jessica's life, and each day seemed darker than the last. She missed working for the Del Rio family. She missed the excitement of commanding her own kitchen. She missed creating dishes that brought people together. Most of all, she missed Marcus with an unbearable, unexpected ache that she couldn't run from. And when nothing made sense anymore, the world bleak around her, she did the only thing that always helped.

She brought in reinforcements.

"Giselle, I am one step away from becoming a hot mess," she said, sitting next to her friend in one of the chairs that hugged the firepit at one of the glamping spots. The guests left yesterday, and the next ones didn't come for a couple of days.

Tucked into the chair with a blanket atop her, Giselle frowned. "I find that hard to believe." The twinkle lights surrounding the outside of the canvas tent, along with the fire crackling in the firepit shooting embers high into the dark sky, cast a warm glow out over the glistening lake. "But do explain." She pulled the wool blanket a little higher onto her lap as crickets sang into the night.

Not even sure how to get the thoughts out of her mind correctly, Jessica inhaled the rich aroma of pine needles and called on every ounce of her strength to admit… "I miss him."

"Marcus?" Giselle asked.

She nodded. "It's like logically I know the reasons why he walked away and hasn't called me, because they're the same reasons I let him walk away and haven't called him. But… I can't shake how much I miss him."

"Of course you miss him," Giselle said softly, as if this was no surprise to her. "You care about him. You were seeing him for almost a month."

"I guess," she replied with a shrug. Only now she was realizing that she'd gotten in far deeper than she'd let herself admit.

Steam rose from Giselle's ceramic mug containing the hot chocolate they'd just made on the fire. "Maybe you've just had blinders on a little bit?" her friend offered. "I knew right away that there was something special about Marcus when you met him. I could see it written all over your face. You were all bright and sparkly."

Jessica laughed. "Bright and sparkly?"

Giselle gave a firm, unwavering nod. "With him, yes,

that's exactly what you are. After I met him on games night, it was pretty clear cut then you seemed so happy."

And *that* was the problem. "But being happy with a guy wasn't in my two-year plan. I'm working on my career, remember? Making a name for myself. Trying to get out there so I can score a job that will bring in an income. Which I need to cover my expenses so I can use the money from the glamping business to hire more staff to handle the work here." Because the glamping business meant something to her, and meant something to the guests that visited, and she didn't want to let those earlier dreams of hers go either.

Giselle watched Jessica closely for a long moment. Then said, "The glamping business still isn't enough for you?"

Jessica glanced at the chopped firewood set next to the fire and sighed. "I could be happy just doing the cooking here," she said, finally looking to Giselle again, "but my dream changed and I'm just not fulfilled anymore. I want to reach more people, create more experiences, on a larger scale. I don't need to become a famous chef in New York City, but I want to make my mark on the world. I want my name to stand for amazing food and bringing people together. I need more than the glamping business can give me."

"There's nothing wrong with that either," Giselle said gently, and then she gave a knowing look. "I felt the same way before launching my skincare line. But sometimes life throws a hitch in your plan. And love seems to always happen when you're not expecting it." She laughed softly. "Look at me and Lyle. I never thought

I'd fall in love with a rancher. But I've never been happier. When love happens, it happens, and there's not a damn thing you can do about it."

Taking a minute to process what came out of her friend's mouth, Jessica took a small sip of her steaming-hot chocolate and sucked a little marshmallow into her mouth, relishing the sweetness. Still, after a moment, she got caught up. "Why are you mentioning the *L* word? I never said anything about that."

Giselle grinned over her mug. "You didn't have to. Like I said, what you feel for him is written all over your face. Bright and sparkly, remember?"

One second passed as the breeze rustled the branches in the trees around the site.

Then another.

And another.

"Just wait one second," Jessica finally said dryly. "Do you think I'm in love with him?"

"Yes," Giselle said without hesitation.

Jessica took that in and then burst out laughing, setting her hot chocolate on the armrest not to spill on herself. "Don't be silly," she blurted out. "That is so not the case here. Okay, yes, I like him and miss having him around, but I'm not that far into this to call it love."

"So says the woman who was all bright and sparkly," Giselle commented with a smirk. "And now who is also turning into an almost hot mess."

"I'm not in love with him, Giselle," Jessica said seriously, pushing her blanket off her lap. "I just miss him."

"If you so say," Giselle said, before she sipped from the mug.

Jessica frowned at the crackling fire. Love? She'd always been too driven professionally to really put in enough effort to fall in love with someone. Admittedly, since she'd never been that committed to anyone, she didn't quite know what all the signs were, but just missing someone didn't seem like anything that serious.

"Maybe you just miss the mind-blowing sex?" Giselle eventually offered.

Jessica wondered what showed on her expression for Giselle to switch subjects to lighten the mood. But she took the out and smiled. "Lord knows I miss the sex."

Giselle barked a laugh, right as the sound of crunching leaves sounded to the left of the trail, when suddenly, Lyle called, "I'm walking closer."

Jessica snorted, shaking her head, as did Giselle. The footsteps drew closer until Lyle finally came out of the shadows heading toward the fire. "Why do you always announce yourself like that?" she asked her brother.

"I don't want to hear anything that you may or may not be talking about," he said, giving a deadpan expression.

Giselle grinned over the top of her mug. "We were talking about Jessica's fantastic sex life with Marcus and how much she misses it."

Lyle froze and glared. "Giselle."

Jessica laughed, picking up her hot chocolate again. Her poor brother. He had it bad with just Jessica, and now Giselle seemed to rile him up too. "Don't worry," Jessica said to ease her brother's discomfort, "it's more painful for me to talk to you about that than for you to hear about it, so anything about *that* shall never cross my lips."

"I'm glad for it, then," said Lyle, walking around the firepit. "Don't talk about any of it. Ever."

He stopped in front of Jessica's chair first and then offered her a chocolate bar. "What is this?" she asked.

"Chocolate," Lyle said, turning to Giselle.

Jessica rolled her eyes. "Yes, I see that, but why are you bringing it to me?"

Lyle sat next to Giselle and handed her a chocolate bar too. "I've lived with you for your whole life and know by now that the only thing that makes you feel better when you're sad is chocolate."

Her heart warmed. "That is a fact."

"Why do I get chocolate?" Giselle asked. "I'm not sad."

Lyle laughed without amusement. "Because I value my life, and I know that if I gave Jess chocolate and didn't give you any, I'd be a dead man walking."

Giselle watched him closely and then shrugged. "Probably true."

Jessica smiled at them both but she opened her chocolate bar and ate a big bite. As the sweetness hit her tongue, she wondered how they made love so easy. She was stupidly happy for them, but they just knew how to make career and love work in a way that she didn't. She took another bite of the chocolate bar and moaned in happiness.

Seated next to Giselle, the side of Lyle's face was lit up by the fire, and he lifted his brows. "Good?"

"Perfect, actually," she said. "Thank you."

He inclined his head before setting his focus on the burning fire.

Silence settled in as she followed his gaze, knowing how proud Mom would have been of him. Her brother found someone to build a life with and the ranch was running smoothly. She couldn't ignore the feeling that crept up telling her that, while her mother would have been proud of what she'd accomplished, she'd have something to say, some word of advice that would help Jessica in this very moment.

Because as much as things were good, something was missing. Jessica could feel it down to her bones.

And that something was more than just succeeding in her career.

Love...

She had it with Giselle. She had it with Lyle. She had it Rosie. And nothing would change the importance of her needing them in her life. But what if she'd gotten something wrong? What if her priorities weren't quite right?

Sighing, she stuck another piece of chocolate in her mouth. The answer wasn't going to come to her tonight. Instead of figuring it all out, she kept to the present, and smiled at her family. "I love you guys."

Lyle's smile broke through the coldness in her chest. "Love you too, sis," he said.

With a mouth stuffed full of chocolate, Giselle added, "Me too."

Just after Marcus finished cooking stir-fry for dinner, he'd been interrupted by knocking on his front door after a long day of finalizing the new line that Marcus felt was a wonderful tribute to his family's heirlooms. Even though his father and he hadn't seen each other yet after what he'd said to Jessica, his father approved the design and things were finally rolling, with the new designs out hopefully early in the new year.

Marcus felt the strands of his anger dissipating at his father's agreement to the ideas with little fuss, something quite unusual for him. But he wasn't letting his father off the hook. Not yet. Not until he fixed where he'd gone so wrong with Jessica.

Though the moment after he opened the front door to Alisha and Maggie, he regretted it immediately, as he now stood in his kitchen, watching them rambling a thousand things to him at once. He frowned. "I haven't heard a single word either of you said," he told them, his stomach rumbling from the spicy scents coming from the frying pan on the stove infusing the air.

Alisha and Maggie exchanged a long look, and then Maggie nodded Alisha on. "You go first. He is your brother."

Alisha nodded, taking Marcus by the hand, away from the stir-fry dinner, tugging him toward the couch. "We have come here to knock some sense into you."

Marcus glared as Alisha shoved him until he was dropping down onto the couch. He lifted an eyebrow at her. "Pushy much?"

She nodded, glaring in return. "Sometimes bossy too, but that's just because I'm right most of the time."

Marcus snorted, getting himself into a more comfortable position on the couch. "And what exactly are you always right about?"

"This whole diamond mess," said Alisha, throwing up her hands in clear frustration. "We all see it written all over your face that you feel like this is all your responsibility, but it's not. Your whole family is in this with you. Even Dad thinks so."

Marcus gazed blankly at his sister. "I don't believe that for one second."

"It's true." Alisha grabbed her phone from the back pocket of her jeans and dialed a phone number. "Okay, I have Marcus here." She offered him the phone.

Marcus accepted the phone and lifted it to his ear. "Hello?"

"Son."

Marcus snapped his gaze to Alisha, and she gave a wide smile. "Father," he said. "What has Alisha done?"

"Hey," Alisha shot back, hands promptly landing on her hips.

"She helped me to understand some things," Dad said. He paused. Then cleared his throat. "I realize now that I might have overreacted at the clubhouse and I regret my choice of words to you and to Jessica."

Marcus lifted his eyebrows, his heartbeat racing. "Is that so?" he asked.

Alisha mouthed: *"See. Told you!"*

Glancing to his food on the stove that was growing colder by the minute, Marcus listened to his father's long sigh. "Your sister helped me realize that while I'm angry at the situation, I shouldn't be angry at you, because you did the right thing."

"I'm glad to hear you say that," he finally said.

He went to rise, but Alisha pushed him, sending him back onto the couch. He frowned at her, as Dad said, "I would have handled the matter differently, yes, that's true." Which was what he screamed at Marcus after the meeting for a good half an hour. "You remind me of myself more than any of your siblings, and I've been hard on you because of it, because I knew you could be better than me. This situation has shown me we are not the same. You are smarter and not consumed by the past. I see now why you made the choice you did."

Marcus could count with one finger how many times his father admitted he was wrong. "The decision was the right one," was what Marcus managed to say.

Joseph made a noise in the back of his throat. "Good, we can put this behind us, then." A pause. Then, "About Jessica."

"What about her?" Marcus asked, feeling heat rising in his chest.

"I truly regret what I said to her," his father said.

"As you should," Marcus said firmly. "No one deserves to be talked to like that, especially someone who has been nothing but very kind to our family."

His father's voice softened through the phone line in a way that Marcus had never heard before. "Alisha made me aware of all she's done, and of the type of person Jessica is. I'll make this right, son."

"Glad to hear it."

Another long, *long* pause filled the phone line. Until his father asked tightly, "We're all right, then, Marcus?"

The answer came all too easily. He stared at his sister and Maggie, who were both practically bouncing up and down. "Make things right with Jessica and we will be all right."

"Good," his father said, his voice lighter, prouder. "We will get through this as a family, just as we have with everything our family has gone through."

"I couldn't agree more," Marcus said.

"Then I'll see you in a couple days for dinner."

A family dinner they tried to do every month, bringing everyone together. "You will. Goodbye, Dad."

"Goodbye, son."

The phone line went dead and Marcus stared at the cell in his hand, his brain having difficulty catching up. "Dad apologized," he muttered. In his way, of course, but *regret* was the closest to an apology that he was going to get.

"Oh, I'm just so happy," said Alisha, bouncing on the spot before she took her cell back. "I told you that he felt bad about what happened at the TCC."

Marcus just watched his younger sister, amazed by her. She was smarter than most of them. He couldn't believe she'd orchestrated peace between him and his dad. Something even Camille couldn't accomplish. "You're too good to me, you know that, right?"

Alisha grinned. "I know. That's why you love me so much."

He rose and hugged her. "I do love you. Thank you for that, Alisha."

"Welcome," she said, grinning from ear to ear.

He went to walk away to put his dinner in the microwave to reheat it, when Alisha again shoved him back down onto the couch.

"Would you stop doing that?" he snapped, adjusting himself again. "And where the hell did your smile go?"

Alisha just crossed her arms, staring angrily at him again. "We are not nearly done with you."

He looked at his sister and then at Maggie. "What now?" he asked.

"Jessica," Maggie said.

Marcus frowned. He glared at Alisha and pointed at her. "Don't you dare call her and stick your nose in there."

Alisha stuck her tongue out at him.

Maggie interjected softly, "Marcus, listen to me. You've made a very big mistake with her."

His stomach growling, he glanced between them. "Please tell me how this is any of either of your business."

"Because I want this feud to end," Maggie retorted, taking a seat next to him on the couch. "The only way to do that is to put an end to the feud for good. And you're just letting it continue."

At that, he lifted a brow. "How am *I* letting the feud continue?"

"Because you ended things with Jessica." His expression must have shown his confusion because she quickly added, "Why did you end things with her?"

He nearly didn't answer them, but their stern expressions told him there was no getting rid of them until he talked. "For a few reasons, not only because she has ties to your family."

"Oh, then you're just scared," Alisha stated, matter-of-factly.

"I am not scared," he shot back.

Maggie placed a comforting touch on his forearm, her voice becoming tender. "I know we're not family just yet, but please listen to me, you're making a huge mistake letting her go. It's the feud messing with your head. Trust me, it messed with mine too."

He hesitated, but still was lost. "How is the feud messing with my head?" he asked.

"Because your mind is telling you that it's a logical thing for you not to be with Jessica because she works for my family," Maggie explained. "That because of the connection you're worried that my family will hold it against her that she's dating someone from the Winters family."

"That is a logical thought," he defended. "Because your family will hold it against her. She's trying to make a name for herself. Who am I to selfishly take that away all because she makes me happy?"

Maggie shook her head adamantly. "And that's exactly what I'm talking about, Marcus. It's not logical. When people care about each other, all that matters is the love between them. This feud has messed with our minds for so long, we think all of this is normal, but it's not."

Only one thing stood out to Marcus. He snorted. "I'm not in love with her."

"Ah, yeah, you are," Alisha countered. Before he could object, she leaned forward and said dead seriously, "Because everyone around you can see how much it's breaking you apart that she's not with you. That's love, Marcus."

Maggie nodded and rose, moving back to Alisha's side. "Just really think about this. That's all I'm saying. Jessica has been good to me and Jericho, and that's why I'm here. For her. Because I did see how happy you made her and how happy she made you." She paused and gave a heavy sigh. "I'm so sick of this feud. I'm sick of watching it tear people apart. The only ones who can break this cycle are us—our generation—so let's break it."

Alisha leaned down into his face and pointed at him. "Get your head out of your ass."

And just like that, they were heading for his front door.

Marcus remained stuck to the couch, hearing the door slam behind them a moment later. He blinked. "What the fuck just happened?"

Thirteen

When Jessica woke early that morning, she drank half a pot of coffee on the go and cleaned her house from top to bottom after she served the guests' breakfast. By the time lunch came and went, she had done her best to push away the ache in her chest that wouldn't quit. But when her sadness kept creeping up, she slid into her gardening gloves and worked on outdoor chores until she was sweating.

All she'd done since the fire with Giselle and Lyle was think…and think…and think. First, over what Giselle had said about the *L* word and then about her life, her job, her next steps. In the end, all that thinking got her nowhere but suffering a deep headache. And now she was soaked in sweat.

Feeling about ready to crawl out of her skin, she'd

come back inside and had a quick shower, redressing in charcoal gray leggings and a burnt orange sweater, when there was a knock at her door.

Nothing could have prepared her for what she saw when she opened it.

She blinked. Once. Twice. "Mr. Winters?" she managed to say.

Joseph wore a tailored suit, looking sophisticated and handsome all at once. "Hello, Jessica. Can I come in?" he asked.

"Ah, sure," she said, hesitantly opening the door wider, never so happy that she'd spent the entire morning cleaning her house.

He entered through the threshold, glanced around her house and then smiled back at her. A warm smile. One in full contradiction of the man she thought he was. "You have a very lovely home," he said.

"Thank you." She shut the door behind her, forcing her hand not to shake. "Can I get you a drink?"

"No, I'm fine, thank you," he said, heading for the couch like he'd been there a thousand times. She supposed that was the type of confidence a man who held the world at his fingertips had. "I only need a moment of your time, if that's all right."

She swallowed the nerves thickening her throat. "Okay." Feeling her insides quivering with every step, she joined him on the couch, folding her hands on her lap. "What can I do for you?" she asked.

His mouth turned down. "I've come to apologize for my behavior at the clubhouse."

"Oh," she said in surprise. She had the feeling Joseph didn't apologize often.

Eyebrows gathering in, he continued, "I took my anger out on you after I found out about the necklace, and then I also took it out on Marcus, and that was inexcusable. I am embarrassed and ashamed of how I spoke with you."

She didn't want to say it was okay because it wasn't. He'd reminded her of old pain. Pain that she never wanted to remember again. "I understand."

His eyes searched hers, and then his voice began to lose its power. "I do not expect you to simply accept my apology. Alisha has told me about you, about how you helped Marcus's search through the archives, and how you've supported him. For that, I'm grateful, so I wanted to tell you that from this day on, I will endeavor to show you that I am pleased and happy that you're in Marcus's life."

Jessica processed what she'd heard and then slowly shook her head. "You've misunderstood. I'm not in his life anymore."

"Yes, I've heard that too," Joseph said, rising. He moved to the door, and then glanced back at her. "It is my hope that changes. If we need one thing in our family, it's more strong and wonderful women." His smile was tender, honest, and Jessica reeled, as he added, "Again, please know my words were in sadness and anger in concern over my family, and I'd like nothing more than to be given the chance to get to know you better."

He didn't wait for her to answer. He simply opened the door, walked outside and closed it behind him.

A moment later, Jessica heard his car start and him driving away.

With her thoughts frozen, she kept staring at the door, trying to believe that Joseph Winters had come to apologize to her. Until the haze faded, and her thoughts turned rapid, one thought after another, busying her mind.

Until her cell phone rang.

Her heart leaped at the possibility of Marcus calling. She leaned over, picking it up off the coffee table. Her heart felt like it was shrinking when she discovered Maggie was calling.

She answered the phone. "Hi, Maggie."

"Hi, girl," Maggie said. "Busy?"

"Not at all," Jessica answered. "Why?"

"Could you come to my parents' house? I've got something I have to talk to you about."

Her mind still hadn't caught up with Joseph being there before Maggie's question sent her thoughts reeling into curiosity over what Maggie needed to talk to her about. Was it Marcus too? The TCC? Marcus's father? About the diamonds? Needing to find out the answer to that particular question, she said, "Sure. I'll come now."

"Great," Maggie said with a smile. "See you soon."

She ended the call, her heart rate hammering, and quickly grabbed her purse off the hook on the wall on her way out the door.

In minutes, she was on the road, keeping the radio off to clear her head. With every mile that passed beneath her tires, and all the leaves she'd driven over, her head spun, feeling like a million ideas were floating around in her head but nothing could settle in deep.

It wasn't until she was sitting on the light blue upholstered armchair in the Del Rio sitting room that reality sank in. "Joseph came to my house," Jessica said aloud, not even sure if she should talk to Maggie about this.

Maggie's brows nearly shot up to her hairline. "Joseph, as in Jericho's dad?"

Jessica nodded, shifting against the chair that was the same color as the flower-patterned wallpaper.

"What did he want?" Maggie asked, leaning in across the small circular table set next to the large window.

"To apologize to me." The words left her mouth, but even she couldn't believe them.

Maggie's mouth slackened; her eyes widened.

Jessica burst out laughing and nodded rapidly. "I'm pretty sure that's exactly how I looked when I opened the door to find him standing there."

"Wow," Maggie breathed, slowly shaking her head. "I had no idea Joseph knew how to apologize."

"Believe me, I was just as surprised as you right now," Jessica admitted.

Maggie added a sugar cube to her tea and then stirred it. "Did he seem sincere?" she asked.

Jessica nodded. "You know what, he actually did." She still couldn't believe it herself. "He said he wanted the chance to get to know me better."

As Jessica added milk to her tea, Maggie said, "Good. I'm glad to hear he came and apologized. I heard he said some horrible things to you."

Jessica sipped her tea and then placed it on the saucer. "What he said wasn't necessarily untrue. I'm not a member of the Winters family, and I'm not like all of you. I didn't grow up surrounded by wealth. And although Lyle and Giselle are both rich, I'm most certainly not rich myself." She gestured to the mansion. "Honestly, as hard as it was to hear, he was just stating the obvious."

Maggie snorted. "No, Jessica, what he was being was a gigantic asshole." She set her teacup down with a *clang*. "He obviously realized that too, since he came to apologize." She paused, studying Jessica before she added, "I'd normally say he would only do so if it benefited himself somehow, but I suspect he's trying to make things right with Marcus."

Jessica cocked her head, knowing she shouldn't ask, but couldn't help herself. "Are they still not talking?"

Maggie gave a dry laugh. "It's safe to say that Marcus was not pleased with what his father said. He went in hard to defend you."

Jessica's heart somersaulted before squeezing tight, stealing all the breath from her lungs.

Maggie cocked her head, obviously reading the emotion on Jessica's expression. "Have you spoken to Marcus at all?" she asked softly.

Jessica slowly shook her head. She didn't dare pick up her teacup again, knowing if she did, it'd shake in her hand.

Maggie's eyes searched hers for a long moment before she reached forward and took Jessica's hand, holding tight. "I don't get it. You two were so happy. We all saw it."

Jessica snorted a laugh. Even she didn't hear any amusement in it. She had been so happy. Nothing felt right anymore without Marcus. Her mornings felt lonely. Her nights even lonelier. "Honestly, Maggie, I am so confused right now, I can't even figure out my feelings myself to explain it to you."

Maggie's hold tightened on Jessica's hand. "No matter what, I'm here for you, if you need me."

"Thank you." Jessica smiled, refusing to let her chin tremble. Though as she stared at Maggie and this new growing friendship between them, the remaining guilt she had for hiding the letter drifted away.

Things were bad now between the Del Rio and the Winters families. If that letter had come out, exposing Eliza as the thief, the hope of mending the feud between the families would have been forever burned.

Maggie deserved blissful happiness, and Jessica would hold that secret to her grave to see it through.

With a final long sigh, Jessica squeezed Maggie's hand and then released her, letting go of all the tension weighing on her shoulders. "Now how about we talk about why you asked me to come here."

"Ah," Maggie said, a little brighter now. "I have some really great news and some bad news. What do you want to hear first?"

"The bad. Then I can end on a good note."

"Solid logic." Maggie smiled. "So, given the dramatic turn of events lately, our family chef has decided to leave her post and focus on her baby. Which means, my family needs a new chef."

"Oh no, that is bad news for you," Jessica agreed. "Is the good news the baby gets more time with her mom?"

Maggie began bouncing in her seat. "No. My parents want to offer you the job in a permanent position."

Heat flushed through Jessica, as she froze in her seat. "For real?"

"Yes, isn't it great?" Maggie beamed.

"Yes, so great," Jessica agreed. She waited…and waited…and waited for the thrill to pop up that she was being offered her dream job.

It never came.

Because she suddenly realized she wasn't the same person a month ago who wanted that dream. A month ago, she didn't know how good it felt to wake up in Marcus's arms. She didn't know how amazing it was to laugh and talk with him. She didn't know what happiness with Marcus truly felt like. She didn't know how it felt to belong to a bigger family that included Maggie too. And like blinders clearing from her eyes, she realized she'd already told Giselle exactly what the new dream was—*I want to reach more people, create more experiences, on a larger scale.*

That couldn't happen in the Del Rio kitchen.

She kept thinking that she needed to prove her worth to the elite of Royal, to get her name out there, and Marcus had walked away from her to ensure that happened. He'd put her happiness, her dreams, over his own. But most of all, she realized he'd shown her the way with the bravery of his company.

Suddenly, that advice her mother would have told her if she'd been here whispered in her ear: *What was her dream job without sharing it with someone? What was her dream job if her heart was sliced in half, with the other piece missing? What was her dream job if she had to give up something great to have it?*

It occurred to her right there that she had her answer: She could chase her dreams forever. Or she could build the life she wanted.

Maggie squeezed Jessica's arm. "Is everything okay?"

"No," Jessica breathed, feeling like she was falling, all the emotions swirling to one solid place that she could touch. "I'm not okay at all."

Love.

She was in love with Marcus Winters. And she didn't have to choose between him and her job.

"I'm sorry, Maggie," she said in a rush, "while I am so honored to be offered the job, I'm going to have to turn it down."

Maggie's brows rose. "Why?"

Telling herself there was only one way forward now, and cursing herself for not seeing her options sooner, she got up and hugged Maggie tight. "I have been so wrapped up in this feud, I was so desperate to stay neutral, but I can't be neutral."

"What do you mean?" Maggie asked, holding on to Jessica tight.

"I will always only choose one family," she said, smiling with the sudden awareness. "Because my heart belongs to the Winters family."

Fourteen

Two long miserable days was how long it took for Alisha and Maggie's advice to sink into Marcus's thick head.

He'd fallen in love with Jessica.

There was no denying it any longer. He missed her body, sure, but he missed so much more. He missed her heart. He missed her support. He missed her fire. He missed how she made him feel. When his father had come at her, he'd never come back harder at his dad in his life.

Now he knew one truth: he wanted to keep fighting for her.

The revelation had hit him while he was sitting around the dinner table with his family. Jessica should have been there, right next to him. A statement he'd blurted out like a stumbling idiot to his family, to all their shocked silence, but in the end, he left the house to Alisha's and Maggie's cheers following him.

He was only too glad he hadn't passed a cop on his way to Jessica's house because he wasn't entirely sure he would have stopped for the ticket.

Once he parked at her porch, he stormed out of his car, leaving the door open, and ran up her porch steps. He banged on the door. Again. And again. And again.

"Jessica," he yelled, his heartbeat thundering in his ears.

"She's not home."

Marcus spun, finding Lyle atop a horse, giving him the judgmental stare that he'd first given Marcus when Jessica had introduced him to Lyle. Until Marcus had won his favor, but that opinion had clearly changed. "Where is she?" Marcus asked.

Lyle shrugged. "Not here."

"Lyle, please, I need to find her," Marcus declared. Even he heard the desperation in his voice.

Her brother watched him closely and then dismounted his horse. "I saw you driving like a mad man. What do you want with my sister?"

"The car can handle it," he said. But the emptiness in his chest couldn't take a minute more not talking to her. He just didn't want to tell Lyle that. Marcus could have given a hundred different answers, but he knew exactly what Lyle wanted to hear. "I want to make things right with her."

Lyle's eyes slowly narrowed. "You had the chance to make things right and you blew it."

Marcus deserved the dig, so he let it roll off him. He

headed down the steps, stopping when his boots hit dirt. "I'll get it right. I'll fix it."

Lyle closed the distance with wide steps. He pointed at Marcus, staring at him in the way he'd likely stared at Alisha's dates. "Make her cry again and you will regret it. Got it?"

Straightening his shoulders, Marcus firmed his gaze. "It won't happen again. You have my word."

Lyle watched him for another long moment before he stepped back, the tension fading from his posture. "She's in the town square checking out a new shop."

"A new shop?" Marcus repeated.

Lyle nodded and remounted his horse. "I'm sure Jessica will want to explain herself. The shop is across from your sister Tiffany's chocolate shop, or so Jessica told me."

Marcus didn't need to hear more. With a final quick goodbye to Lyle, he got back in his car and hit the road a second later, leaving a trail of dust following him as the sports engine roared beneath him. He only slowed the car when he got closer to town, and then followed the speed limits as he drove through the town square, even if every second felt like a minute long.

He pulled up to the curb in front of Tiffany's shop, Chocolate Fix, which was closed, even though pedestrians were looking through the storefront windows. Growing more curious about this new shop of Jessica's, he looked across the road, spotting one of the shops with a sign in their window that read For Rent.

Marcus didn't hesitate. He jogged across the road, grabbed the door handle and turned, only too glad that it opened. The shop was bare, with white walls and a hardwood dusty floor. Once he shut the door behind him, he called, "Jessica."

A beat. Then, "Marcus?"

His chest warmed at the sound of her voice, and everything that felt so wrong suddenly began to feel right again. He followed it, soon entering through the back room, stopping short when he realized they were in a decent-sized kitchen.

She stood in the middle of the room. Her eyes were huge and her skin flushed. "What are you doing here?" she asked.

"What are *you* doing here?" he countered, trying to understand her new shop. "What is this place?"

"You are not supposed to be here," she said, placing her hands on her hips and pursing her lips. "I had a plan, and you're ruining that plan."

Damn did he miss that fire in her eyes. "I'd apologize, but I don't know what plan I'm ruining."

"Well, you see—" she moved a little closer to the metal table next to her "—the Del Rios offered me a permanent position with their family."

He glanced around the space, realizing it was a good size for her to do most of her cooking in. "They gave you this place?"

She slowly shook her head. "I turned the position down. I realized that I've been waiting for this dream job to land in my plate, when what I should have done was create the job myself."

The world spun around him a little as he said, "I don't understand."

A tender smile crossed her face, steadying those spins a bit, and yet that strong burn in her eyes remained. "I decided to open my own catering business and do this alone. I've done it before with the glamping business. I can do it again." She glanced around the kitchen, hope shining in her eyes, "To do that though, I need a shop, so I had a real estate agent show me this place."

His chest tightened at the sheer happiness radiating off her. "You rented it?"

"Not yet, I was just viewing it," she explained, running her fingers along the metal table. "The agent had to run out for an urgent showing, but she said she wouldn't be long and for me to look around to picture myself in it."

Another look around of the kitchen, and then he smiled at her. "I can see you in this place, making your dreams come true."

She smiled, scanning the area. "Yeah, me too."

The distance between them suddenly seemed impossibly far. He took a step toward her. Then another. "Do tell me though, what plan of yours did I ruin?"

She held his stare like she always did, focused, sharp. "Since I decided to open this place, I realized I needed a guinea pig to test new recipes. I wondered if you'd be up for the job."

Heat radiated through his chest, and in three long strides, he made it to her and gathered her in his arms. He dropped his head into her neck and kissed the soft skin there, relishing her shiver. "I missed you," he told her.

She clung to him. "I missed you too."

He didn't know how much time passed as they embraced, and he didn't care to count the minutes. He only held her, feeling like things were finally right again.

Though when he did lean away, he met her gaze and she said, "Your dad apologized to me."

"So I heard," he said. "I'm glad. You deserved that apology."

A pause. Then, "I heard you defended me," she said, in that same sensual voice that caught his attention immediately.

"I'll always defend you," he told her, brushing a thumb against her cheek.

"If that's the case, then," she said, and the air again felt charged between them, "does that mean you're agreeing to being my guinea pig?"

"It depends."

"On?"

He slid his hand to her nape. "If you can handle the insanity that is my family."

She laughed softly. "I can handle them. Even your dad."

"Good," he murmured, "because the chaos with the feud is going to get worse before it gets better, but a life without you is not something I'm willing to consider." Holding her firmly in his grip, he opened his heart. "I love you, Jessica."

Her breath hitched, tears welling in her eyes. "You love me?"

"Without a single doubt in my mind."

She tilted her head, leaning into his touch. "Funny that is, because it turns out, I love you too."

Thoughts faded. Time stopped. Something new

began when his mouth met hers, sealing a promise that couldn't be made with words.

He kissed her thoroughly, until she was wiggling against him, looking at him with hooded eyes.

"You still haven't answered me yet," she said against his lips.

"I'm still undecided." He took her by the waist and hoisted her up on the metal table. "I better taste what you're offering before I make my final decision."

He caught the heat flaring in her eyes and the wickedness of her smile, before he tugged a little, bringing her bottom to the edge of the table. He widened her thighs with his body and pushed up her skirt, reaching for her panties.

As he pulled them off, he dropped to one knee, trailing kisses up her thigh until he reached the spot they both wanted him to go. He buried his face between her thighs, and licked up her sex, and she shivered, sliding her hands in his hair, giving a delicious moan that he'd craved to hear for the rest of his life.

With every swirl of his tongue, and deep suck on her sensitive flesh, he had no intention of finishing her this way. He wanted to taste, to tease, and each lick was slow and planned, leaving her hanging.

"Marcus," she breathed, her legs shaking. "I need you."

Not needing her to ask him twice, he rose and grabbed a condom from his wallet. She had his pants open and his cock freed by the time he opened the wrapper with his teeth. After he sheathed himself, he lifted her one thigh over his shoulder.

Staring at her, he murmured, "You need me."

Tears filled her eyes. "I *need* you. I *want* you. It's only you."

All the plans he had. All the control he thought he possessed. All of it vanished as he entered her, and her sweet heat hugged him.

He dropped his head into her neck, brushing his lips against her pulse point. "Tell me what I want to hear."

She cupped his face. "I love you."

He growled, "Yeah, baby, that's what I want to hear." Leaning away from her neck, he gripped her waist and thrust deep. "It's us now," he told her, dragging his mouth to the base of her neck. She tipped her head back and moaned, as he nipped at the soft skin. "Me and you. Together now."

"Yes," she said, cupping his face to meet his gaze. "Just us."

"Damn, I like the sound of that." He brought his mouth back to hers and kissed her, until they set a rhythm, skin slapping against skin.

The table was banging against the wall as she clung to him, and he could only stare at her beauty that was all his. Her eyes shut against the pleasure, her mouth forming an O. Her moans filled his ears, a sound he'd never grow tired of, and as her brows began to furrow under the force of the ecstasy, her inner walls squeezed him. Tight.

Grunting against the hot sensations overwhelming him, his sac tightened, and his thrusts became faster, harder, as he watched the intensity rise to her face.

Losing control, lost in his pleasure, his eyes finally shut as she bore down on him, her ass shaking against his legs. And as she screamed her satisfaction, he roared, following her over the edge, where they'd go together forever.

Long, *long* minutes passed.

When he could manage it, he opened his eyes to find her warm smile. He slid his hand across her cheek, his chest warming at the emotion shining in her eyes, the happiness in their depths. "I'm sorry I walked away from you," he told her.

Learning into his touch, she replied, "I'm sorry I let you."

Then a voice that didn't belong in the room called, "Jessica."

"Oh, my God!" Jessica shoved him away and jumped off the metal table, lowering her dress quickly.

Marcus spun, snatching her panties up off the floor, and bolted to the closet with the open door. He managed to yank up his pants as the real estate agent said, "Sorry about having to leave you. That never happens, I swear."

"It's totally okay," Jessica said, doing a good job hiding her breathlessness. "Actually, before we leave, do you mind if I have a couple more minutes alone in here? Just to make a final decision?"

"Of course, no worries at all," the real estate agent said. "I need to make another call anyway. Meet me outside when you're ready."

"Thank you," Jessica said.

She stayed statue-still until the noise of the door closing broke through the silence. Turning to Marcus, she burst out laughing. "We really have to stop almost getting caught."

He closed the distance between them and gathered her in his arms. Staring down at her, he saw a world of love, a spicy adventure and his beautiful future staring back at him. "It'll never happen."

She laughed. "Why is that?"

He grabbed a fistful of her ass and nipped her bottom lip. "Because I'll never be able to keep my hands off you."

"Good," she purred against his mouth. "I wouldn't want it any other way."

Fifteen

A couple of weeks later, striding along the trail that led around the lake, Jessica relished the changing leaves around her, the crunch of them beneath her feet, as Marcus sighed at his cell phone.

"The Diamond Gate," he grumbled. "That's what the press is calling this."

"I mean, it's got a ring to it," she said with a laugh.

He looped his arm around her neck, dragging her close. "Not funny."

"It's a little funny," she countered. The families were still in an uproar, but she had noticed that the Winters family seemed to band together a little tighter.

Marcus pressed a kiss to her temple and said, "I'm just happy not to be as involved in the mess as I once was."

"That's definitely the best part of all this," she said, twining her fingers with his resting off her shoulder.

There were a lot of things going on behind the scenes with the necklace being certified. Soon there would be more talk about the stolen diamonds, but Marcus had his family surrounding him now. They were all deciding Diamond Gate matters together, and she could see the weight that had been lifted off his shoulders.

His great-grandmother's letter was buried at her grave, never to be discovered, and Marcus and his father had returned to their slightly strained but amiable relationship that seemed to be getting better now that they were also working together. And she was getting to know Joseph and Camille, and they were getting to know her. She felt welcomed into his family, regardless that she didn't come from wealth and power, and yet was still close to Maggie too.

Life had somehow settled into a beautiful rhythm that she hoped never broke.

But the feud itself had snapped back firmly into place. "Do you think there will ever be peace again?" she asked as her boots crunched the dead leaves.

Marcus sighed and kissed her temple again. "I have no idea. All I know is it's likely to get way worse before things can get better." He tugged her closer, pressing her against all the hard lines of his body. "Luckily, for me, I've got you to help me through his feud."

"Oh, well, that might be hard," she said, razzing him. "Who says you've got me?"

He lifted an eyebrow at her. "I do."

"There's that ego again." She grinned, even though

she loved his confidence. The strength of him. The solidness of his character.

"It's not ego," he said. "It's truth. I know for certain that you'd choose me."

"Oh, really, and why is that?" she asked playfully.

He stopped, turned her into him and hugged her tight enough it made breathing difficult.

When he finally leaned away, he kissed that sweet spot on her neck that he could always find, and he smiled against her skin when she shivered. "I know it, because the only place we're meant to be is together."

When he leaned away, she had tears in her eyes. "No feud could ever stop that," she said.

"No, it couldn't," he agreed.

She leaned in to give him a kiss and he obliged her, but he backed away before it could heat up. "This place is special to you, huh?" he asked, striding off again, his hand reaching for hers. "Your house here?"

"It's home," she said, staring out at her piece of the family ranch and proud at what she'd accomplished over the years. She'd already interviewed two new staff for Camp Up. One was an assistant who would handle the day-to-day bookings, and another was a chef to help Rosie with meals throughout the day.

Within a month, she'd have her catering company, Royal Cuisine, open and running, none of which would have happened without Marcus helping her get organized and financed, being a CEO himself.

Turning to him, she continued, "My mom bought this property. She's here in all of it. I can't really imagine not living here."

"It is a gorgeous place," he said. "Though I think it might be missing something."

She frowned. "What's that?"

"Me."

She stopped, glancing up at him. "You?"

He didn't reply. Instead, he smiled, giving her a little tug toward the lake.

She followed him toward the dock, when suddenly she froze, disbelieving her eyes. Candles were placed around the dock, with rose petals scattered atop.

Her heart leaped into her throat, while her stomach dropped, as she glanced at Marcus. He chuckled, and she could barely see him through her sudden tears she had no control over as he tugged her again.

She felt like she was floating as he led her to the center of the dock, and she stopped breathing when he went down to one knee.

"As I was saying," he said with his charming grin that had stolen her heart, "yes, what's missing here is me, but not as your boyfriend." He reached into his pocket and took out a black box, then opened it, revealing a stunning teardrop-shaped diamond ring, encased in smaller round diamonds that also ran down the length of the band.

Jessica gasped, her legs giving out. She dropped to her knees in front of him.

"I love you, Jessica Drummond," he said, his voice rough. "You walked into my life, told me off, and I've been changed man ever since. My future is no future at all if you're not in it. I want the world to know I am yours and you are mine. Jessica, will you marry me?"

She plowed into him, throwing her arms around him. "Yes, Marcus, of course! Yes! A thousand times yes."

He grunted, catching her in one arm, but finally managed to pull back enough to slide the ring on her finger.

The moment he did, cheers erupted all around them.

Tears streaming down her face, Jessica glanced over her shoulder, and felt the bubble of laughter slip from her mouth as Giselle and Lyle, Rosie, Maggie and Jericho, Alisha, Trey, Misha, Dez and Tiffany all now stood on the pathway where'd they'd been walking.

Trey shook the champagne bottle and popped the cork, spraying the champagne everywhere. Dez couldn't stop laughing at his dad making such a mess. Maggie and Jericho were clapping. Alisha and Tiffany were hugging each other, jumping up and down. Giselle and Rosie were both crying, and Lyle looked about ready to as well.

Jessica smiled at her blood and chosen families, and turned to Marcus. "We're all going to be okay, aren't we?"

"My family?" Marcus asked with a laugh. "I don't know about them, but us?" He wrapped her in his arms. "Yeah, we're going to be so damn happy we won't even know what to do with ourselves."

She pressed herself against him and purred, "Oh, I think we can think of a few things we could do."

"And that's why I love you." He grinned.

Then he sealed his mouth across hers to the cheering and applause and love she knew would stay with them a lifetime.

* * * * *

COMING NEXT MONTH FROM

DESIRE

ONE STEAMY NIGHT & AN OFF-LIMITS MERGER
ONE STEAMY NIGHT
The Westmoreland Legacy • by Brenda Jackson
Nadia Novak thinks successful businessman Jaxon Ravnell is in town to pursue a business location. What she doesn't know is that he's also there to pursue *her*. Will Jaxon's plan to seduce the innocent beauty end with a proposal?

AN OFF-LIMITS MERGER
by Naima Simone
Socialite Tatum Haas is strictly off-limits. She's the daughter of the man Bran Holleran needs for his latest deal. But the passion between them can't be denied—even if it burns everything in its wake...

WORKING WITH HER CRUSH &
A BET BETWEEN FRIENDS
WORKING WITH HER CRUSH
Dynasties: Willowvale • by Reese Ryan
Tech guru Kahlil Anderson plans to sell the horse farm he's just inherited. Not that he's confessing that to manager Andraya Walker. He has other plans for the sexy, determined beauty. But when Andraya learns the truth, will forgiveness be in *her* plan?

A BET BETWEEN FRIENDS
Dynasties: Willowvale • by Jules Bennett
When baseball star Mason Clark retreats to a dude ranch in Wyoming, he comes face-to-face with the best friend he left behind. Darcy Stephens has her own ambitions, which don't include an affair with Mason. Until one fiery kiss changes everything...

SECRET HEIR FOR CHRISTMAS &
TEMPTED BY THE BOLLYWOOD STAR
SECRET HEIR FOR CHRISTMAS
Devereaux Inc. • by LaQuette
Actor Carter Jiménez lost his world to celebrity and now avoids it at all costs, protecting his daughter and his still-broken heart. Can billionaire Stephan Deveraux-Smith mend it? Or will the truth about his wealth and his family's public scandals be too much?

TEMPTED BY THE BOLLYWOOD STAR
by Sophia Singh Sasson
Bollywood star Saira Sethi has fame and fortune, but what she really wants is Mia Strome. Yet no matter how much explosive chemistry sizzles between them, will Mia risk her career for the woman who once broke her heart?

HD2in1CNM0923

Get 3 FREE REWARDS!

We'll send you 2 FREE Books <u>plus</u> a FREE Mystery Gift.

FREE
Value Over
$20

Both the **Harlequin® Desire** and **Harlequin Presents®** series feature compelling novels filled with passion, sensuality and intriguing scandals.

YES! Please send me 2 FREE novels from the Harlequin Desire or Harlequin Presents series and my FREE gift (gift is worth about $10 retail). After receiving them, if I don't wish to receive any more books, I can return the shipping statement marked "cancel." If I don't cancel, I will receive 6 brand-new Harlequin Presents Larger-Print books every month and be billed just $6.30 each in the U.S. or $6.49 each in Canada, a savings of at least 10% off the cover price, or 3 Harlequin Desire books (2-in-1 story editions) every month and be billed just $7.83 each in the U.S. or $8.43 each in Canada, a savings of at least 12% off the cover price. It's quite a bargain! Shipping and handling is just 50¢ per book in the U.S. and $1.25 per book in Canada.* I understand that accepting the 2 free books and gift places me under no obligation to buy anything. I can always return a shipment and cancel at any time by calling the number below. The free books and gift are mine to keep no matter what I decide.

Choose one: ☐ **Harlequin Desire** ☐ **Harlequin**   ☐ **Or Try Both!**
  (225/326 BPA GRNA) **Presents**   (225/326 & 176/376
        Larger-Print   BPA GRQP)
        (176/376 BPA GRNA)

Name (please print)

Address   Apt. #

City   State/Province   Zip/Postal Code

Email: Please check this box ☐ if you would like to receive newsletters and promotional emails from Harlequin Enterprises ULC and its affiliates. You can unsubscribe anytime.

Mail to the Harlequin Reader Service:
IN U.S.A.: P.O. Box 1341, Buffalo, NY 14240-8531
IN CANADA: P.O. Box 603, Fort Erie, Ontario L2A 5X3

Want to try 2 free books from another series! Call 1-800-873-8635 or visit www.ReaderService.com.

HDHP23

HARLEQUIN
PLUS

Try the best multimedia subscription service for romance readers like you!

Read, Watch and Play.

Experience the easiest way to get the romance content you crave.

Start your **FREE TRIAL** at
<u>www.harlequinplus.com/freetrial</u>.